Mosaic

Jacqui Henderson

The story contained within this book is fictional. Names and characters are the product of the author's imagination and any resemblance to actual persons, living or dead, is coincidental.

Text copyright © 2013 Jacqui Henderson

All Rights Reserved

Cover by Tiller

Forward

The Commonwealth War Graves Commission maintains cemeteries around the world for those who died in battle during the twentieth century. By their very existence, they bring alive the many campaigns of the two World Wars and each one is unique.

To walk among the headstones is to remember just how much was given and how much of that gift is in danger of being forgotten.

There are several in Libya, in memory of World War II's North African campaign and to visit any of them is to get a sense of the inescapable sadness for those that loved the many whose lives ended there.

The people buried there came from all over the Commonwealth as well as Europe. Many had never been so far from home, or had even dreamt of visiting such exotic places, but they did not come to relax; they came to fight for a future they believed had a right to exist. Sadly, it was one they would never take part in.

One headstone has this simple inscription:

"Into the mosaic of victory I lay this priceless piece.
My dearest son"

This book is dedicated to all of them and to my father, who would have been pleased that I have finally learnt how not to forget and also to Mum, who would have liked this one.

I would like to thank Kevin Connolly of the BBC (From Our Own Correspondent, 10 November 2012), Penelope Lively (Moon Tiger) and Dire Straits (Why worry), all of whom unknowingly provided inspiration. Thanks too to Alicia, Cristina, Pen and Squares who helped with feedback on early drafts.

A special thanks to the British Pathé News agency and also to the many wonderful records collected and shared on the BBC WWII People's War archive, which provided me with an insight into the time they lived through.

Lastly, to my mother-in-law, Pauline Marie, who brought lots of small, but vitally important things about living in that period alive for me.

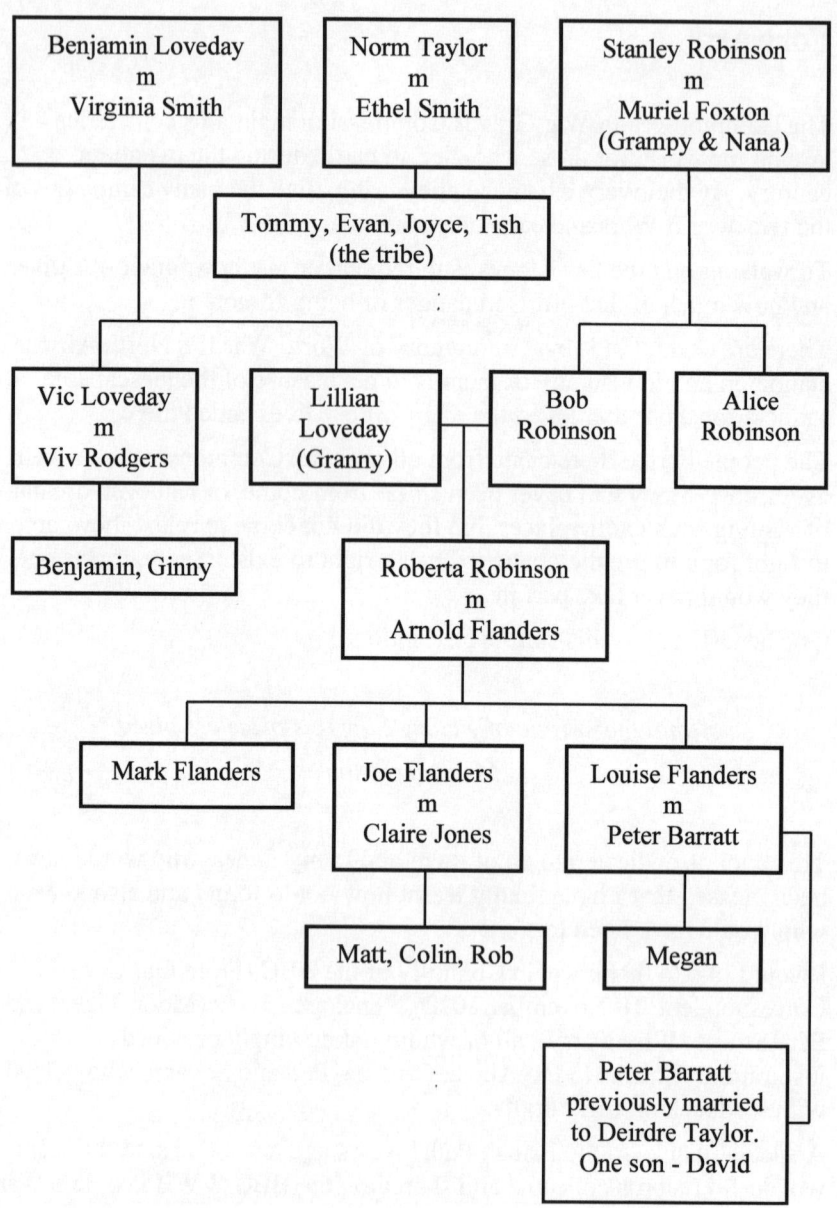

Chapter one

"Megan, wake up, she's looking at you!" Hannah hisses at her best friend, causing the history teacher, Mrs H as everyone calls her, to peer over the rim of her spectacles and focus on the two girls, instead of merely glancing along the rows of bored teenagers as she had been doing.

Hannah's elbow digging into her ribs does more to bring Megan's mind back to the classroom than her words do and more by accident than anything else, she meets the teacher's stare head on. Her blue eyes hold no sign of sullen, adolescent arrogance. Instead they look meltingly young, childlike and confused.

Mrs H softens and looks away. She is after all, as keen for the day to be over as any of the thirty fifteen-year-old girls seated in front of her. Warm afternoon air drifts in through the open windows, making her feel as bleary and fuzzy as they do, not that they would believe her. To them, she is and always has been a dinosaur, while they are swathed in the heat and mystery of their youth. It billows around them, protecting them, while drawing attention to them at the same time and they have access to a magic that she has long ago forgotten the possibility of, or so they believe.

She smiles wistfully, for of course she does remember and most of the time she is happy that all that uncertainty, not to mention all that angst, is firmly behind her. There is however, that corner of her mind, that part of her which is hidden deep within her soul, that is not sensible, that is not forty-nine, that is and always will be young.

Shaking herself out of her reverie, she asks Megan to repeat the holiday assignment. The girl looks blankly at her and panic rises in her eyes as a pink flush spreads upwards from her neck. Instead of ridiculing her, in a moment of pity Mrs H asks for a volunteer to repeat it to the class.

"In case anyone else thought the holidays had already begun..." she says, trying to sound sterner than she feels.

"Stacy..."

She points at one of the front rowers that in her day would have been form prefect, only now such a position no longer exists.

"Between 1938 and 1946, about seventy million people died as a direct result of World War II. Discuss." Stacy repeats to the class in a clear voice. "It's an open project, but we have to source and reference our material ourselves, not just copy and paste straight from Wikipedia. It has to be between three and five thousand words and we need to bring it in for first lesson next term."

Stacy turns back to face the teacher, who nods and smiles at her. Before any more can be said on that or any other subject, the bell rings, releasing them all to the balmy July afternoon.

Megan and Hannah collect their things and walk out together. They have been friends since their first day at school, when they had been seated next to each other, either through accident or design. They never knew which and it doesn't really matter anyway. On the surface they appear to have little in common, but they actually complement each other well, being not quite opposites and in almost four years, they have not had a serious row or falling out.

"You really gonna be gone for the whole summer?" Hannah asks again, her voice full of disbelief and her grey eyes wide in horror. "I mean grandparents are great and all that for a short visit, but not for the whole summer..." She shudders theatrically and grimaces as her mind grapples with the idea of weeks of unending boredom. "I mean, what on earth is there to do there?"

Megan sighs and looks down, allowing her dark curls to flop over her freckled face, hiding her eyes and her thoughts. She does not want to think about any of it, so she masks them, even from her best friend.

"Nothing I don't suppose, except homework. And yes, we're leaving now, straight from school."

"What...? No, but it's only Thursday. Christ, you're gonna miss everything Megs; the end of year party, the summer barbeque, everything. That's so not fair."

She places her hand on her friends arm. "Why? Why's your mum doing this? She never seemed so... you know... before."

Megan shrugs, knowing perfectly well why, but not able to say the words out loud, or even to whisper them to herself.

"At least I get to miss sports day too."

They both pull a long face at the thought of all that activity, on what is usually either a hot day or a wet one.

At the school gate they part with promises to phone and text every day. Her gran doesn't 'do' computers, so there will be no internet access for Megan; no Facebook, no chat and no email. She'll be adrift, totally alone in the middle of nowhere, surrounded by nature and old people.

"It's so unfair..." they both mutter whilst hugging and then waving as Megan reluctantly climbs into the car, which is already loaded with suitcases, bags and god knows what else.

Maisie the cat yowls plaintively and loudly from her box at the back and her mother's slightly flushed face peers at her from the gloom of the driver's seat.

"Everything ok darling?"

The voice is anxious, somehow not her usual one, although nothing has been usual or normal for weeks now. Megan sighs, nods briefly and grunts in a way that her mother takes as an affirmative answer.

"We'll go as far as Gloucester and then stop for something to eat."

Another grunt.

Louise sighs, checks with a sideward glance that her daughter is suitably belted into her seat, and then noses into the traffic, tuning the radio to a station that will give traffic reports and play music that she hopes they can both enjoy. Megan of course has other ideas and sequesters herself away via the use of ear plugs, iPod and that natural teen armour that is both invisible and impenetrable.

Fighting back the urge to yank the thin wires that separate her so completely from her only child, Louise focuses instead on the road ahead while Megan pointedly ignores her, neither of them realising that their thoughts are similar and revolve around a single phrase: 'It's so unfair...' Their confusion and anger, as well as their fear of the future, are exactly the same. Despite the age gap, mother and daughter are united, except they don't know it.

As they sit opposite each other in the restaurant at the motorway service station, Louise tries conversation and Megan tries petulance. Megan's gambit wins.

"I still don't see why I can't stay home with Dad. Just because you two can't get along, shouldn't mean that I get dragged off as punishment. I could have gone with Hannah to France. They invited me, but you won't let me have any fun. Anyway, David will be home at some point. He's not being sent away, is he...?"

"Megan. Your grandmother is ill, very ill indeed. If anyone is being punished, she is, not you."

Louise responds too harshly and is instantly sorry. Sighing softly, she looks away. Megan too feels bad. She knows her grandmother probably didn't mean to get ill, but for a moment she can't be sure.

"David is still at uni doing some extra course or other and he may spend a few weeks with Dad or he may go to his mum's. He wasn't sure when I spoke to him, so he may do both or neither, who knows. And anyway, your father needs some time to..." she pauses, trying to find the right words and then decides upon, "...to sort himself out."

They both know she really meant 'to choose'.

While Megan's face crumples into a scowl, Louise smiles brightly. Perhaps she smiles too brightly, but inside she too is scowling, filled with anger at her husband for putting them through this, now of all times. They both look down to hide the fact that they might cry and for a few minutes silence reigns.

"If Gran's so ill, why isn't she staying in the hospital?" asks Megan, looking at her mother. "I mean, we're not nurses, are we?"

"No sweetie, we're not. But Gran doesn't want to be in hospital any longer, she wants to be at home and you know that no one can make her do something she has already decided that she doesn't want to do."

Her words unite them again and they smile at each other, knowing that the next few weeks are going to be difficult, instinctively understanding that they will need to be on the same side if they are going to survive them.

"So we'd best get going. Bring your can of drink with you; you can finish it in the car."

They pick up their bits and pieces and head back to the car park via the loos, chatting about unimportant things and feeling closer than they have for months.

Louise pulls up outside the dark, familiar farmhouse of Priory Meadows in Little Maddely around midnight and gently shakes the sleeping figure of her daughter. When she opens the car door, a blast of night scented stocks and jasmine fills her nostrils. Then as her feet scrunch on the gravel, a myriad of memories flood her senses and for a moment she is startled. She sits there, half in and half out of the car, acutely aware that the memories are jumbled and in no particular order, but each flash is something she recognises, each a pinprick of pain or pleasure she is familiar with. The assault is indiscriminate and she cannot move, like a rabbit caught in the glare of a headlight.

"Mum...?"

The sleepy, concerned voice instantly banishes them and she sighs in profound relief.

"I'm fine... I've just been cramped up in this seat for too long. Wait here while I get the door open and the lights on."

By the end of the sentence her voice is her own again. She is the adult, she is in charge and her daughter needs her. Or so she thinks as she hauls herself out of the car and fumbles in her bag for the keys. Megan, unaware of the turmoil in her mother's mind, drifts off to sleep again.

Twenty miles away, Roberta Flanders lies in her hospital bed, wide awake and staring at the clock. She is willing the minutes to pass, one at a time until sixty have gone by. Then she starts again. She tells herself that her daughter must be at the house by now, then nods as she pictures her opening the windows, airing the place and letting the ghosts out.

"Hah! Well they won't leave in a hurry, anymore than I will." she mutters to herself, shaking her head slowly and by so doing, managing to feel stronger.

She trusts Louise, although she hasn't always liked her and some might say that she hasn't always loved her daughter well enough, but she has always trusted her, since she became an adult at any rate. She said she would come and take her home to die and so she will. Then with that thought to comfort her, she allows sleep to take her, confident that in the morning she will wake up.

Louise doesn't sleep. Once Megan has stumbled off to bed in what has always been called the nursery, she releases a very indignant Maisie into the back parlour, gives her a litter tray, some milk and food and leaves her to yowl and explore in peace. She winds the old kitchen clock carefully and turns the hot water on, before methodically unpacking the food into the pantry and the fridge. Once all this is done, she takes the bags with her own clothes upstairs, opening each one carefully and placing the contents neatly into the wardrobe and drawers. Then with nothing left to do, she sits on the edge of her childhood bed, trying not to think.

Eventually she coaxes enough hot water out of the ancient pipes and has a very hot, deep bath, before padding quietly down the landing, instinctively avoiding the creaky floorboards and lies naked on top of the bed, letting the soft breeze cool and dry her damp skin.

She pushes all thoughts and memories aside and spends what is left of the night drifting in and out of consciousness, until the birdsong brings her firmly back to the present, which is only marginally better than the past she has been trying to avoid.

She pulls on a dressing gown and goes into her mother's room. It is exactly as it was left, six weeks earlier. But really, it is exactly as it has always been. I don't think she ever redecorated after she moved in, Louise thinks, looking around. It's much more Granny's room than Mum's.

The thought of her grandmother makes her smile briefly. She still misses her, despite all the years she has been gone.

"So different to your daughter... and to me too really..." she murmurs as she begins to strip the bed.

Taking the bundle of bedding firmly under one arm, she opens the windows to let the room air and heads back to hers, where she dresses before taking the laundry downstairs to the scullery. Then she returns and makes up her mother's bed with fresh sheets, knowing full well that she will grumble, but thinks it best anyway.

Once the nurse's back is turned, Roberta surreptitiously moves the toast from the plate into a bag under the cover and shoves it further down, out of sight. The tea is another matter, but she has had plenty of time to prepare for this and just between the bed and the cabinet she has wedged a bottle that she stole from the room near the toilets. Into this she pours the tea and carefully moves her pillow over it. She has done this with every meal for the last two days, although sometimes she has allowed herself the tea.

She will not vomit or have uncontrollable bowel movements. Her body will not do as it pleases and stop her from getting her own way. She, Roberta Flanders, will tell it how to behave. In a while, when everyone is busy, she will place both the bag and the bottle in the cabinet beside the bed with the others. Someone else can deal with it all later; once she is gone, never to return.

Satisfied, she pushes the tray away and wipes the nonexistent crumbs from the corner of her mouth, while smiling at the nurse. This alone should have alerted her that something was wrong. Roberta is never charming and smiles but rarely. She has no respect for the nursing staff, thinking of them as nothing more than jumped up servants and treats them accordingly. Not that Roberta has ever had servants in the plural, but really, that was never the point.

Louise also has little appetite for breakfast and plays with her cereal, putting off the moment when she will have to leave the house and go and collect her mother. Megan on the other hand, is strangely ravenous and has toast as well as cereal.

"Are you positive you don't want to come?" Louise asks, not at all sure which she would prefer: to have her daughter with her, or far away from the graceless circus that she expects she will have to play a bit part in.

"Very sure, thank you! Anyway, I'd only be in the way." Megan replies, all the while thinking, yuk, yuk, yuk, boring...

"What will you do?" her mother enquires gently.

"Erm, read probably."

Megan shrugs without looking up. She hasn't really thought about it and doesn't want her mother to know this.

"Do you have holiday homework?" Louise asks, wanting and needing more of a conversation than her daughter is willing to provide.

"Yes, some French grammar, maths and a history project."

Megan is a good student. Some things come easily to her and learning is one of them, so avoiding her studies is not part of her make-up.

"Goodness, a project."

Louise is concerned. There's nothing here, she thinks. Her practical, maternal mind automatically reaches for a solution. "The library, of course..." she says, thinking aloud.

"Sorry...?" Her daughter is confused.

"There's a library in town, just behind the post office. They will have internet access and books of course."

Megan nods in agreement. She had already decided that books and films were going to be her holiday companions, so to be able to replenish them and also have internet access is an unexpected, if tiny bright spot on an otherwise dark horizon.

"I'll go and check it out then. While you go and collect Gran." she says pointedly.

It occurs to her that the library gives her a good reason to be absent for most of the day, meaning she need not be present for a homecoming she has been dreading, ever since she was first told about the holiday plans.

Louise understands the silent communication and wishes that she too could give the homecoming a miss. But I am the adult, she reminds herself, caught firmly between the two ages of dependence. And I am, if nothing else, so very dependable. This thought flits through her mind while she is handing over notes and coins to her daughter. "The bus stops..."

"I know Mum, don't fuss." Megan flounces out of the kitchen and heads upstairs, calling out, "Good luck..." over her shoulder. Her mother grimaces, but doesn't answer.

At the hospital, Louise finds that Roberta is behaving most unRobertalike. She is meek, quiet and almost agreeable, which makes her nervous. Unable to account for it, she fears the worst. Except, she asks herself, what is the worst? Mum *is* dying, she *will* die and soon. And if she's drugged to the eyeballs, who can blame her? She shrugs and picks nervously at the cuff of her cardigan as they continue to wait for the doctor to come and give the all clear. Her mother sits bolt upright in the chair by the bed, dressed and not complaining about anything.

Louise lets her mind wander. Of course she has read about families making their peace at times like this, but really, she wonders, is that what she wants? Is that what either of us really wants? Are we really capable of such an act anymore? Before she has time to contemplate the question, two little words buzz in her mind. It is, she realises with absolute certainty, just that; an act, because we both know that right up until she is in the car I can change my mind. Louise smiles, relieved. Now she understands and can deal with it, for it is after all, only temporary; her mother will return as soon as the hospital building is behind them.

Megan waits for the bus at the end of the street. Her gran's house is the only old one there, all the others are much newer and she vaguely remembers being told that the land was once the family farm, but that her great grandmother had sold it to developers years ago and then took herself off around the world on the money. Wishing she was anywhere in the world except there, she wonders what her father is doing and toys with the idea of texting him. But what would she say? She is suddenly shy.

He's done this before, she thinks. But we haven't, Mum and I, and it's so not fair. She battles with herself, determined that she will not cry.

Just as the bus pulls up, a boy rushes from somewhere behind her and they momentarily notice each other before taking seats in different parts of the vehicle. He wonders who she is, because he knows the neighbourhood and knows she is not part of it, but then the music in his ears catches his attention and she is forgotten. He doesn't even register on her radar, so complete is her misery.

The library, once Megan actually goes in, is almost empty. She has already spent more time alone than is usual for her, having wandered up and down the small high street and sat in a cafe. She read the end of her book over a glass of something sweet and fizzy, and then amused herself by watching strangers through the window, walking and shopping in an unfamiliar place. After that she stood on the bridge for a while, watching the water as it trickled lazily towards the sea, wishing she could float off somewhere, anywhere would do.

The internet access is quite good she concedes, and she happily busies herself with things that are familiar and part of the world she is already missing. First she checks her emails and writes a long reply back to Hannah, who has given her a rundown of the TV programmes she missed because of the drive, then she leaves some comments on Facebook. Finally, having torn herself from the only contact she has had with her friends for a whole day, she begins to search for information that might be useful for her project.

The subject is wide. Too wide, she thinks, so she begins with the number of seventy million. London, she discovers, has a population of slightly more than eight million. So, Megan calculates, everyone would need to be totally wiped out and replenished every year for almost nine years to reach that kind of number. She shakes her head to get rid of the horrific imagery that floods her mind and instead tries to think of it as more like a computer game, but struggles, because it is too unreal.

She changes the search criteria and is captivated by the idea that around seventy million is the projected population of the UK in 2030, and that right now, if everyone in the country were to be annihilated for some reason, it still would not be as many as had perished in or because of WWII.

"Who were they all?" she asks, writing the question in large letters under the title and not realising that she has spoken aloud.

"Who were who...?" a male voice beside her asks.

She turns to see a boy standing there. His face is not unpleasant and one eyebrow is arched quizzically above his brown eyes. He is pushing the book trolley and she realises that he works there.

She blushes. "Erm, my history project, sorry." she mumbles, momentarily overcome with shyness.

He glances down at her pad, sees the title and nods. "Try Wikipedia," he suggests, "it'll probably give you a breakdown. We also have a whole section on that period. There, just next to that pillar with the yellow poster on it."

He points to it and she nods and thanks him before turning back to the screen. He was right; there is some gruesome number crunching, listing the dead by so many different types and categories that her head begins to throb and the ghastly black and white photos on the page make her stomach churn and heave. The question why...? Screams in her mind, but there is no answer. Maybe there never was, she thinks, sighing heavily.

After making a few hurried notes, she logs out of everything, gathers up her things and heads back out to the warm summer afternoon. She looks up at the clear blue sky and is glad to be alive.

Chapter two

Louise starts the engine and reverses out of the parking space.

"So where's that lazy granddaughter of mine then?" rasps Roberta, breathless from the exertion of getting into the car, but determined to hide it.

Louise decides not to rise to the bait, but as she glances over to the passenger seat, her mouth curves upwards into a small smile. Her mother is staring resolutely ahead. It is a profile she knows well and although her face could never be described as pretty, her sharp, angular features are captivating in their own way. Her once thick auburn hair has long since lost its warmth and strength though, and what little there is left is wispy and colourless.

She can see beads of sweat on her brow as well as on her top lip and her face is grey, despite the thick layer of pink face powder liberally spread all over it. She looks old, much older than she should and Louise suddenly feels sadder than she has ever felt before.

They both know the ambulance would have taken her home. In fact, the doctor would have preferred it and generally it would have been a better bet all round, but Roberta intends to be stubborn to the end. She is going walk into her own home this last time. The neighbours are not to know, so they will not be given the opportunity to speculate. Louise intends to honour her wish, but she fervently hopes that the journey will not make her mother even crankier, as a result of being in pain. That she *is* in pain is clear to see, and that she will not admit to it, is just as clear.

"She's at the library. She has homework for the holiday, a lot of it too, so we thought it best that she cracked on with it."

They both know this is a slight exaggeration, but Roberta understands that Louise wants her daughter to have some freedom from the demands of the sick bed, so she nods, understanding both the spoken and the unspoken communication.

Roberta is fond of her only granddaughter and does not really want her to have a miserable summer, so she approves of her daughter's sentiments, but her thoughts are suddenly disturbed by a shooting pain in her side as the car goes over a bump. She realises she will need all her willpower to get through the journey, so she grits her teeth and steels herself as best she can. Louise sees this and makes no further comments, concentrating instead on the drive to the house she has always thought of as Granny's.

Megan, realising that there is nothing else to do but return to Priory Meadows, slowly makes her way to the bus stop and passes the time waiting for the bus by sending texts to Hannah, who has been letting her know who has done what during the day. Small, but important things, and while she feels far away from it all, she also feels connected to a life she likes to think of as hers.

Her father calls her on her mobile while she is on the bus. He is trying to sound upbeat and interested in what she has been up to, but he is trying too hard and she hasn't forgiven him yet for not insisting that she remain with him for the summer, so she doesn't help him out. The call is therefore short and unsatisfactory for both of them, and when she arrives at her stop she is scowling. Once again, her thoughts are caught up with the general unfairness of it all.

Turning into the drive, she sees the car parked outside the house and the scowl etches itself deeper into her features. She is scared; scared of her sick grandmother and scared of the whole idea of death. She has no knowledge of it and no wish to become acquainted with it either. She pauses in the porch, counts to ten and goes in, calling out loudly as she shuts the large front door behind her.

"We're upstairs..." her mother shouts in reply. "Be a love, make some tea and bring it up."

Later, sitting opposite each other at the kitchen table, they eat dinner quietly, just the two of them. Roberta had a bowl of soup in bed earlier, and now, having given in to the exhaustion of the day, she sleeps. Perhaps not peacefully, but reasonably untroubled.

"Dad called..."

Louise holds her fork in mid-air for a moment, surprised that this piece of news catches her so completely off guard.

"How is he?" she asks, unable to come up with anything else.

Megan shrugs. "Dunno, didn't ask."

Her mother smiles and wonders briefly if this is how the summer will pass; both she and her husband only getting news of the other through their daughter, when and if she can be bothered to share it.

They do the washing up together and head by silent consent into the front parlour. It too has not seen a fresh coat of paint for many years and Louise wonders if she can actually remember anything in this house different to how it is today. They try to make themselves comfortable on the sofa and discover that the TV doesn't work.

"I'll call someone tomorrow," Louise promises, "or maybe we'll just buy a new one." she adds, looking at the hulking great thing squatting on the small table in front of them. It must be at least as old as Megan she decides, at the same time wondering what her mother had done in the evenings to amuse herself.

"You never lived here, did you Mum?"

Louise turns to her daughter. "Well not in the way you mean, no. But I came to visit Granny, my granny that is, a lot and often stayed over, so in many ways it was like a second home. We lived over the other side of the hill and my dad farmed there, but we never owned it of course." That was always one of the problems, she thinks, but doesn't say.

Megan nods; she has been told all this before. She never knew her grandfather, but she has seen photos of him and as far as she could tell, he'd always been ancient. He was almost twenty years older than Gran, a fact she had always found weird and she shudders involuntarily at the thought.

"What was he like? Granddad I mean."

She is suddenly curious and wants to hear about the father and daughter relationship, not the old, well worn stories and platitudes about a man long dead.

"As a dad... was he a good dad?"

Louise thinks it a strange question, but as she looks over to her daughter she realises why she needs to know, then wonders if there is a simple answer. Can we ever really explain people with words? She thinks to herself. Can we ever do their memories justice?

She sighs and turns her mind back to Megan's question. "Yes he was, but he was a different dad to me than he was to the boys."

Her daughter slides along the sofa to sit closer to her. "How?" she asks.

"He was from a different generation, even from Gran's. He was so much older than her and I think because of that, he expected more from the boys. They had a part to play and they had to contribute, well in his view anyway. He always said that boys can't hang around being children forever."

She smiles, remembering how often and in how many different ways this was said.

"When they turned fifteen, I think he saw them as young men and treated them that way, whereas he was in no rush for me to grow up. So by the time I wanted to be treated as a young woman, he still saw me as a child. We had a lot of rows, probably more than with the boys, but despite that he adored me. I know that for a fact, and I hope I always have."

She is stroking Megan's hair and doesn't say anything to her about how her father embarrassed her, how his clumsy country ways made her angry, unkind even and that she, like her brothers, couldn't wait to fly away to another life, although Joe came back more often than either her or Mark. Him being like that let us off the hook, she thinks to herself, trying to justify her absence, but failing.

She searches her memories, trying to find the man that her father had been, but discovers that he is hidden. She realises that she has not thought about him for years and sadly wonders what that must say about her or about them as a family.

"I think he felt cheated by the war." she says slowly. "He always said the country was bankrupted by it, and not just financially. Even though we won, it changed everything, but not always for the better. That, plus the fact that we could never afford our own farm or even just our own garden, made him sad and he worked hard all his life. Maybe sometimes he drank more than was wise, but he wasn't cruel, not to me or to your uncles. They had their own arguments with him of course, just as you and David argue with Dad, but he was perhaps more distant than I would have liked."

She stops for a moment to consider what she has said. Shouting, that's what she remembers most of all, that and slamming doors, then long silences, but not the peaceful sort. The silences she remembers were always brooding and spiteful.

She does not share any of this, instead promises to find photo albums that they can look through together, but not tonight.

"Gran doesn't have any photos out." Megan says sleepily. "Hannah's granny's got pictures of the family all over the place; on the walls, on the tops of things, everywhere in fact. Funny that Gran doesn't. Even Little Nana has some out, and a few of Dad on the wall too." She is silent for a moment as she thinks about her two very different grandmothers. "Will you, when you're old?" she asks her mother.

Louise laughs as she replies. "Maybe, but of course nowadays we take them with our phone, not a camera and then delete them when we're bored with them. All too few make it to paper or into albums, let alone a frame!"

She is sad for a moment as the truth of her words sinks in and then looking around the room, she realises that her daughter is right. All the photos that used to be out when Granny lived there were gone. This was a change that Roberta had made and Louise hadn't even noticed. This thought leads her to another and she decides that going through the house and the paperwork is one of the tasks that she may as well get on with while she can still ask her mother about things. She hopes that the photos will be found when she begins the process of clearing out, for she would like to see them again and share them with her daughter.

Megan carefully pushes the sleeping cat aside, stretches, and says that she is going to bed.

"I'll check on Gran and then do the same." Louise replies. "There will be a carer coming in the morning to get her washed and dressed. That is if she wants to get up of course. And the nurse will come by as well. Do you mind staying in while I go out to get some bits and pieces and a new TV? You won't need to do much, just let them in and out and maybe make some tea or something."

Megan had reluctantly agreed to her mother's request, which is why the following morning she is standing by the window in her grandmother's room, wondering what to say.

Roberta breaks the silence. "Your mum said you were at the library yesterday. What were you doing there?"

"I've got a history project to do." she tells her, while staring out across the rooftops. Then a thought occurs to her and she turns and walks towards the bed. "Do you remember the war Gran?" she asks, hopefully.

"Hardly, I was barely two when it ended."

"But your mum and dad, didn't they talk about it?"

Megan is sure hers would have and innocently assumes that all parents would do the same.

"My father never came back from it and my mother... well, while I stayed here, she went off gallivanting around the world if you please. Nana always said she'd gone funny from it all."

As she speaks, Roberta turns her head away and shrugs. The words have stirred something deep in her innards; something she thought she had banished years ago, that troubling sense of being left behind, of not being enough to hold either of her parents to her. She turns her mind to other, more mundane things as a means of moving beyond the hurt. As usual, it appears to work.

"I've got a thirst. Go and make some tea, will you? Nice and sweet."

Megan goes downstairs, only just hearing the instruction that is called out behind her.

"And check the clock in there for me, make sure it's ticking. She mustn't forget to wind the kitchen clock, it gets temperamental otherwise. I'll remind her when she gets back."

A little while later, Megan returns to the bedroom and carefully hands her grandmother a mug of tea, confirms that the clock is ticking nicely and then asks what else she can do, all the while hoping that whatever the demand is, it will be easy to comply with.

"Read me a prayer."

"Erm... ok, which one?"

Megan is surprised. In all the years she has been aware of her grandmother, she has never thought of her as religious.

"The one that's marked in that book." She points to the bedside table.

Gingerly, her granddaughter reaches for it and opens the page marked by a plastic peg. Roberta smirks, enjoying a private joke that she has not yet decided if she will share or not.

"The Lord is my shepherd; I shall not want..."

"Amen. Thank you, that's enough." Roberta interrupts and Megan looks startled, fearing she has done something wrong and in some way offended the old woman.

The front doorbell rings, preventing either of them from saying anything and Megan eagerly scoots off to see who it is. She returns with the nurse and then escapes to her own room. A little while later, as the nurse is leaving Roberta's room, saying she will let herself out, she is happy to hear her mother arrive back. She is off the hook and wants to be outside, so she quietly makes her way along the landing to the back stairs.

As she goes down the narrow old wooden staircase, she hears her mother in the kitchen and from the sarcastic tone of her voice and sudden burst of real laughter that follows, she knows that it is a private conversation with Cate, her best friend. They speak daily and it is a relationship that Megan is excluded from, just as Louise is excluded from hers with Hannah, and for a moment she almost understands that this 'holiday' will be as difficult for her mother as she expects it to be for herself.

She slips out through the back door and stands on the drive, looking down over the roofs of the houses nearby; feeling lonely, yet at the same time filled with a need to be alone. She spies the garage door and walks towards it, hoping it is unlocked. She has visited this house at least once a year for most of her life and is suddenly acutely aware that she has never been inside the garage.

As she tentatively pushes the small door set in the larger ones open, curiosity replaces all other thoughts.

It's gloomy inside and her fingers run up and down the wall until she locates a light switch. The single bare fluorescent tube plinks and stutters into life. It is covered in dust and spider's webs and has little effect, but it's enough to give her confidence. She pushes the door closed and wanders further inside. The walls are lined with shelves, which are full of tins, baskets, jars, cans and bottles.

There is no room for a car, but then Gran doesn't have one. Instead, the floor space is taken up almost completely with junk, piled higgledy-piggledy everywhere and Megan realises after a moment or two, that it's old farm equipment. From the dust that has clearly not been disturbed for a long time, she also realises that she is the first person in there for quite a while and the thought pleases her.

While she happily loses herself in the largely unfamiliar remnants of another era, Louise is embroiled in an all too familiar reminder of her own past.

"If you fuss about so uselessly around Peter, it's no wonder he's been out looking for a real woman, instead of a bloody nursemaid."

Roberta throws the wounding insult at her daughter, who is holding a glass of water and an assortment of tablets that her mother has no intention of taking.

"Why Mum? Why can't you just take the bloody medicine? Why have you got to be so pig headed about everything? Is this what we're going to do every bloody day, from now until..."

Louise stops short and a flush spreads across her face. Her hand flies to her mouth, but it's too late; they both know what she was about to say. She flops down on the bed, exhausted and tearful. "Why Mum? Why do we always have to fight?"

Roberta does not reach out to her daughter, nor does she comfort her. She hasn't, not for a very long time, not since she was a small baby. She always left that to her own mother, who treated Louise the way that she had never been able to treat her.

Her eyes are bright, but they are also cold and distant as she stares at her daughter and rasps out a reply. "Because that way we know nothing has changed. I am still alive and I am who I have always been. Contrary, that's what your father called me and don't forget it! And don't you come here all pious, hopeful that my dying wipes everything clean and that I go from this life all happy-clappy, leaving you serene from the graft of looking after me.

"There are some things in this life that we just have to do, like it or not. Looking after me is one of them and I don't expect you to enjoy it. Dying is something I have to do. I don't see why I have to make everything easy for everyone, when no one has ever taken the trouble to make life easy for me. So now we know what has to be done, please let's just get on with it. And put those wretched pills away; for the last time, I AM NOT TAKING THEM!"

The exertion of shouting leaves her breathless. Her chest is heaving and her face is drained of colour. Louise knows there is no point in trying to calm her, or reason with her, so she nods, plonks the glass down and leaves the room, fighting back the tears as she stomps down the stairs towards the kitchen.

A heavy-set man is seated at the table. He smiles at Louise as she enters and with that smile the years roll away. They are once again young and carefree, and in it together. She smiles back.

"Same as ever..." he states simply, pointing up at the ceiling.

Louise nods.

"Tea's in the pot." he tells her and pushes a cup and saucer towards her as she sits down.

"Don't seem much point in going up at the moment. I'll go later."

"She'll be pleased to see you; she always is."

There is no bitterness in her voice, it's a simple fact and they both know it.

"Aye, but I reckon she should rest after that little outburst. How are you?"

He stops stirring his tea and watches his sister carefully. She never could hide much from him and he is pleased to see that she isn't even going to try.

For Louise, there is a huge relief in bringing her brother up to date with her woes and the problems with her marriage. It is different from discussing them with Cate, who has only known her as an adult and who thinks of her as successful and in control of her life. Joe has been there for her forever, since she was a baby. He was always the one who protected her, teased her and loved her in that mixed way that only an older brother can. There are few secrets or expectations between them and a lot of understanding binding them together.

"Do you still love him?" he asks when she gets to the end.

"I don't know what it's like *not* to love him. He's been my everything from the moment I met him." she replies with painful honesty. "And I'm not sure how this... this lapse, for want of a better word, changes things, but I feel that it does. The problem is, I'm just not sure how or what it means... for me or for us."

She looks away, staring at the clock without really seeing it and Joe nods slowly. For a moment he is at a loss, filled in equal measure with pity and longing, for he has never known a love like the one she is describing. He is saved by Megan bursting in, who on seeing her favourite uncle, hurls herself at him with evident delight.

The three of them make lunch together, chattering away easily and Megan tells them about the garage and the bicycles she found there. Her uncle promises to sort them out and her mother promises to teach her to ride one. Plans are made to install the two TVs Louise has bought, and for the smaller one to be given by Joe to their mother, knowing that she is more likely to accept it and watch it than if she knew the truth.

Megan is confused by this, but accepts her mother's wishes with a careless shrug. To her, adults are still a species apart and she allows them their foibles without really caring. And anyway, they are not quite interesting enough to hold her attention for long.

Over dinner, she hears the news of her cousins and aunt, all of whom will come with her uncle next weekend. Then later, while he takes some soup up to his mother, she helps hers do the washing up.

Afterwards, while there is still some natural light to see by, she drags her out to the garage to help manoeuvre one of the bicycles into the garden. Louise is appalled at the state of the place and as Joe joins them, she turns to him.

"I hadn't really thought about in here. I mean, I'd assumed I'd go through the house, although most of the furniture is only fit for burning, and there's all the paperwork of course. You know, while Mum is still able to help, but what about all this...?" She spreads her arms out and her shoulders sag at the thought.

"Most of it's rubbish, pure and simple." Joe replies. "We might sell some of it to an agricultural collector, if such a person exists, but most of it will go to the dump. I'd like some of the tools, if that's all right by you...?"

He is suddenly shy; they've never been in this territory before.

"Of course it is, silly." she says, taking his hand and squeezing it gently.

He nods and continues. "When I come back I'll get the boys to help me. You just sort out the house."

Louise is relieved by his offer and some of the anxiety leaves her body.

"Mum, Uncle Joe, look... a rocking horse!" Megan shouts from the somewhere at the back.

Joe and Louise glance at each other, eyebrows raised, before making their way towards her, for neither of them can remember a rocking horse from their childhood.

Much later, as Roberta and Megan sleep soundly upstairs, Louise and Joe sit at the kitchen table and resume their discussion. Louise holds her mug of cocoa protectively and Joe tinkers with bits of bicycle that he has spread out on newspaper on the table. The scene is comforting and familiar and they are easy with each other.

"What did Mark say?" Louise asks.

"Not much, as you'd expect. He has no intention of coming back; not to say goodbye, or for the funeral."

"She won't call him either, I don't suppose." Louise says sadly.

"No, they're too much alike, which is maybe why this happened in the first place. I don't suppose either of them remembers rightly what the argument was over; it's so long ago now."

Joe is frustrated with his mother and his brother, but he is also resigned to the situation. He has spoken to both of them and can do no more. He cannot heal the rift that time has failed to mend, so instead he focuses on the various parts of the bicycles that he has before him.

Louise sighs, allowing her mind to dart back and forth over the years. "Could it have been different, do you think?"

He looks at her quizzically.

"You know, if Granny hadn't sold the farm and had given it to Dad to manage or something. Mum always said that it had been Great Nana's intention. I wonder why she didn't..."

She looks back at him, hoping for an answer that will in some way satisfy the years of silence. She never understood the tension that had existed between her father and her grandmother, but she had always known it was there, bubbling away just below the surface.

"Intention is not the same as writing it down properly." Joe says slowly. "Mum and Granny had their own differences and I think Dad just inflamed it all. He was so angry. Mark got that from him; all that anger, with nowhere for it to go."

"Oh, anger always has somewhere to go..." Louise says quietly, realising that it's what she is full of too and that it is eating her from the inside. She puts her mug down and stands up, resolutely pushing the unwelcome revelation aside.

"Time for bed I think. Are you leaving tomorrow?"

"No, I made two promises today: one to Mum, to spend more time with her and I promised Megan a bicycle. And as I could do with a few hours sleep, I'll finish it tomorrow. Demanding creatures you women." he says, smiling and winking at her.

Upstairs, as they lie in their old single beds waiting for sleep to come, they both think about what Louise has said of her marriage. Joe has always felt comfortable with his wife Claire, because from the moment he met her, it was never giddy. He still enjoys going home at the end of each day, knowing that she will be there and he never worries that she won't. He is as certain of her as she is of him, which is as they have always been.

He wonders if they have missed something, if excitement and turbulence are a better way for a relationship to conduct itself. Then smiling to himself in the darkness, he wonders what they would do with such emotions now, at their time of life. He doubts that he could have managed them in his youth and is sure that they would have swamped and consumed him. He is also sure that there is no place in his life for them now. Content, he drifts off to sleep.

Louise however, lies in her bed fretting, comparing herself to Lucy, a woman about whom she knows little, apart from being sure she intends to steal her husband. She will be younger of course, and firmer, probably brighter and less careworn. She sighs, picturing someone somewhere between herself and their daughter in age and personality looking up at him, captivating him, luring him away.

She had been in a similar position almost twenty years ago. Then, she had been certain of herself, certain that she could take him. Now however, she is full of doubts and unsure if she can keep him. Her only weapon had been to remove herself completely from his life, and her mother had provided the perfect excuse. Otherwise, she may not have found the will or the courage to see it through. She hopes he is missing her and their life together; surely this other woman, this Lucy, cannot hope to recreate it, can she?

A stray thought slips into her mind and slowly blankets all others. Is she missing him? She is not sure, perhaps she hasn't been thinking about him as much she should have done and her body is not as keenly aware of the empty space that he should inhabit as it should be. She is angry, more with him than with this mysterious other, of that she is certain. But what else? What other feelings are noticeable, even if only by their absence? She decides she is still numb from the shock of it all. Yes, she thinks to herself, that must be it. And she too drifts off to sleep.

Chapter three

Louise wakes up later than usual with a brooding headache, one that will not shift, no matter how many painkillers she takes throughout the day, and although she tries to busy herself around the house, she actually achieves very little. Megan instinctively knows to stay out of her way, and as her uncle has decided to spend most of the day with her gran, she curls up on the sofa with some DVDs she brought with her. While watching films she's already seen a dozen times before, she and Hannah text and chat about things that don't matter much to either of them, but it keeps them connected to each other despite the distance. Later, the family share an early supper in Roberta's room, after which she tells them she is tired and wants to sleep. Louise is still fragile and snappy, so Megan hurriedly does the washing up and escapes to her room, deeply dissatisfied with the way her so called 'holidays' are turning out.

Almost by default, Louise and Joe find themselves in the kitchen. It has always been one of the most important rooms in the house and while he continues to work on the bicycle, his sister paces about nervously. He knows better than to suggest that she sits down, but when the day starts fading into evening, he pours them each a large glass of whiskey, which seems to do the trick. They talk quietly while he works, of times past as well as their hopes for the future, but close though they are, they skirt around the subject of their mother's impending death. They are not ready to openly discuss it yet and so the conversation trails off. The silence between them is not uncomfortable and so there is no rush to fill it, but as Louise contemplates Monday, she naturally needs to know his plans.

"What time are you leaving tomorrow?" She asks.

"After breakfast. I need to get to work and I promised Megan a lift into town." he tells her, carefully putting his tools away and wiping the excess grease from the now intact bicycle.

"Good, she can buy a helmet. It's not like in our day, when all you'd meet on the roads were horses, tractors and the odd delivery van."

Joe smiles at his sister. The roads were not quite that empty in their youth, but he says nothing.

Megan wakes up in the morning to the sound of torrential rain hitting the slate roof and all the anticipation of the day vanishes in an instant. She lies there for a while, before getting up and padding along the landing. Someone is already in her grandmother's bedroom and is having a hard time trying to help her. She doesn't know if she should smile or not, because the petulant voices make her feel uncomfortable. Adults shouldn't behave like that she decides.

As she pushes open the kitchen door, she is greeted by the wonderful smell of sausages being cooked and her mother puts several on a plate for her, along with some fat, juicy tomatoes, cut in half and grilled. There are also thick slices of buttered toast.

"Proper country breakfast." Joe says, pushing a mug of tea towards her.

For a little while she is blissfully happy in the fuggy warmth of the kitchen, the noise of the rain now somehow sounding right.

After breakfast the bicycle is unveiled. She is delighted with it and her uncle turns pink as she hugs him over and over again. He says he is sorry that he will not be there to watch the lesson, but promises to join her for a ride the next time he comes.

When Joe and Megan are ready to leave, Louise packs them both off and shuts the front door, determined to make a start on the paperwork. She plans to start with the important stuff, all of which is kept in various old biscuit tins at the bottom of the wardrobe in her mother's bedroom. There are things she needs to understand and she is not sure that Roberta will have put everything into order. She is aware that part of her mother's psyche actually thrives on causing chaos for others and takes a deep breath before going into the sickroom. She finds her mother in fine form however, having earlier almost reduced the hapless carer to tears, and intends to make the most of it.

After buying Megan a cycling helmet and some gloves, Joe leaves her outside the library. Having only boys himself, he is proud to be her favourite uncle and they enjoy their time together. His busy life in Carlisle means they have never had the opportunity to spend enough time to get bored with each other and today is no exception.

The heavy rain has turned to a fine drizzle, but she runs into the old civic building anyway, taking off her damp jacket as soon as she is through the big and imposing doors. She nods in recognition to the tall boy behind the desk and settles at one of the computers for a while, happily lost in emails, chat and Facebook, before taking her notepad over to the section he pointed out on her previous visit. She takes some books to a table and begins to leaf through them, not at all sure what it is that she is looking for, so she makes random notes as she goes, hoping that at some point it will all come together.

Her stomach reminds her that breakfast was a long time ago and when she checks the time on her phone, she is amazed to find that it's nearly five o'clock. She carefully puts the books back in their correct places, gathers her things and heads for the exit, surprised to find that the boy is doing the same.

"I've just realised where I've seen you before." he tells her as they walk in the same direction and head across the bridge "You were at the bus stop in Little Maddely the other day."

She thinks back and nods, having a vague recollection of him. "Yes, I'm staying at my gran's, Priory Meadows."

"Ah... Mrs Flanders, the dragon lady."

He smiles and his face is lit up by it. She smiles back and immediately looks away, aware that he is suddenly more attractive than he had been only a moment before.

"Yes, she can be a bit of a dragon." Megan admits.

They wait for the bus together and are pleased to find that the conversation flows beyond the exchanging of names. His is Jake and he lives with his mum in one of the newer houses that were built on what used to be the orchard, and will be heading off to college in the autumn. They discover that they both like the same bands and had few expectations for the summer, although they each tentatively begin to have some now. His best friends have gone to Ireland camping, while he needs the money he can only get by working. As they get off the bus, they both hope to see the other again soon and once he is out of sight, Megan sends Hannah a text, pleased to have something interesting to report for a change.

She finds her mother in the kitchen, throwing a salad together for them and heating up some soup for Roberta. They both notice that the other is ok and are relieved, so chatter about nothing much, giving little nuggets of information about their respective days. On the table is a pile of books and Megan asks what they are, idly picking the top one up and opening it.

"Photo albums mainly, I think." Louise answers. "I found them in one of the landing cupboards, they belonged to my granny. Gran must have put them there when she moved in."

Megan sits down and stares at the black and white images on the first page. There are place names written beside them, with captions and dates, and they show snippets of a life that was already long gone by the time she was born. She wonders about these slightly faded photos of strangers sitting on a blanket, having a picnic under a tree in 'Lower Tupping field' - June 1953.

"That girl there is your gran. She would have been nine or ten at most and the old couple are my great grandparents, Nana and Grampy Robinson. His family farmed here for generations, but I never knew either of them." Louise tells her, putting a tray together.

"Here, take this up to your grandmother, she'll be pleased to see you. I'll fry some fish and we'll have dinner when you come down."

Having found little of interest to watch on the new TV that now dominates the front parlour, they flick through the photo albums until they find one filled with pictures of Louise as a teenager. They laugh together at the fashion of the mid 1980s and the 'big' hairstyles that she seemed to favour back then. Wide eyes that are almost, but not quite familiar, stare out from a face that is close in age to Megan's and she looks carefully at her mother, trying to see the similarities between her and the person in the album. One is someone she feels she knows, while the other is a stranger, a person who cannot be. Parents, by their very existence are always old, yet here is proof that it was not always so. Louise understands her daughter's dilemma and also knows that only time will help her make sense of it, so she says nothing.

While her mother is upstairs helping Roberta settle down for the night, Megan looks through some of the albums again. One in particular catches her eye, because it is different from the others. It is slimmer, with an oriental front cover, and as she opens it she finds writing, not pictures. The first page tells her it is the diary of one Lillian Loveday and the first entry is dated December 1933, but before she can read any more of it, Louise returns, carrying two mugs of cocoa.

"Look Mum, a diary. Who was Lillian Loveday?" Megan asks, holding it out and taking one of the mugs.

"Your great grandmother: my granny. Read it to me."

For a moment, Louise is lost, wistful even. She was very close to Lillian, much closer than to Roberta and she wonders what she will recognise of the person she knew and loved so much.

"Ok then, listen..." says Megan, breaking into her thoughts.

24th December 1933

Vic gave me this for me birthday, such a treat to have him home for it. He says that now I'm out in the world, I should keep a record, cos one day it'll all be forgot. So much is changing, or so he says. Can't see it meself mind, leastways not from here!

Wonder what I'll put in it? I mean nothing much happens to me, just ordinary stuff really, nothing out of the way. I ain't no grand lady with a proper desk in its own writing room, always set up and waiting for me to sit at and record me thoughts and daily doings. Hah! Wouldn't that be a fine thing now!

So, let's start with who I am, though it's unlikely I'll forget! But others might come after me and maybe they'll want to know. Me name's Lillian Loveday and I was born on 24th December 1918. Me, Mum and Vic have lived here at number 48, on the fourth floor of Prince Albert House ever since I can remember.

Of course now, Vic only stays when his ship comes in. He's in the Merchants, but we're near the Pool, so he ain't usually got too far to walk. Or if he comes in somewhere else, like Liverpool or Southampton, he thumbs a lift home if he's got enough time for a stopover or even better, when he ain't got another ship to join yet.

Anyway, Vic's me big brother and I don't want him getting a big head, but he's a good lad, as Mum often says. Got his wits about him, as well as a good heart and he knows what's what in life. He takes care of his own and stays out of trouble. I miss him when he's gone, but we have a right laugh whenever he comes home again. And the tales he can tell us! Well it's an education, really it is, and often better than the one I got at school!

Anyways that's him. What about me? I'm fifteen today and was lucky when I left school back in June, cos straight off, I got a job down the market. Mum's got Dad's war widow pension and she takes in sewing too, so we do all right really. Leastways compared to a lot of folk, we do really well, specially as I get to bring bits of fruit and veg home most days and Vic brings what he can back with him from wherever.

Me dad got that Spanish flu when he was at the front a few weeks before the armistice, so he never knew we'd won. He never knew me neither, but Vic was seven on his last visit home, so he remembers him. He says I've got his eyes, which is nice I s'pose.

Anyway, today is me birthday and here's me birthday wish. I'd like to stand on a beach and look out to sea, maybe even stand in it and feel it whooshing around me ankles. But not on a rough day, not one of those stormy days like Vic describes, no thank you. But I'd like to see the distance with me own eyes, just once.

≈

The words captivate both of them and Megan looks at her mother, asking her if when she was at school, she too had left before she was fifteen. She is not sure if this is a good idea or not, for part of her would love to free of from it all, while another part actually enjoys the routine of learning.

Louise laughs. "No, I most certainly did not and I'm sure that your gran didn't either. But there again, she might have. We'll have to ask her in the morning."

As they troop off to bed, Louise smiles as she notices that her daughter is still clutching the diary. "And if it's dry tomorrow, we'll have that bike riding lesson!"

Before turning off the light, Megan decides to read a few more pages. She wants to know more about this girl in the diary and eagerly absorbs the next few entries.

Christmas 1933

We've been round at Auntie Eth's and we had such a feast of all those special things! Chicken, roast potatoes, brussel sprouts and all the trimmings and Mum made a great big cake. Uncle Norm managed to lay his hands on some great party hats. I was a queen and Mum had one of those jester hats, she did look funny and Uncle Norm and Vic had turbans, so they was sheiks from the desert! What a laugh we all had. After the singsong we was fit to bursting and Vic brought nuts and strange exotic bits of sweets and biscuits from Italy. The rest of the tribe and us had a right laugh, playing games with sweets for prizes. Uncle Norm was s'posed to be the ref, but he kept nodding off!

≈

26th December 1933

We slept half the morning and woke up still full and a bit worse for wear, but we all agreed it was a lovely Christmas, specially as Vic got to stay over for a change. No work for me today, what with it being Boxing Day, so I don't have to worry. Blooming cold out there and anyway there's no way I would have had me senses about me at 5am! Vic set off after a bit of breakfast and went to see about a sailing that's being organised to the Windies. It leaves tonight, so if he don't come back for his tea, that's where he'll be bound for. He said it'll be lovely and warm there compared to here and he'll come back so brown we'll say he's a native! Mum said to bring more spices, cos she can sell them on, down at the bakery, but we always keep some back for her cakes. Such a treat when her arm don't give her gyp and she feels like baking. That's when we've got all the bits of course. Mmm, makes me mouth water just thinking about it.

As ladies of leisure, cos that's what me and Mum are going to be today, we're going have a big slab of cake with tea in a while, sitting by the fire. I might read to her later and we'll eat the leftovers for supper. No cooking today, we promised ourselves.

I wonder what being fifteen is going to be like. Will I meet 'him' and if I do, will he love me properly? Will I have enough money to buy a really good dress to go dancing in? I mean I've got a whole twelve months of being fifteen, surely something good and wonderful can happen in that time?

≈

New Year 1934

Didn't get to bed til this morning, such a merry group we were. Me, Elsie, Maggie and Rita danced our way into the New Year we did. Peter Sills tried to cop a feel, but I soon put him right, a kiss is as far as it goes and then only at midnight. Elsie says he's keen on me, but I dunno, can't imagine spending the rest of me life with someone I went to school with!

I could sleep for a week, but Auntie Eth and the rest of the tribe will be here soon for a slap up tea and Mum's calling for me to get the kettle on and the oven warm for the crumpets, to get them good and rised I shouldn't wonder. This new electric oven is a right treat, so clean after the coal. It was good of Vic to pay for it, made Mum smile it did. Pity he ain't here, but he got a job on a sailing with one of his mates heading over to Spain. I think that's where he said, anyway he was keen to be off, maybe next year though.

≈

26th January 1934

Me, Rita and Maggie went to the Odeon on the Broadway to see 'A ticket in Tatts'. We laughed all the way through it. It was set in Australia, lovely looking place it is too, such a big sky, I mean really, really big and there was a bit on the Pathé News before the film, showing the harbour at Sydney. Mags said she's going to find herself an Australian sailor for a husband and make him take her there. Good luck to her I say.

I'm not sure I'd want to marry someone from so far away, cos it's likely I'd have to go there rather than have him settle here. Not sure I'd want to leave everyone behind and sail off on me own into a new life. But then what if he was real special and I really loved him? Would that be enough to take me away from everyone else? It'd have to be a big love, like in the really good books and films! That being the case, I know I ain't met him yet!

≈

10th February 1934

Mum's feeling a bit better now. The damp weather really got to her chest, but she was up again today, so I reckon we're over the worst of it. Had me real worried for a couple of days when she didn't have the strength to get up from the bed it did. She tries to say she's fine, but I know she ain't. Mrs Jessop at number 26 had to go to the TB clinic and last we heard, she ain't doing so well and I got really scared. I mean what if Mum got TB and had to go away or even worse, died of it? Don't do to fret over what ain't happened, that's what Mum says, but still, a person can't help having thoughts popping in and lingering can they?

Thankfully I was able to get loads of onions from the market and she says that really helped, cos she wouldn't let us use any of our savings to get the doctor in. Auntie Eth came by every day while I was out, so that was good too. I reckon between them they know the best onion and milk broth recipes!

≈

18th February 1934

Sad day. We had Maggie's funeral today. Can't believe she's gone, just like that. The bloke what was driving the van will be up in front of the magistrate next week, but that won't bring her back, will it? There's talk about introducing a test for anyone what wants to drive, but that's too late for her an all.

A diary ain't the place to speak of death. I don't want to write about Maggie like this. I want to bring her back on these pages, so as I'll always know where to find her. I want to remember the days at school and how she could do that impression of Mrs Gladwell, that always had us in stitches, near wetting ourselves sometimes we'd be. Or how she could never remember nothing in history and said it didn't matter anyway, it was the future what mattered and how she loved to make up stories about what the future would be like for us all. Course none of that'll happen for her now, so she'll never know if she was right or not. It's not bloody fair.

It was a bit of good luck that we both got jobs down at the market and was able to cycle there and back everyday together. I never, never want to forget how I loved to watch her dance and listen to her sing. Such a voice, 'the voice of an angel' her ma always said, rightly so and all. And those freckles, how she hated them! All the lemon juice in the world didn't make them go away, she'd never believe us when we told her they made her pretty, the prettiest of all of us, what with her tiny waist and long legs. She was me friend and I couldn't save her.

It's not right, all of me life ahead of me without me best friend, how can that be? I can't get me head round it. It ain't fair or right, it's nothing but bad.

≈

Megan notices some small discoloured patches on the page and realises that Lillian had been crying. She wonders what she would write about Hannah, if something terrible happened to her and finds her own eyes welling up at the thought. She carefully closes the diary and turns off the light, falling asleep with her head full of another person's life.

The sun streaming through the windows wakes her and she quickly chucks the covers off, startling the recumbent Maisie. Downstairs, as she passes the old office, she hears her mother's voice but not the words. Her tone is odd and she decides to go straight to the kitchen rather than disturb her.

She is still munching through her cereal when her mother comes in. Her face is flushed and she tries to smile when she sees her daughter, but Megan is not fooled and correctly guesses that it was her father on the phone. Before she can ask anything though, Louise confirms that today is the big day.

"We'll begin as soon as you are dressed. Then you'll be able to come and go as you please, without having to use the bus for everything."

She begins to tackle the washing up and is thus able to have her back to her daughter. She is trying not to cry or sound angry. After all, it is not Megan's fight.

Roberta hears laughter and gleeful shouting from outside and forces herself, inch by inch, out of bed. From the window, she sees mother and daughter below in the garden and watches dispassionately. One is trying to teach, the other is trying to learn and they are both helpless with mirth. She is willing her granddaughter to master the vehicle, which she recognises as her own, given to her by her grandparents when she was of a similar age. "No, younger..." she mutters to herself. "I was younger."

She has no intention of sharing any of this with Megan, mainly because the image that floats into her mind is of her own mother trying to convince her to ride down to the river with her for a picnic. Roberta had been dismissive and unkind in her reply and Lillian had shrunk away from her, visibly shocked at the words that had come out so easily, intended only to wound. Standing there, Roberta remembers that she had once been proud of her ability to hurt, but now, looking back, she wonders if it has been a gift or a curse.

"The past matters to no one except those who were there, and sometimes not even to them." she mutters, turning away and shuffling back to her bed, thereby missing the first complete circuit Megan has done without wobbling or falling off.

A little later, feeling reasonably confident but armed with her mobile phone just in case, Megan heads out through the garden gate into the street and off down the hill, to practice and experiment.

Louise is suddenly alone and in need of something to do. She will not let her mind turn back to *that* conversation, and remembering the old rocking horse in the garage, she takes herself off to search for it.

When she finds it, she decides to work on it and return it to its former glory, pleased to discover that she can easily clear a space around it. She needs a project, and not just the dreary chore of clearing a house that hasn't been a home for too long. She makes a mental list, then goes back into the house and calls up to her mother that she is going out for a while and heads off to the nearby DIY superstore for the necessary materials.

As she prowls around the aisles and browses the shelves, she is able to go over the conversation she had earlier with Peter. His words sit in her mind alongside the instructions on various tins and she finds this the best way to consider his request. They had agreed on no contact for a month, on the basis that they needed time apart. That had been *his rule*, when she told him she was leaving. *His rule,* not hers and it was typical of him to break it. Not only has he phoned, but he wants to meet up, because he has things he wants to discuss.

Louise is acutely aware that she is not ready to discuss anything and fears that he will coerce her into agreeing to do something that she should not. But she wants to see him, she wants to touch him and she wants to see herself reflected in his eyes, for only there has she ever felt real.

'Ensure that surfaces are free from dust or grease before application' she reads, knowing that there is still too much dust and grease all over everything in her life. She grabs a selection of paintbrushes and tries to contemplate a future without him, but she cannot. She stands stock still, clutching the handle of her trolley and forces all the feelings back into the crevices of her heart. She is not ready.

When she had been 'the other woman', his wife had chosen to stay and fight for her man. She had been tearful and Peter had despised her for it, seeing it as a weakness, but Louise had stored the knowledge away for when it might be needed. She realises now that she has always known this time would come, because Peter is that kind of man. That is why she had loved him so fervently; it was never going to be forever.

"But my forever doesn't have to end, not just yet..." she mutters to herself, and pulls out her mobile, texting him a few short words.

'No. Too soon.'

Having pressed send, she heads for the tills, trying to breathe normally and counting slowly as she exhales, wondering what Cate will say when she tells her.

Left alone, Roberta drifts in and out of consciousness. It is a pleasant state to be in, because there she is able to find people she lost long ago. In her mind a popular song from her youth serenades her and she smiles as she remembers the title and the moment she first became aware of it. 'Unforgettable...' she hums quietly to herself. She no longer remembers all the words, but it doesn't matter. The mood and texture of the time it conjures up come easily to her and the hour or so passes peacefully.

When Louise returns, looking haggard and cross, and asks what she wants for lunch, Roberta finds she is almost hungry. She is only mildly curious about what has caused her daughter's bad temper and is determined not to lose her own pleasant frame of mind, so she dismisses her with a wave and a request for soup. She returns to a happier time, when she could attract and keep people in her life, rather than scare them away, then banishes this thought by gently shaking her head and smiling, as nicer memories pour in to take its place.

When Megan takes the tray up to her grandmother, she is still flushed from her cycle ride and over lunch she tells her all about it. Roberta asks questions about the neighbourhood, which her granddaughter is happy to answer.

Later, she offers to read to her, but the offer is declined. She suggests bringing a jigsaw puzzle, but this too is turned down. As she begins to cast about for other things that may keep her amused, Roberta comes up with a request of her own.

"Music. I should like to listen to some music." she tells her. "Nat King Cole, that's what I'd like. Do you think they'd have that in the library?"

Megan nods slowly. "They might, but I'm not a member, so I can't take things out."

"Well I can't get there to join, so you'd best come up with a solution."

Roberta pushes the tray away and smiles at her granddaughter. She has faith that she will somehow rise to the challenge, for she has always seen something of herself in her, which has always pleased her.

"I found your mother's diary yesterday." Megan tells her as she is clearing the lunch things.

"Nonsense, is it?" asks her grandmother.

"No, I don't think so, although I haven't read much yet. She's only fifteen in the bit I'm reading."

"Well, you see how it goes and if you still find it interesting at the end, maybe you can read it to me." Roberta says in her offhand way.

Megan is surprised at her lack of curiosity, certain that if someone told her they had found Louise's diary, she would be eager to see what was in it. Adults, she decides, are a strange bunch and she leaves, holding the tray carefully, so as not to spill or drop anything.

She finds her mother in the garage, red-eyed and manically sanding down the ancient stained wood of the rocking horse. The radio is blaring and Megan realises that she needs to be alone.

"I'm going to the Library." she shouts and makes her way back out. She hesitates for a moment, then decides to take the bus and runs back into the house, picking up Lillian's diary to read on the way.

2nd March 1934

Been a busy time lately, so not written much. Me hands are red raw too, it's been so cold and of course with the scrubbing of the veg down the market where there ain't no nice warm water, ohhh nasty. Holding our mugs of tea is the nearest we've been to any heat during the day. Still, we usually manage a bit of a laugh, so can't really complain.

≈

4th March 1934

Been a bit moochy as Mum says, and she's right, I have. All the time I'm looking for Mags, thinking about what we'll be doing in the evening or for the weekend, making plans and whatnot and then I remember. She's gone. She's dead. Not like in a film, but really gone and she ain't coming back. I still can't really believe it.

How can she not have made it to sixteen? Supposed to be a sweet time, the sweetest, that's what the songs say, who said it was all right for her to miss it? That's what I'd like to know! How can all those hopes and plans come to nothing and just be wiped out in a moment of carelessness?

≈

6th March 1934

Been thinking about those women that we met up with last week, the Women's Hunger Marchers they were. Mum and Auntie Eth said we had to support them, cos just because we're lucky enough to have work and food on the table, shouldn't mean we turn our backs on them that don't. We made a big pot of stew to hand out to them at the shelter. Got talking to one, Margery her name is from up Derby way. She's got four kiddies and neither she nor her husband has got any work. They don't get much assistance cos the means testing says they've no need of it because they still have plates and cups and suchlike that they can sell. Problem is, the village is so skint there's no one can afford to buy them. She goes to sleep listening to the hungry crying of her babes, trying to block out the sound of the rats and things scrabbling about looking for crumbs. She says the inspector said their house were a slum, but like she said, 'tis home for them, where else would they go?

Me and Elsie couldn't think of being in such a position. Don't seem as though the world is quite right. We have so much down south and they have so little up north. Although Margery did say there's always rich folk up and down the country and in London we'll have the poor ones too, and I know she's right. There's the slums over in Gaskell Street, makes me shudder whenever I have to go past them. Mum and me we have to say that sorting it all out can't be that simple, I mean if it were there'd be an answer by now wouldn't there?

≈

8th March 1934

We had a lovely tin of pink salmon for tea with some nice fresh crusty bread and a bit of cucumber, just like them rich people in the books. Crazy world we live in, that's what Mum said, so she decided we'd have a bit of our own madness that won't hurt no one and we really enjoyed it. We had it at the big table in the parlour, not in front of the stove, on the best plates too and we opened the window. 'Spring is almost here!' Mum announced in her posh voice, made me laugh she did, I mean we're still all bundled up.

It was nice though, just the two of us nattering away about our day. Nothing special in one way, but losing Mags so suddenly and for no good reason does make a person think and does make me try to appreciate the good things in life, like a tin of pink salmon for our tea!

≈

13th March 1934

Just finished 'The Seven Dials Mystery' by Agatha Christie. Got it for sixpence at the market on Saturday and couldn't wait for the day to be over so I could get stuck in to it. Bought meself a bar of that new Whole Nut chocolate, good it was too, first time I've found it at a decent price. Didn't go out at all once I was back from work, even missed the cinema, the book was that good. Mum didn't get a peep out of me all evening, but she enjoyed the chocolate, so I was forgiven!

To be a lady like Bundle, now that would be a lark. I can see meself in them posh frocks being all lah-di-dah, gadding about here there and everywhere like I owned the flippin place and getting up everyone's nose. Then just when they'd nearly had enough, tralaa! I sort it all out for them! Lords and such would take me dancing, what a laugh me life would be. As it is I got asked out to the spring dance over at the Docket by Charlie Church from the market. Reckon it'll be fun so I said yes.

≈

16th March 1934

Got a letter from Vic today. His ship ran into trouble so they took shelter in Naples, or 'Napoli' as it's called by the locals apparently. It has to stay there for repairs and of course he don't get paid for that, so he got himself taken on as crew on another ship what's bound for Lisbon. Course he don't know when he'll be back now, or even where he'll head after there. Such a life he leads! By the time he's thirty he'll have been round the world several times, seen all them places, eaten all that strange food and who knows what else! But if I were a boy I'd be the same, I'm sure of it. All that world out there, just waiting to be explored. Makes me shiver just thinking about it!

He sent this photo of him and his mate with a couple of local girls who they'd been larking around with. He said they were really sweet but dirt poor, said he'd never seen so many people with less than nothing then he had in Naples. Apparently, one pound buys five American dollars and you can get as much for one dollar as you can for a pound pretty much anywhere. That must make him a rich boy! Bet he likes all that swanning about on shore with all that money. Mind you, he works hard and he's generous with it, so I don't begrudge him a minute of his swanning or a penny of his money.

It was a different stamp to the last time he sent a letter from Italy, so I cut it out real careful and stuck it in the album with the others. Quite a collection Mum's got now and it tickles her whenever she gets them out for her trip round the world from home, as she says.

Must tell Elsie and Rita that we should get a picture of ourselves taken, it's all the rage now after all. Something fun to remember ourselves by when we're old and grey, surrounded by grandchildren and the like! Pity we didn't do it before, when Mags could have been in it too.

≈

A faded black and white photo of four young people smiling for the camera is stuck below the entry and Megan stares at it, wondering which one is Vic and which one is his nameless friend. To her knowledge, neither her mother nor her grandmother have ever spoken of Uncle Vic and she wonders for a moment what happened to him. Perhaps he never came back and is still out there somewhere, forever young and handsome, sailing the high seas like the hero of a fairytale. She giggles to herself at this bit of nonsense and turns the page.

2nd May 1934

Charlie's a good dancer, I'll give him that and we danced for nearly the whole time. It was a great night out, the lights were pretty and the bunting hung around the hall made it real special. The band played all our favourites, 'stay as sweet as you are', 'flying down to Rio', 'stars fell on Alabama' and me favourite, 'I only have eyes for you'. Mind you, Charlie had eyes for anyone with a fine pair of legs on em! But that's all right by me, we both know he ain't never gonna be the love of me life, but we had a good night out and some supper later in one of them new cafes on the Broadway with Elsie and Fred. Now there's a romance that's blossoming!

Maybe it's about how you look together that tells a person if he or she is the right one. I mean Elsie is pretty enough anyway by most people's standards, maybe a bit too curvy, but not plump and Fred is a bit on the short side. Not much on his own you might think, but anyone who sees them together must see that sparkle they give each other, it's unmistakable. I just look at them and see that it's right. But how can you look at yourself with another person and see that? I mean, a mirror or a photograph might not capture it right. It's all so confusing.

≈

25th May 1934

So Bonnie and Clyde are dead. It's all over the news, even on the Pathé at the cinema. Not sure if they were really heroes though, despite what some folk say about them. In books or films being pretty goes some way, but in real life you have to be more than that, surely? Anyway, what good came out of what they did? I mean all the people what they killed were just doing their jobs and they had family too. Like I said to Elsie and Rita, 'What if they killed me, just cos I wouldn't give them a pound of onions and carrots?' I mean, that wouldn't be fair would it? I wonder if they'll be remembered? Maybe that's why they did it. Die young and live forever. Funny thought that, not sure I like it at all.

Auntie Eth's been in bed with some tummy bug or other for over a week now. Mum's been over there most days looking after the tribe and I've been helping after work too. Uncle Norm's looking worried and they're talking of getting a doctor in, but it'll cost a bit, it always does, be about three bob I reckon, then there'd be the cost of the medicine too. Still, between us we've some saved up, so for me tuppence worth, I said we should.

≈

Chapter four

As Megan glances out of the window, she realises she is nearly at the centre of town, so she tucks the diary into her bag and gets ready to get off the bus. She hopes Jake will be at the library and blushes slightly at the thought.

She is not disappointed. He is stacking books onto the trolley and he waves to her as she comes in, which gives her the confidence to walk straight up to him and explain her grandmother's request and her problem about not being a member.

"Music is over there, on cassette and CD. I can always take it out for you if we have what the dragon lady wants." He grins at her as he uses the local nickname for Roberta.

She smiles back. "I'll go and look."

Nat King Cole's greatest hits is on both cassette and CD, but she is unable to recall what equipment her grandmother has, so she takes them both over to where Jake is working.

"I'll be finished here soon, are you doing research today, or do you fancy an ice cream in the park?" he asks, trying not to sound too hopeful.

"Ice cream wins over research any day." Megan replies shyly.

She leans on the trolley, handing him books until the section is sorted and only a few remain, then follows him round the shelves to biographies and leafs through a book about Bette Davis while he works. She is intrigued by the strange beauty of the old movie star, whose name she has heard of but cannot place.

She realises he is standing in front of her, clearly waiting for an answer to a question she has not heard. "I'm sorry, I was miles away." she says, slightly embarrassed.

He loves the worlds that can be found in books himself, so he doesn't mind in the slightest. In fact he finds it charming.

"I just asked if you found anything for your grandmother."

"Yes... yes, I did." Megan holds out the two items. "Are you sure you don't mind? I mean you hardly know me."

"True, but I know where you live!" he says jokingly and takes them from her.

They sit by the duck pond with their backs against the trunk of a tree, eating ice cream and chatting easily, using the time to find out more about each other. He was eighteen in January and she will be sixteen in September. He is an only child and his father died when he was two, so he has no real memories of him. She is genuinely sorry to learn this, while he in turn, is sorry to hear that her parents are possibly heading for a divorce. He wants to do voluntary work abroad when he finishes his studies and then hopes to go on and have his own veterinary practice at some point later in life, but a country practice, looking after big animals, not just pets.

She doesn't yet know what she wants to do, but loves languages. A job is not something she has given much thought to and sitting with Jake in the late afternoon sun, she finds it impossible to contemplate a different life.

She tells him she spent the morning riding her bicycle around the neighbourhood, but she doesn't tell him she only learnt how to ride one a few hours ago. He is thoughtful and then admits that he has not ridden for years, but that summer seems to be the perfect time to start again and together they plan an outing for the coming Saturday.

"The forecast is dry," he informs her, "and it may even be a real summer's day! You bring the sandwiches and I'll sort out some drinks and other things. What do you say?" He jumps to his feet and holds his hand out towards her to help her up.

"Deal! What time?"

They settle on ten thirty and wander towards the bus stop, chatting easily about music and films that they both like.

As the sun moves away from the grubby skylights in the garage, the light changes and fades. Louise clears up and stands back to admire her work. In many ways the horse looks worse than it did when she started, but she knows this is unavoidable. Preparation is important if the end result is to be worth it, so she pats the bare wood where the mane ought to be and assures it that it will be splendid when she is finished.

She turns off the light and walks back to the house, going first to check on her mother who is engrossed in a soap opera on her new TV.

"There you are at last!" she grumbles as her daughter stands in the doorway. "A woman could die of thirst up here. Some nurse you're turning out to be." Roberta says accusingly, but not harshly.

"Cup of tea Mum...?" Louise suggests.

"Magic, those words are." her mother responds with a hint of a twinkle in her eyes.

Smiling, and feeling lighter than she thought she ever would again, Louise goes back down to the kitchen and puts the kettle on. She contemplates the contents of the fridge, then decides on a simple pasta for dinner.

Later, alone in her bed, she allows herself to remember meeting her husband for the first time. She'd had the good luck to secure a work placement at an agency where Peter had been a key client and from the moment he arrived for a meeting, she had been intrigued by his looks, his quirky sense of humour and his piercing green eyes. By the time he left, although barely a word had been exchanged between them, it was clear that he was interested in her. She had been amazed, for her sexual charms were largely unexplored and her experience was limited. He was older and he oozed something that left her breathless. She was young then and called it love. She wonders what she would call it now, but stops short of trying to find the right words.

He was married and David had been what...? Less than a year, a toddler? She tries to remember but cannot be precise. It doesn't really matter though; after all, by their third meeting she didn't care. She had wanted him as much, if not more, than she had wanted anything in her life. The hard won freedom she had secured from home with the help of her grandmother meant nothing in comparison and she gave it up in an instant to be his.

She is certain this new and named other, this Lucy, feels the same. He always has this effect when he chooses to, which leads her to wonder if Lucy is the first since she has been in his life and she empathises with David's mother, although of course they had been married for much less than the thirteen years she has proudly called herself his wife. That had been another hard won battle, for having just got his divorce through, he was in no hurry to marry again. They had Megan, a joint mortgage and were living together.

"Why?" he'd asked more than once. "It's not such a big deal these days."

But it was and still is, she reminds herself, a very big deal indeed and as such, should we just walk away from all those promises and commitments without a backward glance? She sighs, wondering if it would be enough just to forgive him and carry on as though nothing had happened, but she instinctively knows that she cannot do that either. It did happen, there is no getting away from the fact, and she is still uncertain how she really feels about it.

In that moment, everything she has built crumbles in front of her eyes. Her life seems to be one of those surrealist paintings where every misshapen object in it has a dark, hidden meaning, a meaning everyone else knows and has known for some time, but she hasn't. Silently weeping, she drifts off into a troubled and fitful sleep.

Megan wakes up to voices, car doors slamming and the sound of feet scrunching on the gravel. It is light outside, but a feeling of panic envelopes her as she groggily pushes the covers and an indignant cat off her leaden limbs and goes out onto the landing. Her mother is standing outside Roberta's door, talking to someone inside, someone male.

"Mum...?" she asks, her voice small and childlike.

Louise puts her arm around her daughter's shoulders and leads her away, down the stairs towards the kitchen.

"Gran had a bit of a turn in the night. I think... or rather I hope she'll be ok. That's the Doctor with her now and the Macmillan nurse. I need to be there, can you sort yourself out?"

Megan nods and watches her mother disappear back up the stairs. She had somehow managed to forget that her grandmother is dying, a fact that she really doesn't know what to do with. As she begins to get her cereal ready, she spies her bag hanging on the hook by the back door. In it is the tape and the CD from the library and she is reminded that she hasn't had the chance yet to present them to Roberta and that now it might be too late. A sob rises in her throat and she stifles it back down.

Lillian's diary is also in the bag. She carefully takes it and her breakfast out into the garden, walking barefoot across the grass to the far side, where there is an old table and a couple of rickety chairs haphazardly perched on a few slabs of paving stone. She settles down, props the book open against an old bottle that has been left on the table and dreamily spoons the cereal into her mouth.

New Year 1935

Can't believe that's a whole year been and gone just like that. Truth be told, I'd forgotten all about me diary till Vic asked in his last letter how it was going! Made me go red with shame, cos it was such a lovely thought of his to get it for me. So this year I'm going to try harder and write more often. It'd be a good idea, as I realise that since me last entry in May, I've already forgotten all sorts of things that have happened and now I'm sixteen! I do know though, that I didn't get to fulfil me birthday wish.

We went to Kent, fruit picking in the summer down by the river, but I didn't get to the sea. So this birthday just gone, I made the same wish. Maybe you got to really really want a wish to come true, not a flit in the dark sort of thing, but something that you want right down in the marrow of your bones. So by making it more than once, you get to be really really sure!

Vic ain't been back at all and from his last letter it don't seem he's too sure when he might. He's been doing a regular run between Shanghai and Boston for months now, but Mum and me, we hope he gets back sometime this year before we forget what he looks like. Or like Mum said, at least do different runs, cos she ain't had no new stamps for a while now to stick in her album!

He sent a parcel over for Christmas with a mate of his, full of dried fruits, spices and some lovely oriental pictures painted on silk. Really special they are. Auntie Eth cried when she opened hers. He also sent some books back for me, says they are so much cheaper in Boston than here, some new authors for me to see what I think, then we got some magazines too. Cor! What a wonder they are, so different from the ones we get here, not that we buy them, but sometimes you find one. The clothes, well me, Joyce and Tish sat there in amazement, really special some of them are, but the scene the photograph or picture is in is dead normal. Mum says she's going to work out a pattern for one I like, as I need a new going out dress. We agreed that she's done as much as she can really with the one I've got. That'd be wonderful and I'm sure she could do it, she's got magic fingers and I ain't the only one that tells her that!

Mum and me, we bought a radio this winter so we can be snug at home. A right laugh it is too, all sorts of programmes to listen to and music as well. We've even stood up and had a foxtrot around the parlour on more than one occasion! But there's plays and music hall turns too, something for everyone and every mood. And it all comes out of a wooden box with lights in it!

So here we are, January 1935, a whole new year in front of us and I'm still working down the market. Elsie and Fred are real serious and plan to wed next year when she's eighteen. Everyone said it wouldn't last, cos he's so much older than her, but it has and I agree with Elsie, it will last, they're made for each other! I do believe, even though it ain't happened to me, that a person knows when they meet the right one. I know I ain't yet, so that's a start I s'pose.

All that aside mind, life just trundles along like how it's s'posed to. Not that I'd turn down an adventure like in the films or them radio plays, or even like the mystery ones that Agatha writes about. Mum says I shouldn't wish for one though, as I might just get it and then what'd I do?

≈

2nd February 1935

There's a new lad delivering to the market, Albert Tompkins, he stopped to chat with me every morning last week. Nice lad, talks sense and you can have a laugh with him. He was keen to know all about Vic, said he'd always wanted to go to sea but after his dad died he had to take on the family and provide for them proper like, so he does this instead. Lovely blue eyes he's got. They twinkle when he smiles, which he done a lot of while we was talking.

Elsie's been teasing me, says she can see 'the signs' and then she laughs at me. She can laugh all she likes! But I have to say, I do look out for him of a morning and I'd miss our chats if they was to stop.

≈

9th February 1935

Albert came home for tea yesterday and Mum says he seems like a nice lad, so she's happy for me to go dancing with him next week. He asked her all proper like, before he'd even asked me! Elsie and Fred are coming along too, so we'll make up a party for supper afterwards. Mum says she'll have me new dress ready by then too, so it can be a real special night. I tried it on this evening, so she could pin the hem and make sure it tucks in just right, to make me hips and waist look slim. It shimmers and rustles like something from a dream and as Mum says, it's a proper grown up dress and American too!

He's only really seen me in me tats at the market and when he came for tea I had me good skirt and blouse on, but it's a bit dreary. I'm really looking forward to a real night out with him, I hope it all goes all right and I don't spoil it by doing something daft, that'd be just like me!

≈

14th February 1935

We all went down the Docket for the Valentine's dance. It was lovely, the band played all the slow numbers and Albert and me drifted about the place in each other's arms. He's a lovely kisser, I could spend all evening just being kissed by him. I'm going to lie here all night, just remembering our time together. It was the best Valentine's, the best dance, the best everything I've ever had and he was smiling as he left me at the door too, the best.

≈

15th February 1935

Had to get up as normal this morning, it being Friday, right hard that was too! Still, it was worth it. Albert was there delivering and we had a quick cuddle behind his van while no one was looking. He said he'd had a lovely time and we made plans for tomorrow night. He'll come and collect me at seven and we'll go over to a place he knows behind the Broadway, where he says they have a good dance band. It'll give me and Mum a chance to clean me dress up a bit or even alter me old one a bit, so's to be in something different. I can't wait. At least on Sunday I can have a lie in. Dancing twice in one week! Not only did he pay for Thursday, he's already said not to worry about tomorrow, so he must have a bit and be doing all right for his self.

≈

17th February 1935

Feeling a bit down really. It all had to be called off at the last minute as his mum's not well and he had to get the doctor in. He sent a message round with a lad a bit before he was due to come. Said he was right worried and he'd see me at the market on Monday all being well. Mum was lovely, said as I was all dressed up we'd go and see a feature and then have a bit of supper together afterwards.

We saw 'Naughty Marietta' with Nelson Eddy and Jeannette Macdonald. Real rich it was, lovely costumes and both of them declaring in words and song that they'll never marry. There was pirates and nobs and all sorts going on and of course a happy ending, just when you despaired of it ever turning out all right. We had a lovely time, got right caught up in it and then at the end came back to earth with a bit of a bump. Took me mind right off Albert and I felt bad. I mean, what if his old mum dies or something in the night? Mum said I was being daft, I hope she's right.

≈

19th February 1935

All's well in the Tompkins household. I saw him today and he said his mum's pulled round really well. He tried to have a bit of a cuddle behind his van, but I kept me distance a bit. Like Mum said, don't always go a-running, let him come to you. We arranged to go out on Friday. Hope I get to see him before then though.

≈

22nd February 1935

He gave me a bar of chocolate yesterday, two yellow roses today and a reminder that on Friday there will just be me and him. Makes me smile he does, that's for sure. Blooming cold it is, so a girl needs something to thaw her out a bit!

≈

2nd March 1935

Old Mrs Norris along the way has been sticking her oar in where it's not wanted, so she has. She says she's seen Albert stepping out with someone else over the other side of the gasworks. Mum says while she doesn't think it likely, I ought to take care, just in case like. When I asked him if he'd been over that way he said his cousins live that side and often he goes to visit, to take them a bit of money and suchlike, as they're not well off. When I told Mum she said nothing, but pulled that funny face that she does sometimes. I don't care what they think, he put my mind at ease, didn't turn a hair when I asked him straight out. Told me I was his favourite girl and that's good enough for me.

≈

18th March 1935

If this is what love is, then that's fine and dandy by me. What can I say to explain it? I mean I'll want to remember this time if we carry on through the years, so we can laugh about it later.

Well, I like it when we're together, he makes me smile, he likes to do the things I like to do, he dances well and wants to work hard to provide for his mum and his sisters. That's the reason why we can't see as much of each other as we'd like. I mean he's got two jobs and a third one too on occasion. Given that others struggle to have one at the moment, that's not something to grumble about, as I keep saying to everyone who seems to want me to think bad of him. I wish Vic was here, he'd know. Or Mags, we could chew it over together, her suggestions for sorting out how I feel would make me laugh, I know that!

≈

27*th* March 1935

Me and Elsie had a girls night out and went to see 'The Gay Divorcee' with Fred and Ginger. It was a right laugh and Mum says she's going to see it with Auntie Eth later this week, which will be nice, as me and Albert can have a night in with the radio, if he's not having to work that is of course. I'll invite him over for a bit of tea and we can settle down after Mums gone out.

Got a lovely long letter from Vic this morning, sounds like he might be thinking of settling too. He keeps mentioning this girl Viv in his letters. Mum and me checked, and she's been in the last six! Hope he sends a photo soon. Mum says it's about time, what with him being twenty five this year, but still, we'd both like for him to be settled nearer.

≈

7*th* May 1935

Oh what fun we had celebrating the jubilee. The whole flats had a street party, with bunting and flags and decorations made by the kids on long tables, which were all heaving with good things to eat and drink and Mrs Caldicott made loads of her famous lemonade. We all brought something and we all left fit to bursting. Everyone was there and grudges were forgot for the day. We sang and toasted His Royal Highness several times. Tommy and Evan did their famous comic turn together and had us all in stitches and Gloria from number 6 led the singing on her piano, which we'd pushed to just outside her door.

Twenty five years he's been on the throne and everyone says the world has changed while he's been there. Didn't see Albert though, he was over at the party in his street, but we had nice tea out today to make up for it and plan to go dancing on Friday up at the Astoria. Mum's going to change me dress about a bit, so it looks like a new one.

≈

As Louise is saying goodbye to the doctor and the nurse, she spies her daughter deeply engrossed in something at the end of the garden and is thankful. The crisis is over for the time being, but it has brought the reason for their stay into sharp relief. She makes mugs of tea and carefully picks her way through the overgrown grass towards the shabby patio, thinking that she must find a gardener or someone soon.

"Ahh, there you are..." Louise exclaims as she comes up behind Megan. She cautiously sits down on the other chair and hands her one of the mugs.

Megan slowly rejoins the present and listens while her mother tells her what has happened. She was afraid to ask and visibly relaxes as Louise explains that Roberta is still in the land of the living and is sleeping peacefully.

"She is dying and it is possible that next time she won't survive, but it depends, and we have to be ready for the possibility. We haven't really talked about it, not honestly, so I suppose now might be a good time. What do you think?"

Louise watches her daughter carefully as she speaks, not at all sure what she should say, or how she should broach the subject of death when she feels so strongly that when you are fifteen, this sort of thing should not touch or taint the essence of life. For a fleeting second she misses her husband, knowing that he would handle this better than she is doing.

Megan's mind is still partly anchored in Lillian's world and everything in the real world seems a little distant to her, but she senses her mother's insecurity and wants in some way to make it better.

"Mum, to be honest I don't know what I think, or even what I should be thinking, never mind feeling." she replies slowly. "I mean ok, so Gran's dying and that's sad and horrible, but today she's alive, isn't that enough to be getting on with?"

Louise considers these pearls before nodding in agreement. "Yes, it's more than enough to be getting on with. After all..."

"Oh I nearly forgot." Megan interrupts. "Yesterday at the library I got a CD and a cassette for her. What have we got here that she can play them on? I ought to give them to her today to listen to, oughtn't I?"

It is her turn to be insecure and her mother's turn to make it all right.

"Yes you should, it will please her. Let's go and dig around and see what we can find."

As they walk back to the house, Megan tells her about the picnic arranged for Saturday and together they discuss what needs to be bought to make sandwiches with. As they plan, Louise is pleased that she has made a friend so quickly. Cate has been threatening to visit and it seems that Saturday would be as good a time as any.

Upstairs, oblivious to everything, Roberta drifts in and out of a drug induced sleep. She is listening to the smoky voice of Nat King Cole that Louise has thoughtfully put on for her and decides that it is all very pleasant indeed. She argues with herself about the medication she should be taking and while not altogether sure that it will lengthen her life in terms of weeks or even days, she is suddenly aware that they might make whatever time she has left more bearable. This understanding helps her realise that she is not quite as ready to leave earthly things behind as she had thought

"No, not just yet." she whispers into the pillow, curious as to what her daughter will decide to do about that charming but untrustworthy husband of hers.

Roberta knows, even if Louise doesn't, that her daughter is strong enough to leave him and get on with her own life, just as she was in her time, and her mother and grandmother were before her. But Louise has a choice, they didn't and she wonders if that makes it different. If Arnold hadn't died when he did, would she have left him?

Her mind flits about in a most pleasing way, unfettered and free of emotion and she finds that she likes the sensation tremendously. She allows it to settle on the vaguely known Susan Moresby, who had been Arnold's mistress for over a decade, but who had never once, to Roberta's knowledge, tried to entice him away from home. What kind of woman she wonders, not for the first time, settles for that, that what...? Freedom?

She tries the word out carefully in her mouth and after a moment decides that it is the correct one. Would she, Roberta, have understood him better, supported his wishes and dreams more enthusiastically if she had not had to cook his meals three times a day, every day for every year they were married, or wash his socks, or listen to him snore? Could things have been different she wonders. Might he not have had to go in search of another if she had been happier? Who rejected who first she wonders, and then her mind touches the real question, as though it were an exposed nerve in a tooth. Did I drive him to her?

It is a deep and troubling thought, but she is not afraid of it. She faces it and decides to ask Louise to track down her husband's mistress. She wants to meet her, talk with her, drink tea with her, at least once before she goes.

Downstairs, Louise has arranged for an all day carer to come at seven thirty on Saturday morning and is chatting to Cate, planning to collect her from the station. She updates her on what has happened in the last twenty four hours and is pleased that she will have some time to just be herself; not the mother, not the daughter and certainly not the wife. But then she realises that she is no longer sure just 'who' Louise might be.

Cate laughs at her. "Well I'm sure whoever she is, she will appreciate a good natter over some chilled white wine and a meal she hasn't had to cook!"

Louise smiles as she agrees.

Megan is also deep in conversation, but with Hannah, who is sharing everything that has happened during the last days at school and discussing in the kind of detail meaningful only to the young, the imminent BBQ. While she is sad that she can't go, she is also determined not to let it spoil her friend's plans and throws herself enthusiastically into the debate about what outfit, which shoes and what should and should not be said to whom, should the occasion arise.

After lunch, Megan cycles down to the local supermarket to buy the few bits her mother has asked for. Roberta uses the opportunity of their being alone to tell her daughter that her father had been having an affair and that it was only his death that prevented it being known to her or her brothers. Louise is stunned by this revelation and sits down heavily to let it sink in. But before she can ask any questions, her mother tells her that she wants her to contact the other woman, because she wants to meet her, to see her for herself and to find out what else they have in common.

"Are you serious?" Louise asks, aghast.

"Never been more so." her mother says, stirring her tea a little more fiercely than usual.

"But..."

There is so much Louise wants to say, but her mind is in chaos. Questions are tumbling over themselves, yet none of them come out of her mouth.

"But nothing. We were married for almost thirty years and for at least ten of them she was in his life too. I'm curious, that's all. I've hardly given her or your father a thought for a long time, but now I find I want to understand a few things and this is one of them.

"There's a tin in what used to be his wardrobe. It's in the nursery now, the bigger of the two in there and it's got his bits and pieces in it. You and your brothers will have to decide who gets what, but in the tin there's a scrap of paper with SM and a telephone number written on it. See if she's still alive and if she is, invite her over. Tell her I won't bite, couldn't if I wanted to mind, but I reckon she'll be as curious as I am. After all, ten years is a long time, so it weren't no passing fancy for either of them now, was it?"

Louise concedes this fact and immediately a part of her mind turns to Peter and Lucy. Is she a passing fancy, and does it matter if she is? The thought is pushed away. Later, she mutters to herself, there will be time enough later to think about that. Instead she looks back at her mother, who is watching her.

"Why have I got to phone her? Why can't you?" she asks.

"She may need to be collected and if I were her, I'd feel more inclined to accept if I had heard the voice of reason from somebody else. It's a strange request after all." She pauses before adding, "And I thought it might help you think about your situation; talking to her I mean, what with her being the other woman."

"Mum, I was the other woman myself." Louise gently reminds her.

"Well then, you'll have something in common, won't you?" There is a hint of sharpness in Roberta's voice.

"Tomorrow, I'll phone her tomorrow." Louise promises reluctantly. "But don't say anything to Megan." She gets up as she hears her daughter coming up the stairs.

The three generations have a simple supper together in Roberta's bedroom. She eats less than a sparrow, Louise notes and then they watch a film on TV about an angel that falls in love with a human. Of course it has a sad ending and as Roberta says, they were on a hiding to nothing from the very beginning, which makes Louise smile and confuses Megan. She is still at an age where tragedy can almost be better than a happy ending.

Saturday begins with sunshine and promise for all of them and Louise is at the train station collecting Cate when Jake calls for her daughter. The nurse and carer are both with Roberta, so Megan feels it is ok to just shout upstairs before heading outside with her backpack, to join Jake on the road outside. She steers her bike carefully out of the garage and he raises an eyebrow when he sees it, for his is much more modern and she swipes at him playfully.

"We'll keep up with you just fine!" she assures him in her best haughty voice, making him smile.

While Megan and Jake tear around the country lanes and across the fields, Louise and Cate explore the small town of Great Maddely, browsing in shops and the market, chatting in that easy way that only friends of many years standing can do. They finish each other's sentences and seem to speak at the same time, but are in fact in tune with each other and neither are in any doubt that Cate is there to support Louise any which way she can, and to make sure her friend has a nice relaxing day.

Roberta too is having a lovely time, making the carer run up and down the stairs, fetching this and carrying that, asking her questions that she knows cannot be answered and demanding conversation as a form of entertainment. It is only after lunch that she finally drifts into a very pleasant drug induced sleep, thus giving the poor woman some respite.

Cate steers Louise into a nice looking Italian restaurant, tucked away behind the large, imposing church, certain that a nice bottle of wine will be found there, for which Louise is grateful. She needs to talk to her about her feelings for Peter, which she can't quite access anymore and it is making her panic, so a quiet corner table suits her needs perfectly. She also wants to talk to Cate about the conversation she had with Susan the day before, but first she has to tell her what little she knows of this woman, who had been her father's mistress.

Jake and Megan, light in spirit and breathless from the exertion, settle on a spot by the river for lunch. They find some shade under a tree and Megan, a city girl through and through, decides it is absolutely perfect. It is a favourite spot of his, one that he and his friends frequented often as children, so for different reasons, it is also perfect for him.

They unpack their goodies, setting out a feast of sandwiches, crisps, apples, water, lemonade and shop bought cakes. A slim book falls out of Megan's bag and Jake picks it up, asking what it is.

"My great grandmother's diary." she explains. "It's quite interesting, but I never knew her of course..."

As they eat, Megan tells him a little about what Lillian had written of her life in London during the depression in the 1930s.

"May I?" he asks, as they lounge comfortably on the riverbank.

She nods and he opens it at the page she has marked, flips back a few pages, then reads some of the previous entries aloud before putting it down thoughtfully.

"Lillian doesn't love this chap and he most certainly doesn't love her. If I were her brother I would warn her off him." he tells her quite seriously.

She laughs. "What, even now? Even these days, you'd warn your sister off someone?" she asks, incredulous.

"I imagine a brother nowadays takes his responsibility just as seriously as he did what... seventy or eighty years ago, so yes I would. At the very least I would want to know him better, he sounds a bit dodgy to me."

She purses her lips but says nothing. David is a pretty useless brother, but to be fair to him she concedes, they only share a father and he has only ever visited; he has never lived with them. On further reflection, she also realises that she doesn't really know him at all and that therefore he cannot know her. She looks at Jake and smiles, telling him that he would make a better brother than the one she's got and also that maybe he'd have a better sister than she's been. He cannot know the answer to this, being as he is, an only child, but he's quite certain that he doesn't want Megan for a sister. He isn't ready to share this though, as he doesn't know her well enough yet, so instead of answering, he picks up the book and with her sitting at his side, they read on together.

25th June 1935

Vic sent me some advice in his last letter. He told me to be careful and that while it's a good thing to listen to me heart, I ought not to ignore me head. He reminded me that he's walked out with some lovely girls in his time, but he knew when he met Viv that she was different, that she could be the one he'd want to spend the rest of his life with. He said for him it was about what part of yourself you trust another person with and what part of someone else you trust yourself with. He trusts his self with her dreams and in turn he trusts her with his.

Made me think that did. I mean how did Elsie know that Fred was special? What makes me think that Albert could be? Do I even think that? I dunno the answer though, truth be told.

≈

"There!" exclaims Jake. "There, what Vic tells her, that's right, don't you think? That's the best advice anyone could give another person."

Suddenly he looks shy and Megan finds both his spontaneity and his honesty touching.

"Yes..." she says slowly, allowing the idea to float in her mind. "Yes, I think so. You have to know what part of another person you can trust yourself with, otherwise how will they know that they can trust you?"

I wish I'd known Vic, she thinks wistfully as she stares up at the fluffy clouds floating across the blue sky. What would he have been? An uncle...? Or more likely, a great uncle. She suddenly realises that she would never have known this young man who was protective of his sister, because had he still been alive when she was born, he would already have been ancient.

Jake continues reading aloud and they smile as the romance between Lillian and Albert continues and life in the wet summer of 1935 unfolds for them. Their lives are fascinatingly different from their own, and yet at the same time there are many things that are familiar. There is a horrible moment when Lillian cuts her finger at the market and gets blood poisoning. Jake tells Megan that there were few antibiotics in those days and they weren't cheap, so infections could kill. She is horrified and as relieved as Lillian and her mother when it finally healed.

Both of them are surprised by the surge of emotion Lillian feels when she finally gets to paddle in the sea and stare out across the distant horizon towards France, which she says may as well be the moon, for all the likelihood that she will ever visit it for herself.

For Megan and Jake though, the sea, both at home and abroad, is an easy part of their life. Beautiful yes, but ordinary, not mystical or wonderful in the way Lillian writes of her first sighting of it at the age of sixteen.

Megan is reminded of the film she watched recently. It is one Jake knows and likes very much and he instantly knows which part she is thinking of. It's at the end, where the fallen angel has lost his reason for becoming human, but he is still able to swim in the ocean at sunrise and feel it's aliveness through his skin, while the angels can only watch, trying in their unknowingness to imagine the sensation.

It sparks off a debate between them, because they cannot decide if they feel pity for Lillian or sorry for themselves. There are after all, two possibilities: perhaps they have lost something despite their knowledge and comparative wealth, or perhaps their lives are richer than hers. After some discussion and no real progress they read on.

For Megan, Albert's ending of the relationship comes out of the blue. Jake however, has been expecting it and he goes back a few entries, pointing out the signs to her and she finds that once they have been explained, she can see them for herself.

She takes over reading while Jake lies back on the grass, his head propped up on the now empty backpack. His eyes are closed and he listens as her clear voice picks up the story. He is enjoying himself, pleasantly surprised at how peaceful it is to be with Megan.

2nd October 1935

I asked Elsie how she would feel if Fred told her it was over between them. She said her world would end. That was a strange thing to say. I mean Elsie is so practical and down to earth, not like Mags used to be, all up in the air and romantic. But Elsie couldn't even think the thought. Panic filled her eyes, I saw it for meself, I really believe she can't imagine it.

Ah, but then I realised that Fred really loves Elsie. You just got to see the two of them together to know that, so he wouldn't do something to hurt her, no more than she would want to hurt him. That made me realise of course, that Albert don't love me, so how can I love him? He was right to say all those things and be free his self. I mean what point is there in staying together? I'll always thank him for making me birthday wish come true and for all them nice times we had, but the rest of me life? No, I don't think so.

Still, I know me heart ain't broken and just like I said to Mum, that's a good thing to know!

≈

Suddenly Megan realises that her father doesn't love her mother. She doesn't know if the word 'anymore' applies, as she doesn't really know if it's possible to stop loving someone you have really and truly loved.

But she is in that moment, certain about her father's lack of feeling for Louise and she wonders if her mother knows it too. She feels a deep sadness that she has no place for and although it fills her, it's not a part of her. They probably both still love her, but she's not sure that this love is strong enough to mend theirs.

Jake watches her and seems to know that he cannot reach her, so instead he allows her a few moments to be alone with her thoughts. Then he gently points out a large emerald green dragonfly that is flitting around a reed cigar. They both watch it and she is appreciative of his thoughtfulness.

"Come on..." he says playfully, jumping to his feet and holding his hand out towards her. "We may not be by the sea, but we can paddle in the river and see if we can find some of Lillian's magic for ourselves."

Laughing, she agrees and together they slip and slide down the muddy bank, egging each other on to wade deeper into the cool, clear water.

Chapter five

On Sunday, the household of Priory Meadows is a busy one. Megan is firmly ensconced on one of the rickety chairs at the end of garden, confident that she is out of earshot of the house. This is important, because she and Hannah are having a furtive conversation on their mobiles. They are discussing both the end of year school BBQ and the picnic by the river in minute detail, both of which happened the previous day.

Hannah and her family will be leaving in a few hours for their annual sojourn in France and once again she begs her friend to join them. This time however, Megan finds that the local countryside has cast its own spell over her and she is actually happy to stay. As she declines, Hannah understands the real reason why.

"But he's older than you. Won't he want to go to the pub and stuff?" she asks hesitantly and more than a little concerned. Neither she nor her best friend are 'wild childs' and have little experience of either boys or alcohol and no experience of drugs at all, much to the relief of their parents.

"It's ok, we're just friends, so he can do all of that anyway, just not with me." Megan reassures her.

"But still, he sounds nice..." Hannah tells her and Megan agrees, before turning the conversation back to the BBQ and the goings on of their classmates and the other people who'd been invited.

Louise is staring at a map, trying to work out the best way to get to the home of her father's mistress, because her mother wants to drink tea with her before she dies. The idea is so ridiculous that Louise is ashamed of her nervousness and she chides herself, thinking that she should be smiling. This is after all, so typical of her mother's mischievous nature. She puts her coffee down and picks up the car keys, shouting upstairs as she goes, that she should be back within the hour.

Roberta has the carer blow-drying her hair just so. She knows that the time for looking her best is long past, but even so, she will not meet her husband's 'other woman' looking as though she might shuffle off during the conversation. She has decided to wear a blouse and skirt for the occasion, that not long ago fitted her nicely. Now they just hang on her skeletal frame, but it's better than a dressing gown and she will do her make up in a little while. But first she needs to rest for a moment, to get her breath back and her thoughts in order. She asks the woman to put Nat King Cole on and make her a cup of tea, which should give her a good ten minutes to herself, she thinks. Once the carer has gone downstairs, she closes her eyes, shifts into a more comfortable position in the chair and dozes.

Louise sits in the car outside number twenty four Summertree Gardens. It is a small, but pretty house and she knows that inside, Susan is watching her, because she saw the lace curtains twitch slightly as she pulled up. Roberta has never had lace at the windows, so here is a difference, she notes.

After slowly counting to ten, she opens the car door and makes herself walk up the path towards the house. She has no idea what she might say and is both angry with her mother for asking this of her and angry with herself for agreeing to it.

The front door opens before Louise reaches it and a small, pretty woman comes out to meet her.

"I have often wondered about you my dear; your father was so very proud of you. It is such a pleasure to meet you at last."

Her voice, although hesitant, is soft and slightly musical and the smile seems genuine, reaching her large grey eyes that are framed by laughter lines.

"I'm afraid... well I don't... what I mean is..." Louise comes to a stop, both physically and verbally and smiles apologetically. "To be quite honest, I didn't know you existed until last week." she says finally.

Susan laughs. "I did wonder. Arnold was always very proper about things. Would you like some tea, or would you prefer for us to be off?"

Louise wavers. There is something about this petite woman that is instinctively likeable and she is curious about her home. Part of her wants to know what it's like, while another, bigger part, is loyal to her mother. She finds this strange, but she cannot ignore it, so after a moment of indecision she looks at Susan and says, "Let's be off. As I explained on the phone, Mum isn't very well and she really does want to meet you."

The older woman nods and smiles, then turns and disappears inside, reappearing with a cream summer jacket and an umbrella. It is floral, in greens and pinks, a full sized one and has a frill around the top. It is exactly the sort of umbrella that Roberta wouldn't be seen dead with and Louise begins to understand.

Susan hesitates at the car, unsure if she should get in the back or the front, but Louise opens the passenger door and she slips gracefully into the seat. She does up the seatbelt and once Louise is in, she asks her how she feels about her; the fact of her, because of course she doesn't really know her yet.

Louise wavers, unsure what to say and how much she should share, then decides to be honest. "I was my husband's mistress for a few years, until he left his wife and married me. So really, I have no right to condemn you. But one never thinks of one's parents in the same way as one thinks of oneself. I think I'm struggling with that and the fact that Mum wants to meet you now, after all this time."

Susan nods and senses that there is something else, but is unable to determine what it is. "For my part, to finally meet you and Roberta is quite exciting. I heard snippets about you from your father, but it was a side of his life that I could only listen to. I could never share it and really, that was all right, but I am a naturally curious creature, so of course I couldn't help but wonder.

"There were no people that we had in common, so you see our paths never crossed. The two sides to your father's life were so very separate, which is how he wanted things, yet here I am now, after all this time. It's quite amazing how things go around, don't you think?"

She laughs disarmingly and Louise cannot help but smile, finding herself captivated by this tiny woman and wondering what on earth Roberta will make of her.

As they wind along the country lanes, Susan shares something of her life. She starts by saying that she is eighty-three, a fact that surprises Louise, for she is quite sprightly and her skin still glows. Before Arnold Flanders, she had been married briefly herself, but it had been overly intense in the wrong way and she woke up one morning knowing she couldn't stay, so had quietly slipped out with only her handbag, fifteen pounds plus a few coins and the clothes she stood up in.

She laughs as she remembers. "Only when one is young, or when old age catches you unawares, can you have a sense of gay abandon about life; a simple expectation that things will somehow be all right. I lived in Surrey in those days and that morning I hitchhiked to London. It was easy then, everyone did it and I was dropped off at Paddington. The first train out that morning brought me here, and around here is where I have stayed ever since.

"I lost both my parents in the war, so I only had myself to please, so to speak, and that has suited me throughout my life. Marriage was never really for me and your father was already married. Indeed happily so. So you see we suited each other and I was never any danger to your family. I was for him and he was for me, that little bit extra in life." She looks sideways at Louise to see if she understands.

Louise is nodding. She does understand, but she also realises with a recently discovered intensity, that somewhere in the preceding years she and Peter had lost that something extra in their lives. She had turned to work to find it, while he had turned to Lucy. She pushes the thought away; another one for later. Instead she asks the question that has been sitting on the edge of her mind, the reason she has been looking through the photo albums.

"What do you remember of my father? The man he was I mean. You see, my memories are always clouded by the fact that in them he is just that; my father."

Susan thinks for a moment, trying to find the words that will conjure up the man she loved, in a way that might also be accessible to his daughter.

"Arnold was a proud man, a man to whom manners meant something. He used to say that they defined you within your place in this world and he felt that nothing was given in this life; you had to make your own way. But, and this is important, those same senses of being proper, honest and hardworking also meant that he had a deep reserve of kindness and he enjoyed things deeply. Food, beer, love... he'd earned them, so he enjoyed them to the full."

She pauses and smiles, clearly remembering some private moment.

"He could feel, really feel. Now what I mean by that is, he didn't hide from his nature. He knew himself in a way that too many people don't and sometimes that was hard for him, sometimes it was too much, but at other times he could laugh a deep belly laugh, which filled him and everyone else around him.

"He knew he wasn't educated the way others were, but he knew what he knew and he put that knowledge to the best use he could. He was... simple and earthy in the best possible way."

Louise wants to cry. Everything Susan has said she has always known, yet for her it had not been enough. She had been ashamed of him, whereas Susan saw his character traits as something to be admired, to be loved and to be proud of.

She is suddenly glad. Glad that he found her and glad that he'd had that time with her. In a strange way she is glad that she too has found Susan, before it is too late. Perhaps through her she can come to know and love her father in a different way, even though he is no longer there to know it.

As they pull into the drive, they are chatting about less important things, and as a young man steps back to let them pass, Louise realises that he too is heading for the house.

They all reach the door at the same time and he introduces himself.

"I'm Jake, from Pear Tree Close. I've come to see if Megan wants to go to a local history exhibition. It's got a lot of old photos and it's meant to be quite good" he tells them.

"You'll have to ask her. By the way, do you know anyone round here that would come and do some gardening?" she asks, hopefully.

"I can cut the grass and do basic stuff, but if there are flowers or veg that you are passionate about, best not let me near them!"

They agree an hourly rate and he promises to come by after work the following day. Louise crosses another item off her mental to do list and opens the door. She calls Megan and then takes Susan up the stairs towards her mother's room. She is full of trepidation and with good reason, for Roberta is not easy to second guess at the best of times.

After introductions, she goes down to the kitchen and returns with a tray, laden with tea, milk, hot water, shop cakes and biscuits. She sees that Roberta and Susan are still eyeing each other warily and talking about the house, but no blows have been cast. Crossing her fingers, she heads for her own bedroom to change, with the intention of working on the rocking horse.

On the landing, she pauses outside her mother's room and when she hears laughter, she is curious. But it's not enough to make her pop her head round the door; she just smiles and continues on to the garage.

Megan and Jake find her there a little later and Megan confirms that they are going to the neighbouring market town for the exhibition.

"It will help my project." Megan insists a little unnecessarily, adding that they won't be back for lunch.

Louise smiles. "Such an interesting age..." she mutters to herself, then turns the radio up loud and attacks the horse once more with sandpaper and gusto.

Shut off from everything else, she allows her mind to go back and forth over the years she has been married, trying to pinpoint when it changed, searching for when her husband stopped being the prize and became ordinary to her and when she became just his second wife to him.

At lunchtime she takes some sandwiches up to the two old ladies and finds them deep in conversation. She is surprised that they no longer seem to be talking about her father, as well as the fact that they hardly notice her as she exchanges one tray for another. She has her own lunch alone in the kitchen, listening to The Archers Omnibus and for a while she feels almost at peace with herself and her world, noting with interest that it seems smaller than it used to.

As the programme finishes, she realises the room is silent, which means the clock has stopped. Sighing, she finds the key and winds some life back into it, then carefully moves the hands forward to the correct time, deciding that the tick is a very satisfying sound.

The photographic exhibition is interesting and bigger than either Jake or Megan had been expecting. They are enjoying each other's company and are learning more about times past, in the area that he has lived for all of his life and a place that she has been connected to for all of hers. Megan is surprised when she sees a series of black and white photos of her grandmother's house at the top of the hill, surrounded as it was then, by fields and trees. Somehow, seeing them there, blown up on the wall of the gallery makes it more real than the many smaller ones in the albums. As a city girl, it had always been hard for her to think that her family had been farmers, who in their own way had been bound to the land. Yet standing in front of these photographs, she feels a spark of something and from it a glimmer of understanding begins to grow.

Jake breaks into her reverie, laughingly pointing out that his home is where a rather spectacular pear tree used to be and reminds her that in Lillian's day, they would not have been neighbours.

"Well no. But of course Lillian originally lived in London, like me and Mum. I still don't know how she came to be here at all."

They stand for a long time in front of a photograph of First World War Pals. They are mainly young men and most of them are clearly only the same age as Jake, but there is one face in the middle row looking not much older than Megan. The ones right at the back look older, but still they look young. All of them had been local men and boys; all from the same village and from the caption below the photograph, they learn that only six had returned at the end of the war.

Jake tells her that some local family names had ended in the trenches in France, names that had been in the area for generations, wiped out in a pointless war. They look carefully at the faces, wondering which six had survived and why they had been the lucky ones.

Deep in thought, they move to the next series, which depicts haymaking and harvesting. They agree it looks like fun and the pictures lift the sombre mood that the previous one had burdened them with. The harvesting process is shown over a period of almost a hundred years and they both feel sad that in a few weeks they will not have the opportunity to help gather it in. Machines will do it, faster and more efficiently no doubt, but in their eyes the romance has been lost.

"And the chance for people to work together. I mean, look at them all in the photos." Jake rather animatedly says, waving his hand around the room. "The Pals, the workers, the people at the village fair and the farmer's market, they all knew each other. I work in the library and I know only a handful of people to stop and talk to in town and only three people in my street. The rest I only know by sight and I've lived there for most of my life!"

He is saddened by this, but Megan doesn't really understand why and tries to comfort him by saying that most people are probably not worth knowing, but he stands and looks at the laughing faces in the photograph for a little longer, while she wanders off.

Megan doesn't really know the area where her grandmother lives. She has come once a year for most of her life, sometimes in the summer, once or twice for Christmas, other times for half term in spring or autumn, but little is really familiar to her. So she was thoughtful after he had said these things, because it marked out a difference between them, a gulf even, and the feeling stays with her for the rest of the day and into the evening.

Later in bed, she calls up the conversation and goes over it again in her mind, slowly coming to the conclusion that city people and country people are different. People who live in small towns and villages seem to believe that you should know everyone, while she is certain that where she lives, this is not only impossible, it is not even desired.

She only knows a handful of people that live in her street, never mind the area, and this has always been normal to her. She thinks back to the photographs of the harvesting and wonders how well those people really knew each other and decides it must be like her class at school.

There are more than three hundred pupils at her school and twenty nine other girls in her form. She knows all their names, but only some of names in the other forms or in the years above and below hers. She actually spends time with maybe five of them and the only person who really knows her is Hannah. She falls asleep, having decided that life hasn't really changed that much at all, reminding herself that Lillian only talks about a few people in her diary.

While Megan sleeps, Roberta and Louise are talking softly and easily. When Louise took Susan home, Roberta went to sleep, because although the visit had been more enjoyable than she would ever have dreamt possible, it had tired her. She slept for hours, fully dressed on top of the bed, missing her dinner and worrying her daughter. Now though, they sit together with a cup of tea. Roberta has bathed and is in her nightdress in bed, while Louise is in her pyjamas in the chair.

"Susan told me that you've invited her to come whenever she feels like it."

"I did indeed. I mean, I've not got long and I liked her." Roberta says honestly and stirs her tea pensively before confiding something. "To be honest, it was nice to talk about your father with someone who knew him as well as I did. Sometimes you can get stuck in your thoughts and you need another person to bring something else, something that you knew all along, but had put to one side and had forgotten where you left it."

"That is a strange thing to say, but it makes sense." Louise says. Then she smiles, wondering if rather than looking for her husband, she should seek Lucy out if she wants to find him again.

Her mother's tired voice breaks into her thoughts.

"I admire her, I think I always did and part of me would have liked that freedom. I was angry with him mind, when I found out. Terrible row we had over it all, but less than a week later he was dead and all I could think was, at least he'd had the decency to die in his own home rather than hers, so I put it all aside. I didn't forget it, I just didn't think about it anymore."

"Did you talk to Granny about it?" Louise asks. After all, she had told Roberta about her own marital problems, the upshot of them at any rate, and a few of the details.

"No I bloody didn't. Weren't none of her business. Anyway, she didn't live much longer herself, but at least then I had somewhere to go. You forget, when your dad died I lost our home. After all, it came with the job, part of his wages really. Even though he was virtually retired, young Mc Gregor let us keep the place while he was still able to do some bits for him, but I knew my days were numbered after he was gone."

Louise is suddenly aware that it's true, she had forgotten it and that none of them, not Mark, not Joe and especially not her, had offered their mother a place to live, so Granny's death had been timely in a way.

"Have you forgiven him? I mean now that you've met her." Louise asks, standing up.

"What a strange girl you are. You think everything is on a straight line. Well let me tell you it isn't. And what I still feel or don't feel for your father isn't any of your business either." she says firmly, handing over her cup and saucer and then settling down to sleep again.

Louise isn't hurt by the words or the tone; she just clicks off the light and smiles. Some things never change and in a funny way she feels that it's right that they don't.

As Roberta drifts into that nowhere place before sleep takes her, she asks herself the same question. Has she forgiven Arnold? For what though? And for which bit of disappointing her she wonders. She sighs softly, deciding it doesn't really matter. After all, life has been one big disappointment and she has few hopes that death might offer her something different.

"But that wasn't all his fault now, was it...?" she mumbles to herself.

He'd provided well for his family and in her own way she had loved him and he had loved her, she'd always been sure of that.

No, she wouldn't lay all of it at his door, that wouldn't be fair and he didn't deserve it, not then and not now.

As Louise drifts into unconsciousness, Susan's words come back to her. 'No dear, you were never a mistress. At least, from what you've told me, I don't think you were. You were always just the next wife. You had to wait a few years, but for most of them you were already living as though you were. There is a difference you know, so we are not the same...'

An idea floats in her mind briefly before darkness engulfs her and she decides that she needs to ask Lucy what she considers herself to be.

Megan wakes up early to the sound of rain hitting the roof. The house is still quiet and the bedside clock tells her it is only six am, so she is sure that everyone else will still be sound asleep. The trouble is, she is wide awake.

Rather than struggle back to sleep, she goes downstairs and makes thick slices of toast, liberally spread with butter and marmalade. Then she pours herself some juice, before heading back up to bed with her breakfast and a couple of the photo albums. She wants to see more pictures of the house and farm as it used to be.

In one of the albums she finds a picture of Lillian in the orchard, an older Lillian, older than the one sharing her life with her. In it she is holding a small child that must be Roberta, but then as she looks at the date, she realises it can't be. Megan pushes the album aside and reaches for the diary. She is getting ahead of herself and it feels strange to know more about what is coming than the person who is writing about her own life.

24th December 1935

Well, what a year it's been and here I am, seventeen years old with no birthday wish to make! Funny that. I mean not to have anything burning away inside me that I really want to do, or see, or be even. Seeing the sea and the sky above it, standing in it and feeling that coldness, that movement. Well, I'd had that wish for most of me life, so I s'pose it'll take a while for a new one to take its place. I mean, I'm still enjoying the fact that I did it, that I got me wish come true. I know that some people live a whole lifetime and never get that, so maybe I don't need another one. Maybe that would be greedy and anyway, if I do get another chance, well I want that one to be as important as seeing the sea with me own eyes was.

Christmas is going to be a bit sad this year. Uncle Norm still ain't right and although Mum don't like to say it out loud, I can see by her face that it's serious and there's every chance he might not make it. We'll go over there tomorrow, but I think it'll be quieter than normal. Don't really know what to say or think.

Vic said in his last letter that he and Viv hope to be over this coming year. He sent a picture of the wedding and she looks lovely. They look so happy together and of course we all want to know each other, but while he can work his passage over here, hers will have to be paid for and of course we ain't got as much saved as we used to have, now that Mum's having to help Auntie Eth out a bit, as Uncle Norm can't work no more.

Sometimes I see Albert at the market, as he still delivers there and we're friendly like, but when he asked me to the Christmas dance, I said no. Seemed daft, like going over old ground, so in actual fact I didn't go. Money's a bit tight at the moment and me dress is looking a bit shabby. I know Mum'll tart it up and it'll look brand new when she's done, but she ain't got the time right now. To be honest I feel a bit off with life, not sure what I want or why I want it. Mum says it's called growing up!

Well I hope it passes soon, that's all I can say!

≈

29th January 1936.

Well, I'm not enjoying this year so far at all. Even though it's early days yet, it ain't started on any good notes at all.

Uncle Norm passed away on the 19th in the hospital over on Victoria Street and the King his self died on the 20th. While we got a new King with his son Edward, Auntie Eth's got no one and still got all four kids at home. Tommy's left school a few months early of course and got a job, but I know Uncle Norm was hoping he wouldn't need to. I know they had their minds set on an apprenticeship for him over at Williams' but that don't pay enough for years, so it was a proper job he needed to get. But that's life, ain't it? We all got to eat and pay the bills and of course all their savings went on seeing the doctor and the medicines, for all the good they did.

Auntie Eth's on the lookout for more work. There's not a lot right now, but as she says, at least she's still got her cleaning to keep them going. We're sharing whatever I get to bring back from the market with them, so that helps too. The two pounds and three shillings a week I get don't stretch that far though and Tommy won't get that much to start with I shouldn't think, so it's going to be hard this year I shouldn't wonder.

Perishing cold it is too, even with Dad's big old overcoat on the bed me and Mum are sharing to stay warm. We're both glad of the thick bed socks we knitted up from an old cardy of hers last month I must say, but getting up in the dark six days a week is hard and there's ice on the inside of the window most mornings. I fell off me bike the other day too, mainly cos the road was so slippy with that black ice and I was still half asleep. Got a right bruise on me shin and arm, sore it is too.

Still, we got a lovely Christmas parcel from Vic and Viv. There were loads of stamps stuck all over it and two of them were ones Mum didn't have, so she was well pleased. It came a bit late, but in a way that was better. Lovely green cardigan in there for me, not home knitted, but shop bought, real lovely it is too, I'm keeping it for best. Mum's been trying to work out the pattern and given a bit more time she will! There were a few new books in there for me too, so I won't be wanting to go out for a while. And there was the news that they're in the family way, so although we probably won't get to see them now, I get to be an auntie. Who'd have thought it! He'll make a lovely dad, both me and Mum said so.

Elsie and me are getting together once a week to plan 'the wedding'. It'll be in June and it gives us all something to look forward to. She's so happy and Fred looks proud as punch too. Mum's making the dress, so it'll be really special. She'll make one for me one day too she promised, but like we said, dress comes after the proposal, so first we got to have someone that proposes to me and he has to be someone that I really want to say to yes to. So we got time!

≈

14th February 1936

Rita and me went to the cinema last night and saw a lovely soppy film, 'The amazing quest of Earnest Bliss'. Took us right out of ourselves it did. First time I've seen Cary Grant acting, seen pictures of him before of course, but not acting. Now if he'd sent me a card today, there'd be something to celebrate! On the newsreel there was some bits about the new King too. I must have seen him before, but I don't really remember him which is odd, given that he is handsome. Looks like a charmer too! But Rita says he looks shifty! Fancy saying your King looks shifty!!! Made me laugh out loud that did.

Anyway, we was talking afterwards and I said I missed the old King, it was like you knew where you were with him and she said I'd come over all wistful. (Lovely word that is, I like it, makes me feel like a princess of old!) I thought about it and I think she's right. I mean it's not the King his self I miss, cos I never knew him, but it's me own old life I miss and he was King for of all it so far.

Vic's all settled over in Boston and I'm glad he's happy, he deserves that, really he does, but it will never be the same again, not as it was. We won't hardly see him no more I don't s'pose and although he was always away a lot, we was always expecting him home. Now of course, Viv'll be expecting him and that's good and just as it should be. But I miss him and America is such a long way aways and so expensive for us to get to. Course now we ain't earning so much, not now Mum's not able to take in so much sewing and of course Vic can't send a lot, cos he's got his own home to pay for.

Uncle Norm's gone, so everything changed over there too, and it'll never be the same again now, how could it be? Mum's there most days, cos Auntie Eth's still not coping well, so home ain't right neither. I'm over there a lot for me tea after work and Mum and I hardly ever settle down with the radio no more, cos when we get back of a night there's always so much to do here still, even with us out most of the time the place still gets dusty and untidy and washing still needs to be done. Then there's all the mending and darning. Try as I might not to, I can't help but catch me clothes as I work and replacing them is just another expense we can't afford right now. We unpicked a couple of cardies last week and are knitting one good one from the wool we saved. It'll be better than new and Mum says I've got to stay warm, can't have me going down with a chill or anything, we ain't got the money to call a doctor in right now.

Elsie and Fred will be wed soon and that's wonderful for them, but Mags won't be best bridesmaid like she should've been, being sister of the bride an all.

I know this is one of those times when nothing is as it was and I know you can't go back, but I'd like to, really I would, if only just for a while.

≈

Megan puts the diary down and rests her chin on her hands. She would too, she thinks to herself, understanding what Lillian means. Nothing is exactly right in her world either. There is no prospect of a lovely beach holiday somewhere with both her parents, or of David dropping in with a friend or girlfriend in tow. Nothing around her is really that familiar and she realises in that moment that her life seems so far away, not just in terms of miles, but in a different sort of distance, one she can't quite put her finger on and it troubles her.

To add to all this, her grandmother is dying and she cannot quite love her enough, or feel as bad about it as she thinks she should. Her parents will probably divorce and she will have to choose who to live with, how to spend time with them both, and all of this will leave her no time at all for her own life, whatever that might be.

Huge tears roll slowly down her cheeks. She is glad that Lillian understands, because for a little while she is uncertain if Hannah would or even could. But Jake might, she concedes as she wipes them away and the thought makes her smile.

Roberta is still exhausted from the previous day and doesn't want anything, except to be allowed to continue sleeping. She shoos Louise and the carer away, asks for the door to be closed and drifts off again. At least when she is asleep, the pain is less intrusive.

Louise is aware that in the short time she has been there, her mother has faded noticeably. She is therefore pleased when Joe phones, telling her that he and the whole family will be down for a long weekend and that they will arrive on Thursday evening.

Her sister-in-law Claire is much more house proud than she has ever been or is ever likely to be, so with a sigh, she arms herself with cleaning products. Then after a bit of an argument with Megan, the two of them begin the long task of spring cleaning the house.

After lunch, Megan is let off cleaning duties on the proviso that she reads to her grandmother. She is not sure which she would least prefer to do, but Roberta is pleased with the idea, so she reluctantly settles into the chair in her grandmother's room with a book that Louise found in the back parlour, one which she thinks will be suitable for both of them.

It is a light story and despite the difference in age and life experience, they each get enough out of it for an hour or so to pass quite pleasantly.

"Go and make some tea, there's a love. You must be parched by now." Roberta says to a grateful Megan, who scoots off to see if her mother would like some too.

The three of them sit together for a little while, chatting about the forthcoming weekend and Megan listens with interest as Roberta and Louise recall things about her uncle Joe. She notices the light that settles in her grandmother's eyes as she talks about her favourite child and is curious. Then without realising what she's doing, she asks 'the question', the one that has been hovering at the edge of her mind for some time.

"Gran, are you afraid to die?"

There is stunned silence for a moment, then Louise admonishes her daughter sternly.

"Megan! That's a terrible thing to ask. Apologise this instant."

"Why? Why should she apologise? It's an honest question." her mother interjects thoughtfully.

"I'm sorry," says Megan, "I didn't mean to ask, really I was just wondering, just thinking and it kind of popped out."

She is tearful and doesn't want to be the reason for an argument, just when everyone seemed to be getting along so nicely.

Roberta looks at her granddaughter, but is not cross. "All right, but first you answer me this: are you afraid of the fact that I'm dying so very publically, rather than hidden away and forgotten in some hospital room?"

Louise is about to intervene. This is not a subject she feels is suitable for either of them, but her mother gets in first.

"You don't have to stay... go and carry on with whatever it was you were doing. I'm sure we can continue this conversation without you. I'm not even sure it concerns you."

She is dismissive of her daughter, while at the same time her eyes are watching Megan, who is giving the question some serious consideration.

Louise tries to huff and puff, but when she realises that neither of them are paying her any attention, she quietly collects the mugs and leaves them to it, muttering that she'll pick up the pieces later, but no one is really listening to her.

Deciding that she is heartily sick of cleaning, she heads to the garage to inspect 'her' rocking horse, as she likes to think of it, and wonders again who it belonged to and why it had been hidden out there.

Jake finds her there several hours later. He is looking for gardening tools and Megan had suggested the garage. The rain had stopped not long after lunch, so there is every chance that he will at least be able to do some trimming and tidying, even if the grass is still too wet to cut.

"Goodness..." exclaims Louise. She had been lost in her own thoughts as she worked and is flustered for a moment, caught unawares. "I've no idea, but it's a logical place to begin."

She stands up, wipes her hands and they begin to search for anything that might be useful.

Megan joins them a few minutes later. "Gran says it's all in the potting shed at the end of the garden."

She and Jake leave the garage and head off in that direction across the unkempt lawn. Louise is relieved to be left alone again, but after a while she decides to go up to her mother's room. She stands in the doorway and mother and daughter eye each other warily for a moment.

"Did you tell her the truth?" Louise asks.

Roberta nods. "There's no point in lying, and anyway, at that age life is all that matters. They don't give any thought to the other side of the coin, not unless they have to. What's more, she's a city girl to the core, so life is what courses through her."

Louise goes in and sits on the edge of the bed. "Isn't it what matters at any age? Isn't life what it's always about?" she asks.

"You're a farmer's daughter. You know about seasons and cycles, so you know that all of life is about waiting to die. It's the one certainty for any living thing. No malice, but no mercy either, that's what nature teaches you. Life? Hah! It just swallows you up whole and prepares you for death."

Roberta stops speaking and uncharacteristically reaches for her daughter's hand, holding it lightly before continuing.

"Neither fear nor anticipation changes the fact of it. Nor does asking for forgiveness change any deed of mine. I did what I did and I said what I said. It was my life to live, but it seems that now it's almost over and it really is as simple as that."

Her grasp is weak and her skin is dry and Louise wants to cry. She fights back the tears as she looks at the misshapen hand holding hers and neither of them says anything more. Roberta closes her eyes and after a moment or two, Louise quietly slips out of the room and shuts the door behind her.

Jake is waiting for her in the kitchen and he confirms what she already knew; the ground is too wet for grass cutting, but if she gives him some clues about what else she'd like done, he'll get on with it. They walk around the garden together and a plan is made. There's enough for him to be getting on with and she gives Megan a shopping list, despatching her to the local supermarket on her bike. With everyone busy, she goes back to the garage to put things away and to think.

In her mind she turns over the thoughts she has been storing away, the ones she has been avoiding and realises that the time is fast approaching when she must sit down and talk with her husband. She knows this as well as she knows her own name; what still eludes her, is what it is she wants to say.

Chapter six

Susan turns up in a taxi while Louise is making dinner, but quickly assures everyone in her musical, breathless way that she doesn't mean to stop long. With her she brings various herbal teas and the sort of biscuits that most people would describe as healthy, rather than yummy. Roberta, to give her credit, does her best to be polite, which makes Louise smile. She is of course encouraged to stay for something to eat and then later watch a soap perhaps.

"Yes, yes of course you will." Roberta insists, adding that Louise will run her home.

Louise nods in agreement and leaves them to it, promising a pot of tea in a little while. She notes that like Prince Charles, her father had chosen a mistress who was older than his wife. She is certain that Lucy is younger than her, but at the same time, wonders why she assumes this.

Jake appears, to say that he's done, and he too is given an invitation to stay for dinner. His mother is away and cooking is not something he enjoys, so he happily accepts.

While Susan and Roberta eat upstairs with the TV on, Louise, Megan and Jake eat in the kitchen, with a nonsensical quiz show on the radio in the background. They talk easily amongst themselves and make plans for the coming weekend, when Megan's three cousins will be there. The eldest is older than Jake, while the middle one is roughly his age, give or take a few months. The youngest is almost the same age as Megan and Louise is hopeful that they won't get bored and that Jake will be a good addition.

When the carer comes to help Roberta get comfortable for the night, Louise leaves the 'young people' in the kitchen doing the washing up, and takes Susan home. In the car, she senses that the older woman is sad and cautiously asks why.

"Your mother has so few friends. I know as we get older, someone has to outlive everyone else, but I don't think it's the case with her; really she's still so young." Susan sighs, pausing for a moment before continuing. "Arnold always said she wasn't any easy woman to get to know, or stay on the right side of, once you had. I think that was part of her mystery for him, but also part of his pain and now here she is at the end, and here I am with her. Such a waste... we should have done this years ago. I should have made contact; I've been curious too..." She pulls a rather dainty hanky out of her bag and dabs her eyes.

Louise nods, but cannot think of anything to say, so just concentrates on her driving. After a few minutes of silence, she remembers that Joe and his family are due to visit and she tells this to Susan, explaining that it will cheer Roberta up enormously.

"Mark was the first born and my father's favourite. He's settled in California now and we don't get to see him as much as..." She trails off unhappily, but before Susan can ask any questions she brightens and continues. "And then of course Joe has always been Mum's favourite and I was Granny's. So you see, him being here will be good for her, and his wife Claire is a lovely woman. Mum has never really been able to find fault with her."

As she drops Susan off outside her house, she impulsively invites her for tea on Saturday. For some reason, she thinks she should be part of the family while there is still time. Susan accepts, but says that she will come by taxi; she doesn't want to be a bother.

Louise enjoys the drive home. The car windows are open and the cool evening air carries summer scents and noises that are both comforting and interesting. When she arrives at the house, she lets herself in and finds her mother fast asleep and her daughter sitting alone on the sofa in the front parlour, flicking through the channels on the TV. She pours herself a glass of wine, then settles down beside her and they watch the news together, noting that there seems to be little going on in the world that can be called good.

"Do you want to talk about what Gran said?" Louise asks softly.

"I dunno, I'm still trying to work out the difference." Megan replies.

"Difference...?"

"Yes, Gran said that no one is afraid of dying, same as most people are not afraid of falling asleep. She said that what most people are really afraid of is not living anymore, knowing that life will go without them. And because we can't imagine that, well... that's the really scary part."

"Ah..."

Louise smiles. Trust Mum she thinks, able to hit the nail right on the head, just when you least expect it.

"Is that right, do you think?" her daughter asks thoughtfully. "I mean, it's hard to imagine life going on without us actually being alive, isn't it?"

"Yes, I think so, but I also think that many people are afraid of living. Living properly I mean, and that's scary too, don't you think?"

"God Mum, that's a bit deep..."

Megan laughs at her and turns the TV back on, settling down to watch the end of a programme; thereby putting an end to the conversation, but not to the thinking.

It is my truth though, Louise admits to herself later, as she brushes her teeth and studies herself in the old, crazed mirror above the equally ancient basin. Peter was always meant to be the way for me to live my life to the full. Instead I hid behind him, hiding from it, only engaging in it through him.

Now though, she cannot hide from the thought, because it is out and she begins to understand what it is she might say to him. But at the same time, she knows that she is still a long way from being ready.

Megan lies in bed, thinking about the fact that that she has been alive almost sixteen years and for that whole time, Lillian has been dead. She has played no part in Megan's life, not in the big things or in the little things. But then of course, how could she?

I wasn't alive for her life either, she thinks to herself. Isn't that the same? But it's too big a question for her to answer and she reaches instead for the diary, knowing that Lillian could never reach for hers, even if she had one.

2nd March 1936

Mum's decided that now that there's no chance of Vic coming home to live again, we could save ourselves some money and move in with Auntie Eth and the tribe. Between us we could be quite comfy and only have the one place to take care of. Makes sense really I s'pose, cos Mum and me are running between the two flats anyway. The rent's gone up again, along with a lot of other things and with only the money I bring home of a week and Dad's pension, (which don't seem to go up at all) well its hard making ends meet some weeks. But I've lived here all me life and I'll miss it.

I hope all them memories don't disappear when we shut the door for the last time. Mum laughs when I say that, but I do worry. I mean, ink fades on paper, I seen it on all those letters Mum and Dad wrote to each other while he was in the trenches in France. They're in her treasure box, but the writing is pale now and hard to read. Does that happen to memories too I wonder? I really miss Mags at times like this, she'd say something funny and we'd laugh and me worries would slip away, she could always do that. Hah! Maybe she's answered me question after all! I still think of her a lot. I still remember her and all the things we used to do, so there we are, not all memories fade. Perhaps only some do and surely they'd never the be the really important ones?

≈

15th March 1936

Well here we are across the way, all settled in and a jolly lot we are too. Me, Tish, and Joyce got one bed to share in the big back room and Mum and Auntie Eth share the other one. Tommy and Evan got the box room to share and we managed to get our table into the parlour, as they've got their own in the kitchen. It fits nice there and Mum's always been proud of that table. Between us we only got rid of one chair that was falling to bits anyway and now there's enough money to keep the whole place warm, not just the kitchen, so we'll be snug as bugs next winter! Auntie Eth says she only suggested it so she could get her hands on that nice stove Vic bought.

Made us all laugh that did. Nice to see her smiling again, it's not often mind, but it's a start.

Got a lovely letter from Vic and Viv with photos an all, so we can see their new place. Lovely wooden house it is, a house! They got four good sized rooms inside and a lean to, as well as a garden out the back where they plan on growing some vegetables and such. Fancy! They're getting the baby's room ready. It's all the rage to give the baby its own room over there, but then as Mum says, they got more money and Vic had a fair bit saved anyway, even with helping us out. So they look cosy too.

Mum says Dad would have been proud of his only son. I think Uncle Norm going has brought it all back for her. She's been talking more about Dad than I've ever known, and of course there's the wedding on the cards too. It's sad that she don't have a picture of theirs and we don't have a single picture of me dad. At least Auntie Eth has a few of Uncle Norm and anyway, the cousins will always have memories of their dad like Vic has of ours. But I don't and I do wonder what he was really like in his personality, as well as his looks. No point getting too down in the dumps about it though. I mean I ain't never going to know now, so there's an end to it really.

≈

11th April 1936

Mum's birthday! Pity Vic couldn't be with us, but we had a lovely time anyway. Me and Auntie Eth made a cake and a special tea, with ham sandwiches and others with fish paste and cucumber, Mums favourite! I got her a new pin box for her sewing and a pair of silk stockings. Dead chuffed with them she were.

≈

12th April 1936

Me, Elsie and Rita saw 'The Beloved Vagabond' with that French actor Maurice Chevalier, lovely it was too and between us we bought a big bar of milk chocolate to eat while we watched and sang along!

On the Pathé news there was a bit about a new kind of holiday place opened by that Billy Butlin. It looked amazing, really luxurious and fancy. Elsie said how nice it would be for a honeymoon. It's up on the coast in Skegness, so the train fare would be a bit too, but for thirty-five shillings you get to stay for the whole week, get three meals a day and loads of entertainment and fun. Couldn't believe our eyes! Course, thirty-five shillings is a lot when you don't have much, but me and Rita were thinking, I mean between now and the wedding, with all the people they know, surely we could raise enough to send them there. Mum and Auntie Eth and Elsie's mum said it were a great idea, so we're all going out and about all innocent like, to see what we can raise! Just between us five we've already got the first three and sixpence.

≈

Megan feels sleepy and puts the diary down, but she is smiling as she turns the light off. She can't imagine being sent to Butlins and liking the idea, yet Lillian's enthusiasm is unmistakeable and her dreams that night are of the seaside, but one she does not recognise. Stages are set at the back of the beach, filled with people taking part in strange competitions, while other people are walking around with huge megaphones, shouting out strange messages to brides, hundreds of them, all lined up in the water, holding their skirts above their ankles as the waves roll in.

The following morning, as she is reading to her grandmother, she remembers the diary and is curious. "Gran, how much was thirty-five shillings?"

Roberta is surprised by the question, but she dutifully does a quick calculation, telling her granddaughter that one old shilling was worth five pence in today's money and that a pound had been twenty shillings. She then gives the answer before asking why she wants to know.

"One pound seventy-five... Wow, that's nothing, nothing at all..." Megan thinks aloud. "The other day I bought three nectarines for the same money; just three..."

"I ask again, why are you interested in that particular sum of money?" Roberta demands.

Megan explains and her grandmother is thoughtful for a moment.

"Did they do it? Did they send her friends to Butlins for their honeymoon?" she finally asks with her eyes closed, so Megan can't see the combination of frustration and confusion in them.

"I don't know, I haven't read that far yet."

"Well let me know when you have. In the meantime, a cup of tea would be lovely; nice and sweet please."

With that she dismisses her granddaughter, so she won't see the tear that is rolling down her cheek and lays in the quiet of her room, wondering about friendship, specifically the sort her granddaughter had found in her mother's diary. Roberta has always been wary of people, sure that they would hurt her if she let them come too close, so from an early age she built barriers and carefully guarded gates that few had gained admittance through. Nana had cautioned her about the pitfalls of life, and in their different ways, both of her parents had abandoned her, so she'd always been certain that she was right to do this. But now, when it is too late to change anything, she wonders about it and as she drifts in that nowhere place before sleep, she almost has the answer.

Roberta is sleeping when Megan returns, so she leaves the tea beside the bed and tries to sneak out of the house past her mother, who is wielding the Hoover, looking cross. Louise will have none of it though, and after a heated argument, Megan stomps back upstairs to clean the paintwork in the other big bedroom and the small second bathroom at the top of the house.

By the time Jake has finished cutting the grass, front and back, the whole house is cleaner than it has been for some years. Mother and daughter are reunited by their shared efforts and Roberta remains thoughtful, so is not demanding a great deal from anyone. Louise warms some soup up for her mother and orders a couple of delivery pizzas for everyone else.

She takes a few slices and a glass of wine into the back parlour, with the intention of calling Cate. When she gets there though, she finds that the birdsong wafting in through the open window, along with the smell of freshly cut grass and the gentle buzz of insects in the flowers outside is very soothing indeed. She sits and enjoys the peace, smiling as she watches Megan and Jake take the food, still in the boxes, and the ridiculously large bottle of fizzy drink to the end of the garden.

It is a lovely evening, and as they eat pizza, they make plans for the weekend, to keep her cousins amused. He asks her how her project is going and she admits that she has not given it much thought at all.

"Come to the library tomorrow morning. Then if you like, I can take some books out for you and we can get some lunch in the park." he suggests hopefully.

She likes the idea. "Ok. Shall I bring some sandwiches? Only..." She hesitates, not sure what there might be in the house.

"No need, there's a little cafe near the duck pond. It's quite cheap and they have all sorts of things."

He carefully takes a large slice from the box and they laugh as the cheese stretches.

"How is Lillian getting along?" he asks as they close the lid, unable to eat any more.

She brings him up to date, but dusk is beginning to settle and the midges are getting the better of them, so they wander back to the house.

"We can read some more over lunch tomorrow, if you like?" she suggests.

He nods in agreement and smiles as he heads for the gate. Then with a wave, he makes his way home, down the hill to where a magnificent pear tree once stood.

Megan goes in the house and it takes a while to find her mother, as she is tucked away in the old office, deep in conversation on the phone. It sounds rather serious, and unable to attract her attention, she heads upstairs, intending to have a long, hot soak in the bath. She can hear the carer in with her grandmother, so decides not to pop her head round the door after all and instead carries on to the bathroom at the top of the house, so as not to be in the way.

Louise wakes up with a groggy head. She knew the previous night that finishing the bottle was not going to be without its consequences, but she had done it anyway and so she will have to suffer. She grimaces and lies there for a while, recalling some of what had been said the night before. While she can acknowledge that going away in the summer is a perfectly reasonable thing to do, she cannot quite bring herself to believe Peter when he says that Lucy will not be one of the party.

If they do divorce, the other people he is going with would be in his camp, not in hers, so therefore his insistence that she asks them to confirm what he was telling her, was not really good enough.

"And anyway," she mutters crossly as she hauls herself out of bed, "isn't that the point? Trust has gone out of the window! I shouldn't need to ask, I should just bloody well believe him."

As she comes out of the bathroom she is appalled to discover that it is past ten o'clock. Feeling guilty, she goes straight to her mother's room and is relieved to discover that she is bathed and has already had some breakfast, courtesy of her carer and her granddaughter.

"You look like something the cat's dragged in." Roberta tells her.

Louise shrugs, says she will bring fresh tea, and heads downstairs. She finds a note from Megan and notices that the clock has stopped again. Muttering curses, she winds it and has to nudge the pendulum several times before it will tick continuously.

The little cafe in the park is busy. There are lots of mothers with small children and buggies. The mothers sit and the children race around screeching, so Megan and Jake buy burgers, some crisps and a cold drink, then head across the grass. They'd already chosen a rather lovely spot for their lunch, below a horse chestnut tree near the river, which runs through the park on that side. Her backpack is full of the books that Jake took out for her, so that she can work at home if she wants to. She has already made copious notes, but still hasn't decided what her project is actually about. He's got internet at home, so he offers her the opportunity to do her online research there if she wants to.

She is suddenly shy, and accepts while biting into her greasy burger, hoping that he won't see the confusion in her eyes. He does though and feels bad, so trying to make her forget, he asks if she has brought Lillian's diary. She has of course, and getting it out of her bag allows her the much needed minute to regain her composure. He takes it from her, and while she eats, he reads. It's exactly the right thing to do she decides; it gives them both the opportunity to be comfortable in each other's company once more.

18th April 1936

We had a count-up this evening and we've already got enough to send one of them and some towards the other one. Elsie's mum and Fred's sister have also been collecting, so perhaps with what they've got we're nearly there! It is so hard not telling them, but me and Rita are sure they ain't got wind of nothing yet. We keep trying to imagine their faces when we announce it!

Weather is very cold still. We've all had enough of it, there's usually a frost on the ground when I leaves of a morning, blooming ridiculous! I usually warm up a bit while I'm cycling to the market, but that soon goes and as soon as I stand still for more than a couple of minutes the cold sets in and is a devil to shift again. Don't like to go out once we're home and warm, but sometimes it can't be helped, there's usually things that still need doing.

Had a bit of a cough all week, so Mum always has an onion and milk broth waiting for me when I get in. It seems to be doing the trick nicely, along with the honey she makes me swallow three times a day. She's looking more perky too. Joyce and Tish help out a lot indoors, so she has to do less now, which is good for her. I catch her rubbing her arm when she thinks I'm not looking, cos clearly it's still giving her a bit of grief, despite the menthol rub she puts on.

≈

28th April 1936

Got a lovely letter from Vic and Viv, full of gossip about this new King of ours. They put some cuttings in too from different magazines over there. We don't hear none of this stuff about him and that American woman, Wallis Simpson. Divorced she is, more than once too, imagine! Mum says that had Dad lived, this year would have been their pearl anniversary and that's not that unusual round here. I mean of course like anywhere, there's a few who weren't happy. Mrs Jenkins at number 38 kicked her old man out years back and Sally Braithwaite ran away from hers and came here to start again and the Wintertons are a miserable lot, but no one's divorced! Must be an American thing we decided. But it was good of them to send it though, as it means we get the gossip first. Although Mum did say that maybe it weren't true, that maybe them Americans made it up because they were jealous of not having royals themselves. Difficult to know, so we only shared the cuttings with Auntie Eth. I did tell Rita though and she laughed. She'd always said he looks shifty!

≈

Megan and Jake find this strange, because they've seen blurred pictures of Prince Harry's bum in the newspapers. For them, the royals are, and at the same time are not special, while clearly Lillian is in awe of them and for her they hold a place in her life that is never questioned.

"No TV in those days of course," says Jake, "or at least I think only a few people would have had one then. That will have made a difference; once everyone started having regular and easy access to news."

"But they had the news at the cinema and she had a radio. Wouldn't there have been news about it on that?" she asks.

He shrugs. "Maybe, but I'm not sure. And anyway, the radio is different from the TV or the internet and I'm not even sure how often people went to the cinema in those days. I mean, could you just pop in for the news, or did you have to pay to see the film?"

"Yes, I suppose so... I mean, you'd have to pay now, wouldn't you?"

She is trying to imagine life with no mobile phones, no TV and no internet, but she can't, so thinking about what Jake said, she picks up the diary.

18th May 1936

Well everything's ready for the wedding in two week's time. Of course everyone has Maggie has on their minds and no one wants to spoil Elsie's day, but I know she's thinking of her little sister too, how can't we?

Pleased to say I've got me voice back. The dress Mum made is a dream come true. Elsie looks like a proper princess in it, really she does. It'll get her plenty more orders I shouldn't wonder. If there's a wedding coming up in the neighbourhood they'll want Mum to do the dress after they've seen Elsie in hers. She's done me a lovely outfit too, real special it is, it's a green dress in a lovely floral material nipped in at the waist, big on the shoulders and the skirt floats outwards almost by itself. There's an orange clutch jacket to go over it and we managed to find the sweetest hat to go with it and I'm saving a pair of silk stockings specially. All we got to do now is the cooking the day before for the party. It's going to be a right proper do it is, make no mistake!

We got them booked into Butlins for a week afterwards and we got them both booked out from work, but they don't know. Elsie's dad will announce it at the party as part of his speech.

Rita's been seeing a lot of Peter Finkly these past few weeks, so I've not been out with her much and Elsie's saving hard. They've had their name down for a flat for a while and it came through last week. Fred's already moved in and they've taken in a lodger. He don't want her to work once they've got a family, so they need to make as much as possible now and save it while they can.

Mum and me have been busy knitting things for the baby and we sent it all off yesterday, so they'll have it before it's born. Early July Vic said, I can't wait. He said he's taken a job that should have him home by the end of June, so he'll be there to mind them both afterwards. Viv's mum don't live that far away, just a short bus ride, so she'll be there too. Mum's *right sad that she can't be there, but he said he's bought a camera, so at least there'll be plenty of photographs and Mum won't miss as much as she's fearing she will.*

≈

As Jake is listening to Megan reading the details of the wedding, he hears the clock on the town hall chime two.

"Bugger!" he exclaims, leaping to his feet. "I'm late."

She smiles as she watches him race across the park towards the library. Once he is out of sight, she leans back on the tree trunk and happily reads all about the wedding, Elsie and Fred's assessment of Butlins, and the arrival of Vic's son: Benjamin John Loveday.

None of the photos that Vic sent are stuck in the diary, which she thinks is a pity, so she decides to go through the albums when she gets back to Priory Meadows, to see if they are in there. She stretches, gathers up their rubbish, and heads in a more leisurely fashion than Jake had been able to towards the bus stop, reminding herself to bring her grandmother up to date, as she had been asked to.

Chapter seven

"What do I care?" Roberta mutters crossly, rejecting the offer of being read that part of the diary. "It's not as though I knew them..." She picks up the remote control and turns on the TV, leaving Megan standing there, not really knowing what to do.

She is confused and a little hurt at her grandmother's offhand response to the news that Elsie and Fred did get to go to Butlins for their honeymoon and as her grandmother is clearly engrossed in what is happening on the screen, or at least pretending to be, she takes herself off to her room. She still has the holiday project to do and blocks out the present very effectively with music, reading about the past and delving into the photo albums, saddened by the fact that she can't find any of the photos sent by Vic.

Louise is restless and moves from room to room and task to task, without really achieving much. She gave up trying to do anything on the rocking horse hours ago and as the afternoon moves towards evening, she takes herself off to the end of the garden and phones Cate, needing the reassurance that only a real friend can give her. Cate is only interested in Louise, Peter is by the by, and that is exactly what she needs to make her feel better about herself.

Around seven, there is a loud rumble of thunder and Louise dashes for the house. Upstairs, Megan sits at the window and watches the lightning zigzag across the sky in the distance. Unlike at home, there are no buildings to block her view and the boiling greyness of the clouds that now obscure the hills captivates her. Jake is just getting off the bus, wishing he had a jacket. There is no point going to Priory Meadows; he won't be able to do anything in the garden, so instead he turns for home.

Roberta recalls previous storms and smiles to herself as the electricity falters, then fails. As the noise of the rain engulfs the house and thunder rattles the windows, she tells Louise that she is not hungry and wishes to be left alone for the evening. The lack of TV doesn't bother her, the drugs are having their effect, and she is left with her thoughts, drifting back and forth through her life. It is easy for her to alight here and there, spending time with those she has missed. She finds she is able to be both the person she is now and the one she was then, which she decides is a bonus. She tells her nana what a pity it is that this gift has come so late in life. Her nana agrees and then sings her a lullaby.

After a cold dinner, Louise asks her daughter to tell her about Lillian. She does not wish to be alone in the gloom and wants to know what has been happening to her granny. Megan reads a few entries with the aid of a torch and they talk about the differences in their lives and the hardship that seemed normal for so many ordinary people in 1936.

Louise suggests that the next time Megan is in the library, she looks for the film 'Gone with the Wind', because she does not understand Lillian's great enthusiasm for the book when she receives it from Vic, even though she writes a lot about it after she has read it.

"It's a classic, one of the greats and I'm sure Gran would enjoy watching it too. Your aunt Claire certainly would." Louise tells her. "It's a love story, but with a difference and it's told with such style!"

As the year ends for Lillian and the power returns to Priory Meadows, they read about the king's abdication and the shock it leaves the Loveday family in, as well as most of the nation. This, Megan tells her mother, is a key difference in everyday life. She is sure that neither she nor any of her friends would turn a hair, if when Charles became king, he were to abdicate in favour of William.

"I mean really, what does it matter now?" Megan asks her mother.

Louise is sure that it does still matter and that the monarchy is not just about the past, but she cannot for the life of her explain why in a way that satisfies both of them. She settles for something that feels right to her but means little to her daughter.

"It's part of what binds us together as a society; a link to who we were and why we are who we are now I suppose."

Megan shrugs and reaches for the remote control, much as her grandmother had done earlier in the day and quickly gets engrossed in the tail end of a programme.

Turning on the lights and going to the kitchen to make cocoa for Megan and pour another glass of wine for herself, Louise thinks about her brother Mark. She has not spoken to him, not properly, for years, yet they had no argument, nor was there a falling out. Louise didn't take sides, but perhaps Mark assumed that she had. She has always got on well with Izzy though, and in recent years has shared more with her brother's partner than she has with him.

Mark living in The States meant that it was easy to just drift apart and sometimes calls went unreturned for weeks. Christmas cards were exchanged, but news became more banal and shorter with every year that passed. No one's fault really, she thinks, just the way it has become. We were never that close anyway, even as children.

It is all so different from Lillian and her brother Vic. Perhaps it's because there are three of us, she muses as she pulls the cork out, but there should have been three of them. Louise remembers Granny saying that there had been one in between her and Vic, but that the poor little soul had died before it was a year old. While she is no longer certain if it had been a boy or a girl, she is certain that if Joe can't convince their brother to come and say farewell to their mother, she won't be able to. But is that reason enough not to even try? She asks herself.

Thursday begins with sunshine and much activity. Beds need to be made and shopping needs to be done. Roberta wants her hair washed and styled, so a home hairdresser is found and an appointment made for the afternoon. The Doctor comes on a routine call and is pleased to find the patient in good spirits, although looking frailer than the last time he saw her, which had not been that long ago.

Jake comes after work to do some more pruning and tidying and Megan helps him as best she can, although gardening is a new activity for her. Their small patio garden in London requires very little, and there has never been any need or inclination for her to learn.

After she has waved goodbye to Jake, she wanders into the kitchen and pours herself some juice. Her mother is cutting vegetables and she nonchalantly tells her that her father phoned her earlier and invited her to join him in Greece.

"Do you want to go?" Louise asks, trying to make her voice neutral.

"I've already said no. Are there biscuits? I'm starving."

Megan then heads upstairs for a quick shower before the cousins get there and Louise smiles to herself, noting that sometimes her daughter can be like her own mother, in the way she can kill a conversation stone dead. She continues chopping and mulls over this new piece of information.

He won't have expected her to say no, she thinks to herself, and on that basis is left with no other option than to believe that Lucy will not be going with him. "But isn't this what I wanted? Isn't this how I hoped things would go? Didn't I hope that he'd miss me and give her up?" she asks the empty kitchen, looking at the clock as if expecting it to reply.

It's exactly what she had set out to achieve, she concedes, but now that it appears she has, she can't quite find the joy she had expected and unceremoniously shoves the carrots, leeks and potatoes into pans, realising that she is going to have to talk to him before he goes. She needs to know what he is thinking about their future, in order to determine her own thoughts and feelings.

She hears the sound of tires on the gravel drive and voices, then the back door is pushed open.

"Hello...?"

All thoughts about her husband disappear as her nephews come trooping into the kitchen carrying armfuls of stuff. In between much hugging and sharing of snippets about the drive and the weather, their parents direct them upstairs and Louise goes ahead, throwing doors open as she goes and Megan appears on the landing to help the boys take bags up to the top floor.

Joe and Claire head straight for Roberta's room and Louise smiles as she goes past, heading back down to the kitchen, for the murmurings and general tone sound good. "This will perk Gran up no end." she tells Megan as they meet in the hall.

Her daughter is thoughtful. Being an only child, she has never had to vie for her mother's attention or love and her father seems to have split his time between his two families rather well, so Megan has never felt jealous or left out. But she cannot pretend that she has not noticed the deep, genuine pleasure that her gran clearly feels for her uncle Joe and his family, a depth of emotion which is noticeably absent whenever she and her mother arrive.

Claire appears in the kitchen and offers to help, choosing her words carefully as she talks about Roberta. She is unsure about how much Megan knows and doesn't wish to cause a problem. Dinner will be served in the dining room and Roberta has said she will come down for it. The boys, Colin, Matt and Rob appear and between them all the table is laid, with much teasing and joking, so that everyone is able to forget the months since they were last all together and the reason for being so now.

Roberta, frail but proud, comes into the dining room on her son's arm, carefully taking her place at one end of the large, no longer used dining table. She doesn't eat much, but glows throughout the meal, smiling at the general banter going back and forth. Her eyes often stop on her son and she nods, as though agreeing with something she has said, if only to herself.

Later, Joe takes her back upstairs and after the carer has got her ready for bed, he sits with her until she falls asleep. Louise and Claire do the washing up together, away from the boisterous chatter going on in the front parlour, and discuss Roberta, Mark and Louise. Claire is warm and generous and does not pry; her interest is born from genuine concern.

She wouldn't even know how to gloat, Louise thinks to herself, but then tears start to roll down her face and she tries to wipe them away, but her hands are encased in rubber gloves. Claire gathers her sister-in-law in her arms and just holds her for a moment, letting her cry.

"I'm so sorry. We've left you alone to manage this, and that's not fair. We'll have to work out a better way of doing things for as long as... well, you know. Anyway, you need a break. Time off, so to speak." she tells her.

"No really, I'm fine, it's just..." Louise turns back to the soapy bowl, trying to think just exactly what 'it' is.

Before any more can be said, Joe joins them. "I've got a collector chappy coming tomorrow morning, to have a first take on what's in the garage. Then the boys and I will take what's left to the dump." he informs his sister proudly, needing her to know that he hasn't forgotten his promise.

"But not the rocking horse," Louise says firmly, "it's my project."

"Right you are..." he says, smiling. "Anyone for a nightcap?"

He gets a bottle of whisky out of the cupboard, but only two glasses, knowing that his wife will prefer tea, then the three of them sit at the kitchen table, talking softly until everyone else has gone to bed. The house is at last quiet and the gentle tick of the clock is the only sound breaking the silence.

In the morning, Louise wakes before dawn and once again considers the offer Claire had made to her. It doesn't take her long to decide to take her up on it and leaping from bed, she starts to pack a bag and sends a text to Cate.

'On my way to London for the weekend. Can I have your spare bed?'

'Grog... but yeah' is the reply a few seconds later.

Smiling, she steals out of the house before anyone is awake and sighs, but in a nice way. She happily hums along to a tune on the radio as she turns the car out of the drive, heading away from her responsibilities, if only for a couple of days.

"Bless you Claire." she whispers.

At a more civilised hour, the rest of the household, minus Roberta of course, convene in the kitchen. Claire is cooking up a hearty breakfast and Joe is explaining his plan for the day. The collector is due at ten and he and Colin will spend the morning in the garage with him, sorting out what he wants from what will go to the dump.

Megan and Claire will head into town and pick up provisions for the weekend, while Rob and Matt will start clearing the real rubbish from the garage; the bottles, the tins, the old newspapers and suchlike. The afternoon will be spent doing dump runs and on Saturday everyone will be free to do as they please.

Megan tells her cousins about Jake and the planned bike ride. Colin and Joe have a plan of their own; a day fishing, but Matt and Rob like the idea and thankfully they have brought their bikes. There had been the bits of three bikes in the garage, but Joe had only been able to build one roadworthy one, so he'd thoughtfully encouraged the boys to bring theirs.

Everyone goes about their chores and when Megan and her aunt return, laden with things that Louise rarely buys, Claire prepares lunch and sends her niece up with a fresh pot of tea for Roberta. Joe comes in later and relieves her, saying he will have his lunch with his mum and she happily scoots off downstairs for hers.

The rest of the afternoon is spent bagging up rubbish and loading the unwanted farm equipment onto the trailer, which when full, is taken off to the local recycling centre while the next load is got ready. And so the hours pass happily and soon everything bar the rocking horse is gone and they sit or sprawl on the grass, with the smell of Claire's baking wafting enticingly from the kitchen.

Tea is had outside and Megan is in her element, bickering playfully with her cousins, eating cake and enjoying the sunshine. She is grubby and sweaty from the hard work and aware of her body because it aches quite pleasantly. She is not used to so much physical activity and decides she likes it. Her parents are forgotten and their problems do not touch her. Only the moment matters and the moment is good.

Jake arrives to do a bit more in the garden and after a brief introduction, is automatically included into the group. Even though he is an only child, he is very sociable and finds it easy to be with people. Roberta listens to the voices and the laughter drifting into her room through the open window and smiles. For a moment she too feels peaceful, as the noises melt into others from another time and she closes her eyes, happily lost in that place that is neither past nor present.

Much later, as Megan lies on top of her bed with the window wide open, she reaches for Lillian's diary to take her mind off the sultriness of the night. She hopes there will not be another storm, for she is looking forward to the bike ride and picnic arranged for tomorrow. Her uncle Joe had said that if it was going to storm, it would do so much later, assuring them that he could still taste the weather from years of practice, when what it had in mind had a bearing on how you spent your day. Megan noticed how wistful he'd sounded, and wonders how much of his old life he misses, while being absolutely certain that her mother misses none of it.

2nd March 1937

Me and Mum treated ourselves last night and went to see 'Fire over England'. Been a while since we done anything just the two of us like and what a treat it was too. Such a grand film with plots and sub-plots twisting away and the hero Michael is so handsome. Laurence Olivier his name is, not seen him before, but such a good actor. We was there with him all the way, sure that he'd be found out and killed. We was on the edge of our seats when he went on that mission to save the country and got caught in all that fire on them ships that he'd set alight to. Well we was convinced that he was a goner, but no, and he got the girl that he loved all along. She was lovely, a real beauty, Mum and I both said so.

I wish someone like that Michael would come fighting his way into our life round here! Where are all the heroes these days, or were they always just us but in different times? I think of Bonnie and Clyde and others like them, but I don't think they're real heroes, just a different type of villain really and ain't we got enough of them already? As Mum is always saying, we got to live a real life and be glad of it an all, but surely someone gets to have romance and adventures and that being the case, why shouldn't it be me?

Anyway, afterwards we went and had a bit of supper at the cafe and Marge was there playing the piano, so we all had a singsong, really cheerful like. We got a couple of bottles of stout from the off licence and took them back and had them with Auntie Eth and the radio and fell into bed well pleased with ourselves.

≈

19th March 1937

Hope spring comes soon, we've all had enough of the cold. Still, the flat's lovely and warm, even in the morning when I get up and Mum's chest has hardly played up this winter at all. It was good to tell Vic that in our last letter, cos he does worry so and of course he knows that the flats all have damp walls in 'em. From what he says, Boston has a fearsome winter, snow so deep you can fall in it! No thank you! Mum and me we're firm on that, if we go, we'll go in the summer.

Wouldn't that be something, to go travelling, to see the world just for fun, to go swanning about here and there, like a couple of proper nobs! Made Mum laugh, she thought I was only joking and maybe a bit of me was, but another bit, a really big bit, was hopeful that one day it might be the case. Don't know how I'd manage it mind, I'd have to marry a nob and there's always been a bit of a shortage round here of that kind of gent!

≈

2nd April 1937

Oh, what to say? Rita's in the family way and her still not married, nor likely to be neither. Pete says it's not his and has done a bunk. How can he say that about Rita? She's not fast, not at all. She told me she only did it cos she thought she loved him and more importantly cos she believed he loved her. Now of course she knows he weren't worth all her high feelings, but she says she'll love the baby, cos he or she was made for the right reasons and it can't be helped that the father is a wrong 'un.

She's really afeared, that's for sure, but she told me her mum and dad say they'll stand by her. They weren't too happy at first, course they weren't, but now all the shouting's been and done, well they are family, ain't they? She told me that she and her mum had a chat about going to see old Ma Wilcox. She don't charge much and if you go early enough, well there's less likelihood of a problem afterwards. But she said just the thought of flushing it away like that had them both in tears, so after that, everyone rallied round. We all know that what Rita's mum says, is what's going to happen, so her dad had to put all his huffing and puffing and threats aside!

Course Pete's name is dirt round here now and his poor grandma is lost without him now that he's scarpered. What a to do and there's poor Elsie and Fred hoping every month for a sign that a baby is on the way and each month nothing. The world's all wrong and no matter which way I try and look at it, it just don't seem right to me.

Gladys from work said it was all romantic, that Rita was the wronged woman and that Pete would have to see the error of his ways and realise that he loved her. Or if he didn't, that Rita would die of shame or a broken heart. Like I said to her, that's all fine and dandy when it's a book or a film and not real people, but this is our Rita she's killing off without a blooming thought. Stupid girl! I've always thought she was a bit odd, but still.

Made me think though, I mean life ain't like a book, is it? I hope she'll be all right and not do anything daft. Not that I can talk, no idea what I'd be thinking in the same situation, but probably not considering topping meself!

≈

11th April 1937

For Mum's birthday this year we went to the cinema, just me and her and we saw a feature, with Errol Flynn. Hah! Mum's in love all over again she says! After, we went and had fish and chips. It was really nice, we agreed on that, we can usually have a nice time together, not like some mums and their daughters, spitting street cats they are together, but not us.

≈

18th April 1937

Well, the good and the bad they always come together! Elsie and Fred are expecting! It's early days still, but she told me last night. If all goes well, she'll give up her job in three or four months time, so she can take it easy and then poor Rita got the sack, cos her bump is showing and her boss says she gives the place a bad name, what with her not being married. So now she's got to find something else to do to bring in a few bob. Mum said she'd share the sewing jobs with her, she's got quite a bit on at the moment and Rita's always been a neat sewer, not like me!

≈

14th May 1937

Where to start???Vic was over, he actually got to come home. He was with us for six whole days!!! He took me and Mum to the coronation of King George and Queen Elizabeth, what a do that was. We stood on The Mall and saw them both in the carriage, proper carriage it was too, pulled by gleaming horses. We only saw it from a distance mind, but there we were, watching them go past to make it all formal. They really are King and Queen now. Such a tiny lady she is, but when we saw it on the Pathé later, you get to see just how pretty she really is, more so than that American woman and most important of all, Vic was with us for it. Bit of history in the making he said, a brand new age and he didn't want to miss it!

He brought lots of pictures and stories of life with Viv and Ben. Imagine, our Vic a dad. He beamed every time he spoke of his family. And the stories of life in America, cor, what an amazing place!

It was so lovely to have him home. We sat up well into the night every night talking, we even went to the pub together and shared a bottle or two of ale. He took me to a dance at the Docket as well and tried to show me some of them new American dances. What fun we had. I didn't want to share him with anyone but Mum.

It was like he'd never been away, he was interested in everything and everyone. Course he and Fred are old mates from their school days, so that was nice for them both to be able to go down the pub together, both married now they are and Auntie Eth and the tribe were so happy to have him with us. Tommy worships him and he ain't one to hide the fact that he does!

And now he's gone again, but maybe he'll get to come back again soon. He said he'd try to get a regular place on a ship doing the Atlantic crossing. I hope he does, I really really do.

≈

The diary slips from Megan's hand and slides onto the floor as sleep finally overtakes her. Lillian, bold and warm, inhabits her dreams, taking her from the bedroom and out across the fields to stand under the pear tree and look down towards the valley. There, beyond the fields is a city, so big and shiny, like nothing Megan has ever seen. The sun glints off the roofs and windows and the skyscrapers seem to keep growing as she watches. Lillian throws her head back and laughs, but says nothing, then runs away so fast that she cannot keep up with her.

Megan feels vibrant and alive in her company and wakes up early to the sound of her own voice. "Lillian wait, please wait..."

Chapter eight

Over an early breakfast, Joe and Jake spread the map out at one end of the kitchen table and study it, while everyone else noisily joshes everyone else. They both know the area well and Joe feels nostalgic as they discuss routes and landmarks. It takes him back and he likes the feeling, as well as the young man that he is entrusting two of his sons and his niece to.

They have decided that he and Colin will drive to a spot on the river about a mile upstream from the weir. They will take the mountain of food that Claire is still preparing and set themselves up for a day's fishing. The others will cycle towards them via the woods and along the top of the valley and they will all have lunch together.

Claire pooh-poohs the idea of joining either party and tells them firmly that she would like nothing more than a nice day indoors, chatting and reading to Roberta. Everyone falls silent, for they had completely forgotten their grandmother and they feel bad about it. Joe realises this and in his bluff way makes everything all right again. They're just young he thinks, not cruel, and there is a difference.

Once they have all gone, Claire makes a big shepherd's pie. It can be frozen if her husband is lucky with his fishing and brings supper home, but just in case... she thinks to herself, just in case. She clears up in the kitchen, then makes tea and takes it up to her mother-in-law. Roberta is pleased to see her and they spend an hour or so chatting peacefully about Joe, her favourite subject and one that Claire is not averse to either. Roberta has always known that her daughter-in-law loves her son and that she makes him happy. It is more than she had hoped for him, so she has always been generous with her.

As Roberta dozes with the curtains drawn, but the windows open, Claire decides to have a bit of a tidy. She always needs something to do and in some ways, keeping house is her hobby. The fact that this is not her house doesn't matter; her family are staying there and their comfort is important to her.

The air is already quite sultry and she hopes everyone will make it back before the storm arrives, then remembers Joe's pronouncements on the weather and smiles. His forecasts are usually good, often better than the ones on the TV, so she has reason to believe that he will be right, but nonetheless, as she looks up at the cloudless blue sky she worries.

In Megan's room, she carefully remakes the hastily made bed and notices a book on the floor. The cover looks oriental and she picks it up, curious to see what it is. When she opens it she discovers that it is the diary of Lillian Loveday. She met Lillian a few times, years ago and she came to their wedding. She remembers her as charming, more so than Roberta, but back then she hadn't really understood the dynamics of her husband's family.

She sits on the edge of the bed, opening it randomly and Lillian's youth and inexperience leap off the page as she describes her life in 1936. Claire can easily imagine this younger version of the elderly but sprightly woman she once knew. After all, she had always been there, just beneath the surface and not for the first time, she wonders who Lillian might have been had life been different and a little kinder to her.

"No, not life..." Claire murmers, correcting herself. "The world. Had the world been a different place, that's what we mean when we talk of that time."

Roberta is calling. Her voice is feeble and only because the air is so still and hot that even the insects are quiet, does Claire hear her. She puts the diary down and goes to help her out of bed and to the bathroom.

After lunch, Claire digs around in cupboards and eventually finds a fan, which she takes to Roberta's room and they sit in its welcome breeze, chatting about shared events from the past. The sound of the doorbell intrudes on their conversation and they both look puzzled; it is too early for the carer and the family would come round the back, where the door is open. Claire smoothes her skirt and goes downstairs.

In the porch is a small, elderly woman bearing a cake that is covered with what looks like a heavy glass dome.

"Hello dear, you must be Claire. I'm Susan." she says cheerfully, but Clair's evident confusion prompts her to say more. "Louise invited me for tea. It is Saturday, isn't it?" She is suddenly flustered and a little unsure.

"Yes, yes of course." Claire replies. "I'm sorry, how rude of me. Here, let me take that. Come in, come in. Susan, wasn't it?"

Susan follows Claire into the kitchen and cannot help but notice the silence.

"Oh, is Louise out...? Perhaps I am early. Tea is always at four o'clock for us old baggages, but of course times change and in some things I am so unmodern." She laughs and as Claire deposits the cake on the table, she turns to face her guest, instinctively liking her.

"I like tea at four as well, I must confess. But we, my husband and I that is, have given Louise the weekend off and in the rush she must have forgotten to mention you, or more likely I wasn't listening, so I was surprised to find you there. Are you a friend of Roberta's?"

"I hope so. We've known 'of' each other for a long time, but we only actually met last week. How is she today? May I...?" she asks, indicating a chair.

"Yes, do, of course..."

Susan removes her jacket and hat and places them neatly over the back of the nearest chair and carefully sits down.

"Forgive me," says Claire, "you've caught me completely on the hop. I'll make some tea and we can go up. She is tired and frailer than I was expecting from what my husband had said after his last visit. I never thought she would go downhill so quickly. She's always been such a strong presence in our lives and well..." She pauses for a moment and collects herself, then looks once more at Susan. "But how curious... what do you mean, you've know 'of' each other?"

Susan perches on the edge of her seat and leans forward slightly, as if she is about to share a secret, which of course for Claire it still is.

"I was your father-in-law's mistress for almost twelve years, right up until his death in fact. Your mother-in-law was curious and wanted to meet me, so she invited me here last week and we seem to have got on like a house on fire, which given that we shared the same man for all that time should come as no surprise really!" She leans back and laughs conspiratorially.

Claire is shocked, but does not wish to be impolite. Roberta is quite capable of this kind of curiosity, she is sure of that, but she is equally sure that Joe doesn't know about the affair. But is it an affair when it lasts for so long, she wonders, or does it have another name? And if so, what might that be? In her family there have never been any of the dramas that have played such a part in her husband's and here is another skeleton, boldly stepping out.

"Oh my... well... I don't know what to say..."

Susan, seeing the distress that her confession has caused and being by nature a kind person, takes charge and deftly changes the subject, anchoring Claire to more familiar ground.

"I think Roberta will be able to have a little cake with her tea, don't you? It's not very rich and it's made from wholemeal flour, so it's not overly processed. I do think these things are important, don't you? Of course a little of what you fancy in moderation is good for the soul. That's what my old granny used to say, and I do so agree. Why live a long time and be miserable? That's my motto. Although I have to say I'm very partial to just a bit of bread and honey with tea. Brown bread of course and the homemade jams around these parts are so good, don't you think...?"

Her gentle chatter allows Claire a few moments to compose herself and she fills the kettle, spoons tea into the pot and pours milk into the jug. These movements are natural and second nature for her and together they slice the cake, set the tray and then head upstairs, by which time Claire is rather curious herself.

The first thing she notices is that Roberta is genuinely pleased to see Susan and they slip easily into a conversation that hadn't quite been finished last time she was there. Claire can see that she will be surplus to requirements, so after a few moments she excuses herself and leaves them to it, smiling and shaking her head in wonderment at the peals of shared laughter as she heads back downstairs with her tea.

She goes into the kitchen, but finding it too hot, goes back upstairs to her room where there is more of a breeze. She eyes the bed speculatively, feeling a little naughty and remembers the diary. It would be nice to read some more she thinks, so she goes to fetch it. Once back in her room, she rearranges the pillows, slips off her shoes and relaxes on the counterpane, something she rarely allows herself to do during the day and opens a page at random.

24th December 1937

I start me nineteenth year not just an aunt, but a godmother twice over. We'd all hoped that little Rose would wait and put in an appearance on me birthday so we could share it, but it was not to be, she popped out a few days early. Still, she and Elsie are both doing fine and Fred's as proud as punch. She's got his eyes but her mum's nose and she's going to be a real looker, that's for sure. We've all been joking that she and Connor will make a lovely pair. Wouldn't that be a hoot! He's already got a full head of hair and such inquisitive eyes. Thankfully he sleeps well, cos Rita's only just got over having him. Finally she's got some colour back in her cheeks and at last she seems to have found her laugh again, taken months though. Thank goodness her mum's been fussing over the two of them, I hate to think what would have happened if she'd been all on her own, but as her mum's had six herself, she knows what she's doing.

Funny though, all me closest mates and me big brother being parents already. I don't feel old enough, Mum says you never do, so there's no point in waiting! Still, it is all a bit strange, changes things in some ways. I mean they all got different concerns now, so when we're chatting they're no longer just thinking about themselves, they got their family to consider too. While me, well I've still only got me to think about and Mum a bit of course, but that's the way it's always been and always will be. Am I being left behind, or am I the lucky one?

Mum, me and Vic went up town to see the musical that everyone is talking about, 'Me and my Girl' at the Victoria Palace Theatre. Real posh place it is too and what a laugh we had. Vic got us the tickets for Christmas and me birthday. Good seats they were too. We got all dressed up and he made us take a taxi there. Fancy! Said he's been doing all right, so he wanted to share it with us. Always generous Vic is. The song 'Doing the Lambeth Walk' is so popular that the whole audience sings along with it. We had a bit of supper afterwards in a little place round the back, don't know how he knows these places. Lovely it was and then we snuck in real late, trying not wake Auntie Eth. Tommy was waiting up for us and Joyce wasn't asleep as I got into bed, so I told her all about it.

I'm going to miss Vic when he goes again, but at least he is getting back now and then and he's left Mum the fare and says she's to come to visit soon. He told me to make sure she does, after all, she's got a grandson out there and she should know him. He was sorry he didn't have the money for me to go too, but I understand, really I do.

Wish I could go too, but maybe next time, who knows. After all, things might be looking up! I mean third class ain't too expensive these days. Imagine if I could do that, sail across the ocean all the way to the other side, just like Vic does. Makes me toes curl when I think about it. One day, surely I'll be able to do it one day.

≈

2nd *January 1938*

We all saw the New Year in with Elsie and Fred at their place, cos they didn't want to leave little Rose alone and Rita brought Connor with her. She's lost so much weight since the birth though. I've been round to see her a lot since he was born, but it's only really seeing her next to Elsie that it hit me. I said to Mum that I'd take some of the fruit and veg I get round to them for a few weeks, we've got enough after all and she agreed. I know some women do die after giving birth and I know she's feeding him herself. I mean her mum'd take him in for sure if anything happened to her, but I couldn't bear it, we already lost Mags. We're young, we're meant to be living, not dying.

As the New Year rolled in, the three of us, me, Rita and Elsie had a little toast to Mags. If she's up there she'd have seen us and told us we were being daft!

Too many people were talking about that dictator in Italy and how they and Germany are warmongering again. I hope it's just the case of too much beer and whatnot inside them. When I look at those babes I don't want them to know a war. Connor ain't got a father to lose of course, but still, it wouldn't be fair. Surely the world is big enough for all of us? Anyway, we chimed the year in and all hope for the best of course!

≈

5*th* January 1938

Mum's been out today and arranged for a sailing in a couple of weeks, one that'll get her there a few days after Vic's back, so he'll be able to go and collect her from the boat and take her home to meet Viv and little Ben. What a treat that will be for her. I don't know who is more excited, me or her, and I ain't even going!

≈

7*th* January 1938

Me and Mum with Auntie Eth and Joyce went over to Kensington, to the big Pontings store there. 'House of Value' it's called and what an eye opener! We got a nice suitcase and a new coat for Mum for less than eighteen bob. It's going to be cold over there, Vic warned her before he went back. Hats and scarves we've got aplenty between us, but her coat was a bit threadbare and mine's too big for her. We got her some overboots as well and we picked up a few nice glass vases too, in boxes they are, as gifts. One is for Viv's mum, but as Auntie Eth said, there might be other people she'll meet or who might give her something and she won't want to be caught out and left feeling bad. We had a pot of tea and a bit *of lunch in Lyons at Charing Cross on the way back too. Spoilt ourselves good and proper we did!*

≈

18th January 1938

Saw Mum off on the train down to Southampton. I've never known her so nervous. She repacked her case at least four times and that's just while I was watching. Got all the presents nicely wrapped up for them all, got all her papers ready, we double checked everything and then off she went, all teary and smiley at the same time. Auntie Eth told me the only time we've sent family off on a boat train was Vic when he first went to sea and of course the menfolk in the war. Made me think that did. But then she's just being daft I decided, I mean Mum's going to visit family, all the way across the ocean to see the other side, how amazing is that! My mum! We both said that next time we're going together and we're going to start saving as soon as she gets back.

I'm missing her already, we've never been apart. She's always been there and now I keep going to say something and then remember! I've already got enough bits I want to tell her to write a long letter, which I might just do tomorrow anyway.

≈

2nd February 1938

Got a letter from Mum this morning, having a lovely time she is. Vic and Viv are making a real fuss of her and she says Viv's mum's a real gem. Sounds like she won't want to come back! The photos of her glowing with pride holding Ben are a sight to see and she said the crossing was really nice, not stormy at all and the people were real friendly, especially the Yanks. Made Auntie Eth and me smile it did.

≈

14th February 1938

A valentine's card got pushed under the door during the night with just me name written on the envelope. Most mysterious it is, as I really have no idea who it might be from. It's a lovely picture of violets and forget me nots, but nothing *written on the inside, nothing at all. I waited all day to see if anyone wanted to make his self known to me, but nothing out of the ordinary happened and no one said a thing or even smiled at me in a funny way. I'm going to bed still as puzzled as I was when I had me breakfast this morning. I can't even think who I'd like it to be from!*

≈

2nd March 1938

Saw some of the kiddies going to school with gas masks hanging at their sides, gave me quite a turn it did. I know the law was passed back at the start of the year, but even so, we ain't at war, nor does it look like we're going to be any time soon. So why?

Cyril Banks asked me to the spring dance on Saturday week. I've seen him moozie about the floor, he's good, so I said yes. Should be fun. Elsie and Fred are coming and they're going to leave Rita in charge, she said she don't want to come as it won't be no fun with no one to dance with. She got a bit teary, said she'll never have her own home or husband now, but that at the same time she wouldn't part with Connor for the world, he brightens her day a treat he does. But still, she told me to be as careful as Elsie was with who I give me heart to. I reckon she's right too. It's no more than Mum and Vic tell me and she has more cause to say it.

But how do you know? I mean Rita ain't no fool, but she got fooled good and proper. Others say that in the moment you don't care and if you're lucky, well it'll all work out all right one way or the other. I'm not sure though, course I've not felt 'the moment'. That was part of the problem with Albert, seemed he felt it quite often when he was with me, too often if you ask me!

Maybe I'm not quite right, but without Mum here, there ain't no one really that I can ask. Maybe I'm just having a daft minute!

≈

Claire puts the diary down and sighs sadly. She is the mother of three boys and would have loved a daughter, but it was not to be and even though times have supposedly changed since the 1930s, she wonders if Rita would have found it easier to be a single mother now. She knows that both she and Louise would advise Megan against it and would want her to be careful, as careful as everyone warned Lillian to be.

She and Joe have brought their sons up to be respectful, but all the same, they are boys, so she assumes that their heads must be full of sex and their bodies full of hormones. She sips her tea and grimaces, for it has gone cold and she toys with the idea of going downstairs to make a fresh one, but then the decision is made for her, as she hears the sound of tyres on gravel, accompanied by whoops and shouts. Slipping her shoes back on, she smoothes the bed and goes out onto the landing.

As she passes Roberta's door, she remembers Susan and pops her head round, finding them still deep in conversation. It reminds her that Joe doesn't know and she wonders if it is her bit of news to share with him or a secret to keep. Undecided, she heads downstairs, ready to fulfil her role as wife and mother, the role she chose many years earlier and would choose again. Despite the provisions she sent them off with, they will all be hungry and thirsty, so she focuses on that instead of drama and deception, both of which make her uncomfortable.

Louise is sitting in Cate's kitchen, nursing a large whiskey, her second. She is pleased she left Megan with her aunt and uncle and hopes that her daughter is having a better time than she is. But the point of this weekend was never going to be unbridled passion or gaiety, she reminds herself, feeling that such things will probably never be part of her life again, as she stifles a sob.

Her tearstained face troubles her friend and she silently reaches across the table and gently holds her hand. "...and what happened then?" she prompts.

"Well there we were, sitting in the pub discussing our marriage as though it were a film we had both seen, but not at the same time. And then halfway through the discussion, it's like we discovered that one of us had seen the original and the other had seen the remake. So the story isn't quite the same and we both seemed to have missed little but important bits of the plot." She sighs, takes a large gulp of her drink and then tells her friend the hardest part of all.

"He admitted that Lucy isn't the first. He said he'd been seeing someone else when we met and then he told me that there had been another, just after Megan was born. Then he went on to say that it didn't count because we weren't married then and anyway I ought to understand, given that I had enticed him away from Deirdre, who he was still married to at the time. Can you believe that? How could he say that? And more importantly, how could I have missed all of that?" she wails.

Cate shakes her head, muttering obscene insults.

"Then..." Louise continues, a little too loudly, "then he says... calm as you like, that Lucy only happened because I was so busy with Mum, work and Megan, that he felt ignored. Ignored!" she shouts at no one in particular. "I mean there I am, driving hundreds of miles a week, back and forth up the bloody motorway because my mother is dying and then doing the shopping, fitting in work, keeping the house tidy, ironing his bloody shirts, being a mother, dropping in on his mother because he conveniently forgets to go and help her out, and *he* bloody well feels ignored. Excuse me for being human!" She flops down onto the table, huge sobs wracking her body.

Cate sits and stares at the wall, seeing nothing, just holding her friend's hand, unable to make it right.

Chapter nine

Megan lies in bed, feeling happy and tired after a long day, one she believes will be remembered as a good one for years to come. In fact, it was exactly the kind of day she had despaired of having this summer. They had behaved like wild things and had hurtled along green lanes, then through the woods and down to the river. There had been so much laughter and even Uncle Joe had seemed younger and more relaxed than usual.

Her cousins had shown off of course, because their bikes were so much better than hers, or Jake's, for that matter, but that had been normal. Really, they were just trying to outdo each other, no one else, and she was as easy with them as they were with her.

What had been a little unusual, was the fact that at different points throughout the day, she couldn't help but notice that Jake treated her differently to her cousins and not just because he wasn't family. Once again, he had been invited to stay for dinner and on a couple of occasions she had caught her uncle and aunt looking at each other, or at her and him and Matt had smirked more than once.

She is aware that something is different in her life, but she is not sure how to describe it and wishes Hannah were there, not because her friend would understand necessarily, but because together they could unpick it and examine it in minute detail. Texting is not the same, she thinks with a sigh, then turns over and feels on the floor under the bed for the diary, but it's not there.

She gets up and looks around the room properly. She can't find it, and now she is wide awake and even more in need of something to read. Thinking she must have left it in her bag, she heads downstairs, towards the kitchen. Halfway down, she hears her aunt and uncle talking in the front parlour. Funny word, 'parlour' she thinks and spells it out to herself then repeats it over and over again, noting that the word means less each time. It is a description of a room that is used nowhere other than in this house. At home they have a living room and the family room. Hannah's parents have a family room and a drawing room, but no one apart from her gran has a parlour. And she has two; front and back.

In the hall, she is about to call out to let them know she is there, when she hears the pain in her uncle's voice and stops in the shadows, uncertain; not really wanting to listen, but not sure how to go past the open door.

"All those years, a lie... My own father... How could he? A mistress, right under our noses... poor Mum..."

Her aunt is making soothing noises. "It's not for us to judge Joe, not really... I mean, she seems sweet enough."

"Not judge? My own father cheating on my mother for almost twelve years... How can I not judge? How can I just let it go? I ask you... and to think I offered to run her home... how would that have gone, do you think?"

"Well... what did your mum say when she explained it all to you?"

Joe huffs and says nothing. Instead he stands up and paces around a bit before sitting back down again.

"Look my love," Claire says, reaching over to him, "Roberta has clearly forgiven everyone. You should have heard them laughing together and..."

A floorboard creaks and she breaks off, mid sentence.

Megan pops her head around the door. "Sorry, I was just looking for my bag. I think it has my book in it. I er..."

Claire's hand flies to her mouth as she remembers. "That's my fault dear. I tidied your room earlier and found it and started reading it. You do mean Lillian's diary, don't you?"

Megan nods.

"It's on the bedside table in our room."

Grateful for the chance to escape, she scoots off upstairs and her uncle wonders how much she heard, and if she knew anyway.

As she settles on her bed, she contemplates what she did hear and surmises correctly that they were talking about Susan. To Megan, she is of course more than ancient and the whole idea of someone so old being a mistress, which must involve sex, is so horrific to her that she shudders and pushes all the associated thoughts out of her mind. She is not curious, but she is sorry that her favourite uncle is so hurt by it. Then with more than her usual level of enthusiasm, she dives into the diary, eager to lose herself in something more palatable.

28th July 1938

We've all been scouring the market for old copies of The Times, well us girls have, anyway. It's a real prize when we find the next instalment of Mrs Miniver and get to read it over our tea break and see what she and her family have been up to. One of us gets to read it out loud to the others. Makes me smile that does, as she, Mrs M, I mean, has got more class than all of us put together, so whoever reads it has do a voice to make it sound right. Sometimes they gets it wrong, which has us in stitches. We've banned Gladys from reading it, cos we can't concentrate at all when she does.

It's so nice, cos it's not a book, but a story. Not a short story as such, because it's always about her and her life and what goes on in it from one day to the next, how she solves her problems and suchlike. Different, but we're all hooked. Over tea of an evening I tell Mum and Auntie Eth all about what happened next and they look forward to it as much as I do!

I'd love her life, all that time to be herself, even though she's married and has children, although her boy is away at school. Fancy being away from home so young! I would have hated it. Mum said she would have missed me and wouldn't have sent me anyway! Imagine though, Auntie Eth said it might've been fun, cos you'd be with your friends all the time. Made me think that did. I mean, having days and nights for years with Mags, Rita and others might've been fun, but I'd have missed Vic and Mum more, I'm sure.

≈

Megan laughs, realising that for Lillian, this is exactly what Bridget Jones had been for her mother, who had been very enthusiastic about the column when it first came out and Megan wonders if she will be able to find the Mrs Miniver stories on the internet.

2nd August 1938

Phew, it's so hot, but still, we're all looking forward to our holiday. Hop picking we've settled on for this year, a whole week in Kent, should be fun. Mum and Auntie Eth have arranged everything and Rita and Connor will come with us too. She's still helping Mum out with the sewing and every morning she goes with her mum to do some cleaning at Garriton's, so things are looking up for them.

A holiday is just what we all need though and it'll be great to get away from all this talk of war and suchlike. Even Vic's got the bug it seems, judging from his last letter at any rate. Made me a bit cross it did. I mean I'm sitting here looking out of the window, there's not a cloud in the sky and downstairs everyone's going about their business same as normal, so why? Why have we got to even think such thoughts? Don't make any sense to me at all.

≈

6th August 1938

Joyce and Charlie are still walking out together, I think it might be getting serious. I'd promised not to saying anything and I kept quiet, but she had to tell Auntie Eth the other night anyway, as Mrs Schofield saw them behind the bus station on Wednesday. Made us all laugh that did! But still, I had another chat with her in bed last night and warned her to be careful. He's older than her after all, so he ought to know better, but you never can be too sure, might be his mind is full of only one thing. Although when we went dancing, he never put a hand out of place, I'll give him credit there. I told Auntie Eth that too, to put her mind at ease a bit.

Made Mum look at me a bit funny though, as if to say, 'and what about you?' Truth is, the lads round here are a laugh and I enjoy the odd dance or a visit to the cinema with them, but nothing else. I guess the one for me is still out there somewhere. Hope I meet him before I get old and grey though!

I don't want to be the last one to settle down, I don't want everyone giving me odd looks and feeling sorry for me, but I *don't want to end up with someone that's all wrong for me neither. Maybe he's not out there waiting, maybe I'll have to get used to the idea of being everyone's aunt and never a mum meself. Maybe that's me fate. I hope not though.*

≈

Megan's thoughts turn back to Jake, lingering quite pleasantly on the way he smiled at her, or the way he waited for her whenever the track through the woods or by the river got a bit too muddy or dodgy. Once again she is aware of a strange new feeling seeping through her and she lets the diary drop beside her onto the bed as she closes her eyes, allowing her mind to take her back through the day until sleep claims her.

Claire pops her head round her niece's door as she goes to bed herself and is pleased to see her fast asleep. The window is wide open and the breeze has turned; now blowing the curtain so that it flaps about inside the room, seemingly with a life of its own. She slips in and shuts it slightly, sure her husband is right and that the storm will come during the night. She also knows he will lie awake listening to it, turning over in his mind what his mother had told him earlier, piece by piece.

There is nothing she can do; he must find his own way through this and she hopes that it doesn't take him too long. After all, as she gently reminded him earlier, time is something that Roberta has very little of now. Claire doesn't want their final goodbye to be clouded by events from the past that are really nothing to do with him, but she knows he can't quite see that yet.

Joe lies awake next to the sleeping but comforting form of his wife, while a long way southeast, so does Louise. The fug of the alcohol has worn off, the anger has subsided and she is left with only the bare bones of her marriage to pick over in the darkness. She listens to the cars whooshing past outside. Peter has always outshone her, but now, for the first time, she realises that she is not a powerless rabbit caught in his powerful glare and understands that it is not him that keeps her there frozen, but herself.

She mulls over the two words, 'powerless' and 'powerful', repeating them over and over to herself, wondering how one moves from one to the other and where the line that divides them is. Eventually, the answer inches its way into her consciousness. It is 'choice' she decides. I chose him. I chose to be the person I thought he wanted me to be. Then her mouth slowly forms the words she has been hiding from. "I chose to give up who I am, in order to keep him."

The last few months, or possibly years, she reflects, flinching a little uncomfortably at the notion, which she knows to be the truth, she has been changing. She has been trying to reclaim parts of herself, if only by feeling angry or resentful about certain things within their marriage, which of course is why she turned to work so eagerly. Once the chance to do something meaningful outside the home came up, she grabbed it with both hands. She was greedy for it, demanding that it be hers, in the same way that Megan had demanded things when she was two, even though she did not yet have the words to express herself.

Now, she can see with absolute clarity that she too was dishonest. She made excuses to Peter, making her job sound temporary or insignificant, so he wouldn't see the reality. She didn't realise it, but it was a way of finding herself again and she is sure he wouldn't have wanted that, hence the lack of honesty.

She takes a deep breath and asks herself a question. Can I choose to be myself and still choose to keep him? It's too big, she thinks. I'm not ready yet. She puts it away, but doesn't bury it. It will be answered, just not tonight.

The rain hammers down and is whipped about by gusts of wind, but within the thick walls of Priory Meadows, Roberta sleeps through it. The exhaustion of the day, mixed with the sleeping pills and painkillers, ensures that she will remain peacefully unaware of very much until Sunday morning. The boys are in two of the rooms at the top of the house and they wake and sleep again in quick fluid movements, only their dreams disturbed by the ferocity of the weather outside.

Claire wakes and moves closer to her husband's side, thankful that the sultry air has been banished. He strokes her hair, grateful for her presence in his life and in that moment, knows that while he is and will always be his father's son, he is not his father. Holding her closer to him, he finally goes to sleep and she smiles in the darkness before drifting off again herself.

Megan sits up in shock, trying to stifle a scream, then realises that it's a very cross and wet Maisie that landed heavily on her chest, nothing more sinister. Neither she nor her aunt had considered the cat, so now she feels guilty, but at the same time glad that the angry furball managed to find her way up and in through the window.

Once Maisie is dry, fed and settled in the back parlour, Megan takes herself off to the kitchen to make a big mug of cocoa. She wonders again how anyone can live without a microwave and then heads back up to bed, holding the mug carefully. She is slightly unnerved by the shadows leaping on the stairs, even though she knows they are caused by the wind buffeting the outside lights, but still her imagination sees something else. She knows there are other people in the house, but she feels totally alone.

A sprinkle of rain flies into her face as she passes the landing window and she pulls it shut, feeling exhilarated by it all. She stands for a moment looking over the rooftops, superimposing the view with images she has seen of fields and trees, before a flash of lightning shows her only what is really there.

Back in her bedroom, she is wide awake again. Clutching her cocoa and sitting cross-legged on top of the bed, she pulls the diary towards her and flips it open.

2nd October 1938

Well, we heard it on the radio, we saw it at the cinema on the Pathé News and we read it in the newspapers.

'Peace for our time.' That's what Mr Chamberlain said. He also said that the desire of our two peoples is never to go to war again. Amen to that, that's what me and Mum said. Amen to that once and for all.

Problem is, yesterday they marched into some place called 'Sudetenland'. Apparently we calls it Czechoslovakia, but let's face it, most us didn't even know it existed until yesterday. Thankfully the newspaper had a map in it so we could all see. Bloody miles away from us it is.

Fred says it's nothing to worry about. He says that it was part of their country before the war and Austria didn't mind, so why should they. I hope he's right, but others down the market say it's not the same at all. Austria is Austria and full of Germans, but this place ain't. They say it's the beginning and war will come, maybe not this year, maybe not next, but that Mr Hitler will get too big for his boots and we'll have to go and put him in his place. I hope they're wrong and I hope Fred's right. I hope Mr Chamberlain knows what he's talking about, cos I can't stop thinking about it. I wish Vic was here. I wrote him a long letter last night. If he tells me not to worry I won't, but I'll be lucky to get a quick reply.

≈

18th October 1938

I'm so fed up with it all. All this talk spoils everything, even a nice night out at the pictures is ruined. I'm right glad I've got Agatha's 'Death on the Nile' to keep me company for a few nights, something to get me teeth stuck into.

I did hear that they are going to make 'Gone with the Wind' into a film. That will be magic if they do. The actress they've chosen as Scarlett is one of us Brits, the same one I saw in the film 'Fire over England'. She's so pretty, I'm sure they've made the right choice, can't wait to see it.

I been lost in me own daydreams of what if that had been me? Would I have been so mean to Rhett? He weren't no angel that's for sure, but who wants to fall in love with an angel!!!!

≈

13th November 1938

We've all been talking about what happened in Germany the other night. It's been in the papers and on the news at the cinema where you got to see pictures of the mess after all them shops was smashed. I know what they did was in their own country to their own people, but still it makes you think that if a country can do that to its own, what else will it do? There are plenty of people down the market who said someone high up in the government over there said publically that he would not want to be a Jew in Germany right now. They said he sounded proud about the fact, like it was a good thing to say. Sends a bit of a shiver down your spine that does.

Can't say I know any Jews around here apart from old Mrs Diamond's family at number 35, and they're not really any different to us. Except everyone knows not to disturb them on a Friday evening, but that aside, it don't seem to me that she's that religious, the family mix as much as anyone else, but then here in the flats there's all sorts and we all get along. If we don't, it's not usually to do with religion, more to do with thieving or insulting, but that's just normal.

I am worried now. Me and Tish sat up late last night talking about it all and what it might mean for us, specially for Tommy and Evan. I'm so glad Vic's over in America, out of the way he is.

I know Mum always says there's no point in getting in a state over something that ain't happening and might never happen anyway, but me and Tish ain't so sure now. I lay there for hours, wide awake, couldn't drop off to sleep no matter how much I tried.

Mum always says that Dad and all the others went in 1914 cos they were full of rightful pride and certainty, but that Dad said the reality of them trenches was like nothing he'd wish on no one, not unless there was a really good reason for them being there.

Surely we did it then, when we fought for what had to be fought for and despite losing so many of our lads, not to mention me own Dad, we won. It's over, ain't that enough?

≈

18th November 1938

I lost me job. Can't believe it. Mr Dickens and I had a right row about the way he treated Joyce Peterson so he fired me as well. Just like that. I mean she didn't do nothing wrong, just stuck up for herself when that smarmy brother of his put his hand where he had no right to put it.

Anyway, when I told him that, he looked at me right funny and gave me what he owed and then sent me packing without a by your leave for all the years I've been there. She'd only been there a couple of weeks, but still, she was right to slap him. I mean a girl's got to make these things clear. Like I said to Mum, I would have done the same and he knew it, which is why he's never tried anything on with me, so I don't really regret it, not in that sense anyway.

I went back the following morning to say sorry, like Mum asked me to but he wouldn't hear of it and no one else, not even Old Sully would take me on, said there were no need for extras right now. There's always a need for extras, specially with Christmas coming up.

I can't believe it. I feel like I've let everyone down, if I don't find something quick like, we're going to have a rotten winter, never mind Christmas and it'll be my fault, even though I know no one will actually say that. We'll all know it though.

≈

27th November 1938

Mr Smith asked me to come every morning this week to clean his shop, while his wife is off visiting her mother and he said everything was a bit up the creek at the moment. No one's sure what's happening and what with all those people leaving Germany, Austria and other places over there any which way they can, there's loads of cheap labour on the market. He told me you can hire a man for the same price as a girl these days, sometimes less. Imagine being that desperate. When you look at it that way, what you can do? So at least now I know why they were so quick to fire me and why no one wants to take me on. I went up and saw a couple of the girls at teatime and they said the same, slightest excuse and bang, you're out and the following day there's some foreign bloke doing what you used to do for less. Still, as Mum says, we're together here, all snug and Vic's over there all safe and sound, so all's well, which is not how it is for so many others.

Mum and Auntie Eth also said not to worry, they said to let a bit of time pass, then go back and see what's what then. Mum tried to make me feel better by saying that we got some savings and they've been putting stuff by for Christmas, so we won't go without, but even so, I've never done nothing else. I was happy there, I can't see me working in a shop or cleaning, drive me mad it would and I can't sew for toffee.

Why's everything going so horrible all of a sudden? Still, as Mum says, at least we've got our health. I keep telling meself that she's got a point and she's been trying to keep our spirits up. She made me favourite cabbage and mash last night with a lovely meaty gravy and a hunk of bread to mop it up with. I know I'm lucky really, just wish I could shift this feeling of doom and gloom.

≈

12th December 1938

Well maybe things might just turn out all right. Fred got me some work for a couple of months up at his place. He says it'll last until at least the middle of February, might even go on a few weeks longer, but we'll see. I'm assembling some bits and pieces with some other girls. Don't know what they're supposed to be, they're all such funny shapes once all the bits are fitted together, but it don't matter. As he says, ours is not to question why! When we're done they get boxed up and taken off to wherever, for the next bit to be done by someone else and we then get more to put together. He pays me two pounds ten shillings a week, no questions asked. As Mum says, it'll see us through until I find something else. Fred takes me in the van every morning and usually brings me back at night. I've been there just over a week now. Must say I miss the sky, although it's lovely and warm in his shed, if a bit dark by the afternoon.

The other two girls are nice enough, older than me. One's married and the other is planning on a spring wedding. They've been doing stuff for Fred and his partner for a while now. They say it's always different, sometimes there's a few weeks with nothing, but something else always comes along.

They say the main thing is just to keep mum about it all. Reckon I can do that, but it's a bit strange being with new people after all those years down the market. I mean everyone there knew me, we didn't always have to explain ourselves and the laughs we could have when we was cold and wet and fed up. I miss them, even though I do appreciate what Fred is doing for us. I mean we can't survive without me earning a few bob, so I shouldn't be stuck up about it all, but still.

≈

19th December 1938

Well, Little Rose is one year old today. Fancy that! Elsie says she's in love with mothering and is quite happy for the next one to come along whenever he or she is ready to put in an appearance. She does look happy I must say and they're doing all right for themselves too. We had a little party, of course Rose didn't know it was for her, but she smiled at us all and she's well kitted out with a whole new wardrobe and lots of stuff for the winter!

Little Connor was down with croup, so Rita couldn't bring him. She's not been doing so well herself just lately, got a terrible chesty cough, but Mum takes over some sewing for her to do then collects it, so she's still earning a bit. We knitted up a couple of bits for Connor, while we was doing some to send over to Ben. She was dead thrilled, but it's such a responsibility having a little one all by yourself to care for, I wouldn't change places with her. I know it ain't what she intended for herself, nor what her mum and dad wanted for her, but still, lovely though he is, I am so glad it ain't me!

≈

23rd December 1938

What a laugh we had tonight. Mum brought a couple of bottles of ale home without me knowing and I brought fish and chips for us all, cos Fred gave me ten bob extra today. So a right good mood we was all in as we settled down to listen to the radio. Tish showed us a new dance that she said was all the rage, but how'd she know? She don't go dancing yet, she's too young! Still, we all stood up and had a go and oh, the laughing, we had stitches from it all!

≈

24th December 1938

I only want one thing, I don't want no war to happen.

≈

Megan mulls over the single line entry, thinking she knows Lillian well enough to understand the sentiment behind the sentence. She puts the book down and drains her cocoa mug, wondering how she would feel if she thought a war was coming now. Her mind draws a blank and she has to remind herself that she has studied the Second World War in history at school. She has seen programmes and films, so she knows what Lillian, the Lillian that wrote that line, could not have known as she was writing it.

For a moment, one of the horrific pictures from the Wikipedia page flickers into her mind and she pushes it away, trying instead to think about Fred and Elsie with little baby Rose. The cocoa has the desired effect and by now she is shattered, and falls asleep almost instantly.

Chapter ten

Claire hovers uncertainly in the back doorway between the kitchen and the garden. She can see that the trailer is ready to go; loaded with bikes and some of the things from the garage that Joe wants to keep. The boys are eager to return to their own lives, as indeed is she, but leaving Megan in charge, even for such a short while doesn't seem right to her.

"Are you sure? I mean, we could..."

"Of course she's sure. Isn't that right Megan?"

Joe has been to say goodbye to his mother and as he comes into the kitchen he embraces his niece.

"Of course I am." Megan confirms. "And anyway, Mum called and said that she's less than an hour away and there are no reports of holdups or anything." she adds, happily wriggling out of her uncle's arms and moving to her aunt's side. "After you're gone, I'll take Gran her lunch and we'll be fine together, honest. We'll watch something on the TV till Mum gets here."

Claire hugs her, smoothes down her fringe and smiles. "I forget that you're so grown up now! Don't forget to tell your mum that we'll be back next Friday, although it'll be late, so don't wait for us for dinner. Anyway, it'll probably be just the two of us, so we'll eat before we set off or grab something on the way maybe. But we'll speak during the week of course, so..."

Joe gently propels his wife out of the door towards the drive. "Come along, don't keep fussing..."

The boys take their cue and pile into the car, waving and shouting farewells to their cousin. Then after a minute they are gone and there is silence once more, leaving just the faint smell of diesel lingering on the damp air.

The light drizzle threatens to turn into something more persistent, so Megan goes back inside. A tray is already set up with cake and sandwiches. Her aunt has made a selection, in the hope that there is something there that Roberta will eat, but in amongst them she spies tuna mayonnaise and tomato and smiles. It's one of her favourites, even though she ate a hearty breakfast not that long ago and is still surprised by how much her uncle's family eats in a normal day. There is only the tea to be made and after a couple of minutes she carefully goes up the stairs to where Roberta is waiting.

Her grandmother is hungry, but not for lunch. What she wants is some diversion from her thoughts and the pain. She is already missing her son and not at all certain that she will still be alive on Friday. She has taken more painkillers than perhaps she ought to have, but they are beginning to have an effect and although the pain is not subsiding as such, it seems to have shifted to place where she can more easily ignore it. She does not tell her granddaughter that it is the pain she is most afraid of.

She expects dying to be quite easy, which is what she meant when she spoke of it. Not living is what will be difficult, however she assumes that particular difficulty is more of a concern to the living and that it will disappear with death. But pain and suffering, these are things she does not want to deal with or endure.

Her thoughts fly once again to her nana. She has memories of the familiar and much loved figure sitting in the garden; silently crying, tears running down her face. The young Roberta is distressed and runs up to her, although she's almost certain that it's not a new event that is the cause of her grief. She is immediately gathered into a hug and then waits, trying to be as still as she can, for the words that always come.

"I'll never know if he suffered or not. It's the thought that I wasn't there with him and that if he did... well he suffered alone. That's not right and is what besets me so. My baby... he was always my special little boy..."

Apart from Nana's gentle snuffling, they sit like that in silence for a while. There is never anything that can be said to make her feel better, for the information she requires is not there to be had. Roberta has always been certain that her presence was important to her grandmother and that although she was a child, she was in some way able to comfort her just by being there.

It is a recurring event from her childhood, one that was visited often over the years. She has only recently come to understand just why her grandmother felt the loss so keenly, right up to the end of her days. She also understands that if and when the pain gets too much for her, it will be her nana she will cry out for, just as she has always supposed her father did.

Megan eats the sandwiches and Roberta picks at the cake. They have surfed the channels, but found nothing that really interests either of them. The sound of the rain on the roof and the windows creates the impression that they are cocooned, cut off from the real world. It is a pleasant feeling, one that makes them both feel drowsy.

"I could read to you..."

Roberta considers the suggestion. "What are you reading at the moment?" she asks cautiously.

"Your mother's diary, which I'm not sure you will want to hear." Megan replies, equally as cautiously. "But there are other books downstairs... maybe one of them. I could go and find one, or have you read them all already?" She doesn't move and they silently regard each for a moment.

"You find it strange I expect. The fact that I have no interest in my mother's nonsensical ramblings must seem odd to you, but there again, you have a curious nature that is different from mine." Roberta's voice is harsh and before Megan can say anything, she supplies the answer herself, but in a softer tone. "I would find it strange too if I were in your shoes. I will try to explain, although to be honest, it's not something I've ever tried to do before. Let's give it a go anyway... "

She smiles at her granddaughter, who waits patiently, not at all sure what is about to come and even less sure if she wants to know, but is unable to move or to change the subject. Roberta is the family elder and must therefore be deferred to.

"You know that your mother loves you, don't you?"

Megan is quick to nod. She does indeed know this; it is a simple truth, but one that runs deep in her bones. She is therefore shocked by what her grandmother says next.

"Well, my mother didn't love me or want me. She never did, not before I was born and certainly not after."

Roberta stirs her tea thoughtfully and Megan continues to wait, curling up more snugly in one of the two big old fashioned armchairs beside the bed. She feels a need to protect herself and wrapping her arms around her legs seems to do the trick. She is now ready to listen and Roberta has decided what it is she wants to share.

"I imagine there are few circumstances in life where a mother could ask to be forgiven for not loving her child. Rape might be one I suppose, but I'd hazard a guess that it's only 'might'. No two situations are ever the same after all, maybe there are others, I don't know. My father didn't rape my mother, let's be very clear about that. As I understood it, both from her and from my nana, my father's mother, they were in love; deeply so in fact, so that was not the case at all. Whether it would have lasted... well we'll never know. Nana and Grampy had their views I'm sure, but they never shared them with me. Anyway, Nana told me that when my mother, your Lillian, found out she was pregnant, she went into shock.

"She found her all curled up, tight like a ball, she always said, underneath that big pear tree in the orchard, sobbing her heart out and calling for her mother. Hysterical she was and there was no reasoning with her, that's how bad it was. It went on for hours, the screaming and the crying. She told Nana that she didn't want the baby, that's to say me, and that she wanted it ripped out from inside her. She didn't want me to be born. Can you imagine that? No, me neither, but that's the truth of it.

"Nana was horrified. After all they'd endured, she always said that I was the one ray of sunshine that came through. But not for her, not for my own mother. I may have been many things to her, but I was never that.

"Of course I wasn't ripped out of her and she went full term with me and never tried to harm me, not while I was in her and not afterwards neither. But Nana said that throughout it all, the pregnancy I mean, it was like she wasn't really there anymore. Some spark of hers had been clean wiped out and it were like she'd gone somewhere, to a place where no one could reach her. No surprise really I suppose. After all, Nana always said that during those times you were hard pushed to find a spark of anything good anywhere. Dark times they were, such as I've never known in my lifetime, not really. I was so young, so I have no real memories of them and I hope that in your lifetime, people don't wander back into them...

"Where was I? Oh yes, well once I was born she turned away from me, Lillian I mean and I don't remember ever being held by her. I don't remember her telling me a story at bedtime, she never bathed me or dressed me, nor did she ever feed me herself. She was there, but always distant. Watched me she did, often intently, but never from up close. I'd feel her eyes boring into me sometimes, but whatever she was thinking she kept to herself. I don't mean to say that she was silent, because she spoke, but it was like she wasn't part of the family. Mainly, I've always thought, because she didn't want to be. Then of course she'd be gone every year for a couple of months, over there visiting that part of the family that never lifted a finger to help us when we needed it. Then there was all that travelling here, there and everywhere, using up the money on what she said were her charities, kids that had nothing, in places like Africa and suchlike. Didn't matter where she spent it, or on what, the fact of the matter is she made sure there'd be none left for me and your grandfather.

"So you see, all those childhood things were done for me by Nana and what a wonderful woman she was, right to the end of her days. Without her I don't know what my life would have been like. She was there for me, *always*, in just the same way you expect your mother to be there for you. I loved her and she loved me. She used to tell me that I'd saved her; that without me, her life had no meaning."

Roberta smiles at the memory. It is important to her, it always has been and it still anchors her to this world.

"After she died, Nana I mean, I couldn't bear the thought of living here with just her, with your Lillian that you think so highly of. Thankfully, Arnold, your grandfather, came along and well, the rest as they say is history. It would be nice if I could tell you that somehow we found a way of getting along, but the truth of the matter is, we couldn't. She never approved of your grandfather and she made her views known loud and clear, but as all those books you most likely read will tell you, true love will always find a way. Hah!"

They smile at each other, united by the notion; one in innocent anticipation, the other in selective reverie.

"Even though most of the farm was sold off before Nana died, your grandfather and I didn't get what was due to us; what had always been promised.

"But all of that aside, it was when Louise was born that the knife was turned good and proper. You see, what she had never been able to bring herself to do for me, she wanted to do for your mother, regardless of what I might have wanted. Not that we discussed it, we'd gone too far to discuss anything much by then, but still, she was my mother and grandmother to my three. Arnold's two brothers didn't come back from the war and his father was already dead by the time we got wed, so the whole lot on his side were gone by the time Joe was three and that just left Lillian as family. Well here, anyway.

"When your mother was born she changed, Lillian I mean. She couldn't get enough of her, it was like she was drunk all the time. I was quite poorly after the birth; I got one of those infections and whatnot, so they kept me in for three weeks. Back then we didn't expect fathers to cope and he was busy anyway, so Lillian took the boys and the baby in, until I was well enough to have them back. Then of course, when Joe was nearly seven he fell out of that great big pear tree down in the orchard, while she was supposed to be minding them.

"In a coma he was and in hospital for weeks, if not a couple of months after that. I was so sure that I was going to lose him. I hope you never know that feeling Megan, it's not something any mother should have to go through."

She shudders at the memory and feebly waves a hand in front of her face as though to banish it.

"Anyway, Mark was nine by then, so he stayed with his dad and your mum came here. She'd only just turned three, far too young to be left with her father and anyway what would he have done with her while he was out in the fields? I came over most days of course, here and over to the house we lived in then, but most of my time was spent at the hospital. Funny really, Mark was always such a little man whenever he was with his dad, and as for your mum, well...

"You'd have to have seen it to believe it, to understand the difference between when I was a child and how she, Lillian that is, was with your mother. How she held her and cradled her when she was a baby, how she loved her. The clothes she bought for her and the toys, the laughter at bath time..."

She falls silent and her face contorts. There is bitterness there, even after all the years that have passed and Megan sees into the deep pool of darkness and shudders.

On seeing her granddaughter's physical reaction and realising what it is in response to, Roberta collects her thoughts and continues with the story.

"Drove a wedge between us in many ways she did, made the gap uncrossable, because when things got tough at home, Louise would come a-running over here, to her. Then what was I supposed to do? You'll know yourself of course, you'll have arguments with your parents, only natural at your age, but you don't leave home, do you?"

She falls silent for a moment and Megan is aware of a great sadness radiating from the frail body propped up in the bed. She cannot find the words that need saying, for she is too young and she does not know them yet. Instead she sits and watches the old woman, waiting, knowing that she will take control again one way or another. It is her duty and she does not disappoint.

Roberta looks up, smiles at her granddaughter and brings the story to the end she wants it to have. "And now here you are. You look a bit like her, Lillian I mean, but you have my strength and your mother's softness. Most important of all, you have yourself. So you see, while there never was any love lost between Lillian and me, without her you would not be here and that would be a shame. Now, this tea's gone stone cold. Would you make me fresh one please? Nice and sweet..."

Megan is thoughtful as she makes her way down towards the kitchen. The woman that her grandmother described does not sound like the person she has come to know; the one who clearly adored little Rose, loved being an aunt and was concerned about Connor. How can they be the same person, she wonders. Hearing the scrunch of tyres on the gravel outside, she takes another mug from the cupboard. Is it possible for a person to change so much? The question troubles her and she hopes not, but can't be sure.

She pushes all thoughts of Lillian to one side and turns her mind instead to what she has been told of her own mother. That too is confusing. She is aware that Roberta has given her something; something that is probably important, but she doesn't really understand it. Nor does she really know where to keep it, so that it is out of the way until such time that it might be useful. It floats, cluttering her thoughts, and she finds that it annoys her.

Louise bustles in carrying a couple of bags, which she dumps on the floor. She is soaked from the short run from the car and quickly peels off her jacket and shoes, leaving them in a heap next to the bags.

"Oh, is that for me? Just what I need... thank you love. All alone? Joe and Claire get off all right? Gran been ok? Not given you any trouble I hope. Did you have a nice time? Such nice boys, aren't they? I forget..." She shakes her head at some memory or other and tiny droplets of rain fly from her hair, sparkling as they catch the light.

Taking the mugs to the table, Megan quickly fills her in on the weekend.

"Sounds like you didn't miss me at all. Dad sends his love by the way. Here, give me that; I'll take it up for Gran, see how she is and all that, and I'll get changed at the same time."

Louise is bright and cheery; too bright and too cheery and her daughter sits at the table alone for a while, wondering what on earth is happening to her world and if it is possible for her to rein it all in before it gets even more out of control and unrecognisable.

A knock on the back door and the scraping sound of it being pushed open breaks into her thoughts before they get too maudlin.

"Hello... anyone home?"

Jake appears and Megan is suddenly smiling, as is he when he finds her alone.

"I thought you might like some company. I brought cards, fancy a game?" he asks, shrugging off his wet jacket and producing a pack from his pocket.

"I don't know many games..." she confesses.

"I know loads. I'll teach you."

He sits down opposite her and starts to shuffle the pack. They pick up a thread of conversation from the previous day and are quickly lost in their own world.

It is the sound of Louise's shout, or was it a scream? That has Megan and Jake running out and into the garage in alarm. They skid to a halt, surprised to find her standing in the middle of the space, hands on her hips and looking at the rocking horse, repeating over and over, "Well I never..."

Megan is a little put out. From what she had heard from the kitchen, at the very least she had expected a... a... what? A masked man with a chainsaw or something? Then giggles at the ridiculous idea.

"Mum...?" she asks, trying to gain some composure.

"I'm sorry, it was just such a surprise. I know Joe said he'd deal with it, but look; it's all gone, everything, and now there's all this floor and all this space!" She laughs, but the sound is brittle and it echoes strangely.

Jake wanders over to the horse and admires it. "Was it yours?" he asks.

Louise shakes her head. "No, never seen it before, but it's just what I need. And it is so well crafted, so beautifully made, that it's a pleasure to work on."

"What colour will you paint it?" Megan asks, coming closer.

"It will be an appaloosa." Her mother declares. "During my pony phase, that's what I wanted, not golden palominos like all my friends. I saw a film, years ago, 'Run Appaloosa, RUN!' it was called and it made me think that a pony like that would be just the thing to have real adventures with."

She turns away from them, lost for a moment in a mood that she thought had vanished forever, pleased that she has found it again. "Yes," she murmurs, "an appaloosa..."

They leave her twiddling with the radio and go back to their card game, which Megan quickly wins. The rain has stopped and through the windows, sunshine can be seen as the sun begins to peep from between the clouds. Jake suggests a bus ride into town; there is a cinema there and there might be something on that is worth seeing. Megan happily agrees and disappears upstairs to change her top and drag a comb through her hair. She pulls a jacket out of the wardrobe and heads back downstairs, stopping on the way to pop her head round the door of her grandmother's room.

Roberta, deeply engrossed in something on the TV, absentmindedly waves goodbye.

She grabs her bag from the peg by the back door and they head outside, finding Louise in the middle of the garage, enveloped by noise. Music is blaring from the radio and she is using an electric power tool that she brought from London. Megan is pleased to see her mother working with a dedication that she has not seen in her for a while and decides it is positive.

Louise decides that her daughter's friendship with Jake is positive too, so she waves them off happily. Later, some supper and a TV film with her mother might be a good thing she thinks; there are some things she would like to discuss. Assuming of course, that Roberta is both willing and up to it.

Chapter eleven

Megan pops her head round the door of the front parlour to tell her mother that she is home and is going straight to bed. The room is almost in darkness and she turns the light on, startling them both. Louise thinks that she looks flushed, but says nothing, remembering her own youth, that brief time before Peter...

"Night love..." she says, slightly absentmindedly, holding the glass of wine that she has not really been drinking, while staring at the TV, which she has not really been watching. In her mind she is turning over the fragments that her mother gave her. That they were given unwillingly was all too clear, but how much truth was attached to them was not, so she keeps turning them over, hoping to find something that she has missed.

"Joe was right..." she mutters. "Mum and Mark are too alike."

They had both told her to stay out of it, telling her that there was nothing that could be done, yet neither of them had told her what it was all about. What was it that had been so terrible that they had not spoken to each other for years?

Try as she might, she cannot imagine falling out with Megan so badly that it would separate her completely from her child, or for that matter, from her mother. Some harsh things had been said over the years and some deep hurts inflicted, but still she is there. They remain mother and daughter, and when called, she came. But her brother will not be called and will not come. Why...? She wonders again.

Roberta is dozing. The pain is too acute for proper sleep, despite the cocktail of tablets that she has taken. She drifts in and out, back and forth, not sure what is real anymore, but it doesn't really bother her and this surprises her. She has never been one for imagining; she has always liked her reality plain and simple, but now it seems she has changed.

Louise's demands and questions have brought it all back and she thinks it is an unfair position to put her in; now, when she can do nothing to change it even if she wanted to. But would she? More to the point, could she?

She allows her mind to float back to that afternoon, now so long ago. It was a few days after the funeral and she had been standing at the kitchen sink, washing up the lunch things and looking out onto the garden. Rain was streaming down the window, so that the view was lost to her and their eldest was sitting at the table, holding his head in his hands.

Of the three of them, Mark had been closest to his father and as a toddler it was Arnold he wanted, not her. When she brought him down in the morning, his eyes would dart about in eager anticipation, always looking for his father and his simple joy or disappointment, depending on if Arnold was still there or had already gone, would be written all over his little face. His chubby arms would reach up for him as soon as he came in through the door and his first word had been 'da', not 'ma'.

Almost as soon as he could walk, he wanted to be doing things with Arnold and the memory of his screams and the tantrums he threw when he had to be left behind for his own good, still make her shudder. She had matched his anger, and her shouting had drowned out his cries for his father, or the other cries, the ones in reaction to the slap of her hand on his bare flesh.

She had felt rejected by her firstborn and the piercing heat of that pain, brought on by one so small and so determined, is still able to wound her. There are some things that time does not diminish, but that rainy afternoon, not long after they'd laid her husband in his final resting place, she'd exacted her revenge. She'd made him pay for the hurt she'd suffered, the hurt he'd inflicted on her throughout his childhood and beyond.

Joe had often been caught in the middle of their arguments and maybe that was why he came to see himself as the peacemaker, yet to her knowledge, he had never enquired what their last row had been about. Over the years he had asked her, and no doubt him as well, to put it behind them, to shake hands and move on, but not to kiss and make up. He never asked that, not even when he was small.

Louise had never got involved and had stayed out of it for reasons of her own, but now she has decided to step in and it has opened more than Roberta had known was still there. From the little that Louise had said, he still suffers too, but what she can no longer be sure of, is just how she feels about this.

She hears the floorboard at the top of the stairs creak and the bathroom door opening. There is the sound of water splashing into the bath and of another door opening and then footsteps. Another door opens, slips shut, is opened again and after a moment the bathroom door shuts again. She surmises that it is her granddaughter and smiles. She does not begrudge Megan her youth, for she is far enough removed from her to be something separate and this distance is natural, not resentful.

These thoughts have distracted her and she fumbles among the covers for the remote control and then flicks through the channels. She finds a programme that she can lose herself in, but only as long as the pain doesn't get any worse, for when she looks at the clock, she calculates that she still has two more hours to go before she can take any more tablets.

Megan settles down in bed and sends a text to Hannah, but it can't even begin to cover the elation and confusion that she feels. She waits for a moment or two, but there is no reply. Every time she closes her eyes, she is transported back to the moment where Jake kissed her and she kissed him. He'd held her hand all the way back on the bus and she is hoping that her kissing technique was ok, because of course she didn't let him know that she'd only been kissed once before, at Hannah's party. Alex had ignored her the next time they met, which had knocked her confidence a bit, but that hadn't been nearly as nice as this time...

She checks her phone again, still nothing. Should she text him she wonders, but what would she write? Too keyed up to sleep, she fishes about for the diary, needing something else to think about.

3rd January 1939

Evan got clobbered by Constable Fuller yesterday. Sharp whack round the ears he got and a right bruise is coming up so it is, but as Auntie Eth says, his dad would have been mortified to hear that he'd been messing about like that and he would have boxed his ears good and proper too! But she told him straight, she don't want no thieving in the family neither. While we may not always have quite enough of everything, what we have is ours and me and Mum agreed with that. Pride ain't that easy to get back once it's lost and he's too young to know what's best for all of us. Mum got quite peeved with him as well, quite right too. I'm ever so glad she rarely gets like that with me and Vic, a bit fierce she was!

He looks a bit down in the dumps today and he must be missing their dad. Tommy's taken him aside, well he's the man of the family now and he does his best, but it must be hard for them. None of us were ready to lose Uncle Norm.

Fred was late picking me up this morning and seemed a bit out of sorts all day. I brought meself home on the bus and stopped off to see Elsie and Rose. She couldn't shed any light on anything, but like she says, she deals with home, he deals with work. That's what they've agreed and that's the way they like it. Still, had a nice cuppa with her before I came home, her baking is coming on a treat too.

≈

18th January 1939

Rita and me went to see a lovely film this afternoon. Mum took Connor while we were gone and we took a bottle of stout and fish and chips home to share with her afterwards. We both loved the film, a girl suddenly comes into loads of money and her sweetheart calls it off, cos of course he's still poor so he says he can't marry her. Then these other blokes come on the scene, but of course he still loves her so doesn't think they're good enough for her and all sorts starts to happen and in the end, just when we was thinking it would never work out all right, it did!

The news is so depressing at the moment, all about home defence measures, how to use a gas mask and whatnot. I keep saying to everyone, we are NOT at war! 'Peace for our time', that's what Mr Chamberlain said, peace for our bloody time and he ought to know. I mean he is the bleedin' Prime Minister.

≈

8th Feb 1939

Well maybe we are at war, but not with Germany. Two underground stations were blown up by that lot what calls themselves the Irish Republican Army, terrible damage they did and some people got hurt. I mean those people aren't the ones that make the rules. Kath at the shed says her Brian says it's because those that vote, vote for the ones that make the rules, mind you, his parents were Irish so maybe he really thinks that. But Tommy and me, we don't vote yet, won't get that chance till we're twenty one and it could have been us down there going about our business. So how does that work out then?

Mum says she's too frightened to use the tube now and she'll stick with the bus, even though the journey to collect the sewing from Mr Banks takes an hour longer as she has to take three buses instead of the one train. Everyone's really scared now.

We were looking at one of them posters that are everywhere at the minute. 'Keep Calm and Carry On' they say and me and Rita decided that maybe the new decade will be better. I mean 'the forties' sound good don't they, like they should be fun. The fabulous forties or the fantastic forties or even the unforgettable forties! You can't do that with the thirties now, can you? I mean the thrifty thirties don't sound the same at all and let's face it, that's pretty much what they've been. We'll be glad to see the back of them, we're all agreed on that!

So we'll just get through this year, that's what we said and next year everything will start to improve. We both need some changes after all, some of the romantic sort we said. Just one good bloke each, that's all! Not too much to ask now, is it?

≈

15th February 1939

I've been blooming knackered since I can't remember when. Fred's got so much work on we've virtually been sleeping at the shed. Still, I've made more than three quid in overtime, so me and Mum ain't complaining. We went and bought some nice material and she's making us both some playsuits for when we go to the country in the summer. We did say that if the work keeps up like this, we might even go to Butlins ourselves. Fancy!

≈

24th February 1939

Opened the door this morning and there was Vic standing there, beaming he was. Lovely surprise. He hadn't let us know because he wasn't sure he'd be able to stop off, as his ship was just doing a quick turn around, but he did a swap with a mate of his who needs to be back in America sooner than what his ship would have got him there for. So the bonus is we've got Vic for three whole days, then he has to go up to Liverpool, as now his ship leaves from there, but he hitches, saves money and he meets interesting people he says. Maybe I should try it, but I think I'd be too scared. What if one of them came on to me, what would I do then? As it is though, there's too much going on around here to think of swanning off anywhere just at the present!

He's gone for a pint with Fred and a couple of other lads, so he'll be rolling in later Mum says. Nice to have him home, I think Tommy benefits from it and hopefully Evan will too. Vic can put him right after all.

He brought a lovely parcel from Viv, silk stockings for both of us, some books for me and a lovely pile of wool for Mum, so soft and such a lovely red. She says she's going to knit herself a lovely posh cardy from it. Lots of photos of Ben too, up to all sorts of antics he gets now. Mum has a smile from ear to ear!

≈

2nd March 1939

We are going to Butlins!!!!

When me and Mum were joking about it, Vic got all serious and left us an envelope, said we had to promise to go. Bless him. With the money we've got saved as well and me overtime, we think we can all go and still have a bit left over.

Auntie Eth is thrilled at the prospect and when I was telling Elsie, she said we'd love it. There's so much to do there that there ain't no chance of getting bored and all the food is paid for and there's so much of it, so there's no chance of going to bed hungry neither. Mum's going to look into it and book it for June, it's a bit cheaper then and like she says, the train won't be so crowded.

≈

14th March 1939

Oh the tears and tantrums. Joyce and Charlie have broken up, she caught him with Lucy Skinner over Chalfont Street way. He's been round every night, with flowers and whatnot, but she's not having any of it. She said he's broken her trust in him and that's that! I had her down for having a bit more romance in her soul, just goes to show you.

Rita's coming with us to Butlins, little Connor too and Mum's keeping back some of her sewing money to pay for it. That'll be lovely, we're going to have such a good a time. The time of our lives! That's what we keep saying to each other.

≈

22nd March 1939

We're assembling bicycles would you believe, down at the shed. Fred's given me one too, said it's time I had a new one, bless him. I gave me old one to Tish, cos she's picked up a bit of work after school, delivering bits and pieces for Mrs Cassidy. The people she delivers to give her h'apence and sometimes a penny for her trouble and Mrs Cassidy pays her a shilling for the afternoon and every bit helps.

≈

Megan's phone burrs softly and she reaches for it, expecting it to be Hannah, but is surprised to see it is a message from Jake.

'UOK?'

She stares at it for a moment, sensing that he too is uncertain and that he wants it to be all right as much as she does. She hugs the thought to herself, as though it were something tangible.

'Yes. U?' She replies and holds her breath while she waits.

'Very! Lunch 2mro in the park?'

Smiling, she agrees and lets the diary fall from her hand. She snuggles down and allows herself to relive their first kiss, while at the same time hoping that tomorrow will bring more new wonders.

Much later, Louise pops her head round the door. She had seen the light on and is surprised to see her daughter fast asleep with her phone tightly clasped in her hand. When she tiptoes over, she notices the diary open on the cover and picks it up, then takes the phone and places it carefully on the bedside table.

Just before switching off the light, she looks at the sleeping face of the person she loves more than she ever thought possible. She knows that her baby is growing up and will soon start to stake a claim on her own life. Louise is determined to travel that path with her for as long as Megan will allow her to, going from leading, to walking alongside and then inevitably, at some point she will fall behind. As she leaves her daughter's room, she heads for her mother's. There is a different journey being undertaken in there, but she wishes to travel this one too, for as long as she is able to and for as long as her mother will allow her to.

Roberta is sleeping, but her breathing is laboured and uneven, fainter than it should be. In the warm light cast by the bedside lamp, her skin tone looks pinker than it really is, but the lines on her forehead are deeper than they ought to be for a woman of her age. She is also too thin and her cheekbones protrude in a way that they shouldn't. Louise sits in the chair and studies Roberta's face carefully. Without any makeup it is naked and in it she sees reminders of different faces at different times in each of their lives. Those faces are hidden now, but not completely lost and Louise has to fight down the urge to gently trace her mother's features with her fingertips.

There is a stillness in the room, and not just in the air. It is coming from somewhere inside them and Louise finds that she doesn't want to leave. She is still clutching her grandmother's diary in her hand, her index finger holding it open at the page Megan had been reading, so she sits back and starts reading it herself.

3rd April 1939

Weren't much of an April Fool if you ask me and the gloom the news has brought is really bad. Taken the shine out of the day it has, not that I actually see much daylight in the shed.

They've announced conscription. Six months compulsory military training for all men aged twenty to twenty one. Why would they do that if they didn't think we need a bigger army and why would we need a bigger army if we ain't going to war?

There's a lot of people speaking publicly about putting the effort in and keeping the peace and about not starting or joining in with any more madness. I've been to a couple of meetings meself and a lot of what they say makes sense. They say Mr Hitler is running his own country the way he and the Germans see fit, which is no different to what we do. They say that we marched into countries that weren't ours for the taking, that's why our empire covers something like a third of the world. I never knew that, well I must've learnt it at school, but when they say it, seems more somehow. But that was a long time ago and some of those places didn't have any people, well not civilised people anyway. I mean Australia, or Canada, I'm sure we were told they were empty, vast wildernesses, I'm sure I remember Mrs Turner saying empty and vast. I always liked them words. Anyway, I don't think Austria or Czechoslovakia was empty!

Then they say that in the war sixteen million people died, imagine that. Ten million fighting men dead they reckon and another six million ordinary people, just cos of the war. I can't begin to picture that many people.

Here, we lost a million of our lads and that don't include all them that died of that flu that did for Dad, but he wouldn't have been in them trenches or even in France at all I don't s'pose, if there hadn't been a war on.

Why? Why would anyone want to do all that again? It just don't make any sense to me at all.

≈

12th April 1939

As we was all together last tonight to celebrate Mum's birthday, we agreed to change our holiday and go in May instead. That way we'll be sure to have it, just in case the world goes crazy. Still, it's given this household something else to talk about and we're quick to turn the radio off whenever the news comes on, cos we don't want nothing spoiling our holiday! Me, Tish and Joyce have been practising the new dances, so that we can do them proper at Butlins, good laugh it is too. Tish is so good with the latest hairstyles, she's got the fingers she has. She can roll up my hair in less than ten minutes and it stays put too!

≈

27th April 1939

Vic got an overnight stay with us. He was full to bursting with news, Ben's going to have a little brother or sister and they're already saving up for Mum to go over soon after it's born. She says springtime would suit her, or maybe even summer, the winter was too cold for her! But you can see she's thrilled at the prospect of another trip and another grandchild.

He says that over in America, there's talk of war coming to Europe, but the Yanks don't want no part of it this time. If it comes, he says the president says it's not their war, it's ours. Blooming well makes it sound like a parcel. Well, it's not a parcel any sane person wants!

Let's hope that the President of the United States of America has some clout with this Mr Hitler. I mean a president has got to be someone worth listening too, especially if he's saying the same thing as Mr Chamberlain. I mean we did win the war, surely Mr Hitler and all those German people ain't forgot that?

≈

3rd May 1939

I might have to stop going to the cinema, cos I can't get the pictures of the refugees from Germany out of me mind, but people here and in other places don't want more people who need work, money and food. There just ain't enough of it to go round as it is. But the kiddies, who'd turn them away? We can't and we won't, that's for sure.

From what we could gather, they was mainly Jewish, but without their parents, being sent off to a strange country on their own. There are some adults on the decks and I am sure there must be a few whole families, but still, how bad must it be over there if you'd prefer to send your kids so far away? Horrible, that's what Rita and Elsie said, it must be truly horrible. They can't imagine handing theirs over, unless it was so bad you couldn't trust yourself to protect them anymore. I don't know what to think now. That's the truth of it.

≈

8ᵗʰ May 1939

I saw a bit on the Pathé about this Sir Oswald Mosley. He was inspecting, like a general of an army (if you please), the women's faction of his party. They're called fascists, like the Nazi party in Germany and seem to think that what Mr Hitler is proposing is a good thing for everyone. He says the German people don't want a war with us, any more than we want to go to war with them again and says the world is big enough for all the superior powers and races and we Brits of course are one of them.

Me and Mum were talking about it on the bus afterwards, as we took her mountain of sewing back to Mr Banks and to collect the money for our holiday. It's so difficult to be sure, but he, Sir Oswald, is gentry and well educated, he's also in the government, so there's a fair chance he knows more than what we do. Vic says that the Duke of Windsor, who'd be King if he hadn't gone and abdicated, says pretty much the same thing, while his brother, who is the King, ain't really saying much one way or the other, just like the government. I mean, while they're not saying, yes get ready everyone, it won't be long now because we'll be off to war soon, they're doing things like conscription, building ships, designing new rifles and whatnot, which must mean we are. We got into a right pickle with it all, so Mum and me decided in the end to just look forward to our holiday!

≈

12th May 1939

Tomorrow, we get on the train at twenty past eight in the morning at Kings Cross and we'll be having lunch in Skegness!!! Beach, sea, sea, sea, and lots of other things to do too and always <u>the sea</u>!!!!!

≈

Roberta's voice suddenly breaks the moment. "What are you doing sitting there? I'm not planning on dying tonight you know!" she snaps, trying to give her voice more strength than she really has left to give it.

Louise is flustered and the peacefulness and pure joy that Lillian's words had conjured up vanish. She drops the diary into her lap and looks at her mother, momentarily confused.

Roberta sees what she has been reading. "Go on get out, and take that bloody thing with you. I can just about tolerate the interest from Megan, but from you too? That's just insulting. Go on, bugger off and leave me in peace."

She turns her head away and Louise doesn't know how to reach her, so she leaves and with a sigh, quietly shuts the door behind her. She is not sleepy and standing alone on the dark landing she hovers, not knowing what to do. She decides a bath will help, so heads towards the second bathroom on the floor above, so as not to disturb her mother.

Chapter twelve

Louise cannot lock herself away in the garage, because she and Roberta have not yet got over the incident from the night before, and there is always the possibility of her mother having a funny turn just to make her feel bad. Roberta doesn't even want her daughter's company and took her bad mood out on the carer, who did everything as fast as possible so she could leave, but that just worked her up into more of a mood.

As soon as she had finished her breakfast, Megan fled to the library, saying she needed to work on her project. She had sensed the atmosphere in the house and decided to leave them to it.

For different reasons, by ten o'clock both Roberta and her daughter have bad headaches, but for Louise it is only her head that hurts and she knows it will clear. For her mother, that luxury no longer exists, nor will it ever again, and the pain triumphantly seeps into the rest of her body.

Susan's unexpected arrival for morning coffee changes everything. Roberta is happy to see her and Susan is happy to be able to give Louise some time off. She in turn is relieved, for now her mother will not be alone and she can take herself off to work on her project.

When Megan reaches the library, she is shocked to see Jake looking miserable and wonders if it is somehow her fault. She considers not going in and hesitantly stands in the doorway, but before she can slink away, he sees her and smiles. The smile is just for her and it gives her the much needed confidence to walk up to him and boldly ask what is wrong.

"Jim Smetherton's dead." he tells her, and while he is clearly upset by this news, her mind draws a blank.

"Oh... I'm sorry, was he a friend of yours?"

"No, he was a photojournalist. He came from round here and his family still farm up at Yarrow Woods as far as I know. He mainly covered wars and the aftermath of them. You know, when the rest of the world had lost interest, he was still there documenting life for ordinary people. He was world renowned and won lots of awards, but he always said that was never the point. He did a talk at our school a few years ago when he came back to visit. Here... let me show you some of his work."

He comes out from behind the counter, takes her hand and leads her towards the computer area, then logs on and finds a photographic website showing some of Smetherton's work. Megan slides into the seat and begins looking at the photos and reading the notes that are with them. Jake stands beside her, his hand lightly resting on her shoulder. He is reading too, feeling that the world has lost someone important.

Megan is impressed by the clarity of the photos and the emotions they convey, and one in particular catches her eye. It is of a group of five young girls in what is clearly a classroom. They are about her age, but definitely not from a world she recognises. All of them are dressed in what look to be hand-me-downs and all of them are carrying guns. Two have them slung over their shoulders, with just the muzzles showing, two rest them on their laps, while the other holds hers easily in one hand.

They are smiling for the photographer and you can almost hear them say cheese, but it is not a school photo, at least not the sort Megan recognises. The things they hold so causally are not books, or iPods, or smartphones. Their everyday technology is somewhat different to hers, as is their everyday life and he captured it so perfectly that no words are needed.

The picture stays with her as she settles at one of the tables with a pile of books. She makes copious notes of strategies, dates, battles, attacks and counter attacks from more than half a century ago, while all the time the image of the recently taken photograph remains in the back of her mind.

At lunchtime, the food goes largely forgotten, as does everything else. People walking past see them locked in their own world and look away, perhaps remembering their own first love, their own youth and passion. Most, but not all, smile.

Once home, she is nervous and fidgety, unable to settle. He is going to come round after work to do some gardening and she tells her mother that she has invited him to stay for dinner.

"Good, I like him." she replies.

Megan's project now has lots of facts, but the nub of it is still missing, so she puts it to one side and makes a long cool drink, then takes herself off to the rickety chairs at the end of the garden to spend some time with Lillian and wait for Jake.

18th July 1939

They've re-formed the Women's Land Army, to help cover the jobs in the countryside now that so many of the lads are on military training. The harvest needs to be brung in, plus the winter planting needs to be done if we're not all to starve next year. There's a poster at the town hall of a girl out in a field holding a pitchfork and Mum says I should apply. The pay's good, there's board and lodging thrown in and as she says, I'd be outside again. I've not said nothing to her, but I s'pose she knows me best. I mean, she is me mum! Working at the shed is getting me down, cos I never see any daylight and I don't like to go outside too often. Fred says it draws attention to the place, which he don't want and the others will think I'm skiving, which I don't want. Mum said we should go over to the office and find out about it. After all, it's volunteering, not conscription!

≈

22nd July 1939

I passed me medical and they've said they can use me. I don't know what to do now. Mum says she'll be fine, it's not as though I'll be leaving her on her own. It'd make a nice change to spend some time in the countryside and I can still send money, cos I won't be needing much if me board's thrown in. It'd be different, wouldn't it? I mean as Mum says, I've always had a hankering for something different. Me and Vic are the same that way. We must get it from Dad though, cos Mum likes to stay put. Maybe that's why he volunteered so early on in the war, maybe he just wanted to see something different. But look what happened to him! Although of course, lots of people died with that flu, not just in the trenches, here too in the hospitals and in their own beds. Rita and Elsie say I should give it a go. There's no one here that holds me heart,

I've not got the responsibility of motherhood yet and they say they'll come and visit. I think I'll sleep on it.

I wish Vic was here, he'd help me think this through properly. He'd know what's best, but he'd make me think too. Still, no point wishing, he ain't here and a letter would take too long to go there and back. By the time his reply gets here, I'll have gone bonkers with all that thinking!

≈

3rd August 1939.

I only went and said yes. Mind you, I walked around outside for at least an hour before I went in and saw the woman again. She said I'd made the right decision and apparently I'll get a letter soon with a posting. Funny that, a 'posting', just for me. Later though, as we had our tea, I told Mum that I've a got a right case of the collywobbles now! She laughed and said I was being daft, but I know she understood.

We went out to celebrate, although to be honest I'm not altogether sure what it was we was celebrating! But we had a real nice night out anyway. Everyone was there, Mum, Auntie Eth, Tommy, Evan, Tish and Joyce, Elsie and Fred, Rita, and Brenda from the shed with her new beau Georgie. We went dancing too! What a lark that was, with Mum and Auntie Eth standing up together! Fred gave me and Brenda the morning off, said we'd be no use to no one and he was right. Took a while to shift me head up off the pillow it did.

≈

7th August 1939

I'm off tomorrow on the first train to a farm in a place called Little Maddely and the farmer, a Mr Robinson, will collect me from the railway station. I've got a railway ticket, me uniform and Auntie Eth and Mum have knitted up more socks, scarves, hats and gloves than I know what to do with. I keep showing them the sky and the sun, which is streaming through the windows, but as Mum says, it's different up north. I'm all a-jittery, I've never been nowhere on me own before.

I hope I'll be able to settle all right and not make a fool of meself. I wonder if there will be anybody to make friends with, people of me own age. I almost wish I hadn't said yes. I wonder if it's too late to pull out. I've got no nails left, I've bitten them all down to the quick.

≈

Louise brings a tray over and joins her. There is cake and Megan smiles appreciatively. Her mother carefully sits down on the other chair and they enjoy the late afternoon sun together.

"How far have you got?" she asks.

"She's just about to come here for the first time, as part of the Women's Land Army. I read a bit about them for my project. How old were you Mum, the first time you went somewhere far away on your own?"

Louise helps herself to a slab of cake and thinks. "Totally alone...? When I went to university in London, so I was nearly nineteen."

"Were you scared?"

Louise thinks it an interesting question. Fear is something that either prevents one from doing something, or propels one to a place of safety and she wonders what university had been for her.

"Yes, I was. Well, I was certainly very nervous. My dad didn't want me to go so far and there was a place nearer to home where I could have done a similar course, but in one way the whole point was to leave. Granny helped me out and gave me the money I needed, not to have to work as well as study. That had been one of his arguments. If I had to work, I wouldn't be able to concentrate on my studies and it would be a waste. You see, I was the first to go to university. Neither he nor Mum had and as you know, Lillian left school before she was fifteen, so it was a big thing for him. And for me too, actually." Louise's voice drops slightly as she remembers the weight of the responsibility. "Mark and Joe never really got the chance..." She stops speaking and wonders if they had wanted to go but had been prevented, then realises that it is a question she has never asked them and feels guilty.

"Jake's coming to London in the autumn, he's got a place at the Royal Veterinary College." Megan tells her mother proudly and then looks away.

A soft peach blush creeps over her cheeks and Louise understands. She wonders how it will go and if it will it last. Will her daughter be happy or will her heart be broken? After all, first love can last a lifetime or be gone in an instant. She smiles sadly to herself, but says none of this. Instead she lets Megan know that she can invite him home whenever she pleases.

Louise hears her named being called and sees Susan just outside the back door. She is waving, but makes no move to join them, so she leaves her daughter and goes to find out what is needed. After a brief word, she quickly goes upstairs to assist her mother, who needs to use the toilet and is struggling to get out of bed by herself. Despite the incontinence pads she wears, Roberta resents the indignity of her situation and forces her body to comply with her will whenever possible. Sadly, both the will and the opportunity to do this are becoming less, but still she tries, and Louise understands.

Alone again, Megan turns back to the diary.

9th August 1939

Well, what nice people. Mr and Mrs Robinson have made a real effort to make me feel welcome. I got me own room at the top of the house, quite a big room with blue flowery wallpaper, a fireplace, a wardrobe, some drawers and a lovely comfy bed all to meself, which after all this time sharing is a bit strange. Still, I'm sure I'll get used to it, even in winter, as the eiderdown looks good and thick and there are extra blankets in a drawer. Imagine that, so many blankets in just one room.

There's a bathroom with a toilet next door and for now I don't need to share, as there's another one on the floor below for the family and an outside privy by the back door. Imagine!

It's a big old house, with a front and back parlour. Nice stuff in both and I can use the back one whenever I like, they told me. They also said I can use as much hot water as I want. Fancy that. I won't take the mick though, that'd be rude and Mum'd be mortified if she thought I'd done that.

It's really quiet and dark outside at night and I'm not used to the noises the house makes. It's all a bit scary really and I'm all alone up at the top, so I've not slept that well so far.

≈

10th August 1939

Mr Robinson took me all over the farm today, it's a big old place. They've a few dairy cows, some pigs and a few sheep as well, but mainly it's given over to crops. Oh and there's chickens everywhere! We're going to have to start work early, as harvest time is here and everyone's worried that the rains will come before it's all in. Trouble is, as I said to them, I've got no problem with getting up at the crack of dawn, but me hands have gone soft with the work in the shed. At least at the market I did plenty of physical stuff. Mrs Robinson said me body will remember and there'll be a nice hot bath waiting when we get back! She said her sister was a Land Girl in the war, even though she came from round about these parts. She's down in London now, over Pimlico way though, so not near us at all. But her saying that made me feel better, I reckon she understands a bit about how I'm feeling.

They've got a son and a daughter. Alice is a year younger than me, she seems nice enough but she's been out in the fields herself, so she's tired. She came back late, ate and went straight to bed every night. Their son Bob is older than me and he's on his military training, but they hope he'll get back for some leave soon. Mrs Robinson showed me some pictures of them when they was kiddies. Sweet looking pair they are and the boy has a naughty smile in so many of them, right mischievous he looks, while she looks like butter wouldn't melt in her mouth. Alice is still pretty though and I wonder if he's still as cheeky!

≈

15th August 1939.

 Mrs R was right, me body does remember, but that don't stop it from aching. I've places that hurt that I never knew was there. We're up before the lark, then we get back around eight in the evening, wash, eat and go to bed. To be honest I've never eaten so much and can't remember ever being so hungry! Mollie, the housekeeper, is fearsome, she don't take no prisoners, but blimey she can cook! She does us all a big plate of bacon and eggs every morning before we go to work and sends a big lunch out at midday that we eat in the fields. She's Mike the foreman's missus and she told me they've been with family since they got wed, though she's only been working at the house for the last ten years. Her sister does the cleaning and her niece does the washing. I wash me own smalls though, don't seem right giving them over to someone else to do.

 We've been lucky so far, the rain has held off. I've managed to write a couple of lines to Mum and to Vic, but that's about it. Not even picked up me book to read, me eyes are usually closed before me head's on the pillow.

≈

22nd August 1939.

 It's been pouring down. Still, we've got most of the stuff in that we needed to before the rain. There's still plenty in the ground, but rain won't hurt onions or carrots, so we're having a bit of a day off. I say a bit, cos of course the cows still need to be milked, the eggs still need collecting and them smelly old pigs still want feeding. I'm getting good with the cows though, Mrs R says I've got the knack, firm but gentle.

 Got a lovely letter from Mum this morning with all the news. Joyce has finally forgiven Charlie, taken her long enough, so if he really loves her he won't be doing nothing like that again! Vic's been over as well and Mum's given him me new address, so I'll hear from him soon I hope. There was a note in there too from Rita, she sounds well perky, said Tom Cassidy's been round a few times, he says to see her brother, but he's often out, so he stays chatting to her instead. Fingers crossed. Do her the power of good that would and he's nice enough. He's steady, maybe not the brightest, but he's not got a temper or a mean streak neither and with all those little brothers and sisters he'd be a dab hand with Connor too!

≈

3rd September 1939.

Even though it's Sunday we still have to work, but about eleven o'clock, Mr R took us all back to the house and we sat around the radio, listening to the Prime Minister's broadcast and then after that we heard the King speaking to the nation.

We are at war with Germany. That's what they both said, so it must be true. That Mr Hitler marched into Poland and we said you can't do that and he did anyway.

They both talked about us having to defend a principle that's important and that it's an evil thing we're fighting against. The King his self said this is the second time for most of us that we are at war. He said that many things had been done to try and find a peaceful solution, but it was in vain and he called for courage and faith.

So we have to defend Poland. Why? We're not even neighbours, what have we got in common and would they come hot footing over here to save us? Would we even expect them to? We're s'posed to be famous for fighting our own battles, or so it seemed to us back in school. That's what being British is all about, or so Mags always said. I miss her, I really do, she'd have joined up with me, I know she would.

Courage and faith, I wonder where we're going find them, Poland? As far as I've been told, all they have there is coal and wood and lots of it.

We sat there in stunned silence and me blood ran cold, made me think I might never be warm again. I have never wanted Mum more than I did when I heard them speeches. 'Courage and faith' His Majesty said, that's what we need. Big things to find they are. We won before and I'm sure we can win again, but I <u>am</u> scared.

Mr R was furious. He fought in the last war against 'The Hun' as he calls them and he lost a brother, a cousin and an uncle. He kept shouting 'they're not having my son' and ranting that it was meant to be the war that ended all wars. 'That was why the huge sacrifice had to be made, there was never going to be no more.' He just couldn't stop shouting. 'The war to end all bloody wars and it was surely the bloodiest, a million lads gone, a million of our lads!'

We all started to get a bit fidgety and Mrs R had to calm him down. Alice and I went out for a walk and took their jack russell Captain Bill with us, cos he was right upset with Mr R's shouting. We wandered down to the orchard and sat under the big old pear tree for a while, talking about some of those grand words that they said about the Germans. Brute force, bad faith, injustice, oppression and persecution, but what do they really mean?

After a while we just sat there, we didn't know what else to do, so it was a big relief when Mike called us all back to work. The ground is heavy from the rain, so you got to keep your wits about you. Anyway, it took our minds off everything else for a while.

It's not bloody fair!! I don't know no one that wants this.

≈

Megan has seen the film where George VI makes that speech. The film itself hadn't really caught her full attention, but now, thinking about how it must have sounded to her great grandmother, she shivers, even though it is a warm afternoon. She wonders if the farm had a telephone in 1939, but then remembers that Lillian's mother's flat in London definitely did not. Her mother is as far away as it is possible to be and Megan cannot imagine being so completely cut off from her parents or her friends. Her father is currently in a different country, yet she is still able to speak to him regularly. She had received a text from him earlier in the day and been able to answer it.

She closes the diary, trying to imagine Lillian's life as it was before the world got turned upside down, knowing that at that point, her great grandmother had no idea; no one did, about what was to happen. But would it have made any difference if she'd had an idea of the sheer scale of the horror that was to come? Would it have seemed any more or any less fair?

She shivers again and thinks about the photojournalist whose work she'd seen earlier in the day. Would he still have gone to that part of North Africa if he'd known it was to be his last trip? She cannot know the answer and on that basis, decides that are some things we are not meant to know and that it is probably for the best.

Jake finds her there, deep in thought. He brings a message from Louise: she wants her to go and pick some things up from the little supermarket down the road if they are to have dinner later. Shaking her head to bring herself back to the present, she happily gives herself up to his warm embrace, then goes to find her mother.

Chapter thirteen

Roberta is discussing an event in Arnold's life with Susan, and by extension, in theirs too. She is surprised at how much her husband had shared with his mistress, for she has always assumed that apart from the sex, he ran off to her because they'd had a row, or because there was something in their life that needed sorting out. But as she shares some of these thoughts, she learns that this was not the case.

"Well yes, I can see why you might have thought that, but really, where would that have put me?" Susan adds thoughtfully. "You see, we made no promises to each other, legal or otherwise. What I mean is, we had to enjoy every hour we chose to spend together, otherwise why do it? If he'd just come over to rant and rave about how miserable his life was with you, I would not have wanted to spend time with him. I was perfectly happy in the life that I had chosen for myself, so he had to bring something that was missing from it. Sex had its place of course, but a relationship that lasts for more than a month or two needs more than that, don't you think? And anyway, we were hardly spring chickens..."

They smile at each other, then Susan continues, trying to find the right words.

"He brought himself to me, but only himself; he never brought you as well. You were a fixed point in his life, so I knew of you, but I also know he loved you and there was never any intention on his part to leave you, or on my part to try and induce him to."

Pausing, to see if her words have been received in the way they were intended, she sees doubt lingering on the pallid face in front of her, so gently pushes her point home.

"Try and look and at it this way Roberta, because it really is important to me that you understand. Our time together was always completely separate from the life he had with you. He spoke about the children, of course he did and just before he died, he was, as you know, greatly concerned about the road Mark had chosen, for he remembered the hushed tones that were always used whenever a cousin of his had been spoken of and felt that in some ways it had been better that he'd not come back from the war.

Then he was worried that Louise was making a mistake in her choice of partner, but he didn't know what to do about it, or what to say. He was their father after all and he spoke of them only from his perspective, never from yours. Sometimes he told me what was on his mind about the farm, but he never told me intimate things about your marriage. That was a part of him and his life that I was never privy to. Of course you don't have to believe me, just think about the man you knew; the man you married."

Roberta is silent for a while, thinking about what Susan has said. She turns her thoughts to the man she spent thirty years of her life with and who she had, in her own way, loved deeply. She tries to push past the anger and the hurt, to see him simply as the man he had always been, but she cannot. Instead she changes the subject, saying that she needs help to get to the bathroom.

As Louise is leaving, Roberta asks her if when she unearthed 'that wretched diary', she also found the photo albums. When she discovers that they are in a pile in the back parlour, she asks if they can be brought up, saying that she wants to show them to Susan. Really, she wants to see them for herself, for it has been too long since she looked, and now there is barely enough time left.

Louise is intrigued at her mother's request but also pleased. In the past she had spent many a pleasant evening going through the albums with Granny and even though she is in many of the photos, she cannot recall ever looking through them with her mother. Nor can she recall her ever saying, 'say cheese...', to preserve a moment where her daughter was the main attraction. Any photos that Roberta might have taken only included Louise incidentally.

Downstairs in the kitchen, she wonders which ones she is showing to Susan and why. As she scrubs the new potatoes in the sink, she looks out of the window and sees Megan and Jake clearing the debris from the far corner of the garden. They are laughing, obviously enjoying themselves and she notices that her daughter looks leaner; not overly thin, but her silhouette is better defined. She has some colour to her and her hair glints nicely in the evening sun. Megan has spent far too much of her life indoors she decides, and Jake is therefore good for her, if only because he takes her outside so much.

Susan is going to join them for dinner in the kitchen, for Roberta is tired and when the carer arrives early, everyone is pleased. This surprises her, for she was ready to argue her case and had instead been welcomed by all the family, even by the dragon lady herself.

"Odd lot..." she mutters to herself later as she leaves.

Jake and Susan know a lot about the area, despite being from different generations and Louise finds it easier to remember things as they talk. When Megan tells them about the photographs that Jake had shown her in the library, Susan said that she too had been saddened to hear about Jim Smetherton's untimely death so far away from home.

"So avoidable too." she says. "He died for the want of some first aid, photographing a war most of us don't understand. Or more's the pity; don't give much of a fig for."

She shakes her head sadly at the truth of her own words, before telling them that years ago she had known his grandmother and that they had been close friends. Louise too knows of him and has seen to some of his work exhibited in London.

She wonders why she never took Megan, then realises that it was because she wanted to shield her from the horrors of life for as long as possible. She sighs, understanding that now it is Jake's role, or if not Jake himself, then others like him, to start to remove the carefully built armour around her only child.

After dinner, Louise takes Susan home and Jake and Megan curl up on the sofa together with the idea of reading a little more of the diary to each other. It is not until Louise finds them there later, that they break off from exploring each other's thoughts and mouths. She is not in the mood for her own company, so she joins them and sits on the chair by the open window with her eyes closed, listening as her daughter reads the words written by her own much loved granny.

5th September 1939

Got a note from Mum this morning, telling me not to worry and not to rush back to town. She said that she and Auntie Eth are doing just fine and that nothing has changed, nothing at all. Put me mind at rest that did.

Mr and Mrs R got a telephone call from their son Bob. Apparently he'll be back for an overnight stay on Thursday. He's driving some colonel or other to a do somewhere around here and isn't needed from half past four in the afternoon right until ten the next morning. The whole family is really happy, lifted the mood a treat it has and I s'pose it'll be nice for me to meet him.

≈

The words quietly capture her imagination and Louise smiles at their innocence. Of course she already knows more than either the Lillian who is writing them, or her daughter who is reading them.

6th September 1939

Mrs R, me and Alice caught a few chickens today and they showed me how to kill them quick and then take all the feathers off. I was right squeamish at first, but then like they said, 'You eat chicken in London, don't you? So where do you think they come from?' Sometimes it's a bit funny me being the city girl, but they had a point, so I gritted me teeth and did me bit. Two of 'em are for dinner tomorrow, when their son joins us. Mr R's brother and his wife are coming over from the town too. He's second in charge at the bank there, so quite important. Alice told me that they have no children of their own, so they've always been really good to her and Bob. Mrs R made a point of saying I wasn't to eat me dinner in the kitchen on me own, but was to join them for the evening, just like normal. Really sweet of her to include me, some people wouldn't think to, I know.

The other chickens were all prepared and trussed up for the oven. They're off to be sold tomorrow morning with a few of the calves, we didn't kill them though, they walk themselves there. Mike is going to take 'em and Mr R said I could go too and see the market for meself. I've read about country markets in loads of books, mainly the historical ones though, so to see one for meself at last should be fun. I wonder if it'll be any different to the market at home. I mean, I spent years working there, but that was city not country and there weren't no livestock, or if there was it was already dead and cured and in bits and pieces.

≈

8th September 1939

Bob was really nice. He didn't make me feel like I was intruding on the family and it was really interesting what they were saying about the war. Apparently we're going to France, not Poland, because we're going to help the Poles by helping the French defeat the Germans. He told his dad that he's volunteered to go with the British Expeditionary Force and has been allocated a posting in the Tank Brigade. His dad weren't too pleased, but like he said, 'best to volunteer, cos you only get called up anyway and then you don't get no choice. They'll put you where you're needed and that's usually where there's been the most casualties.' He'd been in the Rifles his self, so he was interested as to why his son had chosen the tanks.

They sound horrible to me. I wouldn't like to be so closed in, urgh! Makes me shudder just the thought of it. But Bob said they're an important part of modern warfare. They support the poor bloody infantry, giving them some cover and protection. He said it's not like the Hun will just let us walk into Germany and take Berlin and his dad and uncle said he had a good point.

After dinner, Alice and he were going outside, so he could have a smoke and he asked me to join them. We had a bit of a laugh out there and left the old 'uns to themselves for a while. Afterwards we went into the back parlour and Alice got her gramophone out, then we rolled the rug up and played some records and had a bit of a dance. I danced with both of them and they danced with each other, so no one was left out. He's *got a lovely laugh and he's a good mover. He held me nicely too, not too tightly and not all creepy neither.*

Course with everyone getting ready for war in France, he don't know when he'll get back again, but he hopes it's soon and I must say, so do I.

≈

19th September 1939

Well, that's the last of the summer harvest finally in. I could sleep for a week, if not two! Mrs R said if I want to go to London to visit Mum, now would be a good time, cos come October, we'll start planting some of the crops. There'll be a lot to be done to some of the fields too, so they'll ready for spring planting and then the apples need to be brung in and sorted. The cider has to be made, herbs have to be dried and so it goes on.

Alice said she'd come with me, she wants to visit her aunt, do a bit of shopping, and there's a chance Bob might be able to get a pass for a few hours and she'd like to see him too. Mr R said it wouldn't be long before the trains were all taken by the military, to move the troops to the docks round Dover way and other places too I s'pose, so he said if we want to go, go now. We said yes!

Got a long letter from Vic, with a picture of a really heavy and enormous Viv. He says she's so big he's not sure if she'll make it to October, either that or she's having twins! He told me it's all a bit confusing over there at the moment. America ain't taking sides, which means they'll continue to trade with both Britain and Germany, but like he says, he can't do a run to the enemy, or if he works in the docks, he can't load one of their ships, cos that'd be like helping them win. He sounds uncertain about what's the right thing to do by his family, both there and here and of course for his country. I've never known him like this, but then I've never lived in times like these, so maybe it's no wonder.

He says that for the minute, he's got some work in the docks, but in a warehouse. It's close to home and he says he thinks it'll allow him some peace of mind, so he don't plan to do more than that until after the baby is born, then he'll see what the world's doing. Poor Vic, he says I've helped him in the past, but I've never really understood how, so I don't know what to suggest to him, honestly I don't. I mean, he's always been the one to look after me.

≈

24th September 1939

What a lovely time I've had so far. Mum came and met me at the station and it was just as well that she did, cos I hardly recognised the place with all the sandbags piled up everywhere. Gave me a bit of a turn seeing all that, cos it made it all more real somehow. But then I saw Mum waving with her best hat on and everything was just right again. She was so pleased to see me and it was lovely to see her and we went and had a pot of tea and some buns in a cafe, just the two of us, before we went home. We stopped off to see the Pathé News and there was all the troops sailing to France, all cheery and waving on the decks. There was so many of them it's a wonder them ships can stay afloat! They talked about rationing food as well as petrol and we left quite tearful, seeing all the kiddies on the platforms being evacuated. I told her that Mrs R had said they'd take a couple, but so far, none had arrived yet.

Despite all that we had a lovely evening in. Mrs R had given me a chicken to bring, as well as a load of veg, so it was a bit of a slap up tea and of course it was lovely seeing the tribe. What a laugh we had, it was like I'd never been away. The air raid siren test was a bit of a shock though, I must say. Made me blood run cold. Mum says it's just a precaution, it warns people and gives them enough time to get indoors, but she said no one expects an air attack. There weren't none last time, not really, so why would there be now? Made me breathe a bit easier, I mean why would they bomb London? What's here except us? We're not even army.

I know I'd been expecting the blackout, I mean Mum had written about it before war was even declared and even at the farm we have it. But nothing of what I've seen so far really *prepared me for the blackout in London. Shocking it was and black, completely black, no real lights to speak of but the stars. Quite spooky it was and lovely at the same time.*

The following day I went round to see Elsie and Rose. How she's grown! It was a bit of mixed news to hear that Elsie is expecting again, cos of course things are different now. Like she says, what if Fred gets called up, or even worse, killed? She was so tearful, took me a while to calm her down. She said she didn't want to be evacuated and separated from Fred, not unless he was called up anyway. I said surely it's the single men that get called up first, Mum said that's how it was last time. Dad volunteered, he wasn't called. But really, what could I say? No one really knows how it's going to be or how long it's going to last. Last time they gave it four months and everyone said it'd be over by Christmas, but it took us more than four years to beat 'em.

Rita and Tom Cassidy are seeing each other officially, but like she says, she's taking it nice and slow. Connor is happy without a brother or sister and he needs a father more than he needs one of them, so no hanky panky until that ring is on her finger! Rita said the same as Elsie over the evacuation lark. She wasn't going to take Connor away from family and put herself in a sticky position unless it was absolutely necessary. Dead serious she was too.

≈

25th September 1939

Me and Joyce went over to Gilly's this afternoon to buy a couple of dresses. They had a sale on, good prices they were too and I bought three for the price of one. Imagine! Just as well, because when we got back there was a note from Alice. Her brother Bob was able to get a pass and was apparently dead chuffed to hear that I was in London too, so she invited me to join them for a bit of supper and a dance. She said he was bringing a mate with him, so it promised to be a real good time. Of course Mum said I should go and she offered to look after Connor, so that Rita and Tom could come with us. Tish has done me hair in that nice new roll that's all the rage and thankfully I got a new dress. I'd left me posh shoes here anyway, as I didn't think I'd need them on the farm! So off I go and it'll be nice to spend a bit more time with Rita and Tom, after all.

<u>Later</u>

We had the loveliest of times. Bob was a real gent with me, wouldn't let me pay for nothing and just seemed to want to be sure that I was having a good time. We went for supper at the cafe on the Broadway, then we went to the Docket for a drink and then on to a new club that Tom and Rita know, where there was a band and we danced till we could dance no more. He walked me all the way home, because of course it was dark. It was lovely walking along streets I've known since I was a kid, but I've never seen 'em without a single light on. We talked about everything except the war, we didn't go there. He asked me so many questions about me childhood, Mum, Dad, Vic. He was especially sweet when I told him about always wanting to see the sea and how I'd felt when finally I did. I mean, he's seen the sea loads of times, but he didn't laugh at me, he just squeezed my hand a bit tighter, like he understood. He even said how lucky I'd been to have a wish come true.

He really understands how difficult it must be for Vic not being here and having his own family to consider over there too. He said he don't envy him, but the way he said it was like he really meant it, he wasn't just saying it cos that was what I expected or because it was the right thing to say and it made me feel better about not being able to give him any advice in me last letter.

He told me he loved the land and how he'd never wanted to be anything other than a farmer like his dad and his grandfather and the ones before even him! Imagine that, all that family lined up behind you in the same place, doing the same thing as you. It fair made me head spin. I never knew any of me grandparents, Mum and Auntie Eth were orphaned when Mum was eight, so she's not got much to remember or tell me. Still, at least they managed to stay together, lots of kids in that situation got separated.

He also told me that he loves engines almost as much as the land, but to his way of thinking the two go together, or at least they do now and will in the future. That was why he'd chosen the tanks. He told me the colonel won't let anyone else drive him long distance, cos he's got himself the reputation of being able to get an engine going again when other mechanics can't. He told me he learnt that on the old tractor that his grandfather had, and we laughed.

He has such a lovely laugh on him and is serious and fun at the same time. I must say the whole night was magic, I really wasn't expecting that.

<u>Even later</u>

Can't sleep for going over every minute of this evening, over and over again. Well everyone said it was bound to happen sooner or later, but why did it have to happen now? I mean, I don't know when I'll get to see him again. He hopes he'll get to come home before he goes to France, but again, no one can be sure about nothing now. I saw those troop ships on the Pathé, full they were. So many are being sent over, so why would he be lucky and get to stay here longer? He said he'd write, but that's hardly the same as being in his arms, dancing with him, kissing him, talking to him. It's not blooming fair. Not going to think about that, I am going to think about just how lovely the evening was!!!

≈

Megan blushes as she reads the last part. Jake and Louise find it charming, but for completely different reasons. Jake looks at his watch and says he has to go, so Megan puts the diary down and they leave the room together so she can have him all to herself for a few minutes in the deep shadows of the back doorstep.

Louise picks it up and rereads that last entry. In fact, she is remembering her first proper date with Peter, when they no longer needed to pretend it was anything other than what it was. Her pulse quickens and there is a stirring deep within her as she recalls the way he looked at her, the way he held her, and the abandonment with which she gave herself to him. She wonders if she is still capable of being that person.

Granny had always said that she'd been different people at different times. "Life does that to a body..." she'd say, or, "You can't change it and you can't go back, so there's no point wasting your breath trying. Get it right at the time; that's the best thing to do. Do it like you mean it."

Other times she'd take her hand and look at her. She would become very serious and say, "Louise, if I can teach you anything, let it be this: You can't bring yesterday back. Yesterday is and can only ever be a memory, so make it a good one. Make it one you can be proud of, otherwise the only person that gets hurt is you. If you're lucky that is..."

Her grandmother's voice seems so clear in her mind that she turns round, half expecting to see her in the chair beside her. It is of course empty, but the words seem to linger in the room and though she has heard them many times before, their echoes begin to make some sense to her. Hearing the back door close, she stands up. She needs to check on her mother and then all she wants is to be able lose herself in a good night's sleep.

Megan goes up ahead of her and stops at her gran's room with the intention of saying goodnight, but as she opens the door she hears her crying and is shocked; unable to go in or leave. Louise sees her frozen there and fearing the worst, rushes past into the room. Then she too stops dead in her tracks, for Roberta is sitting up in bed with a photo album open in front of her on the eiderdown. She doesn't seem to notice either her or her granddaughter, for she is somewhere else and wherever it is and whatever it is she is seeing, is making her cry.

Louise understands, while Megan does not yet, that not all tears are caused by sadness. She indicates with her head and a soft smile that her daughter should go, then walks further into the room until she is standing by the chair beside the bed and can see the picture that Roberta is staring at.

It is a black and white one of the family from years ago and they are at the kitchen table in the first house they lived in. She is in the high chair and has a mucky mouth. Her father is behind the camera and she is waving at him with sticky, jammy fingers. Joe sits next to her, clean and serious looking, as he often was, while Mark stands at his mother's side. They are staring intently at a piece of paper on the table, but it is not clear what the paper is.

Louise smiles. She has no memory of it, but it gives her a warm feeling nonetheless.

"Do you want to be alone Mum...?"

Roberta looks up at her daughter, but does not really see her. "We think we're the stars, the moon or whatever. We think, or we hope, that we're the important one and that life centres on us, but it doesn't, leastways not for most of us. In actual fact, most of the time we're just a little part of the mosaic, nothing more."

She looks down and slowly closes the book, then looks at Louise as though seeing her for the first time. "Thank you for bringing them up for me. Seems even clearer to me now though, that we didn't share much, did we? Not really... Bit late now of course, so no point getting lost in regrets, is there? That doesn't serve any purpose at all."

Roberta settles back into the pillows and closes her eyes. Louise doesn't know what to say. She feels a pain, low and deep inside and slowly it dawns on her that there is nothing to say. Her mother neither expects nor requires a reply.

"'Night then Mum..." she says pointedly and goes back onto the landing, softly closing the door behind her, while thanking God, the universe or whatever, that she has a different relationship with her own daughter.

Megan curls up with the diary and as her mother had done a little earlier, she rereads the last entry. Although her lips are following Lillian's words, her mind is actually reliving her afternoon and evening with Jake. She misses Hannah, but Lillian understands exactly how she feels, so in a way they are able to share the exquisite newness of it all. Her phone burrs and she eagerly pulls it towards her.

'R U asleep?'

'No'

He calls and despite having said a long and slow goodnight less than an hour ago, they find they can very easily fill another hour, chatting, laughing and sighing.

Further along the landing, Louise has already fallen into a heavy sleep, while for Roberta, sleep is a luxury she is beginning to miss. She knows that there will be less and less of it and then too much.

She turns the TV off and Nat King Cole on.

'Unforgettable, that's what you are...'

She sings the words along with him. Her voice has lost its power, but in the confines of her head, it sounds exactly as it had all those years ago.

The first time she heard it was on the radio and it was also the first time she saw Arnold. He was dancing with someone else, but their eyes met and each of them saw something they recognised in the other. She smiles as she recalls his confusion that afternoon. Throughout their marriage, he had never denied it or the shock he had felt at that moment. She however, had not been confused, for even though she was so much younger than him, she had been sure. She had turned away and let him have his dance, certain that he would be hers; it was just a matter of time.

Chapter fourteen

In those vague nowhere moments between sleeping and waking, Megan has a flash of inspiration. Not only does she see the answer to her question, but it also becomes clear just how her project should be laid out. She flings off the covers, startling Maisie, and grabs her bag, tipping her notes out onto the floor along with the books she has borrowed from the library. As she scans through the pages she realises that only a little of what she has is useful, so in some ways she will have to start again. This thought excites on two levels: the first is that she has the perfect excuse to spend even more time with Jake, but the second is just as important to her. She has always been the sort of student teachers adore; she likes learning and generally does her best. She pulls some clothes on without thinking and grabs the diary, then clatters down the stairs to look for her mother. She finds her in the garage, lovingly spraying the first layer of paint onto the rocking horse.

"Mum, I need money."

Louise absentmindedly turns towards her. She had been pleasantly engaged in what she was doing and it takes her a second to refocus.

"Take what you need from my purse. It's in my bag, hanging on the back of the kitchen door. Will you be back for lunch?"

"No. I've finally got my ideas sorted out for my project, so I want to spend the whole day at the library."

Her mother raises an eyebrow and smiles.

"No... it's not like that, well ok, yes it is, but *actually*, I want to study for most of the day. We'll just have lunch together." She is blushing as she speaks.

"Whatever, enjoy..." Louise says simply. She means it, but is also eager to return her energy to her own project. Without another word she turns back to the horse, gives the aerosol can a shake and resumes spraying.

Megan has to run for the bus, but before they have travelled very far along the main road they are held up in traffic. Seeing that they are not going anywhere for a while, she happily pulls the diary from her bag, for after all, it has now become part of her research.

3rd October 1939

The Hun sank another merchant ship on the 30th, Mr R heard it on the news. I'm so glad that Vic's working in the docks over there. I sent a note to Mum and I had to run to catch the afternoon post, but I wanted to get it in there, just in case she's a bit behind with his news. I don't want her worrying.

≈

4th October 1939

Got a lovely long letter from Bob today. Mrs R recognised his handwriting on the envelope of course and her eyebrows went up as she gave it to me, but she did smile. I didn't know what to say really. I mean, I hadn't read it yet!

But now I have. Lovely and chatty it is, course it's sent from the barracks, so he can't tell me nothing about what they're planning to do and suchlike, but I don't think that really matters. He asked lots of questions, so I've had plenty to write back and if I cycle down good and early, I'll get it in the morning post.

We've had a busy day today, got loads of the trees in the orchard cleared. Hah! I never thought I'd be sick of the sight of a blooming apple, but the view from there, down over the valley at sunset really is something to marvel at. Gave me the same feeling as when I stood in the sea. Some things are just so big you've got to feel small, but the smallness is magical, cos you get to see the bigness of other things. Reading that back, I'm sure I'll never make it in this life as a poetess, but the land? Well, I'm starting to think I could be good at that!

≈

8th October 1939

We went to the harvest festival today at the church. Mrs R says they always go for high days and holidays and as the family's been in the area for so long, they've got their own pew and of course I got to sit with them. I'm not much of a church goer, as I told her, we're not believers as a family, but she said to come anyway, as it was a nice thing to do and also to celebrate all my hard work with everyone else. She was right too, it was nice and they'd donated some smashing stuff for the display.

≈

14th October 1939

So, I'm an aunt again. As well as a note from Mum, I got a letter from Vic with a picture. Virginia Lillian Loveday was born on the 6th and named after Mum and me, how lovely is that. Mrs R was so sweet, said she'd get Mollie to cook me favourite beef and ale pie with mash to celebrate. Then she said it was such a pity that Bob couldn't be with us. I had to agree, but I didn't know what else to say. I mean we've only seen each other twice and exchanged a couple of letters, it's not as though we're engaged or anything and really, he ought to tell his parents, that's if there's anything to tell I mean.

I wish we could see more of each other, letters are lovely and all that and better than nothing of course, but it ain't the same. I mean it ain't the best way for two people to get to know each other, to find out if what they might be feeling is real or not.

We heard the news on the radio that the ship Royal Oak was sunk by a U-boat in the naval port at Scapa Flow. I've never heard of the place before, but Mr R said it was thought to be impenetrable. Clearly it ain't, so that gives us food for thought.

≈

20th October 1939

I am bloomin' knackered! We've scrubbed the milking shed from top to bottom, twice, cleaned the pigs' huts out and got the hay that we're keeping for winter fodder under cover proper like, the rest was loaded and sold. The apples are sorted and I can't see straight no more. I never seem to get enough sleep and no matter how much I eat, and there's always plenty, I'm hungry all the time.

But the life here is good, better than working inside that's for sure, I just wish I was closer to Mum, Elsie, Rita and the others. Petrol is rationed, so it ain't so easy to get a lift anywhere now, at least not for Mum, and most of the trains are given over to troop movement. The Canadians arrived first to help. You got to admire them, the way they come when needed 'back home' as they say. You can always count on them, or so Mum says.

Mrs R just popped her head round the door. Bob telephoned to say he's coming home, he's got a whole week's leave she said. A whole week. I hope it'll be ok. I mean, when we're writing we share all manner of things, but we ain't seen each other since that night in London. S'pose we just sit there like lemons, with nothing to say. I'm excited and scared, all at the same time.

≈

29th October 1939

Where to start? What to say? How to hold on to the magic? I'm sure I'll never forget this week that's just gone by. I know I don't want to!!!

He's on his way to France now, his training is over and he's been posted to his unit, which was one of the first to go over. He'll have to catch up with them he says, cos they're on the border, ready for if the Germans advance apparently. But he said the M line is strong and it won't break easy, the French are ready and we're ready too. He, Mr R and his uncle spent a long time looking at maps and whatnot after dinner each night, usually after we'd listened to the news.

Of course Mr R and his brother were there themselves in the fourteen-eighteen war as we now call it. Funny that, cos until now, everyone always talked about 'the war', so something was always before, during, or just after 'the war'. Now here we all are fighting another one.

But him and me? Well, we're strong. He said he was just as worried as I was, in case we didn't have nothing to say. Hah! We'll laugh about that for a long time to come. Couldn't shut us up, well that's not completely true!

We went into the town, to the cinema and saw a lovely old film called 'Joy of Living'. There's this one song in it which he sang to me all the way home after we'd been dropped off by the local magistrate. Fancy! Turns out he went to school with his sons and Mr R is an old friend of his.

Anyway, we walked up the lanes holding hands and he sang the loveliest song from the film, 'Just let me look at you'. We said from now on it would be our song, cos it works both ways!

'Your smile, such an enchanting smile, it's made my whole world right...'

We worked well together in the fields too with that old tractor and he was right, he really could keep it going. We had a bit of a mishap with it a few weeks ago when it packed up and we stopped using it. No one could get a peep out of it, so we've been using the horses instead, but he got it going and kept it going too.

He took me to his favourite spot on the farm, under that big old pear tree at the bottom of the orchard. He was a bit shy about it, like it was a soppy thing for a man to say, but I smiled at that, cos I like it best there too. Once I'd told him that, we climbed up into the branches to watch the sunset together and he pointed things out that we could see. He told me how it changed with the seasons, how it went from green to reddy gold then to white, first with snow, then with blossom and back to green again. Magic it was. We agreed it would always be our place, right up until we're too old and grey to climb the branches, even with a ladder. We laughed so much we nearly fell out of the bloomin' thing!

I asked him if he was afraid to go so far from home. He said no, cos he'd been away at school since he was seven, so he'd been pretty independent even before his training. Sent away to school! Imagine. When he saw me face he laughed and said we could discuss it for our children when the time came. I looked at him hard when he said that and we laughed, but there was something in his eyes that told me he meant it. I like that idea, though it made me blush right down to me toes.

He told the family that they was to take good care of me too, cos when he comes home next he was coming home to see all of us and that was the way he hoped it was going to stay. Made me blush all over again he did, but Mrs R squeezed me hand and smiled at us, real sweet she was. Then she got out the elderberry wine to celebrate. Nice it was too, I slept like a log!

≈

13th November 1939

He's there. Of course he can't say specifically exactly where 'there' is, but he got there safe and sound. He says his time is mainly spent on tinkering with the 'girls' as the tanks are known, cos they're a type that's called Matilda, don't ask me why. He says there was a bit of competition to get him between some of the commanders, so his reputation clearly went on ahead. Each 'girl' has a crew of two and he of course is the driver.

Mrs R's sister is coming up for Christmas with her youngest son. Her eldest is in France too and as she's got enough petrol to drive here and back, she wanted to know if Mum would like to come too. Course Mum would! Auntie Eth said she'd forgive us for not inviting her and the tribe, but the chances are, for a while at least, that this will be the last one that they're all together too. Joyce and Charlie have set a date for the spring, Tommy is all for joining up his self and he'll be eighteen in the new year, so everything's changing. They'll be here on the 22nd and will stay until the 29th. Can't wait, I'll almost have Mum to meself.

≈

18th November 1939

Bob's doing well, but he said tommy rot is setting in, cos there's nothing to do. Though he says the mess of an evening is a bit of hoot, all those lads together from all over! He says the singing is something to hear and in different *circumstances people would pay a lot to hear voices like that in a choir. Made me laugh, cos I don't s'pose they'll be singing many church songs!*

The Hun ain't a-coming as far as anyone can tell. Holland and Belgium are neutral, like they was last time, so there won't be anything happening there. According to the news we're still pouring men and equipment into France, so who knows, maybe it will all be over by Christmas this time.

Then again, out at sea the poor old merchants are taking a terrible battering and they ain't got no guns. They ain't navy, they're civvies. Vic said in his last letter that he's heard of at least four ships he's served on what have been torpedoed by the Germans. Men lost as well as the cargo and for those not lost, they don't get no pay from when the ship goes down till they get taken on as crew by the next one. Apparently being rescued don't count. I don't know what to make of it all.

On the home front, Alice has signed up to join the WAAFies as she calls them. She said it's cos the uniform is so much better than mine! We laughed about it, but Mrs R had a bit of a teary eye and we all hope she'll still be here for Christmas.

≈

22ⁿᵈ November 1939

More lads are being called up, now it's anyone up to the age of twenty seven. That'll mean Charlie, Tom and Fred too, I shouldn't wonder. I've written to both Elsie and Rita, asking for news and telling them that as far as I know from Bob, it's all quiet over there, so not to worry too much that way. I asked Mum to tell Joyce the same, no need for her to worry neither, but I wonder if they'll bring the wedding forward or not.

Mr R said he was going to put in for more Land Girls. They got enough room here after all and I can't do everything with just him and Mike, cos it looks as if everyone else has to go to France after they've been on training and Alice will be gone soon too, she got her papers through this morning.

She's been passed fit and has to report to West Drayton on 2nd December.

≈

Megan leaps up, grabbing her bag. She was so deeply engrossed in the diary that she's gone past her stop, but what she has learnt has helped her plan her project in more detail.

Jake is busy with someone when she finally gets to the library, so she waves and heads over to the big table where she can spread out. He surprises her some time later, when he appears beside the bookshelf she is standing in front of, leafing through a book.

"Can I tempt my studious girlfriend to some lunch?" he says, catching her around the waist and lightly kissing the nape of her neck.

She blushes at his use of the word *girlfriend,* but decides that she likes it.

"You can, but I want to come back afterwards, so can I leave my stuff here?"

They gather everything together and stow it away in the back room, then go out into the summer sunshine hand in hand. She explains her idea for her project to him and he is not only impressed, but it helps him realise that they have more in common than he had thought, which pleases him.

"Have a look in the biography section too, you might find some interesting information from other people who were there." he suggests as they stop at the crossing.

"Good thinking, and there'll be plenty on the internet too, but I'll save that for another day though." she says, smiling at him. "Where today? The park? Fish and chips? My treat."

While Megan and Jake settle under their favourite tree, chatting and eating their lunch, Louise is with her mother, grimacing as she sips one of her milky food supplement drinks.

"You don't have to drink it, it wouldn't matter to me if you sat there with a three course meal. I'm not hungry and I'm not drinking any more of this disgusting rubbish." Roberta plonks her glass down on the tray and glares at her daughter, who was about to say something back, but snaps her mouth shut. What's the point? She thinks, shrugging.

"And if you've got to something to say, you may as well spit it out." her mother adds.

Louise sighs. "Joe and Claire won't be back until Friday. If you want to be dead before then, well just carry on. It's only Tuesday after all."

They are harsh words, but spoken softly. Their eyes lock for a moment and Roberta slowly smiles. "There. You see, you are my daughter after all." Then she picks the glass up and drains it.

As Louise takes the tray downstairs, she can see through the frosted glass of the front door that someone is in the porch, although she hadn't heard the bell. There seems to be shuffling and she hears muffled voices. Intrigued, she deposits the tray on the hall table and opens the door. An elderly couple are standing there, looking confused.

"Can I help you?" Louise asks.

The man smiles at her. His is tall, but has a stoop and he speaks with a thin reedy voice. "We've come to see Roberta."

His wife nods from behind him, adding, "Flanders; Roberta Flanders." Then turning to him, she says quietly, "You forgot her surname, silly. Important things, surnames. You ought not to forget them."

She turns back to Louise, who sees that they are holding hands. She has no idea who they are, but a lifetime of togetherness radiates from them.

They are long forgotten neighbours and the old lady was a member of the Women's Institute for the brief period that Roberta had been a member too. Her mother is not averse to seeing them, although she cannot recall their faces from the surname. She has let go of most of her acquaintances over the years and the one or two real friends she ever had have died and gone on ahead of her, so it is with tired curiosity that she welcomes them into her room.

Once she has provided tea, Louise finds she cannot escape back to the garage, for the unexpected arrival of this couple have brought her thoughts firmly back to her own marriage. She pulls various things from the freezer and the pantry, deciding to make something more complicated for dinner, hoping it will help her think. She has always preferred to think around things, rather than attack them head on.

She decides that it is too easy just to blame him, for she is half of the thing they have created. 'For better or for worse', that was what they'd said, so what was the worst part? Before she can look at Peter and Lucy clearly, she has a need to understand her own role and her own failings. She chops an onion more fiercely than it deserves as she tells her absent husband that she doubts they will agree on them.

"Being tired," she says to the empty kitchen, "is not a failing!"

Megan and Jake find her there an hour or so later, vigorously kneading dough with a force that does not go unnoticed.

"Mum...?" Megan asks a little timidly, shoving her heavy bag onto the hook behind the door. Jake tactfully heads out to the potting shed to get on with some gardening.

"Flat bread," Louise announces a little too loudly, "has got to be flat!"

"Easy..." says her daughter, turning away and trying not to laugh. She lifts the lids of various pans, inhaling the spicy aromas that drift up as she stirs and tastes the contents. "Mmm, this is good, but who else is coming?" She asks, turning back to her mother.

Louise flops down at the table. "I know, it's far too much. Ask Jake if he wants to stay. In fact, invite his mother up too. There's something about a big old farm kitchen that means you want to cook up masses of food. It's all right for Claire; Joe and the boys eat tons, but for us, I mean, we're only two..." she trails off unhappily, trying not to cry.

Megan moves closer. Her newfound romance has given her a little insight into her mother's pain and confusion. She doesn't have the words, but she does have the gesture. Louise takes the proffered hand and holds it against her cheek, smiling. The pain is worth it, she thinks, for she has her daughter.

Jake calls his mother, who is delighted to join them and the four of them sit down to a meal they all enjoy. Louise and Lynne find they have a lot of people in common from their youth and after dinner they take a bottle of wine into the back parlour for a natter, leaving Jake and Megan with the TV.

Much later, as Louise is putting the last of the washing up away, she sees her daughter's bulging bag. It is hanging by a thread rather than the whole strap and as she watches, the fabric tears and it falls to the ground with a thud. Papers and pens tumble out and she picks them up with a sigh, putting them back in the bag. Noticing the diary, she takes it to the table. Some bedtime reading will be just the ticket she decides and takes it up with her, along with a glass of whisky.

30th December 1939

Having Mum here has been lovely. We've had time to talk about everything and nothing and Mrs R has been so sweet to her. While I've been out working, she took her down to the town and out and about a bit to meet a few people and so forth. Being a similar age and all, I'm sure they had plenty to talk about, even though Mrs R and her sister come from a bit of a different class to us, but now, we're all in this together, after all.

Mum arrived with a bit of a chesty cough, but she left with some colour in her cheeks and as usual, Mollie cooked up a feast every day. Mrs R made sure the bedrooms were kept warm and there was no damp in Mum's room at all, so I'm sure that was good for her too and it was sweet of Mrs R to take the time and the trouble.

We heard that the rationing is going to be extended next week, not sure yet what to, but from all the torpedoing of the merchant ships, we're thinking it'll be the things we don't make or grow here. The man from the ministry has been to all the farms in the area setting out how it's got to work this year. We got to feed everyone here and the lads over there too he said, so it's all got to be planned, right down to the last detail. As most of the farmers have got lads out there, they won't be arguing with him I daresay.

Got a lovely parcel from Vic and Viv, it arrived while Mum was here which was great, cos there was some stockings and a brooch in there for her and a few bits for Mrs R as well, which tickled her. Course with the Hun busy in the Atlantic, Vic said it's not safe for Mum to come out just now. I think she was relieved actually, especially when Mr R agreed with what Vic wrote.

There was a letter to Mr and Mrs R from Bob and he mentioned the parcel we'd sent him at the start of the month. Mrs R had got Mollie to bake up his favourite cake and we put in homemade plum and apple jam. I knitted him a jumper he can wear under his uniform when it gets really cold and Mrs R did some socks. Like Mum told her, I've never been able to get the hang of socks! We put in some books too and a pack of cards. We reasoned that if they are that bored, cards would be useful. Anyway, he got it all and he really enjoyed the cake and the jumper fits a treat.

Mum had brought me a note from Elsie, who's over the moon. Fred didn't pass his medical, cos he's too short and he's got flat feet. He's going to do ARP work instead, but as she said, most of the time that's just poncing about in his uniform, directing people who are lost in the blackout!

Mum also said that Tom and Charlie are at their training camps and that Rita and Joyce have both agreed to quick weddings before they head off on their postings. Unlikely to be the same place after all, cos Tom's in the navy and Charlie's a fitter with the RAF. But then he's like Bob, always enjoyed taking things apart and always been able to coax some life back into a machine what's given up the ghost!

If they could all get married at the same time, I might see if I can travel down for them. Mum said Auntie Eth and Evan was looking into him coming north and being one of Bevan's boys down the mines. He's a strong lad and he would be helping until he's called up. I know Mum and Auntie Eth are hoping that if he's doing important work, he won't be called up. That's to say if the war's still going on, cos after all, by *the time he's eighteen it might not be. It'd do him good. Might even be near here, well not too far away anyroads.*

≈

1ˢᵗ January 1940

So here we are in 1940. I wonder what it will bring us.

I don't think they are going to be the fabulous forties after all. I think me and Rita might have got that a bit wrong, despite us both seeming to have found a good bloke each. I mean, there weren't much celebrating, cos all anyone has to talk about is the blessed war.

≈

12ᵗʰ January 1940

Bob's birthday today, he's twenty three. We had a toast with Mrs R's elderflower wine before dinner, she said he's always been partial to that one. Of course, he's not here and nor is Alice. So it was all a bit sad really.

≈

14ᵗʰ January 1940

Mum said in her letter that they've rationed all sorts, but she's got her book. Bless her, she thought we would be exempt up here on the farm, but of course we're not, so for us too it's bacon, butter and sugar of course, for now. We've got plenty of veg and eggs and Mr R gets to keep some meat and milk back for home consumption, but not for selling. He says that he knows, even if the city folk don't, that rationing of all meat and milk products is coming soon and I imagine all the things you need butter and sugar for too. I told Mum to do a bit of stocking up of non perishables and sent her a bit of extra money to help out.

Still, it's not all bad news. I get a letter from Bob every two or three days and it seems he gets mine just as regularly. Now that we've had some time together as well, the letters are different. Seems like we can say more, but without having to explain so much. It's almost as though we're having a real conversation, I just have to wait a while to hear his half!

He said in his last one, that one day, a long way into the future, we're going sit down by the fire one winter's night and reread these letters to each other and remember this time apart. Made me smile that did.

≈

Louise gently closes the cover and turns off the light. She tries to imagine a point in the future where she and Peter sit comfortably together and discuss the current hiccup in their marriage. Will they laugh about it? Will they look lovingly at each other, happy that it didn't break them apart? Or will they pretend it never happened and never refer to it again? She cannot quite picture any of these scenarios and quickly gives up, before drifting off to sleep, dreamless and refreshing for a change.

Chapter fifteen

Louise is woken from deep sleep by the persistent ringing of a distant telephone. It is barely dawn and it takes her a few moments to realise that it is the house phone. She leaps out of bed and runs into her mother's room where the nearest handset is located, and finds Roberta staring at it but not making any move to pick it up, for she is of the generation that still believes that between the hours of nine pm and eight am, it only ever brings bad news.

When she answers it, Louise hears a slightly hysterical Izzy, Mark's partner. Her brother has been involved in an accident and as they speak is in hospital having an emergency operation. Izzy is tearful and breathless and it is difficult for Louise to get the information she needs, so she repeats things slowly, for Izzy to either agree or explain. Roberta listens carefully to every word that her daughter says, but her face remains expressionless.

Eventually Louise understands that while Mark will be in some pain for a few weeks, his injuries are not life threatening. His health plan is good and although the hospital he has been taken to is a long way from the LA suburb where they live, it has a fantastic reputation. She spends a little more time talking and calming Izzy down and they agree to speak again in an hour, when Mark should be out of theatre. She makes sure they have her mobile number, then hangs up and immediately calls Joe, who listens to the news calmly and asks to speak to their mother.

Louise leaves them to it and goes to the bathroom for a shower, needing to reorganise her thoughts. She realises that her life has toddled along for years with no real events to speak of, not since her wedding in fact, then suddenly, in the space of fourteen months, her mother has been diagnosed with primary and then secondary cancer, undergone several operations, not to mention the other invasive treatments, and is now dying. Her marriage is crumbling, Megan is growing up rather rapidly and her eldest brother is in hospital in another country.

"And I no longer know who I really am, or where I'm going in this thing called my life." she mutters to herself.

She sighs into the steam and leans against the tiles, letting the hot water flow onto and over her body. It is very soothing and for a moment she is transported back to another time, a time when there had been another set of reasons to cry and be confused by life. She was young and had drunk too much and her grandmother had found her passed out on the bedroom floor.

"I don't know the cause of your pain love, maybe it will pass, maybe it won't, but one way or another, you will have to make your peace with it." Then she had propelled her fully clothed into this very shower and turned the taps on, telling her to come down for breakfast when she was ready.

Louise smiles. She can no longer remember the cause of her pain, for it had obviously been trivial and probably just teenage angst, but those words had stayed with her for a long time before fading away, and now, just when they were needed, they had found her again. She turns the taps off, takes a deep breath and steps out; finally ready to face the future.

She spots the diary on her bedside table and takes it down to the kitchen, where she makes tea and porridge for her mother. Once she has helped Roberta into the bathroom and she is comfortably settled back in bed with the radio on, Louise goes downstairs and makes herself coffee and toast. She sits down at the big kitchen table, picks up the diary, then opens a page at random and eats breakfast with her granny.

19th June 1940

Finally, after all what's happened these past weeks he's home. We can see him with our own eyes and we can touch him and hear him. The relief, the sheer bloody relief of it all. I never thought such a deep feeling was possible. There ain't no words to describe how I feel, leastways I don't know them if they do exist. Overwhelmed, is the nearest that I can find and that ain't deep enough!

He's got a shrapnel wound in his leg and he's broken his arm and damaged his collarbone, but he says that he's one of the lucky ones. That's a serious thing to say and I know he means it.

I can't believe, no that's not right, I don't want to believe the things he's been telling me. It's changed him, that's for sure, cos he's not the same, but then how can you see all that, experience all that and stay unmoved by it? Even from the bits and pieces we've been able to read and see on the newsreel, we know we ain't the same as we was. Something's been lost, that's for sure.

He said his dad told him that those of us that thankfully have never seen a battle can never understand. Mr R also said there was no point in talking about it to us at home, he told him that he'd just have to keep it inside and manage it as best he could. Then later, only when it's all over, he could try and think it through properly. But he strongly suggested to his boy, to my Bob, that while it's happening, he'd have to push it all aside, push it back and just get on with things as best as he can, despite what's going on around him and what he might see happen to his mates.

When he told me this, it made me cry and he cried too. We was sitting under the pear tree though, so no one saw us. I told him that if this thing is going to change him and if we're still going to have a chance, I have to try and understand, I have to try and help him mange these things as best he can. We agreed that what his dad said was good advice, but we're a different generation and things are different now to how they was in those days, so he tried to tell me, he tried to show me with words what it had been like for him and the things he'd seen.

I can't write it yet, it's still churning around inside me. Maybe in a couple of days I'll be able to. Cowardly of me really, after all, he's lived it.

Mr Churchill told us all yesterday that the battle for France is all but over and the battle for Britain is about to begin, but at least we have so many of the lads home, so surely we can defend ourselves.

≈

21ˢᵗ June 1940

Mr R has given me the afternoons off, says I'm needed to get Bob back on his feet. We've got a couple more girls helping out anyway, though they don't live here. They're part of a group billeted down in the town, in one of the bigger houses there. What with Bob being home, I've not really spent much time getting to know them yet.

Let's see if I can write this properly, here goes.

He said suddenly the peace and boredom at the M Line was gone and it was for real. At first they'd been excited, cos it had been terrible just sitting there, miles from home doing nothing, just waiting. He said too much waiting is sometimes worse than doing what needs to be done, even if it's scary or terrible, but then it started and he said that then he wondered if waiting endlessly, even for all eternity might have been better! He tried to smile at me but I could see it was hard for him. He said in all the noise, people are screaming in pain and you can't help them and he said that's the worst part.

All you can do is focus on your job, do what you're supposed to do, what you've been trained to do. He and his commander were a good team he said, they trusted each other and worked well together and that was important, your lives depended on being a good team.

He said they just kept pulling back because they certainly couldn't advance, they couldn't even hold the line when it came to it. Belgium surrendered and then Holland fell. Without the defences in Belgium there wasn't enough to stop the Germans marching straight in to Holland. Old Kaiser Bill is there anyway, so maybe they won't mind, but maybe they do. Their Queen and government is here, so I am s'posing it ain't friendly like Austria. But like Bob says, it's got two important ports, that's really why the Hun wants it.

His type of tank don't go very fast. Apparently you can run faster! Anyway, his job is to protect the infantry, taking out other tanks and gunner positions whenever he can. When they got a chance to stop they were exhausted, they ate and snatched a bit of sleep whenever they could, which wasn't often by all accounts, not once the show started and certainly not once they really started retreating.

He said that was best in some ways, cos when you're that tired you can't think, so you don't take in what's happening around you. You're glad when you see a face that you know and like and you try not to think about the faces of the people you can't find no more, or when you see a tank with blokes you know inside 'brew up', which although he didn't say, I imagine means explode. He told me that you don't stop to collect the dead, you just keep going, you just keep trying to take out as many of the Huns's tanks, guns and men as you can, while protecting as many of your own as you can.

Anyway, that's enough of that. We sat under the tree and watched these big birds flying across the valley. He told me they were buzzards, they are different from the ones called kites and he pointed at the wings and the tail and showed me how to tell the two apart. They made such little effort to stay up there, circling around and around for hours.

It was peaceful and we was happy.

≈

22nd June 1940

The French surrendered today.

We got the map out and saw that much of Europe and Scandinavia as far as the Russian border is now held by the Nazis or their friends. The Spanish are neutral, mind you, they're probably sick of fighting after their own terrible civil war and the Greeks ain't involved. But that's a scary picture when you look at it on the map. We're so small, but we ain't on our own. When you look at the rest of the world and think that men from Canada, Australia, India even, are all on their way, or already here. So Mr Hitler, <u>we ain't on our own</u>!!!!

Now we'll have the flippin' French government here as well I s'pose, along with bits of the Dutch and Polish navies and anyone else who could get away and get over here to us. The Polish Air Force is already here apparently. Well, at least we can use them.

Mrs R served up a beef and kidney suet pudding, with apple pie and custard for afters. Something to get our teeth stuck into she said, to forget all this nonsense. It worked a treat too, full to bursting we all was and we didn't put the radio on neither!

≈

23rd June 1940

Bob and I sat in the orchard under the old pear tree today. I told him what we'd read about Dunkirk and seen on the newsreel at the cinema. In fact, we went into town specially to see them. It seemed important that we did and he understood.

We knew it was a defeat, Mr Churchill said you don't get a victory from an evacuation, but in a funny way we did. Like the King his self had said the week before, we have to pray and I think even nonbelievers like me did. Mainly I reckon, because we all knew someone who was there and we wanted them brung home safe.

Bob said his unit was some of the last to reach the beaches, they'd held off for as long as they could, giving cover and holding the Hun back and off the beaches, but then they had to abandon all their equipment, while some of them brave Frenchies gave them cover. Men and lads had to wade out into the sea, as the big ships couldn't get close enough to the beach. Lined up they was, waist and shoulder deep in the water for hours waiting to board, trying to stay out of the way of the bullets and bombs that the Huns was spraying and dropping as they flew over the beach and the sea itself, which is how he got hurt.

While they was on the beach, something got hit and exploded and the bloke he was running for cover with, he had his... he had his head sliced off, but he kept running, before he fell over. Bob got a blast of metal which knocked him sideways into a shell hole in the sand, which probably saved his life he said. Anyway, if he was knocked unconscious it wasn't for very long and someone helped him out and he limped to the sea, helped by this other bloke. Waiting to *board in the salty water cleaned his wound good and proper, good thing too we agreed.*

When I close me eyes at night, I see that poor soul running along the beach with no head and I bet Bob does too. He never knew his name, never even saw him before and now he's gone, probably didn't even see it coming.

I told him about the bit of Mr Churchill's speech that I took to me heart. He said they deserve our gratitude, as do all brave men, who in so many ways and on so many occasions, are ready and continue ready to give their lives, for their native land.

After what Bob had seen and what he told me, well we understood and that poor bugger was indeed one of those brave men that we have to say thank you to.

I just held him closer, he's safe and he's home and we're making the most of every minute we have. Promised ourselves a picnic down by the river as soon as his arm is mended, I've not explored down that way and when I came back from London last time I brought me new bike with me on the train. I prefer it to the one they let me use here, I mean it's nice enough, but not quite the right size and mine's, well, mine.

Got a lovely letter from Elsie today as well. Good news, little Bernadette is fully recovered from that rash and Rosie never caught it. Elsie says she's going to sleep for a week now, cos she's been up all hours with one or the other of them. Still, she sounded more like herself when she gave me the gossip, although there weren't much!

Alice will be home for a few days soon too, so Mrs R is looking well perky!

≈

25th June 1940

We went over Mr Churchill's speech again and I saw for the first time why the Nazis wanted Poland and France. They've got the mines and all the wood from the forests and other things they need to be a dangerous war machine. They have the ports in Holland as well as those in Norway. We've got the empire, but the seas and oceans are full of U-boats and their navy and we can't walk from here to India or Shanghai, but all they done was march from Germany into all those other countries.

Mr Churchill said that we will fight everywhere. He said we will not give in and no matter what, we will protect our home and what is ours and that even if we was starving, still we would not give in. Made me think that did. But I understand, I mean we can't, not now, because over thirty thousand of our lads have given their lives already, we can't tell them it was for nothing now, can we?

I look at Bob and think about what he was trying to do, how he didn't care if he got hurt or not, how he just kept going and I think Mr Churchill must be right. If Bob and others can just keep going, then it seems to me that us what's left at home have to too.

≈

26th June 1940

We walked all the way down to the river. Bob, Alice with her friend Angela that she's brought back with her, Mr and Mrs R and me. We took a picnic and a big blanket to spread out on the grass under an old horse chestnut tree. Mollie made us a feast and for a few hours we pretended nothing outside our little party existed. Magic it was. Alice told us that she and Angela are stationed at a big old house near London and from what she said, the place sounds really posh. Fancy!

On the way back, Bob told me that when he'd been on the ship coming back from France, as soon as he saw the outline of England and the white cliffs that they all talk about, he thought of me. Apparently that outline is a sight no fighting man will ever forget and with it, always from now on will be my smiling face. He said it was so important for him to know that I was here and that I was safe. I just squeezed his hand, cos what could I say? I know he won't be here and he won't be safe. He seemed to know what I was thinking though, because then he just said 'We're here, we're together, why waste it by worrying now?'

≈

27th June 1940

Got a letter from Vic. He said he can't stand by idle no longer. He's been seeing and reading about the air attacks on Southampton, Caithness and other places. He says he's heard from men down at the docks that the German pilots machine gunned civilians who were trying to leave the cities in Poland, France and Holland. Made him sick to the core he said, to hear of women and children just mown down as they ran from the burning buildings or the bombs. Could have been Viv or us he said and if Hitler ain't stopped, who's to say it won't be in the future?

He said the merchants need men who know the sea and know what they're doing. He explained that President Roosevelt is allowing trade with anyone who pays on the nose and takes it away themselves. Vic can't stand the thought of the Germans getting their hands on more than us, so he's signed back on. What can I say to him, now that I know a bit more of what it's really like, far away from this lovely peaceful place? Our lads need feeding, they need guns and they need tanks and planes, not to mention fuel. They had to leave so much of our stuff on the beaches in France. We can't fight Hitler with spades and pitchforks! But still, I don't want either of them out there in danger, truly I don't and I don't suppose anyone else wants their loved ones out there neither.

≈

Louise puts her toast down, then goes to the back door and looks out over the rooftops that were not there when Lillian was writing. She had never thought of her childhood homes or the sanctuary her grandmother provided as being set in 'lovely peaceful places', but as she strains to hear the morning noises, it is birds and insects that she hears first. A dog barks somewhere, a car drives past. It's not so different, she thinks.

But London was always where Louise wanted to be. London was her spiritual home; the family home on her grandmother's side, but Lillian had never returned there to live. She had kept herself busy in Little Maddely and was much loved in the community. So many people had come to her funeral and they had been all ages, not just similar to hers, but young people too, as well as people from all walks of life. Louise smiles as she thinks of her, so full of zestfulness, yet somehow always just a bit separate from things and always with a stillness about her that no one else seems to have inherited.

Her thoughts are broken by a familiar and welcome voice.

"I'm starving. What's for breakfast...?"

"I've got just the thing..." Louise smiles and turns round to see Megan standing there in her pyjamas, looking sleepy and pink.

In that moment she can see both the child her daughter was and the woman she will become and hopes she will never swing endlessly back and forth through the dieting fads of her own youth, which still seem to determine how too many people live their lives, including her own on occasion.

While Megan chomps, Louise calls Izzy. Mark has survived surgery, but naturally he is still woozy and will be kept in for a few days; mainly for observation and to make sure his blood count stays stable. Louise is given the hospital number and after a brief chat about other things, Izzy is told to go home and get some sleep.

"You sound exhausted." she says.

"I am, and home is exactly where I'm heading. Catch you later, Lou-Lou."

Louise smiles as she ends the call. Izzy is sounding a little more upbeat and that can only be good for Mark she decides, before calling Joe to give him the update.

Megan pulls her notebook across the table towards her and copies out the last three entries from the diary. "I'm going to use some of this in my project and I'm planning on spending the day at the library again, if that's ok?" she asks, a little shyly. "It's really starting to take shape now and..." she trails off, looking at her mother from under her lashes.

They both know of course that Jake will be there too, a fact that accounts for a large part of her enthusiasm.

"Good idea. If I give you a list, can you stop off at the supermarket and bring some bits back with you? It'll save me having to go out too. I need to do some housework before Claire and Joe arrive on Friday. Gran's doctor is stopping by today and I want to talk to him and if possible, I'd really like to get some more done on my project too!" She smiles as she thinks about the next layer of paint that needs to be applied to the rocking horse.

"Sure. I'll go and get dressed while you write it down. I need more money too; I bought me and Jake fish and chips yesterday. Not cheap, but well tasty." she says with a smile, then leaps up and heads back upstairs.

Chapter sixteen

Louise hears the doctor coming down the stairs and goes into the hall to meet him. He tells her that he suspects a new infection has got into her mother's system, so he has taken some blood and the results should be ready in a week's time. They both think, though neither actually says, that there is only a shared hope that she will be still around by then. He has changed her prescription for pain management to something a little stronger and will call round again in a few day's time.

He has already told Roberta that the current situation could go on for weeks or even months with a slow deterioration, or there could be rapid progress and she may not see September. She had asked the question and had expected the truth, which on getting she finds is pretty much in accordance with what she had thought herself.

"Don't bring me back. When I start to go, just let me be." she told him firmly. "I've told Louise and Joe the same, so none of your resuscitation malarkey if you please. I've got my ticket and I'm almost ready to board."

Roberta sits alone in her room, contemplating the differences between her slow passing and her husband's sudden one. Given the choice, would she prefer his? Would he have preferred hers?

"You get what you're given." she says aloud and although the room is empty, the shadows of people already gone nod in agreement.

Cate calls, and as Louise is giving her friend an update, she makes another nourishing, but vile tasting meal replacement drink for her mother. She tells her of Mark's accident, her conversation with Izzy, then switches without warning to Megan's romance with Jake. She also tells her about the rocking horse and the film she had seen when she was fifteen, which inspired her choice of colouring for it. Almost without drawing breath, she moves onto her hopes for the weekend, when Joe and Claire return. She natters and Cate listens, saying nothing. At the point in the conversation where Louise is starting to wind things up, her friend announces that she is coming up tomorrow.

"You sound weird and I don't like it. Megan and this Jake fellow can granny-sit for the evening I'm sure, because you and I are going down the pub! I'll be at the station at... hang on... at six fifty and I can get the first train back on Friday morning. Be there!" she tells her and hangs up before Louise can protest. But as she puts the phone down, she realises that she wants to test a few things out and Cate is just the person she needs.

Thinking it unfair to burden her daughter with the responsibility of looking after Roberta, she calls Susan and asks if she would mind coming over tomorrow for supper and to sit with her mother, as she wants to go out for the evening. Susan is delighted to be of help and plans are made for Louise to collect her after lunch and for her to stay overnight.

"It's so funny don't you think?" Susan says laughing, "Me spending so much time with you all, even sleeping in his house."

"Dad never lived at Priory Meadows," Louise explains, "it was my maternal grandmother's house and before that the home of her husband's family."

"I must have been mistaken... I thought he said... oh well, no matter, I look forward to seeing you all tomorrow and finally meeting Cate."

They ring off and Louise thinks again what a sweetie Susan is, but as she heads out of the kitchen with the lunch tray and up the stairs, something about the conversation nags at her.

"Were they actually married?" she asks her mother, putting her drink and sandwich on the bedside table.

"Who?" asks Roberta, startled out of her reverie by the question.

"Granny and Granddad. As far as I recall, she always called herself and was always addressed as Lillian Loveday, not Robinson."

Roberta picks up the glass and scowls. Louise is uncertain if it is in reaction to the drink or her question.

"Well they must have been, because my maiden name was most definitely Robinson, not Loveday and anyway, you've been nosing through all the family papers, so you should have found the certificate. I take it you found all her letters and whatnot?" She sips a little of the drink and grimaces.

Louise feels terribly sad, watching her mother force down the milky coloured drink. She always used to have such a good appetite and Joe didn't get his from a stranger.

"Actually I haven't. Would you like some tea to wash that down?"

"Yes I would, and sooner rather than later if you please. There's a big box on top of the wardrobe in the blue room upstairs, the one that was always hers when Nana and Grampy were still alive." She plonks down the not quite empty glass with a sigh. "I can't stomach any more of that. I think I'll have a bit of broth for dinner, nothing greasy or fatty though. And take that sandwich away with you, the smell of that tuna is turning my stomach."

As the day begins to fade into evening, Roberta tries to lose herself in a chat show on the TV. Louise has finished all her chores, so she goes up to the blue room, stands on a chair and finds the box on top of the solid old wooden wardrobe. She carefully lifts it down and blows the dust off, then takes it to the single bed under the eaves to see what is inside.

The sight of the carefully bundled letters, photos and newspaper clippings, tears at her heart. Her grandmother had shared many things with her over the years, but not this box of treasures; she had kept this for herself.

A black and white photo catches her attention. It is faded, but she can still see the figure of a young man sitting on an upturned bucket. He is in shorts, but they are clearly army uniform. It is the desert and he is tinkering with the tracks of what must be a tank, surrounded by spanners and smiling cheekily for the camera.

"Granddad..." she whispers. "Joe is so like you. You'd have got on like a house on fire!"

She smiles at the thought, then realises that Joe is almost twice the age her grandfather had been when the photo was taken. She puts it back in the box and carefully replaces the lid, dithering for a moment, wondering if she should leave it there or take it downstairs and go through it all later with Megan.

The last of the afternoon sun is streaming through the small, arched windows that face west and Louise walks towards them. She can see all the way down to the river and across the valley. The view is very peaceful and she tries to wonder what it might have been like if the war had been lost all those years ago and Nazi storm troopers had marched in.

Bringing her mind back from a past that was only ever a borrowed echo anyway, she sees her daughter coming up the street. She is walking quickly and lightly, a bag in each hand and one casually slung over her back. Louise picks up the box and heads towards the kitchen, stopping briefly at her mother's door and is pleased to see her dozing and listening to music.

While Louise puts the groceries away, Megan sifts through the box and finds letters; all neatly separated into individual bundles, from Lillian's mum and her friends in London and of course from Vic and Bob. It is the ones from her mother that interest Megan most and she carefully slides the top two out from the ribbon holding them together.

"So... Virginia Loveday was my great great grandmother? Is that right?" she asks as she opens one of them.

"Er... let me think, she was my great grandmother... so yes, she would have been." her mother confirms.

"Don't suppose you remember much about her?" Megan asks hopefully.

"No, nothing. She died long before I was born. But Granny, Lillian, often spoke about her and I know they were very close. She missed her, right up until she died herself."

"Ahh, that's really nice..."

Megan is looking at her own mum as she speaks and realising for the first time just how much she loves her. Without having been aware of the transition, in that moment she is suddenly sure that it has become an active love and has matured, because it is no longer childish and passive. She smiles at this new knowledge and settles into one of the sturdy wooden kitchen chairs, that like so much else in the house are a great deal older than she is.

"Listen..." she says, then starts reading aloud.

14th September 1940

Darling girl,

What can I say to you? Of course I miss you and yes, there's plenty of war work to be found in this great big city of ours at the moment. Like I said before, me, Elsie and your Auntie Eth are very busy looking after the kiddies of the mums that want to or have to work. That is them that didn't want to be evacuated, cos there ain't many schools open now, as the teachers have all either gone to the country where the kiddies are, or are doing other war work. That was a good idea of Fred's to set this up, cos we've got over 30 now during the day and another 20 at night. You remember Sandra White, the one with the wonky eye from Gilly's? Anyway, she and Elsie take the night shift and we've moved them all out to near Fred's shed. There's a good shelter near there, so it's safer.

You're safer where you are, although I know no one ain't completely safe anymore, not even the King and Queen. I suppose you heard that the palace got bombed again last night? But I like the fact you're there in the middle of nowhere and from the photos you sent recently, I can see everything is all calm and peaceful, just like it ought to be everywhere, but ain't. I'm so glad to have seen it for meself, that sweet town there was a picture, I hope no blooming bombs spoil it. The little tearoom that Mrs Robinson took me to was a real treat and I want to go again when next I get the chance to come and see you!

Now I know you heard about that shelter that collapsed over the way there and we ain't using the one here at the flats no more, cos it's made of the same cement mix. They now say it was faulty, that's what did for those poor souls, well that and the bomb of course, cos it was a direct hit. It was a bloody miracle that Rita and Connor weren't there that night.

But really, we get plenty of warning and us weeds are harder to kill than those exotic flowers up the way and over the river!

But darling girl, you must know that I've enough to worry about, what with Vic being at sea again and if you were here *you wouldn't be tied to me apron anymore, so I'd have to worry about you too. So you stay where you are love. You're doing important work, work that you're good at. Mr Robinson told me so his self, he said you were worth two of some of the lads he's hired in the past.*

You don't need to worry about sending me money, we make more than we've ever earned just by charging each of the mums a couple of bob. So you save it up for afterwards, when I'm thinking you'll need it because you'll have your own home. No need to keep sending me bits of your ration book neither, cos Fred sees that we're all right. He can get his hands on all sorts, no questions asked and his prices ain't that much more than those in the shops, so we ain't going without much, honest.

The truth of it is, there are too many people with light fingers, what with most folk gone all night down the shelters and you have to hope the wardens are keeping a good eye out for the thieving sods. Mrs Pritchard, I don't think you know her, from Gatekeepers Street, had her best canteen of cutlery nicked the other night, along with just about everything from the larder. Disgraceful it is at the best of times, but now? Hanging's too good for them if you ask me. Anyway, let's not get me started on that or there'll be no shutting me up and you won't get the news.

I got meself a lovely new dress at Gilly's last week, fancy that, me not making me own for once, but I can't say I've got the time. It's not the best fit, so when I've got a minute I'll just sort the darts out a bit better, but it was a real bargain and it's that lovely red that you always say suits me.

Keep yourself wrapped up in that howling cold wind, cos you've inherited the Smith chest, mores the pity, so take care of yourself. Don't stay in damp clothes if you don't need to, that's the worst thing you can do. Anyway, at least you'll have plenty of onions if you do get a chill. Ask Mrs Robinson to see if there's any honey thereabouts, you know it always does you the power of good when you get one of those coughs that don't shift.

You give me regards to Mr and Mrs Robinson and maybe when Bob comes home next on a bit of leave, you and him can spend a bit of the time visiting us here. Hopefully those German sods will have run out of bombs to drop on us by then!

Your ever loving mum.

xxx

PS. Auntie Eth, Joyce and Tish send their love.

Megan carefully folds it up and looks at her mother, smiling. "That's really lovely isn't it? I mean, in the diary I've read what Lillian says about her mum, but seeing it from the other side... well, just makes it even nicer, doesn't it?"

"It does." Louise agrees and thinks that she would have written exactly the same under the circumstances, knowing that sometimes you have to send those you love away, because it is safer and easier than keeping them close to you.

"Read me the other one you've got there while I make some soup for Gran."

Megan opens the second letter, happily complying with her mother's wishes.

24th September 1940

Darling girl,

Sorry I've been a bit quiet, didn't mean to worry you. We've been a bit upside down here, what with one thing and another, nothing to worry about though. We're just a bit tired. We don't get much sleep down the underground station, it's so busy and noisy down there, but we reckon it's safer than the shelters, so we go most nights after we've had a bit of dinner at home first. That's if we get the chance, otherwise it's sandwiches and a big cooked breakfast when we get home in the morning. I've quite a liking for that these days, sets me up for the day nicely and I don't know why I never did it before, but I never fancied it when you was doing yours before you set off for the market. All seems like a lifetime ago now, don't it?

Funny really, it don't seem so long ago when I remember how scared I was of Irish bombs while I was down there and now we go there to stay out of the way of the flippin' German bombs!

Joyce and Tish are working shifts at the factory, so sometimes they have to come along a bit later, or if their shift runs all night they go straight home, but only after the all clear's sounded, we made them promise us that.

This'll make you smile, one old girl down the station said she was there when the Queen came to visit what was left of their street and someone said to her majesty, 'Why do you take the mick and come here dressed up to the nines, when we ain't got nothing left?' And her majesty looked straight at this person and said quick as you like, 'When the King's people come to visit me, they always wear their best clothes, so when I go to visit my husband's people, how could I not do the same? It would be rude and ungracious of me not to extend the same courtesy to those that have already suffered.'

This old girl was laughing as she told us, said it shut that other one up a treat. Lovely lady the Queen, a real lady don't you think? They ain't left us, the whole family is staying and facing it with us. You can't knock them for that now, can you? I bet that American woman wouldn't have done the same if she'd been Queen, I bet she'd have upped sticks and gone to Canada, like the government suggested to Their Majesties, but they wouldn't go, didn't send the little princesses neither.

You wouldn't recognise the place at the moment, so it's better that you don't see it, or smell it. Whole streets, all burnt out and buildings reduced to piles of rubble. Not just houses, but great big office buildings, warehouses and that old bond place too, you know, up near the Ferryman, but we carry on as best we can. We keep telling each other our lads are doing what they can, so we mustn't let them down.

Me and your aunt pop in to see the Pathé newsreel on our way back from work most days, but we don't like the idea of staying in there too long, so we've not seen a feature since I can't remember when. Did you see that old mother on it the other night? 'We can take it' she said, even though she was still dizzy and covered in dust from her house being hit like that. Hah, made us all laugh it did! She's right though, so it's what we all say now and it keeps us going! We can take it!

Got a lovely letter from Viv this morning, telling me all about those little scamps and what they've been up to. Seems little Virginia is more like you was than me at that age, a right little charmer who knows her own mind already. Made me smile that did, you were just like that, still are really, just bigger and kinder and you don't scream so much now when you don't get your own way. Oh the lungs you had on you then!

Any news from Bob? Can he tell you where he's been posted to? There's nothing I can say to stop you from worrying. These are terrible times, worse than the last war, that's for sure and I never thought I'd say that. But just take each day as it comes and write to him often. Your dad always said that getting letters from home was what kept them going. Look forward to his letters by all means, but don't wait for them before writing yourself. Don't forget he's got a war to fight, he may not have much time to write and even when he does, well, just you be prepared, they get held up, cos ships, god forbid and keep me boy safe, get sunk. Write a lot, so he always gets one from you and tell him you love him, give him something to come home for, that's the best thing you can do.

Tomorrow after work, your aunt will go over and see Fred and Elsie, to pick up some tinned peaches. Looking forward to those, I can tell you. Of course cream's a bit scarce, but we might have enough bits and pieces, you know, powdered this and that to knock up a bit of custard to go with them. I'll go home and cook and we'll hopefully have some dinner before we go down to the tube station for the night.

Poor Fred's tired out, cos he's working all night and them fires don't miraculously put themselves out at daybreak, so he's lucky to get more than a couple of hours kip before the next round of bombs starts dropping.

Anyway love, must dash, that's the siren. They're early tonight, or I'm late. I'll drop this in the post box as we go past.
All me love as always,
Your ever loving mum.
xxx

As Megan comes to the end, Jake pops his head round the back door.

"Oh Mum, I forgot; we're going out this evening, so I won't be here for dinner." Then she turns to Jake. "Give me ten minutes..." and with that scoots out of the kitchen and rushes upstairs.

Jake and Louise chat easily while they wait and she remembers to pay him, which cheers him up no end. She tells him that she'd like Megan to stay in tomorrow, as she will be out and although Susan is coming to sit with Roberta, she'd just find it less stressful if everyone was under the same roof.

"I'll bring cards." he tells her, just as Megan reappears, looking lovely in jeans and a multicoloured blouse. Her damp hair curls around her chin and she has a hoodie over her arm.

"There's a band playing in the gardens up at Heron Pond House." he tells Louise.

"No alcohol. That's all I ask," she says firmly, "and back by midnight."

"Don't fuss Mum!"

Then they are gone, without a care in the world.

"Exactly as it should be..." Louise says to herself, shutting the back door behind them. Then she turns to the stove and removes the pan of thin soup from the hob. She strains it through the sieve and pours it into a bowl, slices some brown bread and arranges the tray with a mug of sweet tea as well and takes it up to her mother.

Roberta is pleased with the plan for the following day. Susan is bright, cheerful and undemanding and it will take her nicely into Friday, when Joe will return. She is feeling more hopeful that she will survive that long.

"I spoke to Mark this evening." Louise tells her mother as she exchanges the empty mug of tea for a full one. Although Roberta says nothing, Louise instinctively knows that she is curious, so continues to tell her the news.

"He says he's a bit sore, but that's to be expected really. He can start eating solids in a day or two, they've told him that his stomach should be able to cope by then, but it's his leg that's driving him mad. It's hot there of course, but then unlike us here, everywhere is air conditioned so the itching must be the stitches I imagine. Anyway, he sounded like himself again and Izzy sounds less hysterical."

Roberta says nothing, and Louise decides it's a good sign. "Do you want me to sit with you?" she asks.

"No, there's a programme I want to watch, then that silly woman will be here to help me get ready for bed and hopefully she won't arrive until after it's finished. So no, if you don't mind, I'd like just to watch that. It's the last episode and I was chuffed to see that the series is being repeated and well, you see, last time round, I missed the last two. Funny that, I'd expected to miss them this time too." she says, winking at her daughter. Louise smiles sadly at her, then heads back to the kitchen to make her own dinner.

The peace and quiet lulls her into a pleasant state of mind as she prepares her meal; chopping, grating, sautéing. She sips at a glass of wine and plans how she will achieve the right kind of markings on the rocking horse, making a mental note to go to the big DIY store over the weekend to get some of the things she will need. The carer nods to her as she leaves and before she slides the risotto onto her plate, she takes a glass of water and another mug of tea up to her mother, who is almost grateful for the thought.

Louise sits down alone at the big kitchen table, with only the ticking of the clock for company, and seeing the diary open where

Megan had left it after copying out some of the entries, she pulls it towards her and reads as she eats.

5th July 1940

Bob's been given the all clear from the medic here and is waiting for his orders. They could come any day, so we're making the most of every minute. Normally, me and Mrs R run to meet the postie, but now we avoid him, cos he ain't that welcome just now.

≈

10th July 1940

I went with Bob to the station this morning and we said our goodbyes. His unit's been kitted out with new tanks that are ready to roll and he'll go straight to rejoin it. He said he'd write as soon as he knows anything and then he said he'd write even if he didn't know nothing. We was being so silly, laughing and cuddling and we was serious without being serious. Funny that we can do that, despite where he's going and what he's got to do when he gets there, or maybe it's because of it, I dunno really.

What I am certain of is, that we're both sure and we both know how we feel. He ain't going with no worries on that account and he ain't leaving me with any. I trust him and he trusts me and that goes almost as far as love and I know I love him. I know that, because I ain't never felt like this about anyone before and I also know that when he looks at me, he ain't neither! His smile makes my whole world right, just like our song goes.

≈

18th July 1940

The Hun are flying their planes over the channel, they think because we left France in a bit of a hurry, we can't defend our home and we're ripe for the picking. Well they're wrong about that.

Alice phoned to say not to worry if we don't hear from her. They're up to their necks with work, but she's inside the command room, not ground crew as such, so we're not to worry. It's hard not to though.

I've got so much work to do, me body aches with tiredness at night and sleep comes quite quickly. The other girls are a right laugh. There's three of them, Pauline and Daisy are from North London and Erin's from Liverpool, so we city girls are putting our backs into the countryside. We're going to feed everyone!

≈

23rd July 1940

Got a letter from Bob. It's North Africa he's heading off to. He sailed on the 20th, but I don't think even he knows where to exactly. We made our own code up for the world before he left, one that the censors wouldn't know. As I said to Mrs R, it's good that he's a country boy, otherwise with his colouring he'd burn real quick under that desert sun.

It's a long way though and the only way there is over an ocean full of U-boats, which none of us try to think about. Mr R said he thought that the navy would be giving an escort to all our boys and all that equipment. I hope he's right. Just as well we're a naval country. I mean, all those convoys coming and going all over the place with food, men, oil and goodness knows what else, it's a wonder we got enough ships!

Got a quick note from Vic. He had a twenty four hour turnaround in Southampton, so no time to go a-visiting, but he sounded happy and more like his old self which I suppose is something. Course he's back out at sea too now, so my hopes for his safety go that way as well.

≈

8th August 1940

When we're not in the fields, we're glued to the radio. Those Hun just keep on coming in their planes and our lads just keep on going up to meet them. Mum says sometimes you see a dogfight, as they're called, up above the city or the river and her heart just flies up to her mouth and stops there. Sometimes she's not sure which plane goes down on fire and which pilot has been able to get out before it crashes. If they live, the Hun pilots are prisoners, but at least our boys are already home. Everyone's looking out for them after all, so they can get treated quickly if they're hurt. Otherwise, they catch a lift back to their airfield and are back up there as soon as they can be given another plane.

Mr R said that they're trying to knock out our air force, so that we can't stop them invading. Well they're making a big mistake there, that's what we all say. Every single one of us is behind our lads what's up there fighting back for all of us.

No word from Bob yet, but there's every chance they're not there yet, wherever there is of course. That's what we keep telling ourselves and then it's back to the harvest. After all, it ain't going to get itself in and as we're going to have a front in Africa, it's got to feed the lads there too.

≈

20th August 1940

Alice came home with a forty eight hour pass. She was grey with exhaustion and I swear I've never seen anyone that tired. She told us that if we thought she looked tired, we ought to see some of the pilots and ground crew, on their knees she said they were. She said she didn't want to sleep though, just to breathe fresh air and listen to silence, that was all she wanted.

After dinner we sat outside and she was smoking one cigarette after another and her hands were shaking really badly, so I asked her to tell me. I told her that Bob had said telling me had helped him, so maybe it would help her too.

She said that her job has been to plot the planes on a big map, so that the air chiefs can plan who has to do what, where and when and her friend Angela is on the radio to the pilots. She says the call to scramble has been relentless and that there have been terrible losses of people, not just the RAF boys but WAAFs even and ground crew people too. The Hun have been targeting the airfield itself and most of them have taken a beating at one time or another.

She said the key thing was to get the planes and the pilots up and off the ground, so they weren't sitting ducks. I asked her if she'd been scared when the bombs started falling, but she said no, not really, you just had to keep focused on what you were doing, because that was why you were there. Fancy her saying that, she's younger than me. I wonder if it's the training, or like Bob said, when you're there, you just have to do whatever it is that needs doing. Can it really be as simple as that?

She said the really frightening part was afterwards, when it was over, your heart just went funny when fewer planes came back than went out. Or after the airfield had been bombed and she went outside to help, seeing people she knew dead or injured, that was hard for her. Well it would be hard for anyone, wouldn't it? But not as hard as Angela's job. She shook even more when I asked why.

Apparently she hears them as they go down, if they can't bale out cos they're on fire, or trapped. So she hears them right up until they die. We both sat in silence for a while. I can't, no, I don't want to imagine that.

Alice said that at least once a week new lads arrive, all fresh faced and eager, then 'phut' too many of 'em are gone and so another lot arrive to take their places. 'Angela hears them going down, while I just push a little model to one side, out of the way. What is this madness Lil?' she asked me, her face all puzzled.

Apparently, most of the pilots are the same age as me, or even younger. None of us shouldn't have to be a part of this, but we are, so what could I say to her?

She started crying then and I just held her. She said they were just ordinary people and that she should be out dancing with all these young blokes, not worrying if next week they'll still be alive, never mind next year. 'There won't be any left to marry soon,' she whimpered, 'that bastard Hitler will make spinsters out of all of us.'

She said that one of the pilots played the piano. He was quite a bit older than the others, maybe twenty eight or twenty nine and was an old school airman, an original. He had thick black hair and a handlebar moustache and it made her laugh, because despite everything he kept it in such good condition. He never said much, just played for hours on end, smoking with his head down. Most of the men he'd arrived with had gone, there was just him and one other left. She told me that on the last night before her leave, when they went into the mess it was quiet and there weren't no one at the piano.

We sat there for hours, she said she was scared and didn't want to go to bed, but eventually she fell asleep against me shoulder and I just sat there with her until Mrs R came to get her. I know I would have wanted Mum if I'd been in her place, so I wrote to her before going to sleep meself.

≈

22nd August 1940

We listened to Mr Churchill say thank you to all them pilots on behalf of all of us. He said that never was so much owed by so many to so few. After everything Alice told me, I knew he was right and I was pleased that he knew it too.

I mean, I know he's an important man with an important job, but what he said needed saying to all those people who maybe don't understand, who maybe don't have an Alice or an Angela in the family and who were lucky enough not lose their lads like that.

What he didn't say though, was that it would mean a quick end to this war and nothing he said leads us to think that might be the case, so it looks like we have to fight on.

Mr R says we have to fight in the fields too, backbreaking though it is. The tractor's gone and given up the ghost again and Bob ain't here to put it right.

Joyce wrote to me to say that Charlie's been posted to Duxford as a mechanic. He's always enjoyed messing around with engines he has, so I bet he's well chuffed to be able to work on planes now. She's hopeful she'll see a bit more of him, cos it's not that far outside London after all and he's put in for married quarters, so there's a chance she'll get to join him. Like we said, every minute together counts for something now, which ain't fair, but it don't change the fact of it.

She said Tommy's been accepted in the infantry and is waiting for his sailing, though no one knows yet where to. It was nice to hear from her and she put in a pot of face cream, saying she thought I might need it with all the sun, wind and rain we've been having. I must say me skin drank it up in no time, so I reckon she's right. I joked with Mrs R that Bob might have a change of heart and mind if I get all wizened up by the sun. Made her laugh it did.

≈

The phone in the hall rings, pulling Louise back to the twenty first century. She closes the diary and makes her way to the stand to answer it, thinking about Jake, who will be nineteen next birthday and who in another time, could have been one of the few. When she picks up the handset, she is surprised to hear her husband's voice. He has been unable to reach either her or Megan on their mobiles and he is worried.

Chapter seventeen

As Peter rambles on, amiably enough but a little incoherently, Louise realises that he has been drinking. The initial pleasure at hearing his voice and the worry in it vaporises and she is quickly irritated with him, something he can hear in the shortness of her tone.

"Look, we're fine. My phone needed charging earlier and I forgot, so it's probably dead by now and Megan is at a concert with her boyfriend, so she..."

"Boyfriend?" he cuts in sharply, "Since when has Megan had a boyfriend?"

Louise sighs. "It's early days, so keep your hair on. He's actually very nice." She smiles as she recalls the sight of them walking up the drive hand in hand.

He grunts in reply and she wonders whose judgement he is questioning, hers or their daughter's. She doesn't respond and after a moment or two of silence he changes tack.

"Why are you doing this to me Lou?" His tone has softened and the words catch her off guard.

"I'm not doing anything to you." she replies carefully.

"Yes you are, you're cutting me out. I don't know what's going on up there. Hell, I didn't even know my daughter had a boyfriend. If that's not cutting me out, then please tell me what is."

Louise says nothing and once more there is silence for a while. Again, he breaks first.

"Look, I've said I'm sorry, I'm not seeing her anymore. These things happen; you know that, it's how we started. Christ Lou, what more do you want?"

His voice is a mixture of irritation and suffering, and she is surprised that neither have any effect on her.

"No Peter, these things don't just happen, the people involved have to want it to happen."

Her voice is even. It is, she realises, a simple fact and one she can both say and mean now without tears.

"You are one of the people involved." he replies. "Have you considered your role in all this? After all, you're not just some innocent bystander."

He's using the velvety tone, the one she always loved to listen to, the one that used to make her think that everything would be all right, because he would know how to make everything right again. She smiles as she realises something.

"Yes..." she says quietly, "Yes, that's exactly what I am considering. That very fact is actually key to all this I think."

"And...?" he enquires softly, as though he already knows the answer.

"And I'm not twenty anymore." she tells him.

"What the blazes is that supposed to mean?" he demands testily, clearly cross again.

"It means that back then, you were my world and nothing else existed for me. I was yours; body, mind and soul, completely and utterly yours and I was blissfully happy for a long time. But things change; nothing can stay the same forever, even you must realise that. Now, twenty years later, I am my mother's daughter and not only does she need me, I actually want to be here for her. After all, there won't be another opportunity. I am also Megan's mother and she is at a very important stage right now, one that will be over all too quickly and I don't want to miss it. I am also me and I find that I like my job, I want to spend time with my friends and I want a husband who will on occasion support me when I need help, and not go running off to fuck someone who makes him feel good about himself, especially when I get overtired and can no longer put him first, because in actual fact he's the one who needs least from me."

There, she has said it and she waits, slightly breathless. She hadn't meant to, but now it is out it feels good, it feels right and she fights down her natural instinct to apologise and to try and take it back. You never can anyway, she reminds herself, once something is said it can never be completely forgotten; it can always be used later.

"I don't understand you anymore Lou." he says, and sighs softly before ringing off.

It is a move that is intended to undermine her, to make her call him back, but instead she slowly lowers the handset onto the cradle and returns to the kitchen. She is shaking, and at first she heads for the cupboard, thinking a small whiskey will help, but then she changes her mind and puts the kettle on instead.

She sits back down at the table with the hot mug and her granny, instinctively knowing that she would be grinning at her, so she smiles back at the empty space across the table.

12th September 1940

I'm so worried, cos the Hun have been dropping bombs on our cities every night. Some of the air raid shelters don't seem to be much cop and one of the ones at home near the flats collapsed, killing almost everyone inside. It was the one Rita and her family would normally be using, thank The Lord they weren't that night.

She said in her last letter she was going to move to Portsmouth with Connor, cos that's where Tom's based. He's got them a nice flat down there and there are other naval wives, so she'll be with women that understand. Hopefully she'll be out of the mess that London's in. I wrote to Mum to say I'm thinking of coming back. There must be war work in a city that big that I can do and at least I'd be with her.

Finally I got two letters from Bob and one from Vic. Honestly, I spend all me time looking out for the postie on his bike. Don't matter where I am on the farm, I get neckache from craning so much. Thankfully, when there is something for me Mrs R sends word.

I got a short note from him saying that they'd had their first show and that he was all right, no more than a skirmish really, just to test the new girls out. Apparently the new tanks need some work, as they're not immune to the sand as they'd all hoped, but he said that it was giving him something to do when it was quiet. I was able to share that one with his parents, even though it was a bit old.

Then in the same post was a really long letter and I didn't share that one. It was funny, him saying that as a farmer he never thought a barren place would be captivating or that the desert would be beautiful. He thought miles of sand would be boring at best and sad at worst. But he says it ain't like that at all, and it seems to me from what he wrote, that in many ways it's a magical place.

His descriptions certainly captivate me. During the day the blue sky goes on forever and at night it turns black, but blacker than any black he's ever seen. He said it was like two completely different places and that little was the same at night as in the day. He prefers the night after the blistering heat of the day, when there is the cold wind and everything is so clear it makes him feel so small, sitting there under a black sky filled with so many stars that it would take more than one lifetime to count them all. I understand that feeling and he would remember it from other chats we've had, either in person or on paper.

He promised me that when this was all over he's taking me out there to show me the desert so I can see it for meself, he said if I thought the sea was big, I should see this. I almost can from the way he describes it and if I close me eyes, I'm there with him holding his hand.

Vic sounded ok, given what he's been through. He said this last trip had been the worst so far. A couple of U-boats had been tracking the convoy and they'd lost a couple of merchants and one navy ship. They hadn't been able to pick everyone up and he knew one of the sailors quite well, sailed with him on more than one occasion and it was only luck this time that they were on different ships in the same convoy.

He said that before he goes back he was going to go round and see the lad's parents, cos they live in Southampton. Apparently he was due to get wed next month, really excited about it Vic said, and why wouldn't he be? I wonder how his fiancée will take the news.

That's so like Vic to do that, it'll be hard though. He said he wants to tell them something about his life at sea, maybe something they don't already know, something to keep his memory alive for all of them, Vic included.

I hate this war, I hate what it's doing to us and how it's making us think and behave. This shouldn't be happening to us.

<u>Later</u>

We went into Great Maddely and watched the Pathé news. Now I'm even more worried about Mum and the others.

≈

19th September 1940

It seems that the bombing in London is relentless. It's been every night for nearly two weeks now and that's after all the daylight raids in the summer. How many more bombs can they have? This waiting for news is driving me mad. Up here, the birds sing, the crops grow, cows mosey about bellowing to be milked and the sun shines (when it don't rain). Somewhere out there and in danger, are all the people I love. No letters for a week now, not from anyone. Mum said in her last one not to come back, it would worry her more, but this is killing me.

≈

25th September 1940

How can Mum be gone? I still don't understand. And why wasn't I there?

≈

20th October 1940

Mrs R said to try and write in me diary. She's right, I can't write to Bob with so much sadness on me mind and closing off me heart, that's just not fair on him, he's so far away. He can't hold me, he can't make it all right, though I know he'd want to. But the truth is, no one can make it all right now.

Vic came to the farm last week. It was so good to see him, cos he understood and he knows how I feel. Of course he feels the same, neither of us can believe it. He was so sad that he couldn't be at the funeral and that he couldn't say goodbye proper like. What could I say to him? Me and Auntie Eth was there along with loads of other people, but Mum weren't there. I couldn't find her, I couldn't find her anywhere, that's the truth of it.

I didn't stay over, I mean I ain't got no home there no more and to be honest, I don't remember much of either journey, there or back. Mr R made all the arrangements, he took me to the station and then picked me up when I got back. We didn't talk much, but I got the feeling he understood.

Vic said the bombs are still falling, every night they come. That's six weeks now, how can there be anything left?

How can everything be gone?

How can there be nothing left but the memories we have of her?

He said he stood there where the flats used to be, where we grew up, where so much of our lives happened and all he saw was blackened and charred rubble. He said he'd hoped to find something of Mum's treasure box, even though he knew it were a daft thought, but still he hoped. I understood that. Of course I didn't go to the flats, didn't have time, but even if I had I wouldn't have, but if I had, I would've looked too. I would've hoped that something of those special treasures were left.

He told me not to go back, cos he said it'd break my heart even more than it's already broke. He told me she wouldn't want that. He said she'd want us to be strong and brave and to go on and be happy and that was the best way we could remember her, by having a good life. I know he's right and I know she'd say that, but how can I be happy?

I told him what had happened, or as much as anyone knew anyway. Apparently Mum'd gone with Auntie Eth and Joyce to the underground, just like they'd been doing every night and halfway there she remembered she'd left her box with all her treasures in it on the bed. Auntie Eth said she took it with her every night, but that evening she'd been flustered, cos the bombing had been day time as well as night time. Everyone's nerves were frayed and of course everyone was exhausted by that time too. What with one thing and another, she'd forgotten it and I know just how special that box was to her, it had all her mementos and memories in there.

Neither me nor Vic is surprised what she'd said to them. 'I'll nip back quick like, while you go and get our spot ready, I'll be back in a jiffy.' Course she was still carrying her share of the stuff they normally take down with them and that will have slowed her down I daresay. She must have got back to the flat and maybe even have got the box and been heading back down the stairs, but we'll never know, not for certain.

I keep reading her last letter. I must ask Auntie Eth if them peaches were good. I wish she'd been able to have cream with them. I wish so many things. I know it's a stupid thing, but she was so looking forward to them and she deserved them, that's why I keep hoping she got to have to them.

I hope it was quick, God I hope it was quick. When he told me about all the charred rubble, no I ain't going to think about that. I'm going to remember her properly, like how she really was.

Mum said I have to write to Bob a lot, cos he needs me letters to give him something to come home for. I haven't been able to write a single word though, not since Auntie Eth phoned Mrs R and asked her to tell me what had happened. I must though, I must. After all, Mum always knew best and I mustn't let her down. I mustn't do that, wouldn't be fair. I'll write to him now, that's what I'll do.

≈

Louise sees a couple of discoloured patches on the page and tears well up in her own eyes. She feels sad for Lillian, the grandmother she loved so much. Sad that she suffered and sad that she had never been able to share any of this. She also feels sad for herself, because there was never the opportunity to comfort her and now of course, she is gone too.

She is sad that her own mother is dying and that they cannot love each other as well as they should and that as far as she can tell, neither of them really knows why. She feels sad that she and Peter have come to this point in their marriage and that so much appears to have been lost, things that she has no idea how to find again, either in herself or in him.

When Megan returns from the gig, she finds her mother quietly weeping in the kitchen. Louise wordlessly points to the diary entry and Virginia's final letter, which is sitting open on the table.

"It was the... last one, that's why it was on the... top." she tells her daughter, hiccupping slightly.

Megan's eyes quickly scan the page over her mother's shoulder and silent tears also trickle down her cheeks. She feels a deep sense of pity for Lillian, who in some ways, she has come to think of as a friend.

"Poor Lillian." she whispers, running her fingers through her mother's short hair.

"Yes... anyway, you're home early, no good?" Louise asks, wiping her eyes with the back of her hand.

"Mum, it's pouring down and it's not that early either." Megan is laughing at her, knowing that she has been totally absorbed in what she was reading. "Look, I'm soaked!"

"Go and get changed into something dry and I'll make cocoa. Have you eaten?"

"Doh! It's gone eleven, so yes..."

Louise playfully throws the tea towel at her daughter, but she dodges out of the way and out of the door.

They sit at the kitchen table together, cradling big mugs of chocolaty milk. Megan tells her mother about the band and Louise tells her daughter that her father had been trying to reach her.

"I left my phone upstairs..." she admits, looking a little shamefaced.

"Never mind, phone him tomorrow. Not too early though, I can't remember which way the time difference goes and he was going out with friends tonight..."

It is not that Louise is trying to be kind to him; really, she doesn't want her daughter to get her head bitten off if he has a hangover.

"Mmm... all right. Shall we read the next entry, to see if she's ok?" Megan nods towards the diary.

"Yes... let's." Louise pulls it towards her and begins to read.

24th October 1940

I got a letter from Bob today. Mrs R had written to tell him and so had Alice. His words were almost like he was here with me. He wants me to promise that should anything happen that upsets me, I won't keep it from him like I've been doing, because it hurts him more not knowing what I'm going through. He said we both have to understand some of what the life that the other is living is really like, good things and bad and even the boring bits, otherwise these months apart might break us and he can't bear the thought of that. We have to be together through everything, that way the miles don't count and the time apart don't matter. 'We have to be together, even though we're apart', that's what he said and that's what we both want more than anything, so I know he's right.

I sent a letter to him yesterday and I'll write another today. We don't always get our letters in the right order, so as usual Mum was right when she said to write a lot and not to wait for his. I s'pose they all catch up with each other in the end.

I feel a bit like a windup toy. I do everything I'm s'posed to, but a bit of me has gone somewhere else, somewhere I can't quite find me way out of. I catch meself thinking 'oh, I must ask Mum that', or 'I must write about that, it'll make her smile' and then I remember.

I still ask her anyway and I tell her things, I just don't have to write them now and sometimes I swear I get an answer, but maybe that's just because I know what she'd say. I don't feel like she's too far away at those times, so I don't care what anyone might think. Other times though, well I miss her so much it hurts right inside.

Auntie Eth wrote to say what her new address is. Mind you, she's out at work all day and down the shelter all night, so it's not much of a new home, but then she's only got what she and Joyce had carried that night, cos they lost everything they didn't have in the shelter with them. She's staying with Charlie's mum, who's on her own now, and Joyce and Tish are there too. Joyce is looking to go nearer to Duxford if possible though, as there's war work out that way that she could do.

Everything what was at home has gone. I can't get me head around that, anymore than I can really accept the fact that Mum's gone, along with the treasure box with all her special memories in it. The round table from the parlour, Dad's old overcoat, that vase she got for a wedding present and always hated but couldn't bear to part with, her sewing boxes and pin cushions, <u>everything</u>, even me good shoes.

The bombs still keep dropping every night, how much longer can it go on for?

≈

Megan wonders how her mum will feel when Roberta dies. Her grandmother is old and her mother is older than Lillian was when she was writing about the Blitz, so she supposes it will be different. They've had plenty of warning after all, but she still wonders if it can ever be that simple.

Louise puts the diary down and looks at her daughter, sensing what she might be thinking. She knows Megan won't ask about it, so she reaches across the table for her hand.

"I don't think it can ever be easy or the right time, but what Lillian says is right, don't you think? You just keep on talking to those that you love, and that way they don't seem so far away. That's what I did after she died. Granny I mean"

Louise pauses, to see what effect her words have, but is not prepared for what her daughter tells her.

"Gran said that Lillian never loved her and that by loving you so much, she drove a wedge between the two of you. Is that true?"

"She told you that?" Louise is shocked. "Well yes, we were close. I can't remember a time when Granny wasn't there, but Mum was always there too..."

As she speaks, she knows she is telling an untruth. It is not a lie as such, but it is not really true either. Roberta wasn't always there and even when she was, she often pushed Louise away. She still does, and it still hurts, but she is not yet ready or able to explain this to Megan.

"Maybe we'll understand more as we read more." she says, standing up and putting the empty mugs into the sink. They both know this a cop out, but they can accept it for now.

"Night Mum..." Megan kisses her mother's cheek and heads off to bed, her mind already thinking about the following day and what she wants to say to Jake.

Louise sits at the table for a while longer, listening to the sound of the rain and the steady ticking of the clock. She is remembering the Lillian she knew and loved and chides herself for forgetting that Virginia Loveday had died horribly in the Blitz. She must have known this; she must have been told it at one time or another, yet she had forgotten. It is possible, she concedes, that at the time she hadn't understood that it was so big or had left such a deep scar.

After all, she had never really wondered what Granny was like before the war, or who she might have been had it not happened. But sitting there in the family kitchen, in the shadows of a different time, at the very table where Lillian, Bob, Vic and even Virginia herself had once sat, she feels it keenly for the first time.

Pulling the diary towards her, she reads a few more entries, realising that all this happened during Lillian's first experience of life away from home. She wonders how she would have felt, if while at university her whole world had been turned upside down and she had been left stranded in her shared room, with nothing but what was in the cupboards.

"Oh Granny, I'm sorry." she whispers into the silence.

She knows that Lillian would of course have just brushed her words aside and hugged her, but she still feels that in some way she has let her down, and for that she is sad.

The last entry she reads before turning off the lights and going to bed begins to show some hope for the future, as though the darkness, while not completely gone, is not overwhelming anymore.

12th January 1941

It's Bob's birthday today, he's twenty four. I've not spent a birthday with him yet, not mine or his. That's not right.

I sat under the pear tree and wrote to him as if he was with me and we was chatting away. I can always find him there and I know that when he reads those letters, he can see me better too.

We know there's been a bit of a show over there, cos we get some reports in the papers and on the Pathé as well as the radio. They ain't always exactly the same, but the more bits you get, the better the picture we have of what might be going on, cos of course they can't tell us everything. We check the wounded and missing lists whenever they're published, just like everyone else does, and only breathe again properly when we see his name ain't there. But there's always lots of other names that are.

It's us against the Italians, cos that part of the desert is under their control and the Hun ain't there, but Mr R says it's only a matter of time before they arrive. He says that they like to be in charge and won't trust the others, even though they're supposed to be on the same side and that bit of the world don't even belong to them!

Waiting for the postie is a bit of a mix, cos he comes on his bike just like the telegram boy. From a distance you can't see which one it might be, so I don't breathe till I see it's the right one and I don't s'pose Mr and Mrs R do neither. We don't actually say that to each other though, just in case it puts a jinx on things.

Funny how superstitious we've all become, we try not to say nothing negative, 'just in case' we say. It's not right, I've never believed in this stuff before, but now in all this madness, it just ain't as easy to be sure about what to believe in.

Bob said they were setting off into the blue, which means he don't know when the post will catch up with him or when he'll get a chance to write again, but I do just as Mum told me and I keep on writing. At this rate, he'll get flattened when the postbag gets delivered, cos it'll have just his post in it!

In his last letter, he told me that when things get a bit dark out there, he thinks of me. He says he's got this photo of us together, one that Alice sent him and in it we're laughing and that to him it's clear we love each other. I'm sure I know the one he means. Alice took loads of pictures with her new camera last time we was all together and when we was having a play fight and laughing so much we was almost crying, she surprised us. I bet it's that one.

He told me that it helps him make sense of what they're trying to do out there. He says keeping the Suez open for our ships to get through with stuff we need from India and such places and keeping the Hun from getting their hands on the oil is the main objective, but behind it, I know he's making the world a safe place for me and our kiddies.

He says all these things to me, even though he's so far away. Mainly he tells me not to worry, but how can't I? He tries though and he always finishes every letter with something he knows will make me smile, something that's just between me and him.

≈

Louise closes the diary and smiles, wondering what Peter would have written to her, both at the beginning of their affair and now, almost at the end of their marriage.

Chapter eighteen

Roberta wakes with a start. The room is still in darkness and coming from a farming family, she knows that dawn is still several hours away. She slowly eases herself into a sitting position and winces at the pain these small movements cause. On the bedside table there are too many boxes and blister packs of pills, a glass of water, a flask of hot sweet tea and a small radio.

Her hands are shaking, but she manages to pour a cup of tea and take an assortment of tablets. After washing them down with water, she turns on the radio and hears a beautifully distinctive female voice singing American country music. Neither the singer nor the song are familiar, but as she cradles her tea, one of the lines catches her attention. 'God never gives us back our youth...'

"Ain't that the truth!" she mutters.

This used to be a favourite time of day, when everyone else was sound asleep and she could slip out of bed and steal some time that was hers alone. Sometimes she would sit outside, other times she would stay indoors, but wherever she sat, the point was to do nothing at all. To just enjoy sitting and simply being for a while, letting her mind wander or be still. No one was there to make demands, the house was silent and there was just her, floating free in the night air. Of course it was a different house and a different time, and she laughs quietly, almost capturing that very particular sensation again, but the pain pulls her back into her body, imprisoned in the bed.

She thinks about the children, turning their names over several times. Mark, Joe, Louise... all of them unique and so different from each other. Mark is definitely a Loveday; dark haired and blue eyed, able to be both passionate and light hearted at the same time. Louise has inherited the doggedness of the Flanders and Joe's steadfastness and mischievous nature mark him out as a Robinson.

She herself is a Robinson, both in looks and colouring and Joe was definitely her child. From the moment he arrived, no one could dispute the bond between them, as they were clearly from the same stock. She remembers Nana telling her how much like her father she was. It was something that had pleased them both and held them together whenever Lillian wished to prise them apart, or the very few times when she had tried to insert herself into their exclusive relationship.

Her thoughts linger on her father, who unlike her mother, was never absent. He was always a part of the family, always included in conversations. Nana had told her all about him, all the way throughout her childhood, leaving her in no doubt that he would have loved her as much as she did.

She fleetingly allows herself to wonder what life would have been like if he had lived. Could her mother have found it within her to love her only child? But there again, she tells herself, if he had lived, she may not have been an only child.

Being part of a larger family was something she could not begin to imagine and had always been bemused by the bickering, loving and playing that went on between her own three. It was alien to her and she recalls a particular game they played in the orchard, a place they always seemed to want to go to whenever they visited. No, she thinks, hang on a minute... it was a place her mother always encouraged them to go and play.

The orchard, along with the adjoining meadow, had not been sold during Lillian's lifetime. It had been left to Roberta in her will with the words, 'Your father can always be found there. If you need him, look under the pear tree.' Lillian had never understood that her daughter had never needed to look for her father; it was her mother who had been missing. They had both always known where to find him, but they had never been able to find each other.

Roberta dismisses the thought with a wave of her hand, just as she has always done, because nothing can be done with it now. But Mark... can anything be done there while there's still time? Or rather, should anything be done? She asks herself and if so, what precisely?

Louise also wakes up long before dawn. The rain has stopped and a slight breeze wafts in through the windows, lazily stirring the thin curtains. She watches them and in so doing, loses the ability to drift back off to sleep. She sits up and sips the tepid water on the bedside table, then needs the loo. On her way back to bed, her mother calls out.

"Louise, is that you?"

Sighing, Louise pops her head round the door. "You ok?"

"Apart from dying you mean?" her mother replies, with a mischievous glint in her eye.

Louise smiles and quips back, "You said we were all waiting to die. You're just a bit further ahead in the queue, that's all." She surprises herself with the words and her hand flies to her lips as though to stuff them back in.

"Go and wash your mouth out!" Roberta tells her sternly, but for a moment mother and daughter are united in a fit of giggles.

"I've got something on my mind." she says, wiping her eyes with the back of her hand and wheezing from the effort of laughing.

"Do you want to talk about it?" Now Louise is cautious, aware that the moment has passed.

"No I bloody don't. What I want is a glass of whisky to help me think. There's some in the cupboard downstairs in the kitchen, the one to the left of the range. At the back, on the top shelf there should be a bottle of single malt. I'll have a drop of that, but no ice mind."

Louise is unsure. "I don't know Mum. I mean, some of those tablets might not mix well with alcohol and..."

Her mother cuts her off. "What'll it do, kill me? I can't eat anything worth eating anymore. I can't sleep without being woken by pain, I can't get out of this damn bed on my own and I'm wearing what you may as well call a nappy. If I can't have a drop of something I fancy, well the Good Lord might as well take me now. After all, he's taken everything else already!"

She is breathless from the exertion and her face contorts with pain. Louise is frightened and doesn't want to antagonise her further.

"All right, all right, keep calm. Just breathe in and out for a bit, while I go and get you a glass."

Once sure she is alone, Roberta slumps back on the pillows.

Louise gives her mother the whiskey, then returns to her room and settles back in her own bed. She has left both bedroom doors open and in straining to hear sounds that are not there, sleep is effectively banished. Sighing, she struggles back up into a sitting position and turns the light on, then looks around the room as though she has never really seen it before.

Normally, when she stayed there as an adult with Peter, they slept in the other big room, the one Claire and Joe will be using this coming weekend. This one had been her room as a child and before that it had been her great aunt Alice's.

The floral wallpaper had once been pink, lilac and green on a creamy textured background and in its time had obviously been expensive. So not done now, she thinks to herself. These days it's almost a sin not to totally renovate one's home every few years, or even better, to move and start with a completely new canvas on which to display your wealth and personality. But here at Priory Meadows, little has changed in all of her life and possibly for much longer than that. Some bedrooms have received a fresh coat of paint over the years, with new carpets, mattresses and lampshades, but not all of them and not often. This room was one of those that had not.

Her thoughts move towards her great aunt Alice. Granny had stayed in touch with her when the rest of the family had abandoned her, including Roberta. A sign of the times she supposes, yet another example of misunderstanding and intolerance. Alice had been petite and pretty, even as an old lady, which is how Louise always thinks of her. She had come to visit on occasions when she was over and Louise remembers Lillian going to visit her and the nieces and nephews, as well as her cousin's kids too; all of them on the other side of the pond, the Lovedays, the Rawlingsons and the Oshiros.

Roberta had always been dismissive of those annual trips and never showed any interest at all. She would not let Lillian take Louise with her and as she didn't have a passport until she was nineteen, it had not been possible anyway. After Louise had left home, they planned a trip together, but then she met Peter and didn't want to leave him, so it was postponed. Then her father died and soon after that, Granny herself, so it never happened.

Louise is sad that in her youth she had not seen the merit of such a trip for what it was. Alice is long dead now, for she died before Lillian, but there will be her children. Ben and Virginia might still be living, as would their children. There is of course, her brother and Izzy too. All of them over there; spread about, but all under the same sky.

Louise had always appreciated Granny's specialness in relation to herself, but had never really understood just how special she was to so many other people too. She had met some of them when they'd come for the funeral, but she'd been too upset to really make an effort to get to know them. She had also been touched by the telegrams, cards and flowers sent by family members and friends who had not been able to travel. Megan and I will go as soon as this is all over she decides. It will be good for her, and good for me too.

As sleep clearly has no intention of returning, she makes her mind up to write to all these forgotten members of her family. She had found Lillian's address book when she was clearing out some drawers in what used to be the office. One of them might still be at the same address and would maybe know where the others were.

As she passes Roberta's room, she sees that the light is off and stands in the shadows, listening to her mother's shallow breathing. She does not know if the whiskey helped her with her problem, but it has clearly helped her sleep.

Once she has written what is effectively the same letter twelve times, sealed them in carefully addressed envelopes and taken them into the kitchen to be posted later on her way out, Louise turns her mind to supper. She needs to prepare something that Susan and Megan can warm up quickly, as well as something that her mother might be able to digest, something that isn't just thin tasteless broth.

She rootles around in the fridge freezer and decides on an eggy pie and also that she needs to do some serious shopping before Claire and Joe arrive. Megan finds her an hour or so later, stirring frozen vegetables into the cheesy egg mix. Her daughter has her phone in her hand, and has clearly been woken up by something she is not happy about.

"Toast or cereal?" she asks, as Megan sits down heavily at the table.

"Cereal. What'd you go and tell him about Jake for? It wasn't yours to tell and now he's all..." She lifts her shoulders and does a pompous sounding voice that makes her mother smile. 'You do realise that you are only fifteen... blah blah... there's plenty of time ahead of you... don't feel you need to rush into these things... how old is he? No, that really is too old... blah blah blah...'

She sighs deeply. "Really Mum!"

"I'm sorry darling, it just slipped out when he said he couldn't get hold of you..."

"That's it, blame me!" Megan interrupts crossly.

"It's a fact sweetie, nothing more." Louise ruffles her daughter's hair as she puts milk and a bowl of cereal in front of her.

"Ok... I s'pose." Megan grudgingly concedes. "What are they?" She points with her spoon at the pile of letters.

"I was thinking that we might take a trip to the States later in the year or early next year. Just you and me." Louise explains the plan and Megan approves.

"That'd be neat." But then her smile vanishes, for if they are to take a proper holiday, just the two of them, then matters must have been decided. She puts her spoon down and looks straight at her mother.

"So, you and Dad... over... I mean..." she trails off unhappily.

Louise sits down opposite her daughter. "To be honest... yes, something is over and I am not sure yet if there is anything new to take its place. For a while at least, we are going to be separate. I'm not sure just how it's going to work out yet; the three of us will have to talk about it when Dad gets back from Greece and before we go back to London. Maybe one of us will take a flat or something and we'll split our time between the two places. But right now, I do believe that we, your father and I, need some time apart to see if we can find a more..."

She pauses, choosing her words carefully. They need to be the right ones for both of their sakes, otherwise something important will be misunderstood.

"... A more grown up and less selfish way to be together. I'm not just talking about Dad; I mean it about me too."

Megan considers what her mother is telling her and nods. Really, it comes as no surprise and she is comforted by the thought that they will continue to try and work things out. She picks up her spoon and tries to smile, but it wobbles a bit.

Louise puts tea and a meal replacement drink, as well as toast and porridge, onto a tray and takes it up to Roberta, leaving her daughter to mull over her own thoughts. When she returns, having showered and dressed, she finds the kitchen empty and the pile of letters gone. She reaches for her mobile and is about to call and insist that Megan come straight back, when the back door opens and she appears.

"Good, there you are. I need you here today." Louise tells her. "I have to go shopping, because we're nearly out of all the basics. After lunch I'll go and collect Susan and bring her back and then I have to go and meet Cate at the station. I don't want to leave Gran alone, so do you mind staying home?" she asks hopefully. She doesn't want to insist, but will if she has to.

"No problem. I've got loads of bits for my project and now I need to start putting it together. I just went to post your letters, that's all. Can I spread myself out over the table?"

She has laid out all the voices she will use in date order and has tied each one to a specific event. They stretch across the table, starting with an eyewitness account of Kristallnacht in November 1938 and end with George VI's speech in August 1945. She has gaps though, and it these that she is busy listing. The siege of Stalingrad, the battle of Tobruk, something about the Arctic conveys, the Normandy landings, the liberation of Auschwitz, the feeding of Holland and the dropping of the atomic bomb on Nagasaki.

She has no voices from the various resistance movements, or from prisoners of war held by the Japanese. The US airmen who had been based in the UK and the many people from the commonwealth nations who answered the call are also silent on the matter, as are those from the forced soviet marches of the Poles after their 'liberation'. Her map of the world also needs some attention, but as she surveys it all she smiles, for it is at long last coming together.

As the nurse is leaving, she informs Megan that her grandmother would like some tea and company. She had been lost in her work and it takes her a few moments to grasp the idea, but before the woman has gone, the request has percolated through. She stands up and shakes her head to help bring her mind back to the present.

She sits with her gran for a while and tells her about the proposed holiday in the States. Then after, as she comes tripping down the stairs to make more tea, the sound of tyres on gravel tells them both that Louise is back.

Alone in her bedroom, Roberta begins to see that there is a way for her to make things right with her eldest son. The remaining and still unanswered question is: does he want things to be sorted out or not? After all, she tells herself, he was the one that walked out that day, never to return. He has never called to find out how she was doing, not even when the final diagnosis was made and she is certain that Joe will have told him, if not Louise as well. Admittedly she'd not called him either, nor had she written, not even on birthdays or at Christmas. "But he was the one that left, not me." she mutters crossly.

Roberta, Louise and Megan have lunch together upstairs, chatting away about the changes in the supermarket, the lack of flavour in tomatoes these days and the plans for the weekend. Louise confirms that it will just be Joe and Claire this time and Roberta is happy; she will see more of her favourite child and that naturally pleases her. After lunch she is clearly tired and while she has a nap, Louise goes to fetch Susan. Megan does the washing up and as she is putting the last of the plates away, she spies the diary and settles down to read a bit more.

22nd April 1941

Finally we got word from Bob. They've had a hard time of things of late, since that General Rommel arrived over there. Funny really, on the one hand he's clearly a more difficult enemy to beat than the Italians, yet there seems to be a lot of respect for the man. Even Bob writes about him differently. I don't understand and I said as much in the last letter to him. I also told him that on the news we learnt that we had over 130,000 Italian prisoners from North Africa alone. That's an awful lot of men. Mr R said there's talk of a POW camp being put near here and that if that's the case, he can put in for some workers. I s'pose it's only fair, maybe they can do some of the backbreaking harvesting and field preparation in the autumn, as that old tractor ain't no help at the moment.

Why can't he be here with us, working alongside us in the fields, coaxing that tractor back to life instead of a tank, instead of trying to stay alive while killing others? Why??

≈

27th April 1941

Got another letter today and it was good to hear that he was having a bit of a rest, cos he wrote from this hotel that he's been staying at near the coast. So for now he's safe and away from the front line, wherever that is in a desert.

He said he's never seen such white sand and the sea is so blue that it dazzles him. He reminded me that he's taking me to see it when this is all over. Imagine, a sea warm enough to swim in, like a bath almost and hardly any waves at all. It's gentle he says and relaxing. I can't believe that!

He wrote that those first couple of nights of sleeping in a real bed again were pure bliss and he has a shave every day at the hotel, a proper one done by a barber, with loads of soap and hot towels and he's had his hair cut too. I told his parents about that over dinner, thinking Mr R would appreciate the sentiment, but no! He said he wouldn't let anyone near him with no blooming cutthroat razor, specially a person you couldn't really be sure about! Made me and Mrs R laugh that did.

Bob said that for seven and six a night, he gets a bed, two meals and a shave in the morning. That's not bad really and I understand that it must feel like a luxury after sleeping on the hard ground next to the tank. It's such a pity that they can't always bring the lads home for their leave time, but no point dwelling on that, the seas ain't safe, so this is best. I understand that, but still.

He had fourteen letters to take on leave with him. It made him chuckle and I did too. I think some of his must have gone missing though, cos he speaks about things he's written before, only I can't find the letter it's in.

Vic's got some shore leave too. He hurt his shoulder on his last crossing, cos the weather was so bad and he slipped and got caught by a heavy bit of rope. Anyway, he's been signed off for a month to have it heal properly. Do him good I said, to spend some time at home with the family and he agreed, even though he won't get no pay. Knowing Vic though, he'll have a bit put aside. I offered to send some if he ain't, cos I hardly use my pay and now... well we won't go there.

Been so wet here, I can't remember the last day it didn't rain. I still go to write to Mum and I still hear her telling me to keep me chest warm. I made up a bit of onion broth last night, cos I did have a bit of a cough. I feel a bit better for it today. Aunt Eth sounded a bit brighter in her last letter, cos really, in that respect we're in the same boat. Mum's always been around for all of our lives. My mum, and her big sister. What'll we do now?

The night raids seem to be over, or at least they're not every night now. Almost eight months people say, just over London, with not that many nights where they didn't come. She says she still can't relax, the sirens still go and the bomb still come, but it's not the same and in some ways it's worse, cos you just don't know what to think.

I think she misses Tommy, Evan and Joyce, but at least she knows where three of her four are most of the time. No one's heard from Tommy for a while, but as I said to her, letters go missing and if she ain't had no telegram, then there's nothing to worry about. Course she misses Mum too, her birthday just recent was hard for us all.

≈

4th May 1941

There's talk of a new rationing system, one that'll include most things, not just food and petrol and it'll be done on a points system. The government has also said that they will set the prices for lots of things, cos we're all in this together and there's no call for some people getting rich on other people's misery. I reckon they're right there, but I'm not sure yet how it'll work.

Alice was home for two days. She looked a bit brighter than the last time I saw her and I told her so. She smiled and said she was just taking it a day at a time and that seemed to be working for her. She still smokes too much and don't eat enough though. Mrs R said the same! We went into town together and had a bit of a mosey round the shops and saw one of them new lunch places that's opened up near the school. Looked popular too and of course it's not rationed in the same way, so if you got the money, in you go!

Bob sent a short note and I can tell, even though he don't say as much, that he's having a hard time. I wish I could see him, I bet he's not eating or sleeping enough. It's so hard to imagine what it's like for him over there. Here we don't even get bombed, the days just start and end like they've always done. Not right really, to be in it, but not, at the same time. Count yourself lucky, that's what Mum would've said, but it's hard to do that when so many others ain't lucky at all.

≈

22nd May 1941

Got a long letter from Elsie. She sounds fine but she's clearly worried about Fred. She was hoping that he'd stop having the nightmares now that the raids have lessened off a bit, but on his nights off he don't get much sleep at all she says. He won't tell her everything that he saw and I must confess I don't like to let me mind wander in that direction too often, but sometimes I can't help it. I mean all that fire, them explosions, buildings falling, all the glass. It makes me shiver. I'm sure the people he found, dead or alive, weren't all nicely laid out, as though they were just having a kip. How do you forget that? How do you just go about your own business? But it's like they all say, you have to make yourself, cos if you don't, it's like saying Hitler has won. So Fred has his nightmares, then he gets up and goes back on duty.

≈

6th June 1941.

He's back!!!

He's here at the tank factory, down at Chobham in Surrey. He phoned this evening to say he arrived just an hour before and we got to speak for a whole five minutes. Imagine, actually talking and hearing each other's voices! He said he don't know yet how long he's here for, or if and when he'll have the chance to get up here, but I don't care. I'm hitching down there. I told Mrs R tonight and she said quite right too! We'll make our plans tomorrow when he phones again.

We got the new ration books now an all. Clothes! They're rationing clothes! I got sixty six coupons for the year. But a dress will take eleven! Me knickers alone are three coupons a go, so I'll be taking better care of them from now on.

Good job I don't need a new coat and that me work clothes are provided by the ministry. Wish Mum was here, she'd make two of me old ones into something new and I'd get a blouse too. I never did have her skill and I don't s'pose I'll find it in meself, not now, not without her to guide me.

≈

Megan smiles as she reads this entry, imagining what she might do if it weren't for the fact that Jake was coming to London in October. While she is not ready to speak of love, she is not ready to give him up either. She understands Lillian's need to see Bob, especially after such a long time apart. For them, all those years ago, so much had happened to the other in the intervening months and they must have wondered if things would still be the same for them. Before she can read any more, she hears the car doors slam outside and her phone burrs softly as a text arrives.

'Missing you. Only a few more hours and then I'll be there.'

She sighs happily as she reads the message and in just a few seconds, she is able to reply that it makes her happy and that she will meet him from the bus. Her mother and Susan come in through the back door, chatting and laughing about something or other and carrying armfuls of fresh flowers that have obviously been cut from a garden and not bought. She gets caught up in their good humour as they both hug her lightly and she eagerly jumps up to find some vases.

Chapter nineteen

Cate is beside herself with laughter as Louise tells her of her most recent conversation with her husband. "Good for you!" she finally manages to say, wiping her eyes and leaning over the gearstick to hug her friend. They are sitting in the car in the station car park, where they have been for over an hour, catching up on all the important gossip.

Louise is laughing too. "I never thought I could... I mean, in all the years we've been together, we've hardly ever rowed. On the rare occasions when there was a slight difference of opinion... well usually, I just assumed he was right and so did he. Whenever he went off because I was being unreasonable, well I followed him, pleading for him to come back and insisting that of course he was right. But... well... this time I didn't take back what I said or call him back. Most of all, I didn't apologise. I left it with him to mull over for a change."

"Well I hope he sees this as a wake-up call. No one is always right. It's impossible; we're human!" Cate tells her firmly.

Louise nods in agreement. "I told Megan that we needed to be apart for a while and that we have to try to find a more grown up way to be together. Really, I meant me as much as him. I've allowed him... no, more than that; I've pushed him into this position. If he's going to step down, that's if he even wants to... well, then... I've got to let him." She says this very slowly, then sighs deeply. "Trouble is, I'm not sure I know how to." Her bottom lip wobbles, much the same as her daughter's had earlier.

Cate looks at her with one eyebrow raised. "Really Lou! It seems to me that you already have. Now, what's for dinner? I'm starving. It may not be British Rail anymore, but I tell you, the sandwiches on the train were left over from the fifties! Is there a half decent Indian tucked away up here in the wilds do you think? I fancy a major pig-out, with loads of plates, full of different yumminess!"

Under Susan's watchful eye, Roberta eats a little of the eggy pie and finishes almost all of the meal replacement drink. They have been chatting about Arnold, but Roberta realises that in doing so, they often strayed onto the subject of Mark. It would be impossible not to, she thinks, for her husband had clearly shared so much of his relationship with his eldest son with his mistress.

"I'm glad he waited until after his father had gone to move to the States. I think it would have broken his heart to say goodbye to him, don't you think?" Susan says brightly. "But how silly of me! You must miss him awfully too." she adds, while pouring the tea.

She assumes, wrongly, that Mark must have been over already, or is on his way, or may even already be here, but that her visits have not overlapped with his. However, she says none of this, thinking it is not her place to pry.

Roberta does think about what Susan has just said, but chooses only to answer the first part, and carefully.

"I don't think he would have gone had his father lived. I think he would have stayed, but around here... how would that have worked out for him do you think?"

She takes the tea, thinking that maybe she did him a favour after all. As she stirs in even more sugar, she decides that this is indeed the case and that he has a lot to thank her for, so for a few hours that tiny nagging voice in the back of her mind is silenced.

The topic of conversation moves onto the flowers that are dotted about the room in vases. Susan is a passionate gardener and it is how she met Arnold. They were both entering delphiniums in a competition at the country fair. Neither won anything, but they had got talking, then laughing and over the course of a summer's afternoon, one thing had led to another. Arnold had loved growing things, while for Roberta it was work, but she had always appreciated the abundance of fresh vegetables and flowers that he produced. She loved to watch him tending their kitchen garden, so gentle with his plants, often so absorbed in what he was doing that he was totally oblivious of her. She smiles at the memory and sees that Susan has similar ones. She knows that theirs had been a shared passion, but she doesn't begrudge either of them their time together, not now.

Her nana could often be found pottering about in her large greenhouse and it was one of the things that she and Lillian did together, so she usually left them to it. There were always flowers in the hall and in the front parlour; always. For most of her life, Roberta has appreciated flowers in vases and the scent wafting around the room on the cool evening air takes her back to a place in time she is happy to go to and she begins to drift off to sleep.

Susan checks her watch and rises, assuming the carer will be along shortly. As she places everything on the tray, meaning to go, Roberta speaks quietly. "The children don't know about him and her. We never saw the need and I don't think anything has changed in that respect."

Susan looks at the wasted figure in the bed, but says nothing.

"He told you so much about himself; he must have told you that too." Roberta says pointedly.

"Yes, he did." Susan confirms. Then after a moment's thought, says she won't ever bring it up, but that she won't lie either.

"Fair enough... fair enough..." Roberta seems to slide into sleep with the words dying on her lips, leaving Susan feeling uncomfortable. She had never felt this way when she was Arnold's mistress and this is the first time it has happened since getting to know either Roberta or the rest of his family.

Downstairs in the kitchen, a raucous game of cheat is being played and she is invited to join them, which she does, quickly gaining the upper hand, much to their amazement.

"My misspent youth carried on for rather more years than is usual." she tells them mischievously, then shows them a different card game. They talk and play while the carer comes, does what is needed and then goes again. Later still, Susan leaves them to slowly and passionately say their goodbyes on the back doorstep, while she takes a flask of tea and a small jug of cool water up to Roberta, who doesn't seem to notice her at all.

When Megan rejoins Susan in the kitchen, a little flushed but happy, she finds her leafing through her school project. "Will you explain it to me?" she asks, genuinely interested.

"Sure..." Megan agrees, then sits down and begins spreading it out over the table.

"The title, as you can see, is way too broad. I mean the first thing I wondered was: who were these seventy million people? They were just the ones who died, so then you have to think about all those others; the ones that didn't. You know, those that lived through it. I mean you can't forget them either, can you?

"Then when Mum and I found Lillian's diary, she was my great grandmother, I began to see that these people were us, or who we might have been if we'd been born in a different time. I mean, there they were, most of them just going about their lives, then WHAM! The world goes mental and nothing is the same any more, not for the rich or the poor or the ones in the middle. And it was awesome, I mean it didn't matter where you were, it seems to me you were either in it or knew someone who was.

"I mean, what must it have been like? So I decided that although history is often lists of dates, you know... this battle, this politician, this king or queen... that sort of stuff. But Lillian was there: her mother died in the blitz, her sister-in-law saw the Battle of Britain and so were all these other people, and seventy million of them died. Like the photo of that woman on Wikipedia, shielding her baby as she gets shot. What happened to that baby? Or to the man that shot her?"

She shakes her head before continuing.

"So I'm trying to find voices of real people, to make the dates, the battles and everything they lived through more real. Real for me I mean, because of course it was always real for them."

Susan is thoughtful. "I don't spend much time thinking about it at all, not now, and in fact I've not thought about it for a long time, I must say. I was so young; ten when the war started, eleven when my mother died, also in the Blitz. My father had an accident at work and died from complications a year or so later, but the job he was doing wouldn't have existed if the war hadn't been on. So many things would have been different without it. I would have known them better, I wouldn't have been evacuated and then who knows what my life might have turned out like..."

She smiles at Megan. "That's not to say I've been unhappy with the way things have been and there's nothing I've done that I regret, but still, there were an awful lot of people who never had the chance to live any sort of life and not just here, but right around the world."

She pauses, shaking her head and Megan sees a tear roll down her cheek. "I'm sorry dear, I don't spend much time remembering. I've always been one for living in the moment, being in the now, not in the past, but maybe that's why. Maybe it's because I've always know the moment can be snatched away from you without so much as a by your leave.

"Funny really... you are so young, yet you are right; we shouldn't forget them, even those we never knew." She pats Megan's hand and tries to smile, but Megan can see it wobble.

"You see..." says Megan slowly, "you're one of those people from out of history, but you're sitting here with me now. You're as real as me, so that means we're connected. I mean maybe I couldn't be here in this world, in my world, if you hadn't been there in yours, then."

Susan has a faraway look in her eye and says nothing, so Megan rushes in to fill the silence. She is not sure if the wobble, which has not gone and if anything has become more pronounced, is a happy one or an unhappy one.

"In fact, you could be my evacuee's voice, well my British evacuee anyway. If you'd like that of course...?"

"Yes, that would be nice dear, what would you like to know?"

Susan moves her head to look at the young girl in front of her, trying to focus on her, but too much is stirring in the back of her mind and she finds it difficult, but thankfully Megan doesn't notice.

"Oh you know, a memory maybe, but nothing too long." she says, taking up the offer and shyly pushing a pad and a pen towards her. "Something that tells other people who weren't there a bit about what it was like..."

Susan laughs. "I'll think about it and bring you something next time, or perhaps in the morning if I can't sleep. Now, what about some cocoa?"

She stands up purposefully, eager to change the subject, surprised by the depth of feeling that is rising up inside her. She had been telling the truth when she said she rarely thought of those times and is beginning to wonder which floodgates are about to burst open.

Megan takes her cocoa up to bed with her, along with Lillian's diary. Susan takes hers outside and sits on one of the rickety chairs at the end of the garden, looking at the stars, lost in thoughts of a world she thought had vanished, but which she realises, is still alive in her mind and possibly in her heart too.

She is still there an hour or so later when Cate and Louise arrive. Louise goes to the house and returns with wine, a tub of chocolate ice cream and spoons, then the three of them sit there until gone midnight, talking and laughing. Cate and Susan are quickly easy with one another and between them they try to help Louise understand herself better.

Roberta hears their voices, but not the words, and is reminded of other times; when she was a child, and Nana and Grampy, uncles and aunts sat out there while she lay in the nursery bed. Her mother must have been there too she reasons, but she can no longer hear the sound of her voice or the tinkle of her laugh. "But then she never did laugh much," Roberta says to herself, "not then, anyroads." That was later, much later she recalls, straining to hear the other voices, the ones that are now long gone. In this way she is able to ignore the pain and drift back off to sleep, for a while at least.

Megan hears nothing of the conversation in the garden below, for she is listening to some music that Jake downloaded for her. They have resaid their goodnights by text and now she is reading the diary, completely lost in a past that is not her own.

28th July 1941

Got back this evening. I forgot to take me diary with me, but no matter, I'll never forget a single minute of our time in Chobham. He's back at his barracks now, but he'll be here next week anyway. He's got two weeks leave before he has to go back over there, but I'm not going to think about that, not yet anyway.

He told me about an Indian chap who's out there with him and we agreed it's amazing just how many people from all around the world and the colonies have come to help us. People who we never knew and we'll probably never know, upped and left their families and their homes and came, just cos we got into trouble when we said no to a bully.

Anyway, this chap told Bob that there's always cycles in life, just as there is when you grow things and after unhappiness, well happiness must come, just as sun follows rain. It always happens in nature and will always happen in life too he said. It makes sense we agreed. If you live a long life, there's bound to be good times and bad, but don't we always hope for good times to come when we're in the bad ones? So that must mean that we already believe in these cycles, even if we never put thought to it before.

Like Bob said, farmers know that you have to have rain, just as you have to have sun, otherwise things don't grow right. In the desert there's too much sun, so less grows, not more. He says it don't rain for years and years there. Imagine! Hah, it ain't like that here!

This bloke also said that he believes anything that is, can never not be. We had to think about that though and Bob laughed at me, cos he said I pulled such faces when I was thinking hard about something! Anyway, he said well just don't forget it, because you never know, one day it might just make sense to you and then you can explain it to me too!

We've been so lucky. He got to come back because they had teething problems with the new tanks and one of the top brass out there wrote to some of the brass here and complained or something like that. Anyway, they said if he had people who could come and show them how to tinker with the designs they'd be happy to listen, so this general puts Bob and another bloke on the first available flight!

When he described what it was like being so high up in the air, well I think I would have been really scared. He described flying over the sea and getting a proper idea of just how big it is, much more than from the boat he said and seeing all that sky at the same time. He said they flew above some clouds what must have looked flat from below, but were huge on the topside. I just can't imagine it, but I keep trying, as I don't s'pose I'll ever get the chance to find out for meself.

With him working all day it meant that while I was down there with him I had to find things to do in the daytime while he was at the factory, but that wasn't hard. I went to the Land Army office in the town and they soon found me some work! I told them I didn't want a billet, cos me and him were snug in our room at the pub on the common. We had to tell a bit of a lie when we took the room of course, but we will be wed soon enough. When he gets up here we'll go and get everything arranged, that way his parents can come. They'd like that, he said, and Alice might be able to get a pass too, if only for an overnight stay.

No, I don't s'pose I'll ever forget our time together, he said he won't neither. We're good together, that's for sure and like he said, without this bloody war we may never have met, our paths may never have crossed. But I reckon they would have one way or another. I mean, when two people are so right for each other, they'd have to find each other now, wouldn't they? Stands to reason I told him and he laughed at me for being so sure, but I know he thinks the same. I'm glad I waited for him and didn't take no chances with any of the others, it almost don't matter that the ring ain't on me finger yet. It's not like with Rita, I'm so very sure of Bob and he's so sure of me. We know we can trust each other with all those fragile bits of ourselves, as well as with the strong bits.

He said he knew as much that first time he came home and found me waiting here. I had to admit that for me it was when we was in London that I knew for certain and he smiled at me when he remembered our first date. What a pair of wusses!

Anyway, there's so much to do here that I need to get on with, so that when he gets here we can have a bit of time to ourselves. Of course Mrs R's over the moon that he gets two whole weeks at home. We've not said anything to her yet, we thought he could tell her when he gets here. Must write and tell Vic, he'll be so pleased.

≈

7th August 1941

Got a telegram from Viv. Vic's ship went down and there's no sign of him. She says he's presumed dead.

≈

Megan has to reread the entry several times before it makes sense to her.

"How?" she whispers to herself. "How can that be? Not Vic..." she says quietly to the empty room. "Not him, that's just not fair, he's a good guy, a really good guy..."

She flips the pages back to the photo taken in Naples. One of them is Vic and she desperately wants to know which one, for it is suddenly important to her that she knows his face. After all, she knows so much about him, but not what he looks like. She carefully eases the photo off the page and turns it over. On the back in faded ink, are the date and the words 'Me and Nat in Naples', nothing more.

Feeling sad, she turns back to the next entry, but silently promises herself and them that she will search all the albums and ask her mother, and grandmother too if necessary, tomorrow. There must be a picture somewhere she tells herself. There must be.

30th August 1941

Mrs R gave me the letter, the one that he left here when he came. He told her it was just in case, cos there were things, important things, that he didn't want left unsaid if the worst was to happen.

Me and Bob took it to read in our favourite spot. I was sorry that I never took Vic there, he would have liked it, but I never imagined we had so little time, or that he and Bob would never meet or share a pint together. Anyways, the view would have tickled him. It's not the sea of course, but lovely in its bigness anyway.

I told Bob that it was so like my big brother to have thought of that. I said I bet he left one each for the kiddies for when they're older and one for Viv too. When we read it, it was just like he was sitting there with us, talking to us. It made me laugh with some of the things he wanted me to remember, like the time I fell in the canal cos I was showing off and he had to fish me out and I cut my knee on the wall as he pulled me clear and then how I belted him for all I was worth as soon as I was on me own feet again. Then there was the first time he came back from the sea and I ran all the way down the stairs to meet him, but when I threw myself at him I tripped and landed sprawling at his feet. What a black eye I got from that! He made me cry once by pretending to be the bogey man when it was really dark one night, I must've been no more than four years old and eventually Mum came in and gave him a slap. He didn't talk to me for two days after that. I'd forgotten all about it though, cos normally he was there to protect me and teach me things, but we must have had our rows, only natural really and I must remember them. He weren't no saint, after all!

He said Ben and Ginny had to know me when this is all over and that it was up to me to tell them all about our life over here, so they would know that he was a real person who'd had a real life. He told me that I had to make sure that they knew how much he loved them and he told me never to forget that he loved me too.

Viv would do that too of course, she'd help the kiddies remember, but she's their mum and she'll have to live her life without him as best she can, but I can be that other voice, the one that knows other stuff, from before. He said he'd made sure there was a bit put aside for the family, but no one knows how long this'll last for, so if I can, can I send some over whenever I've a bit spare? I've already done that, I don't need much of what Mr R gives me every week and I'm well fed here, so from now on, I'll do it every week. I mean, he said one pound buys five dollars, so I hope Viv will be able to do all right on that, I hope she can buy enough with five dollars. At least he could leave them a home. The roof over their heads ain't rented and that must be a comfort. Nothing else is going to be, after all. I still can't take it in. Me big brother gone, swallowed up by the sea he loved so much. How can that be?

He reminded me that he wasn't called, he volunteered. He chose to go back and he wanted to do his bit by doing the one thing he knew how to do well and I know that the crossings are important if we're going to win.

'We know when we set off that not all of us are going to see the end of this, but in doing our jobs we are doing what needs to be done if Hitler is to be defeated and he must be. You know that Lil, you know a world where he wins is not one I want my kiddies to grow up in.' he wrote. He wants them to understand why he went, why he felt he had to go and he wants them to know that it was because he loved them, not because he didn't.

Most of all, he asked me not to forget him. 'I don't want to be forgot Lil. Just because I ain't there with you all physically, don't mean I never existed. Remember me Lil, please don't forget me and don't let them neither.'

Silly beggar, how could I ever forget him? How?? He's me big brother, the one that was there for me when Mum weren't and when she was too. The one who could make me cry or laugh and who would help me even when I didn't know I needed helping. Me brother, gone just like that.

He said I had a duty to be happy. I owed it to him and Mum, and Dad too, even though I never knew him. How can I do that though? Honest, there are moments when I don't know how to carry on with them all gone. That's me whole family gone, taken from me by one war or another. What did I do? What did they do wrong? They were just trying to do the right thing or get by as best they could. That ain't no crime now, is it?

I was so glad Bob was here, cos he understands and we've delayed the wedding, I mean it should be a happy day. Nothing can make it all right, nothing, but having him here with me meant a lot, it really did. If I didn't know just how much he loves me before, well I certainly can't doubt it now.

Getting the news changed something though. When we made love it was different and although neither of us said so, I know we both thought it. Maybe it was a way of making sure that our bodies always remember the other one, not just our hearts and minds, but something real and solid like a body would remember differently and it was important, because it made us more real too somehow.

He's gone now, back to the desert where the birds don't sing, nothing much grows, the rain hardly ever falls to make it fresh and there are so many stars a man could lose his mind trying to count them all. God, if you're real, keep him safe. I've never asked for nothing before, only this one big, very big and important thing. Please keep him safe.

≈

As Louise passes Megan's open door, she hears her daughter sobbing softly. Megan is able to reassure her that she is fine, nothing bad has happened to her or Jake and that her father has not called and been difficult. She holds the open page up for her to read and Louise sits on the bed with her arm wrapped around her. As she reads, understanding dawns on her.

"Do you know what he looked like?" Megan whispers.

"Who? Uncle Vic or Granddad?" her mother asks.

"Vic."

Louise shakes her head. "No, but maybe in the box with all the letters there will be a picture. We'll look tomorrow, ok?"

Megan nods, but the tears start falling faster instead of subsiding. Her shoulders shake and she is beside herself with grief. Louise is worried and puzzled. "What's the matter sweetie? I mean he was older than Lillian and she died of old age."

"I... I... d... don't have enough words." hiccups her daughter.

"Not enough words?" repeats Louise a little stupidly, feeling she has missed something, but not at all sure what or where.

"My project. I only have five thousand words, but seventy million people died. How can I remember them all? I don't know their faces or their names... they all had faces and names. Vic had a face and that woman waiting to be shot, she must have had a name and her baby too." she wails.

"Hey darling, shhh. You can't remember people you never knew, silly. But you can make sure they are not forgotten and that's a really good thing to do, it's enough. Really, it's more than a lot of people ever get the chance to do."

She strokes her daughter's hair and holds her close until the shuddering stops.

"You can't change it sweetie, but you can help make sure it's not forgotten. There." She wipes Megan's face with a corner of the sheet. "It's all about life, it's always about life..." she mumbles quietly, remembering the conversation with her own mother and is even surer now than she was then, that she disagrees with Roberta. "It's not about death at all..."

Her daughter understands some of what she says, but not all, then nods and pulls away, sighing softly as she lies down. Louise kisses her on her cheek, puts the diary to one side and turns off the light.

"Night Mum..." Megan's voice follows her out and before she reaches the landing, she knows she is already asleep.

"Sweet dreams darling..." she murmurs as she makes her way to her own room, wondering if her daughter's sensitivity is a reflection of her hormones, or the situation that her parents have placed her in with their own confusion.

Probably a bit of both, she decides as she peels off her clothes.

Chapter twenty

Roberta is woken early by a sharp pain and lies in bed, feeling restless. While she waits for the medication to kick in, she scowls at the racket the birds are making. It keeps her from dozing and only the thought of Joe arriving later in the day calms her enough not to demand release from this world right now. When Louise eventually brings her breakfast, she is short with her and waves it away. Try as she might, she cannot hide the fact that she is in pain. Her eyes give her away and at the same time her daughter cannot help but notice how pale she is.

Megan is woken by Hannah. Her father has returned her confiscated phone and she is calling to reveal her own holiday secrets and to find out what has been happening to her best friend. She wants to do all of this before her parents wake up, for such is the news she wishes to share. His name is Dominic; he is seventeen and he looks a bit like the actor that plays Sam in their favourite programme, 'Supernatural'. His mother is English and his father is French, but they mainly live in New York. Squealing and laughing, the girls share everything and as Louise passes the now closed door, she smiles, for last night's 'episode' is clearly over.

Cate and Susan have a hurried cup of coffee and a slice of toast before Louise takes one of them to the station and the other one home. Susan has written her piece for Megan's project and she tentatively gives it to Louise.

She had thought long and hard before putting pen to paper. There were a million tiny fragments of those years floating around in her mind, but to make any kind of picture, more rather than less would be needed. She would have to explain herself in a way she has long since forgotten how to and of course she is no longer the same person; life has moved her to a different time, one which requires her to have a different persona.

As she listens to Louise read the words aloud, they seem somehow sparse and cold, but Megan had asked for something short, she reminds herself. She is also aware that they have stirred a childish emotion. A fear without a name is rising within her but she quickly pushes it back down.

Susan Moresby, child evacuee.

I was just ten years old when I was evacuated from London to Lincoln. It was the end of November 1939. I was an only child and had never been separated from my mother before and although I was more scared than anything else, I was a little bit excited too. As we waited on the station concourse at St Pancras, she held my hand tightly and we were surrounded by more children than I had ever seen before. It was a cold morning, but the sky was blue, I shall never forget that.

With me I had a small suitcase, a satchel and my favourite doll Mildred, who like me, had her best clothes on. In my satchel I had a book of Girl's Own stories, some sandwiches, an apple, some toffees, a ten shilling note, a sixpence and two half pennies in change, a new pad of writing paper, a brand new fountain pen and a bottle of ink, twenty six first class stamps and twenty six envelopes, already neatly addressed to my mother. More were to be sent later if the war lasted longer than the six months she had allowed for.

I was to write once a week, starting from the first morning in my new home and I was under strict instructions to get the address of the family I was to stay with right. If the people were mean, beat me or starved me, I was to write that the family were really kind and that it was just like being at Auntie Betty's. That was our secret code. Mum said one mention of Auntie Betty and she'd be up there like a shot to take me away. That was her promise.

That is my last memory of her; standing on the platform waving to me, but she wrote two or three times a week, sometimes more, right up to the day before she died, which was almost a year later. The family, the Chepworths, were in fact very kind to me and we stayed in touch for years after the war and they even came to my wedding.

"Of course when it was all over, there had been no therapy or counselling." she quietly explains to Louise and Cate. "Too many people had been hurt or damaged by it all and there would never have been enough to go round." She smiles as she remembers some of the people she knew at that time. "Most of us wouldn't have known what to do with a counselling session anyway, even if we'd been offered one."

No, she thinks, I dealt with it all the best way I could and there's no point in revisiting it now. It's so long ago...

Megan finally comes down for breakfast, happy to have caught up with Hannah, but finds the kitchen empty. There is a note from her mother next to Susan's, which she reads as she drinks juice straight from the carton, something she is not allowed to do.

Morning sweetie.

I'm taking Susan home and dropping Cate off at the station. Then I need to do a big shop before Joe and Claire arrive, but I should be back about elevenish. Once the carer has been, can you make Gran some breakfast and spend some time with her? I'm going to call the doctor as soon as the surgery opens, to be honest I'm a bit worried. Call me if you need me.

Love Mum xx

She goes back upstairs to her grandmother's room and finds her alone and bad tempered. The carer has been and gone, and yes, some tea would be nice if anyone could be bothered to make some and a bit of porridge wouldn't go amiss either. Then she grumbles about the draught and tells her to shut the window and the one on the landing before doing anything else.

Sighing, Megan does as she is asked and heads back down to the kitchen, not at all sure how to make porridge without a microwave. She carefully follows the instructions on the side of the packet, once she has got over the horror of finding that the oats are not even in individual portion packs.

She makes herself some toast and when the tray is ready, she gingerly makes her way back upstairs and they have breakfast together. Roberta adds a lot of sugar to both the tea and the porridge, but is complimentary on the texture and flavour and the silence becomes more companionable. Once she has eaten enough, she pushes the half empty bowl away and picks up the tea, then smiles at her granddaughter and asks what she has found to do while she's been there. The project is explained in more detail and Susan's piece is retrieved from the kitchen, then it is read and discussed.

Despite the age gap between them, neither can imagine being separated from their families while still so young. They discuss the differences between Susan's evacuation and Roberta leaving for boarding school at fourteen. Roberta shares a few happy memories of those days and Megan feels bold enough to ask the question.

"Do you know where I can find a picture of your uncle Vic, you know, Lillian's brother?"

Roberta sips her tea, looking over the rim of the cup and silence stretches between them again.

"Why...?" she eventually asks.

Megan almost loses her nerve, but it is important and she finds the courage to say what she is thinking.

"He died on one of the Atlantic convoys in the war. His ship sank, so I suppose he drowned, although maybe there are other ways of dying, even on a sinking ship. I mean if you've been torpedoed, there'd be an explosion, wouldn't there?" She shudders as she imagines fire and chaos, but quickly banishes the thought; it is too horrible.

"Anyway, I've read so much about him and his life, but I don't know what he looked like and I'd like to. He said in his last letter to Lillian that he didn't want to be forgotten and that he didn't want his children to not remember him. He asked her to make sure that they got to feel as though they really knew him, even though he couldn't be there and it was up to her to make sure that he was a real person to them and that he'd had a real life. I know why he went on those convoys and now I want to know what he looked like. I want him to be real to me too." Tears fill her eyes as she explains this and Roberta is shocked to discover that the words have dredged up something from long ago.

"Find me that letter." she says quietly. "I want to read it. It'll be in the box with all the other stuff I daresay. And bring a fresh pot of tea up while you're at it."

She dismisses her granddaughter, takes some more tablets and closes her eyes. She is aware that she may have got something wrong and is not at all sure how she might feel about it.

In looking for the letter, Megan discovers a faded photo of Vic. He is holding Ben's hand and Ginny is draped on his shoulder, sucking her thumb, with her head nestled next to his. The three of them are smiling for the camera and she stares in wonder at his face. The letter is easy to find, because of course it is the top one in that bundle.

She puts the photo with the letter and takes the tray back upstairs to her gran's room. Roberta moves over a little in bed and once fresh tea has been poured, the two of them arrange themselves comfortably side by side. No sooner have they taken the letter from the envelope and opened it, when Louise appears in the doorway with the doctor.

Megan leaves them to it and goes downstairs, where the beeping of her phone tells her she has messages. There are five from Hannah, two from Jake and everything else is forgotten as she attends to them. Jake is proposing a film and pizza, something she is very happy to agree to. Later, when she tells Louise, she smiles and says, "Fine, but you have to help get the house ready before your aunt and uncle arrive."

"Deal!" Megan shouts and leaps up, ready for action. Working together, the beds are changed, the washing is done and hung out, the bathrooms are cleaned and the house is hoovered from top to bottom. They break for lunch, which Louise shares with her mother while Megan chats via text to Hannah from the kitchen, but everything is done and dinner is prepared by the time they hear the crunch of tyres on the gravel drive shortly after six pm.

After all the hugging and taking of things upstairs has been completed, Joe heads for his mother's room, while Louise and Claire settle in the kitchen for a chat. Megan disappears off for a long soak in the bath before getting ready to go and meet Jake. She had suggested that she go to his house, because she is curious to see the view from there and wonders how different it might be, now that it is several lifetimes later.

Once ready, she pops her head round her grandmother's door, but Roberta is starting to doze and Joe leaves her and comes onto the landing with Megan.

"Where you off to, all dressed up?" he asks, careful not to ruffle her hair as he usually would, acutely aware that his niece is actually a young woman now. As she answers, he wonders how that can have happened in less than a week. He misses most of what she says, but catches the words, "... walking to Jake's house, you know, it's where the big pear tree used to be." And his mind is suddenly awash with happy boyhood memories.

"I'll walk down with you. I could do with a bit of leg stretching after the drive and then sitting with Mum. Do me good it will and he's a decent lad, so it'll be nice to see him too."

They pass through the kitchen on their way out and Claire smiles as she lays one end of the big table for dinner. As Louise stirs the sauce, she reminds her daughter of the two rules: no alcohol and home by midnight.

They walk down the hill chatting and Joe tells her how it used to be. As children, they would leave by the back door and walk across the meadow, skirt round the duck pond and the greenhouses, then down to the orchard. The farm used to stretch across the side of the hill and down to the river, but by the time he was born, all bar the meadow and the orchard were gone; sold off. Not all of it had been developed though, some of it was farmed, but by others, and a small part of it still is.

"But the orchard..." he tells her, his face aglow, "the orchard was always special. Granny, my granny that is, loved the place; it was almost religious for her. Whenever we came as children she would bring us down here, whatever the weather, to play all manner of games. She'd let us run wild and she even brought us at night, to teach us the stars and constellations." He pauses for a moment, before going on to tell her that they were sometimes allowed to bring tents and in the summer they could sleep in sleeping bags under the stars. "I've always loved the night sky. She brought it alive for me and kept its magic strong."

They stop on the pavement and stare around them at the street of modern houses; each one almost, but not quite exactly the same as the next. Some are two bedrooms, some are three. Some have a garage on the left, while others have it on the right, but the modernity is complete and unquestionable.

They look at each other, their eyes filled with disappointment; both had been hoping for something else. For a moment they are lost, uncertain which way to turn and where Jake's house might be. Then Joe pulls himself together and takes his niece's hand.

"This way. The pear tree was on the edge of the orchard and from there you had a clear view down across the valley. I fell out of that tree when I was a lad; hit my head good and proper!"

He laughs at the memory and Megan compares his lighthearted reaction to that of her grandmother. When she'd told her about the event, it was in hushed tones.

"Gran said you were in hospital, in a coma." she tells him. "She said you nearly died."

"I don't remember the coma of course, but afterwards I had a grand time. Off school for weeks I was. The ward I was in had a television, lots of toys and other children to play with. No, for me it was a holiday, it was only for everyone else that it was a nightmare. That's the difference between being a child and a parent." he tells her, chuckling again.

Jake has seen them coming and is waiting at the door. He and Joe greet each other and they are invited in. From the large patio door in the living room, Joe sees something of the view he remembers, and through him, Megan gets an idea of what Lillian and Bob used to see.

"It's lovely at night." Jake tells them shyly. "Sometimes I go and sit on the shed roof and just look at the stars. On a clear night there are so many."

"You'll miss that when you get to London." Joe tells him. "Hidden they are down there most of the time, same as in Carlisle, but it's easier for me to get out of the city and onto the fells to find them."

They stand for a moment in silence, each lost in their own thoughts as they look out over the valley, then Megan takes Jake's hand and squeezes it slightly, pleased that he has shared something fragile of himself. Joe says he must be off; his dinner will be waiting for him and he is aware that the 'young uns' probably want to be alone.

They leave together, but are heading in opposite directions. Joe assures them he will find his way back to Priory Meadows without a guide and Megan and Jake go hand in hand towards the bus stop.

Claire is pleased to see her sister-in-law looking so much brighter than she had the previous weekend, and even though they spend quite a bit of time discussing the doctor's recent visit and his thoughts on Roberta's rapid deterioration, their sadness is more matter of fact than emotional.

"I've pretty much found all the necessary paperwork, but there are a few bits and pieces that I haven't actually read yet. I thought we might do all of that together this weekend and with Mum too. What do you think?" Louise asks, just as Joe returns through the back door.

He looks at his wife and smiles before answering for the two of them. "I think that's a good idea. We can phone Mark if we need to; he's home again and planning to stay there for at least a week."

Louise's hand flies to her mouth. "Shit! I meant to phone..."

"I told him you were here looking after Mum and that I was calling for both of us. He sends his love, by the way. Have you been down to where the orchard was?" he asks, drying his hands. She shakes her head and as they sit down to dinner, he tells them what he saw and they compare it with what it used to be like all those years ago.

Once the carer has left, Louise and Claire do the washing up, then head into the front parlour to watch TV. Joe goes back up to his mother's room with tea, water and whisky. She is waiting for him and after he has poured them both a nightcap, she gives him an envelope.

"You're a father and you have a good set of values on you. What do make of this?"

The paper is old and Joe takes it out of the envelope carefully and puts his reading glasses on. Then he takes a few minutes to read and take in the full meaning of Vic's last letter to Lillian. Sighing, he looks at his mother. He understands her and he knows that she is uncertain; a frame of mind she has never dealt well with. He does not wish to hurt her, but nor can he lie, so he chooses his words with care.

"It's a wish any father would have. My boys mean the world to me and now they're starting to go off on their own, as is right and natural. But of course I've been lucky enough to watch over them from birth. He," he says, pointing to the letter, "was less sure than any of us can be that he would have that luxury, so he asked the one person who he knew loved him unconditionally to do this for him. If I'd been in a similar situation, when the boys were young, I would have asked the same of Lou. Like him, I know that she would have understood and I know she would have done everything in her power to help Claire make sure they didn't forget me. Claire could have told them all sorts of things about me, but only up to a point, and then only as their mother and my wife. Lou would have added the meat to the bones and she would have given it some gristle; tough things as well as good things. She would have been able to recreate my boyhood and that's what makes us real."

Roberta nods and exhales painfully. She knows he is telling the truth, just as she knows that Joe and Louise have always been close. He adored her from the moment he was introduced to her at the hospital; when she was pink and screaming. She herself had been distant and drugged. It had been a problematic and painful birth, one which left her emotionally numb and physically wretched.

They are now in unfamiliar territory. Roberta has rarely spoken of her relationship with her mother and sitting with her favourite child, she finds that she does not have the words. He is aware that it was never easy for them, but he learnt more about it from his granny than he ever heard from his mother. It is to those memories that he turns, trying to find something that will comfort her.

"She once told me," he says slowly, "that we have all these preconceived ideas about what love is and what it isn't, or what it should or shouldn't be. Perhaps some of them are right, but generally speaking, love is usually more, not less, than we ever thought possible."

He looks up at his mother and hands her the envelope, with the letter safely tucked back inside. "I can read about those times, but they don't make sense to me. I didn't live them, so I can never know what it was really like, or what life might have been like for all of us without it sitting there in our past. We're here because they were there, for all manner of reasons; some good, some bad I daresay. I can't judge her Mum, not the way you do. Her life didn't affect me in the same way, not the day to day stuff... and that's the truth of it."

"You are right son." Roberta puts the envelope and the now empty glass on the bedside table. "Maybe it's right that I see a glimmer of something different... now, before I go. But what am I supposed to do with it? I'm buggered if I know."

Joe bends down to kiss her forehead and she smiles weakly.

"Maybe nothing. Maybe it's enough just to acknowledge that you see it." he tells her, before leaving and going back downstairs in search of his wife.

He has never been ashamed of his own feelings and unlike many of his generation, finds it easy to talk about emotions. But now he finds he is confused and saddened. Vic's letter has touched something deep and he is unsure about what to do with whatever it is that has been awakened. He knows Claire will soothe him and he is certain that between them they will work it out.

Chapter twenty one

8th December 1941
<u>The Yanks are coming!!!!!!!</u>

≈

Louise smiles at the entry and tries to imagine the hope this news must have inspired. Lillian did not write any more for that day, so it was clear that nothing else was needed to convey what she and everyone else must have been feeling.

The next few entries are short and mundane, mostly about life on the farm in the cold winter of 1941. As she turns the page, the front door closes softly. The porch is below her bedroom and through the open windows she can hear Jake's footsteps on the gravel as he disappears into the night, making his way home. It is a tad after midnight and the creaky floorboard on the landing gives away Megan's effort to sneak into her room unnoticed.

"Night love, sleep tight." Louise calls out softly.

"Night Mum..." comes the muffled reply and Louise can sense the smile. No more needs to be said and she looks back down to the diary.

Christmas 1941

I'm twenty three and all me belongings in life are what I can see here in me room, which is in someone else's home. Through no fault of our own, I'm separated from the man I love and who loves me. Mum and me big brother are dead before their time and the world is a place of insanity. So although it might be Christmas, me heart's just not in it at all.

Auntie Eth invited me down to London, but I couldn't get a rail warrant or a lift. Not that I tried that hard to be honest, cos I'm not sure if it would have been any better there. After all, I'd still have been missing them.

Him and me, we've yet to spend a birthday or a Christmas together and well me, Mum and Vic had lots, but there ain't going to be any more coming. A couple of weeks ago I wrote to Viv and said that as soon as this was over, me and Bob are coming to spend Christmas with her and the kids. She wrote straight back and said she was counting on it!

≈

Boxing day 1941

Mrs R and Mollie did a big spread yesterday, roast turkey, pork with crackling, the whole works and somehow Alice was able to get home for the day. The five lasses that have been billeted in town came too, as did Mr R's brother and his wife and they brought the three evacuees they've got with them. It should have been lovely.

After dinner, I volunteered to milk the cows and Alice came with me, cos we both wanted to just leave the others to it. We didn't have to say much, we understand each other and worked quietly. We did talk about the attack on Pearl Harbour though. Viv said her cousin Nathaniel was blown clear off the deck of his ship, straight into the water. Thankfully he didn't lose his consciousness, so he was able to swim to safety and all he got was a bruise!

But he was lucky, a lot of them weren't. Here, we know we're at war, but knowing it still don't make losing someone easier, so how hard must it be for all those families to lose someone so unexpectedly? And so close to Christmas too. But then apparently the Japs don't celebrate Christmas, though Alice did say she thought some of them might be Christian, but it's difficult to say. I mean, what do I know about Japan? Nothing, that's what and now we're war with them too. What the bloody hell is going on?

She's given me two of her dresses. They don't fit of course, cos she's so much smaller and slimmer than me, but I can put them in the clothes exchange in town and get something else, something that'll do for me. She knows I lost everything that I hadn't already brung with me when I lost Mum. It was sweet of her to think of it. She's gone back too now, it weren't possible to stay overnight.

≈

12th January 1942

Happy Birthday love. Wherever you are, know that I'm thinking of you.

≈

15th January 1942

Got a letter from Elsie this morning. She's in pieces, cos Fred's been arrested for profiteering. She says he's been doing nothing of the sort, just a bit of buying and selling as and when it's come up, exactly like he was doing before the war.

After all, we know that lots of people are doing it and he's not making anyone miserable, it's not like he's stealing the stuff. He pays good money for it and then sells it to whoever for almost the same as they'd pay in the shop, except they don't need no coupons. She said what he does ain't much different to the restaurants, you don't need no coupons to eat in them and they've got a cap on what they can charge. He don't overcharge people neither, cos like he said, he ain't no thief.

Elsie's dead scared though, cos apparently if it goes to the assizes court, he could get up to fifteen years in prison!!! I wrote back and said for her to get as many people as she can that Fred has helped out in the past, to write or go in person. I'll write about Mum and her peaches, tell them just how much Fred made her last night so much better than it could have been.

I asked Mr R about it over dinner, but he was a bit gruff. It's unusual for him, he's normally got an opinion for everything and it was almost like he was hiding something his self! Anyway, he said it was unlikely that he'd get sent down for more than a few months if that. It's the fine that could be the problem, he said. Apparently they usually double or treble what they think you've made, not what you paid out in the first place, even supposing you could prove that.

I'll tell Elsie that next time I write, cos she'll need to start putting some aside for the fine. I daresay I could send her a *couple of quid, cos even after I've sent Viv money, I've still got a bit put by for meself.*

≈

27th January 1942

Finally! I got three letters from Bob. Mrs R got two as well. We keep saying no news is good news and as long as there ain't no telegram, we've got nothing to worry about! But still, we do worry and we just try to keep the spirits up for the other one. Anyway, today we got word that he's ok.

The first lot of Yanks arrived here yesterday in them troop ships and they come with loads of their own equipment, tanks, planes and the works. They're a sight to see. I hope bloody Hitler watches the Pathé and I hope he trembled. What with all the lads we got already from the colonies and now from all over America too, well he can't win. He must know that.

≈

1st February 1942

I can read between the lines of Bob's letters, cos we know each other that well. He's writing to me in a different way to how he writes to his parents and of course the censor means there's always so much he can't say up front, but even so, things are really hard over there. The siege might be over, but this Rommel is a different kind of enemy. Bob says he drives a tough but fair battle, but I can't see what he means by that, so one day he'll have to explain the difference between this Jerry general and the last one.

I think we're both glad that he's the driver and not the gunner though. He ain't no killer, but even so, I know he's struggling sometimes. He said no one enjoys the killing and everyone would much rather just take prisoners, but that's not the way to win a war. That's sad though. I mean, wouldn't it be better? Or would that make it like a game? I s'pose it would be like playing gin rummy for toffees instead of money, people don't play in the same way with such low stakes, but it's a pity that Mr Churchill and Hitler couldn't have just sat down with a pack of cards and sorted it all out that way!

We all know that every soldier on our side has a duty to escape if they are taken by the enemy and then get back to the front, any which way they can. It's the only way to win, to just keep on going, so I really do know that he'll carry on for as long as it takes to beat them and he'll always find it in his self to take that next step. There will be a cost, we know that, cos he's lost a lot of his mates and that's something I can understand a bit about, even though I ain't there.

In the last one though, he sounds dog tired. They've been 'out in the blue', so they sleep on the ground beside the tank whenever they can. I must ask him why they say that when they go deep into the desert. Maybe it's to do with the endless sky.

It must be hard enough for them out there as it is, without them worrying about us over here too. Bob says a few of them have lost people in the bombing raids over the cities and that in his dad's time it just weren't the case. There was one or two Zeppelin raids and maybe a hundred civilians died, but nothing like this time. I have to admit, until he said that I hadn't really thought about it, but it puts a different slant on things. Mum wasn't the only one to go like that, not by a long chalk.

He told me some of the things they talk about when they're on rest time. The units he works with are made up of blokes from Australia, India, New Zealand, South Africa, France and even Poland! Imagine! He said it's been incredible to talk with these men from all over the world and how for some of them the stars are the same ones, but for those from down under, the night sky is all different. He promised that next time he's home he's going to teach me all of them and we're going to learn them in the orchard, just us two.

He said it made him feel so proud, being with these chaps, who felt they had to come and fight for the motherland. Makes you wonder really, we agree on that. He also told me that the Poles and the Frenchies ain't heard a peep from their families since they managed to escape and get over here to join us. I hadn't thought about that neither. I have to wait weeks sometimes, but I do get his letters and he gets mine, well most of them anyway. They ain't got no idea what's happening at home, no idea at all, so of course they fight on for as long as they've got breathe in them, otherwise they ain't never going home.

I've written back and told him all about the winter planting, the changes we've done to the milking shed and how the pigs escaped last week and got into his mum's kitchen garden! Thankfully ain't much growing in there right now, so no real damage was done. I told him I've been sitting under our tree of a night, all wrapped up looking at the stars. They're the same ones he can see and he'll know I'm there with him as much as I can be and he's here with me, or as much as he can be.

≈

Louise feels in need of a nightcap, so she slips out of bed and goes downstairs to the kitchen, taking the diary with her. She knows that in similar circumstances, she wouldn't have a clue where to go to find Peter when he couldn't be with her. Trying not to hide from the fact, she wonders if she ever knew and the thought makes her sad. So much is going to have to be different she resolves. If we survive these few months, we have to make it different, she tells herself again, as though to make it stronger and more real.

She pours herself a small glass of whisky, adds loads of ice and settles at the table. Picking up the diary, she opens it at the next page and quickly flicks through a lot of very short entries about the work on the farm, Fred's trial, his three month sentence and almost too much about the weather.

Lillian wrote very little between February and June of that year and Louise surmises that it was because she was alone in so many ways. The conversations she used to have with her mother or her brother, or about them if not with them are over and she senses a slight withdrawal from life in her beloved grandmother, as though part of her has begun to slip away. There is not much of her to be found in the entries, many of which are only single lines.

26th February 1942

Sorted out seedlings in the greenhouse and got the trench ready for the runner beans today. Good job too, cos it'll rain tomorrow.

≈

10th March 1942

We had the ministry inspection today. Mr R was well put out with some of the comments and Mrs R got Mollie to do his favourite spotty dick pudding to compensate.

≈

23rd April 1942

Rita wrote. Everything seems fine down there with her and Connor, although of course Tom is at sea. We all know just how terrible the wait for news can be and there are so many perils out there.

≈

Louise wonders if she had saved herself for the letters to Bob. Maybe it was in them that she could be a real person again and for a moment she is not sure whether to carry on. Perhaps she should read his to her instead; perhaps from them she will get a better sense of who her granny was during that time. She is considering fetching the box with all the letters and photos, when an entry on the next page catches her attention.

21st June 1942

Good news and bad news. The bad came first. Rommel has captured Tobruk and taken around 35,000 or so of our lads prisoner. Naturally our first thought was that Bob was one of them, cos we've had nothing from him for weeks now. No telegram neither, but the fighting must have been fierce and it's possible that the casualty lists weren't put out right, cos so many of the lads have been taken. I haven't been able to sleep for I don't know how long now and I bet Alice ain't neither. She's phoned every day for news and used her contacts inside to see if she could find out anything, but today we got the best news, his voice at the other end of the telephone.

He'd been injured sometime in early May and has been on one of them hospital ships these last three or four weeks.

In a way I'm glad he didn't write to tell us and that we didn't get the information officially neither. Those bastard Jerries target the hospital ships and sink 'em if they get half a chance. Why? They're full of injured men and the women doing the nursing. Brave souls they are, much braver than me working in the fields. He must've known that it would've been worse for us, knowing he was hurt and on one of them for all these weeks.

They docked in Portsmouth this morning and as soon as he could he phoned. Mrs R came running all the way out to the top field to tell me. He's going to phone again later if he can, but he wasn't sure where he was going to be taken next. He's got a wound in his stomach (How? He's inside a tank or he should be) and damaged his collar bone again. Weak spot now that'll be, but he says he's fine under the circumstances and there's nothing to worry about. Of course he would tell his mum that, but I'm willing to believe him too! Portsmouth? I'll blooming well walk there if I have to, it can't be that far!

I haven't been able to stop crying, I'm so happy and the girls are so pleased for me. It touched me, really it did, cos I ain't been good company for quite a long while now, not taking up any of their invitations out of a night, then just ordering them about and keeping me head down while I work.

≈

3rd July 1942

He came home yesterday. He looks terrible. He's very thin and despite his desert tan he's pale. I know that sounds daft, but I know what I mean. Like he says, the trouble with a stomach wound means you can't eat, but that wouldn't have changed his eyes though and they have changed, they ain't mischievous no more, they're old.

Their tank got hit, but thankfully he managed to bail out before it went up. One of the crew didn't make it, but Bob said he was dead already. He could see that, cos although his eyes were open, it was obvious the lad was gone. I shuddered when he said that, cos I realised then that it means he must have seen a lot of dead blokes to be so sure and that can't be right. I mean, he's only twenty five. Anyway, he didn't try to get him out, but he feels bad about it. The lad was a nice kid, just twenty one Bob said and he'd only joined the crew two days earlier, so he didn't know him that well. Anyway, having got out, they were making a dash for cover, when there was an explosion and they went arse over tit. Then he remembers nothing until the next day when he was in the field hospital.

Harry, the commander, didn't make it neither, and well he and Bob had been together since he went back last time. He told me he was going to contact his wife and go and see her. She lives in Shropshire and they got a couple of kids and he said that what Vic had wrote to me stayed in his mind, so he wants to help Harry's kids remember their dad. Made me cry all over again, but not cos I was happy.

≈

4*th July 1942*

It's so peaceful here and it makes it hard to imagine all that war going on everywhere else. Occasionally we get a bomber going over, but it's one of ours, not one of theirs. Me and Bob were sitting in the garden, talking and he said he couldn't get over the quietness, he could hear so much because it was so quiet! That made us laugh, although in a way it's like he can't quite remember how to be his self anymore.

He's sleeping again now, that's pretty much all he's done since he got back. Mr R says that's about right after a big show like what he's been in and that hospitals ain't restful places at all. It made me think though, cos I mean, I don't know what a battlefield is really like. I seen a couple of make believe ones at the cinema and when Mr R said the fighting don't start at nine in the morning after a hearty breakfast, with a nice long break for lunch then stopping for the evening at five, well it made me realise I don't know nothing about what he has to live through day after day, week after week. He ain't alone neither, there's millions of our lads all over doing the same thing, making themselves go on, even when they're empty.

Mr R lets me sit with him. I've said I don't want paying while I ain't working and I've got enough put by to still send some to Viv, but he just waved me aside. He said I usually do the work of two anyway and he only ever pays me for one!

≈

5th July 1942

He's still sleeping a lot, but at least his appetite has come back a bit and that grey colour is beginning to go. When I told him, he laughed, but it didn't quite come out right, it was like he'd forgotten how to. He said the blokes call it battle fatigue and described it as an exhaustion that goes deeper than your bones, when everything is numb and you can forget your own name. He smiled at me, or least he tried to and said that like any tiredness, it passes. So I told him firmly, go right back to sleep then! Everyone is cooking up or making him all his favourite things, trying to get him well again. He told us that all they normally eat in the desert is the rations what comes in tins, same old thing, day in and day out.

Mr R even came up with a drop of the stern stuff, he said it were to put some hairs back on his chest! Made us both laugh, but I left them to it. I mean, there's things that only they will understand and it's right that they share it any way they can.

≈

6th July 1942

I had to leave him this afternoon to go into town. I had some errands to do for Mr R, cos he don't trust no one else with the banking stuff and the payments. Like he says, I got a good head for figures. Mrs R said she was going to sit with her boy while I was out and it'll do them both good I think.

I managed to pick him up some baccy and some mints, the ones he specially likes. I saw Mrs Jelkins from the Post Office while I was waiting for the bus and she said that the telegram boy had had a busy time of late, he'd delivered to six houses, just there in the town. I could see the fear in her eyes, cos her boy Howard is out at sea and he's only nineteen. What could I say to her though, when my Bob is safely tucked up in bed?

Made me wonder as I was coming back, not that I said anything to anybody, but how do we live with all this? I mean, all those people in Europe and the cities here what've lost their homes and much more. How do we just get up and get on with things? I know people do though and even here in all this peacefulness we're not fooled, because it ain't real. I know that, it could all be snatched away from me and everyone else in less than a minute. Sometimes I don't really know what is real anymore, except me and Bob of course and knowing that makes me smile all the way down to me boots!

≈

7*th* July 1942

Last night, when I was dozing in the chair in his room, he woke up and was able to get up without any help at all, which was a good sign. He looked at me and in his eyes I saw something of his old self. Then quiet as mice, we went down to the orchard and sat on a blanket under the stars until the sun came up. He showed me the Plough, Orion and Cassiopeia. They was easy to find, but there was others I don't remember. Anyway, he said we'd do it again the next clear night!

He told me that in the desert there are filthy, fat, buzzing flies everywhere and they cover everything, even your face. I asked him how people live with them and he said that without a war on, there wouldn't be so many. It's because there's so many people there at the moment, the living and of course the dead, the balance of life is all wrong and there ain't enough birds and suchlike to deal with them all.

Well there wouldn't be, I said, not in a desert and he said that the only things that get any benefit from the dead and all the rubbish left behind are the rats and the flies. He looked really sad when he told me that, like he wasn't sitting there with me, but was somewhere else, somewhere where I couldn't reach him. Almost broke me heart it did.

≈

8th July 1942

Lovely day today, sun shone almost the whole time. After breakfast we walked back to the orchard with some sandwiches and suchlike for a bit of a picnic, just us two. We sat on a blanket watching the birds, as though we had no cares in the world at all. I'm still smiling!

I asked him what he meant when he wrote that Rommel was fair and he explained a bit about the rules of war, the Geneva Convention he said it's called. I've heard it mentioned a few times, but never paid it much heed. I mean, war is war ain't it? But he said no, that wasn't right. There were many stories of Jerry soldiers ignoring the rules, but this chap plays straight.

For some reason, apparently some of the German commanders shoot Jewish soldiers rather than take them prisoner, but anyway, this Rommel bloke don't. He says a soldier is a soldier and entitled to the benefits of this Geneva Convention. If there's rules, to me it makes it sound like a game and a game it most certainly ain't.

Seems strange to me to have respect for your enemy, but Bob says it's crucial, otherwise you're in danger of losing your humanness. That's why we're fighting this war, because what Hitler's doing ain't right or fair and we mustn't forget it. He said if we don't have respect, then we could become worse than animals and that's what the rules are for, to keep respect. I can see why no rules might be a bad thing, but surely the worst thing a person can do to someone else is kill them? I don't know what to think, that's the truth of it.

He could see that I was getting into a right two and eight over it all and he said that too many people have already given their lives in order to win this war. People like Mum, Vic, Harry his commander, the young gunner and all the others. We owe it to them to finish it properly he told me, to keep some good in the world.

That's what he's afraid of, he says. He don't ever want to forget what all the good things feel like, all the reasons for making sure that Hitler and his kind don't win and spoil everything that we should respect and appreciate. He came over all serious when he told me that we have to protect all them things that should be good about this life. I just sat closer to him. We're some of what's good I told him, him and me and this spot under our tree. He held me tight and this time didn't disappear off to that place where I can't reach him.

≈

9th July 1942

We, him and me, went back to work today and bleeding knackered we are now! He got the tractor working again, so Daisy was well happy, cos she don't get on with the horses! Alice phoned, to say she's got a forty eight hour pass and will be arriving at the station tomorrow at ten in the morning. Mr R said me and Bob could go and get her. Once she's here too, it'll almost be right, or as right as it's ever likely to be again.

He played some tunes on the piano in the front parlour and taught us some of the songs, but I know he changed some of the words! Mr R raised his eyebrows once or twice, so maybe he remembers them from the last war. It's good to know that they manage to have some fun out there.

≈

12th July 1942

It was good to see Alice, but I can tell that she's suffering, even though she don't say so. She smokes too much and her eyes dart about all the time. I hope she got to relax a bit while she was here with us. It's busy at the airfields with all the bomber raids going out and of course the Yanks are up there too now, although they haven't flown over Germany yet. But they will, she says, and soon too.

She's heard that they don't want to hit the cities, they want to go for specific targets to minimise civilian casualties, so they mainly go up during the day when it's more dangerous for them. The RAF go mainly on night raids, but so far, they go deeper into enemy territory. We've bombed Cologne and Bremen and other cities too, so we're giving the Jerries as good, if not better than they gave us.

I know they killed me mum, but I'm not sure that we should be targeting civilians, maybe the Yanks are right. Then again, like Mr R says, the bloody Hun started it, not once, but twice! They voted for Hitler and they agreed to go marching into places they had no right to march into. But still, the kiddies, the mums and the old folk? I don't know that Mum or Vic would see that as fair or right. Mr R says that the Yanks will have to change their tune if we're going to win this and soon.

But what's the cost of winning and what's the cost of losing? The real cost I mean. I really don't know much anymore, that's about the only thing I can be sure I do know. Mum and me, we'd talk about things, Vic would give us his views and try as I might I can't do it by meself, really I can't. Sometimes, usually late at night, I get all panicky, cos I can't remember their faces, or their voices, or the way they used to laugh. Mum always had a peculiar pucker on her lips when she was studying something hard or difficult. I don't want to forget them and all the things that made them who they were.

Like I said to Bob, missing them don't go away or seem to get any easier. He said when it was all over and we're together properly, then it'll get easier to remember them. He said we weren't going to forget them, cos that wouldn't be right. That's why I love him.

≈

15th July 1942

Bob got a letter back from Harry's wife. She thanked him for offering to go and see her, but said that just now was a bit difficult and maybe next time he was home he could call her, cos it might be a better time to visit and chat. She gave her telephone number and like I said to him, maybe it was all a bit much for her. Viv said she still can't see a seaman in uniform without wanting to cry. I think that helped, cos in a way it must be impossible for him to see it from our side, just like I can only ever get a glimpse of what it's really like for him.

We told Alice about our wedding plans, we've set the date for Saturday August 1st, cos the 3rd is a bank holiday and she's put in for a pass, even if it's only for the day. Mrs R's sister is coming up and she's bringing Auntie Eth and Tish. I don't know how she keeps her car running, but she never seems to be without petrol, despite the rationing!

I'm not having anything fancy for the dress, I got a newish suit that fits a treat from the clothes exchange and a new hat, cos thankfully they ain't rationed. The government says that would be too much and I make them right there. Bob and me, we agreed that the wedding is what it is, but it ain't the most important thing. The fact that we found each other, now that's important!

I asked Alice if she's met anyone special and she looked shocked. After a bit she said that sometimes she goes out dancing, but when any of them asks her to write, she says no. She tells them to come and look for her afterwards if they still want to, but not until then. I know what she's thinking, but it's too late for me to wrap me heart up and put it out of harm's way, I've already given it to Bob and he's given me his to keep safe, and not only till this is all over!

≈

18th July 1942

We've had a lovely couple of days and between us all, we got so much done and in. Knackered we are, but in a nice way. It's satisfying, working the land when it all goes right. This evening we were bringing the tractor up from the lower barley field, up and across the hillside with Bob driving, all the while coaxing the old girl gently, with me and Mr R sitting at the back looking at where we'd been and his little dog Captain Bill trotting along behind. Suddenly Bob stopped and turned the engine off, then made us stand there with him, looking at the pink clouds and listening to the birds finding *their night time roosting places. There I was, me a city girl, yet somehow it was so right us all being there together, being part of the land, part of the countryside, me included. He said it was these sights and moments he missed when he was under that strange yet now familiar sky, but it was also these things that kept him going when he felt he was all wrung out.*

Mr R agreed with him, said it'd been the same for him in the trenches in France all them years ago. He said he's never stopped appreciating the farm, the sights and the smells since he got back, said it made him feel like the free man he was supposed to be. But he was real sad and said he couldn't understand how it'd all come to this. How we could stand there in a place that hardly changed apart from the seasons, yet all around us there was another terrible war going on. He said it was never supposed to happen, but we couldn't tell him the answer, cos we don't know ourselves. Bob cheered us up by pointing out the rabbits and promised his dad a couple for the pot before he has to go off again!

≈

21st July 1942

Molly showed me and Bob the cake she's been making for the wedding. It's only one tier of course, cos of the rationing, but she's iced it lovely. She's promised to cook us up a feast for the day and I know she will an' all! Everyone's looking forward to it!

≈

26th July 1942

Mrs R is in hospital and she's in a bad way. She had a terrible fall three days ago, came over all queer while she was going up the ladder into the loft in the barn. We've postponed the wedding, cos neither of us wants it without her there, I just hope we ain't going to have a funeral instead. Course her sister is still coming up, but there's no need for Auntie Eth and Tish to come. We'll save that for next time I told them and they agreed.

≈

4th August 1942

Mrs R is out of surgery and seems to be doing well. Funny, that fall might have saved her life. She's got a few broken bones of course, but they will heal. The main thing is, that the doctors found that lump and have taken all her downstairs plumbing out, so that ought to put paid to that. She'll be convalescing for a good month if not two, once she's over the worst, but with Molly here, she can come home as soon as she's able. At least Bob can visit her every day and that must be helping her mend, I mean she ain't got to worry about him.

We got the harvest to start getting in of course, but we don't need much sleep, so we have the nights to ourselves! Who needs a ring? I mean it's only a bit of gold when all's said and done. It just represents the feelings and the promises, it ain't them actually and those we have already.

≈

10th August 1942

He's been passed fit, so we wait. Always so much waiting.

≈

13th August 1942

We heard on the radio that General Montgomery has taken command out in North Africa. Bob says this is a good thing, cos he's more than a match for Rommel and that means that we're about to get serious again. If we can retake this Tobruk place and hold it, well Rommel will have to surrender or retreat. He showed us on the map after dinner last night.

I looked at the Nile, meandering along like it's done for thousands and thousands of years. We did something about it at school and I remember a bit, but not much, cos being a kid seems like another life ago. I asked him if he'd seen it, or paddled in it even. He laughed and said yes, he'd seen it, but all the troops were forbidden to swim in it cos it was so dirty. He told us that if you fall in accidently you had to go and see the medic. They call it pin cushion treatment, cos they give you so many jabs!!!

He said one of the most difficult things apart from the heat and the flies was the sandstorms. Sometimes they're so fierce that they take the paint off the vehicles. Imagine! Mr R and me were shocked by that, but like he said, the storms don't take sides, so when it's hard for our lads, it's difficult for the Jerries as well.

≈

14th August 1942

Mr R went to collect Mrs R and brought her home. Me and Mollie have turned the back parlour into her bedroom for a while, cos the stairs are a bit of a no no for a couple of weeks at least. She's all settled in nicely now, but she looks a bit peaky and can't walk or stand up for too long. Alice phoned, to say she's got a pass and will be back to visit in the next few days, she just needs to sort out a lift or a rail warrant.

≈

15th August 1942

Cos he's on the farm and its harvest time, his leave has been extended until 8th September. He's to present himself at Southampton on the 10th and has a travel warrant for the 9th. He reckons that will get him back out there for the early part of October at the latest and there must be a plan for a show soon after that. Stands to reason that the ship ain't just for him, there must be loads of men and new tanks, big guns and all manner of supplies going over and that must be for a reason.

I'm trying me best not to think of any of that, I just keep looking at him. He's here, I'm here we're together now. That is what's important, now.

≈

Louise sits back in her chair and looks around the kitchen. It is very quiet and there is only the ticking of the clock above the mantelpiece to break the silence. She closes her eyes, savouring the moment and realises that the clock has been there for as long as she can remember, like so much else about Priory Meadows.

There has been a farm there since the Norman Conquest; it is mentioned in the Domesday Book, but this house has only stood there for just over two hundred years. She calculates that her daughter must be the eighth or even ninth generation of the family in its various guises to sleep in it. Neither Megan nor her cousins will live there though, because it has already been decided that the house will be sold, along with all the ghosts, many of whom she has no knowledge of. She is reminded of her daughter's recent hysterical words about not having enough details for all the people in her project, but then Louise has no names either, or faces, or details about the lives or personalities of those that came before her mother's grandparents.

But to each other they were real, she reminds herself. They laughed and cried and sat right here, just like I'm doing, just as Lillian did and just as Mum has done for so much of her life. She will be the last one to die there and Louise is suddenly aware of just why her mother wanted to come home.

"She's a part of this family in a way that I've never been. This is her home, in a way that it has never been mine." she whispers, then wonders where 'home' might be, before turning the light off and going back to bed.

Chapter twenty two

The kitchen is bustling with activity as Louise makes breakfast. It couldn't be more different from the night before, she thinks to herself, carefully edging past Joe and putting the milk back in the fridge. The washing machine in the scullery has started leaking and making a strange thumping sound and he has bits of it spread out over one end of the big table, because now is not the time to buy a new one.

"He'll get it working in no time." Claire assures her as she kneads bread dough.

Louise nods. "He always could coax a bit more life out of an old machine, just like his granddad, whereas Dad was hopeless!"

She laughs happily, realising that in the last few weeks, not only has she come to know her father better, but her grandfather has also become more real to her than he had ever been and she contemplates this thought as she puts her mother's breakfast on the tray.

Megan has been rummaging through Lillian's treasure box, hoping to find more photographs. She would like to see Viv when she was younger and maybe there are others of Vic, so she makes piles at the other end of the table, spreading them out, while Jake holds a mug of tea and passes tools to Joe. He'd arrived early with the intention of cutting the grass, something he will do as soon as he has finished his tea.

"Wow, what's this?" Megan mutters, "And this? Oh..."

At first, no one sees any need to answer her or investigate what has caught her attention. It is only as Louise is walking past with the tray that she sees the tears running down her daughter's cheeks. Her eyes glance across the papers and she puts the tray down. Then standing behind her, she reads the three documents that are set out on the table. They are clearly formal, for they are typed, not handwritten and they all look official.

"Joe, come and look at this. Did you know...?" she asks her brother.

"Did I know what?" he replies, coming to stand beside her.

Claire looks up from her kneading and hands him a cloth to wipe his hands on, waiting patiently while her husband reads. She watches his lips move as his eyes go over the documents, not once, but twice.

"What does it mean?" Megan asks, looking confused.

"It seems," Joe says slowly, "that Nana and Grampy Robinson had Granny sectioned and put away in some sort of mental hospital and then they adopted her baby... Mum."

Megan tries to make sense of this new information. "Gran said she was told that Lillian went funny from the war. She said that her nana found her under the pear tree, screaming for her mother when she found out she was pregnant and that she wanted the baby ripped out of her. But why? Why would she want that? She and Bob loved each other. I don't understand." She twists her head round, to look at her mother and her uncle.

"Mum said her maiden name was Robinson, yet Granny's surname was Loveday." Louise says slowly. "They never married, her and Bob, they simply ran out of time. When you're reading the diary, you forget that you already know their ending, but now I see."

She picks up one of the documents. It is a small, faded piece of paper and she slowly reads the words typed onto the dreaded telegram that informed the family of the loss of their only son: Robert Alistair Robinson, who served his country bravely and died aged twenty five, on 2nd November 1942, during the battle of El Alamein.

Almost seventy years later, the words 'deeply regret to inform' still have the power to shock and there is silence in the kitchen. She puts it down and walks over to where she left the diary the night before. Picking it up, she carefully turns the page over and reads the next few entries aloud to the family, who stand or sit with rapt attention. It is, they all feel, important.

10th September 1942

Saw him off at the station. 'Until next time,' we said 'and then we'll have this blessed wedding, come hell or high water!' Can't really describe how I feel. Just as well there's so much to do for the next few weeks, cos I need to be so tired I can't think.

≈

15th September 1942

I'm late.

I've never been late and to be honest I feel different too. I won't write and tell him until I'm sure, but I know he'll be well tickled by the news. It'll put a smile on his face, so I need to be certain. We don't want no false alarms, or even worse, disappointments.

≈

18th September 1942

Got a short note this morning. He sailed on the 11th and it's as we thought, he's gone to join 'Monty' as they call him. This means for certain that there's a big push coming up. He told me again how much he loves me, but they're just words on paper. I need him here. I want to be with him when I tell him we're having a baby. I want us to shout with joy and be happy, <u>together</u>!

Still, no need to go rushing ahead of meself, I'm still not a hundred percent certain. I've written to Elsie, she's had two, so she should be able to give me a bit of advice, cos Mum ain't around to ask. Oh God, I miss her so much. I'm so jumpy and jittery all the time, she'd calm me down, she'd know how, but wanting her ain't going to change nothing. She's gone and there's an end to it.

God I hate this war.

≈

2nd October 1942

Got a note to say he arrived safe and sound. He's part of a new unit and got a brand new tank too. He's already had a little tinker with the engine and got it running a bit better. His new commander is an old hand like him and the gunner's been around a while too. He thinks they'll make a good team and we both know that a team is what they have to be. He sounds all right, but then they're just preparing and testing the girls out. I'm not even sure they've got a skirmish in yet, as he calls them.

He hasn't got any of me letters yet, but they'll be on ships that left after his, so it'll take a while for them to catch up. From what Elsie said, I'm almost ninety percent certain, but she also said that sometimes we lose them for no good reason and that we can't be really sure till we've missed at least two and better to wait for three, which would make me about twelve weeks gone, if not a bit more.

Another eight days and that's when me next one should be. Wishing me life away, but I need to know, I need to be sure.

≈

15th October 1942

Nothing on two counts.

No word from him and I'm really certain. I did write after all, cos I want him to know first. I'll tell Mrs R soon, although maybe I'll let him tell her in his next letter. That'd be nice I think. She's doing really well. We're moving her back upstairs tomorrow and she's started doing little bits around the house again and going for a short walk round the garden every evening with me or Mr R.

≈

19th October 1942

If I weren't sure before, I am now. Christ, I'm as sick as a dog from about four in the morning until about ten. Then I feel great and I'm bouncing around full of energy. It's a bit hard trying to hide it, but thankfully there's been a bit of a bug going round. Daisy's been right poorly and Alice phoned to say she's had it too. It's kept them all off me back anyway.

Wish he'd write. Or rather, I wish the letter I know he's already written would arrive!

≈

22nd October 1942

Auntie Eth sent a lovely long letter, full of news. She's started seeing someone, I won't know him she says, but it's someone who knew Uncle Norm years ago and was in the trenches with me dad, so he's almost family already she says! He lost his wife last year and has been alone since. She didn't say how.

Joyce is in the family way too. Naturally she and Charlie are right pleased. Fancy, Auntie Eth a granny and stepping out at the same time. Made me laugh, I can just imagine what Mum'd say, so I wrote straight back and told her.

≈

29th October 1942

Still nothing from him. We've all been glued to the radio every evening, listening for any news. Sometimes we hear that our lads have taken some place in the desert that no one's ever heard of, but they do say the fighting is very fierce. Please, someone up there look out for him and keep him safe.

≈

2nd November 1942

Got a lovely long letter today, his mum got one too, so we're all in high spirits. He sounds right chirpy too. He got a couple of mine but not the most important one. Still, it'll reach him soon enough. Wish I could see his face when he reads them words. Not sure how much longer I can keep me secret to meself! Unlike Rita, I ain't worried, cos he won't be scarpering. I know how he feels about me and he knows how I feel about him and there ain't no danger of it changing in a hurry.

It's a lovely clear night, so I think I'm going to go and sit under our tree and look at the stars. That's what he'll be doing too, so if I go down there maybe I can find him for a while and maybe he'll feel me and the baby close to him.

≈

The rest of the page is empty and Louise leans back on the dresser, unable to say anything. Megan is overcome with grief, and seeing this, Jake pulls her up from the table towards him and holds her close. She knows the loss she feels is irrational, but nonetheless, she feels it keenly. She also knows it is Lillian's loss she feels, not her own, but it does not lessen the rawness of it as she wraps her arms around him, breathing in his scent and sighing, thankful for his warmth and solidness. Then she realises that this is what Bob must have felt like to Lillian as they said goodbye, unaware that it was for the last time before he was wiped from the world, and with this thought even more tears well up.

Claire is holding the adoption papers, quietly wondering to herself just how many more family secrets there might still be lurking and how this one in particular might affect her husband. She watches his face as thoughts flicker back and forth in his mind. Eventually he breaks the silence.

"Do you think she knows?" he asks his sister.

"No, I don't think she does and I'm not sure we should tell her." Louise answers.

"But she thinks her mother hated her... she thinks she never loved her." Megan reminds them, wiping her eyes on the back of her hand. "If Lillian had been locked away, if she was sick... maybe that would help Gran understand. If she knew I mean..."

"I don't think it'll be as simple as that." Joe says slowly. "Before we do anything, I think we have to find out more and then decide. I mean nothing can be changed, not now; they're all gone, they can't speak for themselves anymore. So if we go down that road, we have to be sure, more than sure even, that some good will come of it. There's no point in making her worry, not now." he finishes softly.

"I agree." Louise says. "She adored Nana and Grampy. She's never said a bad word about either of them and she's always had plenty to say about everyone else. Megan you are to say nothing of this, promise me." Her mother looks sternly at her.

She nods slowly. "Ok..." she agrees with a shrug, clearly unhappy about it.

"Come and help me...?" Jake asks, towing her gently to the back door. He senses that some fresh air will do her good and also realises that Joe and Louise need some time to think things through. He knows very little about the family dynamics, but he was watching Claire and understood from her reactions that everything is not as it seems.

Joe straightens himself and looks carefully at his sister. "I'll take her tray up; your face will give you away."

"Good idea. I've got all the papers in the office. I'll go and get them and we'll see if we can find anything else that might be useful. I've not been through everything yet after all."

Claire walks up to her husband, stands in front of him and gives him a peck on the cheek. Then she gently brushes his shoulders down with the palms of her hands.

"You'll be fine, love." she tells him and he grunts in agreement, then picks up the tray and goes up the back stairs, whistling a tune from Snow White. She returns to her dough, shapes it, then plops it in the tin, ready for the second stage of proving.

"A fruit cake next I think and then maybe a pie for lunch." she says, to no one in particular, going to the pantry to find the ingredients. Her hands need to be busy if her mind is to be still and as she returns, laden with what she needs, she finds that Louise is back at the table with her own armful of ingredients; stacks of papers.

Joe returns an hour or so later. The kitchen is infused with the smell of baking and he relaxes instantly. His sister is sifting through documents, while his wife is reading the diary aloud and through the open doors and windows, the sound of the lawnmower gives the scene a sense of tranquillity, although he knows that no one really feels it. Megan is raking the grass cuttings and she and Jake break into laughter now and then, which makes him smile.

23rd December 1942

Mr R won't let me work in the fields no more, says while there's snow on the ground there's no need and he brings me back whenever I go out. He says I'll catch me death going out barefoot. I keep telling them though, that those shoes ain't mine. I don't know what's happened to me own shoes, but Alice will be here soon, she'll help me find them. She'll understand, Alice will.

≈

1st January 1943

Howling at the moon ain't going to bring any of them back. So many letters keep coming, but none of them tell me where they've hidden me shoes.

Will it be springtime soon? How can that be I wonder?

≈

11th January 1943

I still can't find me bloomin shoes. Why would anyone hide them from me? They keep bringing me pairs and pairs of shoes and boots and slippers, but they ain't mine, none of them are mine. Maybe mine are buried out there in the fields, rotting in the earth along with everything and everyone else, slowly falling to bits, so that no one can recognise what they once were or what they could have been. Maybe that's it, maybe that's why no one can find them and maybe that's why none of them can find me, even though I keep calling them and telling them that I'm here, right where they left me, all alone.

≈

"There's a drawing of a flower, but no more words on this page at all." Claire tells them, before turning the page over. "Ah look, now it's a year later."

1st January 1944

Alice came to see me today. She comes whenever she can, but this time she brought me diary and photos of our daughter. Seems strange to write that. Even stranger if I say it.

'Our daughter.'

'Our daughter, Roberta.'

Roberta Lillian Robinson is our daughter and she's almost six months old.

Did I choose her name, or did Mrs R? I don't remember, but it seems right for her.

I tried to explain to Alice, but it's all so vague. Of course I know I gave birth, a body remembers that, even if the mind wants to forget and I almost remember looking into her pink face, but only almost.

I do remember screaming for them to take her away, but I don't think they understood. How could they have? I don't understand meself. But I know it made as much sense as anything could have back then, when I was swallowed up by darkness and fear. So much fear, I never thought anyone could be so afraid, but they can, cos I was.

I thought it had gone, but looking at her little face in the photos, all that terror came back.

I tried to tell Alice, I tried to say the words, but I couldn't stop crying. I think she understood though, because she kept saying, 'I know, I know, I feel the same. It's not possible to love, not at this time, we have to put it all aside.' Then she was crying too and I didn't know what to do.

≈

8th January 1944

I've been looking at the pictures, every day after breakfast and again before I go to sleep. I gets them all out, lines them all up and then just looks at them. Alice says she's got Bob's red hair and his eyes, all blue and mischievous. But I can see Mum in them too, looking back at me. It's not easy to see, but no one can deny that something of me mum is in me daughter.

She eats well and sleeps like an angel Alice says, which must be a blessing. I mean, Mrs R ain't a spring chicken no more and Mr R was always better after a good night's kip. There's a note here from both of them, telling me that I'm welcome home whenever I'm well enough. They said me place is there, with them, but I don't know.

How can I live there and be so close to her, when I'm afraid to love her? What if something bad happens to her, just because I love her too much? I lost the others because I loved them and I can't let that happen to her now, can I?

≈

12th January 1944

Another birthday apart. One more of yours follows on from one more of mine. A whole year of silence behind us and another year of silence stretching out in front and still this bloody war goes on. When will it end? Will there be anyone left when it does?

I'm letting you down, I know that, but I can't help meself. Without you I can't find the way. I'm so sorry Bob, so very sorry.

≈

20th January 1944

I sat at the window watching the snow today. It falls so softly and makes everything seem so clean. It hides so much, buries it and covers it, so all you see is clean whiteness. That's what I feel like. Like everything's hidden, but so deep that even I can't find it no more and that all me warmth, the warmth inside, is smothered by the whiteness. It's not a bad feeling, or even a sad one. It's no feeling at all. Really, they're all somewhere else, out there, under the snow.

Sometimes, when I'm not looking, I see something, just a glimpse out of the corner of me eye, or I hear some music or smell a scent and whoosh, it rises up and hits me so hard that I'm flat on the floor unable to move. Even if I'm sitting in a chair, I know the real me is flat on the floor, held down by the weight of the snow.

Strange really. Don't know what to make of it. Don't think I'll try to explain it to them though, they never understand what I mean, they just scribble away. Sometimes they smile, but not often. I wish you was here Mum, you'd understand, you could explain it.

≈

24th January 1944

Alice came today through the snow. She's still pretty, but her eyes are haunted by something that I can't quite remember. I told her about not feeling anything anymore and she said she understood. She said she'd packed all her emotions up a long time ago and she was leaving them that way til this was all over. She said if she let herself feel, she'd go mad. Then she smiled and said sorry. I don't know why she was sorry, but I wonder if that's what I've done, put them all away. After all, I don't need them no more, cos there's no one left who'd want them or treasure them, or who I'd want to give them to.

≈

15th February 1944

Dr Smith gave me two unopened letters today. They're addressed to me and were written and sent before he died. Dr Smith said I'm to read them when I'm ready. He said there's no rush, they're mine and no one will take them from me. He said they might help me move on and get over all this. He says I'm still young and I still have a future. Ha! Made me laugh that did. Who on earth has a future in all this madness?

I'm looking at them now. I'm looking at his handwriting on the envelopes and I'm not crying. That must be a good sign I s'pose, but I can't open them, not until I can find the person he wrote them to.

I'm not that person and I don't know where she is.

≈

"Poor girl..." Claire says softly. As a mother, her thoughts and pity are for Lillian, who is young, frightened and all alone. "Poor, poor girl..." she whispers again and puts the diary down, just as Megan comes in through the back door.

"Hello darling, you're just in time. The kettle's just boiled, can you make some tea?" Louise asks her. "I'm sure Jake could do with a drink too and Gran certainly could."

She puts down the papers she has been reading and moves to the bundles of letters from Lillian's box, wondering if the last two are there and if she ever opened them. Would I have...? She asks herself, but instinctively shies away from answering.

"Here..." says Joe, breaking into her thoughts. "Here's Grampy Robinson's last will and testament and his death certificate, and something else. Ah, it's a letter. Hang on, let's have a look at the will first. Listen..."

He looks up and clears his throat. "This is dated 1st September 1960 and according to the death certificate, he died on the 22nd October of that year. So, here we go..."

I, Stanley Wallace Robinson, of sound blah blah blah... on this date, blah blah...

"Ah, here we are..."

Do leave all my worldly goods, which are as follows:

The 1000 acres of arable land known as Priory Meadows Farm, including the house, all outbuildings and any other property that forms part of this estate at the time of my death.

The contents of the house, all the farm equipment and all motor vehicles held in my name.

Any funds that remain in the three bank accounts in my name, once funeral costs for myself and my wife Muriel Edith Robinson have been covered or put aside, should I predecease her.

The proceeds from any sale of property, equipment or produce that might be uncompleted at the time of my death.

I leave all of the above to Lillian Loveday, whose main residence is Priory Meadows. I do this having already explained my reasons to my wife, although she may not recall those conversations in her present state of mind. These I have set out to Lillian in another document, which will be presented to her soon after my death."

Megan puts a mug of tea in front of each of them and stands just inside the door. She has one for her grandmother, but she wants to hear why Mr R, as she thinks of him, left everything to Lillian, so she waits while her uncle takes a swig of his tea before continuing.

"Where's that letter...?"

He fumbles around the papers on the table while Claire swiftly retrieves it and hands it to him.

"Thanks love." he says, smiling at her.

Dear Lillian,

You came into our lives as a worker. You were a hard worker and you had a natural talent for the land and there was a time when we all hoped for different things. Had they come to pass, you and Bob would have taken over the farm anyway, as is the way of things. But that did not happen and a spark went out in all of us.

You gave us hope when we needed it most and at a time when you had lost all of yours. Roberta is a gift and a little light in our life. With her you have given Muriel the chance to be a grandmother and to find something of what she lost, or rather what was taken from her so violently, but there we are, we all lost really.

This world has not turned out to be the one we had happy dreams of living and dying in when we came back in 1918. History is already judging us and to be honest, I do not pretend to understand the blame that is being laid at our feet. However, there have been some things to be thankful for and you and your daughter are two of them.

The fact that the farm has not been profitable for so many years is not your fault. The money we used in taking care of you and Roberta was well spent and I have never regretted a penny of it. But as you read this, you will know as well as I do, that she is too young to be left this responsibility and Muriel is too frail, in mind as well as body. I leave everything to you because there are problems, real problems that I have not the energy, the will or the time to resolve and I know that you will be, above all other considerations, fair minded in your decisions.

I ask that you do your best for Muriel and Alice with what there is. You will have to sell much of the land, for there are debts that will need paying and I am not able to leave you anywhere near the sum required to discharge them. Modernisation has proved more costly than I anticipated and the returns for that investment have been few, given the two failed harvests and other drains on our purse. But you should know that I hold no one but myself responsible for those decisions.

Alice knows that I have always loved her, but she made her choice, as did I when I married her mother. My place has been beside Muriel and I hope she can see that. I know you will do what you can to help her and the children, for she knows of my regret in never having met them. At least through your visits to them I have learnt something about them and knowing you as I do, I suspect I am not a stranger to them either. For that I am thankful.

My other regret is that because of your bumpy start to motherhood, you may not have had the chance to be a real mother. Perhaps I should have intervened more, or at least earlier, when I realised that Muriel took more of Roberta than perhaps she should have and it's possible that you lost something as a result.

However, the sad truth is that I couldn't do it to her and that was a failing on my part, for which I am sorry and I hope it is not too late for you to retrieve something, now that Muriel's mind is failing. Especially now, as Roberta approaches womanhood and Muriel can no longer guide her properly.

Make sure you keep something for the two of you and remember: she has always been your daughter and I hope you understand that we were only trying to help, given that our son could not.

Take care of yourself and if you can find happiness with Arnold, then I for one believe you deserve it. Take no notice of Muriel, for she no longer knows what she means. Just remember who she used to be; who she was before, because that's important.

Thank you.

As Joe finishes, he looks at his sister and they both say just one word. "Arnold...?"

Claire has to stifle a giggle and Megan takes the tea upstairs, leaving her mother and uncle to a discussion that for the moment is of little interest to her. By the time the letter was written, Lillian was older than Louise is now and had moved on to a stage in her life that Megan is finding difficult to empathise with.

As she passes the window at the top of the stairs, she pauses to watch Jake work. He can't see her, so the moment is hers alone and she smiles happily. Tearing her eyes away and forcing herself onwards, she pushes open the door of her grandmother's bedroom and immediately drops the tea.

"MUM! MUM! Come quickly!" she shouts in panic.

Chapter twenty three

Jake and Megan are sitting on the rickety chairs at the end of the garden. He is trying to take her mind off the things going on at the house, while she is trying to banish both the stench of vomit that had hit her senses as she entered the room and the image of her grandmother hanging over the edge of the bed, clearly unconscious.

The paramedic was able to revive her and Louise is with her now. Joe and Claire are in the hall, listening to the doctor quietly explain that Roberta has requested no further resuscitation and that he believes she understands what that could mean.

"Pain management is the main thing we can do. Her vital organs are shutting down, so these episodes may become more frequent, or the next one could kill her. There is no way of knowing or predicting these things, because each person, each body, is different. Comfort is the key thing now; keeping her comfortable and in as little pain as possible. But next time, she has asked that the paramedic does not revive her."

Joe is trembling and Claire takes his hand. She knows that intellectually he has understood for some time that his mother is dying, but only now does she believe that he understands it on an emotional level. She squeezes his hand and he gently returns the pressure. There is nothing she can say and he loves her all the more for not trying to find words when there are none.

Upstairs, Roberta is indignant. She is cross with her body and her frailty and is taking it out on her daughter.

"Don't fuss so... stop that!" she snaps, pushing away the flannel. "Just get me a clean nightie. No, not that one, the one with sleeves. Oh for god's sake! Pink, the bloody thing is pink. On the top... there! Yes, that one."

Her chest is heaving with the exertion of having to change and the shouting has made her breathless. "Tea. I want tea." she rasps, as the clean nightie is finally over her head. "But first take me to the bathroom, you can change the bed while I'm in there."

Louise is flustered, not really knowing what to do for the best, so she follows her mother's commands: bathroom, bed and tea in that order.

Finally Roberta is back in a clean bed, holding a mug of tea and looking at her daughter speculatively. "Where's Joe?" she asks.

"Showing the doctor out." Louise replies carefully.

Roberta nods and sighs. "Mark." she says emphatically. "I know I haven't got much time, but there is something I want you to tell him."

Louise gingerly sits down on the edge of the bed. Her mind is in a whirl and she is not at all sure that she wants to be part of whatever it is her mother is about to share.

"You could phone him and tell him yourself." she suggests.

"He'd hang up. I know I would. No, it has to come from you. You've not been involved in it, so he might listen to you." she tells her quietly, sipping her tea and considering what she wants to say.

"Tell him... tell him that we both know it was a lie, what I said just after your father died. Tell him..." She pauses, then rattles on before she loses her nerve. "That his father loved him and was proud of him, although he's probably always known that. Tell him that I knew it too, but also, that I was hurting a lot. Maybe he can understand, maybe he can't. I don't know anymore." She thrusts the empty mug at her daughter. "That's all I've got to say."

Louise is confused. She takes the mug, but can make little sense of her mother's words. "You just want me to tell him that?" Roberta nods and turns her head away. "I want to sleep now, I'm tired. Off you go."

"I'm not sure, Mum. I could phone him from in here, we could do it together. What do you think?" she asks hopefully.

"No. He'd know and it'd go wrong. And well, to be honest, I'm not sure I could take that." Roberta closes her eyes and as she lies there, Louise is shocked by her pallor and lack of substance. Sighing, she speaks slowly and softly.

"Maybe we should get a twenty four hour carer to come in, or maybe we ought to sit with you in turns. I really don't think you should be alone. Not now, not when..."

Her voice falters. She and Joe need to discuss this, but haven't yet made the time and now suddenly everything is moving quicker than any of them had anticipated.

Roberta laughs, but it sounds wrong, almost obscene and it hurts Louise to hear it.

"Watching me round the clock won't keep the reaper at bay. He'll come when he's good and ready and it won't matter who's sitting with me. Go on, go and phone Mark. I'm curious enough to try not to die while you're gone."

"Mum!" Louise shakes her head and stands up, trying to brush away a tear that she hopes her mother hasn't noticed.

Joe is waiting for her at the bottom of the stairs and it is obvious to her that he is trying to compose himself.

She reaches out and strokes his cheek. "She's tired and wants to sleep. Why don't you give it a little while and then go up?" she suggests. He nods and turns to go into the kitchen with her and she tells him the strange message she's been told to give their brother.

Claire has made a fresh pot of tea and is laying the table for lunch when Megan arrives with a parcel. "This has just been delivered for you." she tells her mother and plonks it on the table. "What is it?"

"It's the stuff I need to do the mane and tail for the rocking horse. I couldn't get it here, so Cate ordered it for me." she says, pushing the box away. "Has Jake finished?"

Her daughter shakes her head and meets her mother's eyes. Louise sees the confusion and reaches for her hand. "Perhaps it was wrong of me to insist that you come. Maybe you should go back to London when Dad comes back, or go and spend some time with Hannah. You could fly over and join them, I'm sure her parents would go and collect you if I explained, or..."

"No Mum. Honest, it's all right... it was just a bit of a shock. I wasn't expecting... you know, but I'd like to stay."

Louise nods. She'll think it about later, but as she brushes the hair from Megan's pale and tearstained face, she realises that parting her from Jake at this stage will not be easy. She is her mother's daughter and Louise smiles as she recalls Lillian's attempts to prise her from Peter's side, with promises of travel and holidays. It hadn't worked then and she suspects that Megan will wriggle just as much as she did if she tries to force things.

"Ok, if you're sure?"

"Sure!" And with that she skips back out again.

"Tell Jake to come and wash up and have lunch with us." Claire calls out behind her.

"Will you phone Mark now, or afterwards?" Joe asks.

"It's a bit early there now." she replies, looking at the clock. "It'll be four thirty in the morning. I don't think what I've got to say will make much sense at any time, but maybe he'll take it better if he's awake and has had breakfast, don't you think?"

"You're only the messenger. It's their fight, don't make it yours." he tells her firmly and she smiles, knowing he is right.

As they help themselves to wedges of still warm leek and ham pie and fresh potato salad, they chatter about other things.

Roberta is sitting up in bed, drifting in and out of sleep. She can hear their voices, but not the words. The sounds of laughter and disagreement on some minor point or other pull her back and she thinks she should feel better about things, having tried to put them right between herself and her first born. But something is nagging at the back of her mind and she can't quite grasp what it is.

"Soon it won't matter one way or the other." she mutters crossly. But it matters now and she wishes she could see what it is that is still wrong, for then she could just go to sleep. She is so very tired and with that thought, allows herself to float again. But she gets caught in amongst the voices; voices that are very familiar, yet at the same time not quite right, and so is brought back again.

"Oh Arnold," she whispers into the pillow, "you never were much good at being there when I needed you."

In the darkness behind her closed eyelids, she catches a glimpse of his smile and finds herself smiling back. "But that doesn't mean we were unhappy. That would be a lie now, wouldn't it?"

They had rowed a lot over the years, shouted all manner of abuse at each other and on occasions even thrown things. She had hit out at him too, more than once, but always they had found a way to make up. He would take her hand and it would be over. Then they would resolve whatever it was and move on, putting it behind them until the next time. Except of course, for that last time.

"Well I'm thinking it wouldn't have been any different; you just buggered off before we got the chance to make it right. But she's nice, your Susan. I like her." she tells him quietly and in her mind she sees him nod and wink at her the way he used to when they shared a joke at someone else's expense. There is some relief from the pain as he does this and she slips gratefully into deep sleep.

She wakes with a start to find Joe sitting in the chair. He is smiling and she smiles back.

"I brought tea." he says, taking the lid off the flask. "It'll be just the right temperature."

She nods and he pours some, then he stands up to help her back into a sitting position.

"How are you feeling?" he asks.

"Ready to go. I'm just going through the motions now. And as for the pain... well let's just say I'm not impressed with that at all. Pass me the pink tablets please, three of them and some water."

He gently presses the pills out of their blisters into the bony misshapen hand she holds out, while she looks at the door expectantly, but it stays shut. Sighing unhappily, she carefully puts them into her mouth and gulps at the liquid.

"It's too early there for her to call. Be patient Mum." he tells her.

"Too early...? I'm dying and it's too early to phone him? To give him a last chance to talk to me, to apologise for his behaviour for all these years? Too early to take a call from his sister about his mother?"

She tries to laugh, but coughs instead and pink foamy spittle dribbles from her lip. He wipes it away, but says nothing.

"Anyway, what's on your mind? You never could hide a worry from me son." she says, taking his hand and holding it.

"It's nothing..." he says, patting hers. "Let's talk of nicer things. Do you want some music on?" he asks, seeing the Nat King Cole CD.

"Later." she says, smiling, but this smile reaches her eyes and for a moment the greyness is gone and a ghost of how she used to look flits across her worn out features. Joe is caught by the moment and asks why she loves this music in particular, for he has never really known his mother to listen to more than the radio.

"It puts me in mind of the first time I saw your father." she says. "He was dancing with someone else, but our eyes met and we knew..." She hums a few bars of 'Unforgettable' and turns to him. "Sometimes, you just know. You did with Claire and I did with your father, but of course it was a little bit complicated. Still, it all turned out right in the end, eh?"

There is a twinkle in her eye and as he sees it he knows, but wants to be sure.

"Where was the dance, where did you meet?" he asks softly.

"Here." she says. "It was here. I'd come home from finishing school. They said I was finished, but I think they were wrong." She winks conspiratorially at her son, who smiles at seeing again a much loved ghost.

"But I came a day early, so no one was expecting me. Grampy had hired him to manage things, but I hadn't been home much. I'd holidayed with friends in Ireland in the summer and then spent Christmas with Nana's sister in London, so I hadn't met him. But all the time, here he was, waiting for me and passing the time with her."

She hums the tune again and closes her eyes. Joe reaches over to the CD player, presses play and the smooth, unmistakable voice fills the room. He continues to hold her hand, and as she drifts off to sleep, he sighs.

Louise pops her head round the door and indicates he should come. He gently releases his mother's hand and they quietly close the door behind them.

"The Arnold in the letter was Dad; one and the same it would seem." Joe says quietly. "Grampy Robinson hired him to manage the farm when Mum was at school and clearly there was something between him and Granny." He shakes his head. "Me? I like a simple life Lou. Nice and simple, that's my motto."

He turns to look at her. "And what did Mark say?"

"Ah..." she says, "well... depending on which you way you look at things, his view is a simple one."

"Which I'm probably not going to like, right? And she's not either, is she?"

They go along the landing to his and Claire's bedroom. Then while Louise sits on the edge of the bed, he stands at the window and looks out over the rooftops into the distance.

"When Dad died, Mum told him that he'd been the cause of his heart attack and that it was his news that did for him. She told him he'd been heartbroken to learn his eldest boy was a pansy. He hadn't been able to get his head around the fact that his own son was 'made the wrong way' and he believed that his sort were disgusting and unnatural. She said she'd never seen him so upset and as it was only a day later that he had that massive attack, well she said it was Mark's fault."

Joe spins round to look at her. "Christ, Lou!"

"I know, how could she? But it gets worse." she says, looking up at him.

"It does...? How?"

"Mum didn't know that Dad had known for ages. He and Mark were always close, so of course he suspected long before he told him, maybe even before Mark knew himself. Anyway, Dad was always really supportive; he didn't hate him or want to disown him. He was worried about what life was going to be like for him of course, but that was because he loved him and he wanted us all to be happy. In a way, he was probably proud that Mark didn't want to hide his gayness and that he was sure enough of himself to be himself.

"Anyway, they had chosen that evening together to tell Mum. So later, when she told him that he'd been the cause of Dad's death, well Mark knew it wasn't true and me giving him that message was pointless. He can't forgive Mum for hating him so much that she'd say that, knowing how much it would hurt him and doing it on purpose. The fact that she was hurting at the time didn't give her the right to do so much damage to another human being, never mind to her own son.

"He said that when he walked out that day, he knew two things with absolute certainty: that she'd never loved him and that he would never come back. Oh Joe... I think of Megan and I know I can say a lot of things in anger and she can hurl a fair bit at me too, but to push her away so completely, with no way back...? To deliberately hurt her so much that she would hate me, really hate me, even for just a moment? No, I couldn't bear that." She wipes a tear away and sighs deeply before continuing.

"She's waited all this time to try and tell him that it wasn't true. But years have gone by Joe, years!"

She looks down at her hands. She has been picking at the wavy motif on the dusky-pink candlewick bedspread and she realises that it, like so much else in the house, is older than either of them.

"What do I tell her?" she asks in a whisper. "I can't pretend I don't know... I can't lie and say I couldn't reach him. What do I say?"

Joe walks across the room and sits beside her on the bed. He puts his arm around her shoulder and for a moment, they are once again aged six and ten, twelve and sixteen, twenty and twenty four.

"Just tell her that you gave him the message and that the rest is up to them."

She tries smiling, but tears start falling instead.

"She's going to die Joe, there isn't enough time to make everything right anymore. I understand Mark. I mean she and I... well you know, it's not easy, but I can't be the same as him, I can't forget that she's my mother and I can't help but want it to end right. But the time is almost past... there isn't enough left."

"There never was, there never was." he says quietly, holding her tighter. "It takes two to fall out and two to make up again. You can't do it all by yourself Lou, no one can."

"But I don't even know what it was I did wrong, she won't tell me." she sobs into his shoulder.

"Hush... maybe you never did anything wrong. Maybe it's all about her and not about us at all..." is the only thing he can say.

He has an inkling of what it is; he has always had, even as a young lad, but feels that it is not for him to say. After all, he might be wrong and do more harm than good, so he just strokes her head and lets her cry, wishing it could be different, but at the same time knowing it never will be.

Chapter twenty four

Claire is alone in the kitchen. She has finished all her cooking and everything has been washed up or put away and with nothing left to do, she picks up Lillian's diary.

6th June 1944

Our baby is one year old today. I have never held her, nor have I ever seen her, not properly. I have only seen her in photographs, which arrive several times a week in the post. Mr R sends them and Alice sends them too, or brings them when she comes.

I've been here such a long time, well over a year. How can that be? Yet I remember so very little. Months and months of memories seem to fill less than five minutes of talking out loud. They say that it's quite normal and it means that I'm almost better. But how can so much time just vanish into nothing?

I must have had thoughts, I must have done things, yet nothing comes to me. Miss Watkins says it's the medicine what make you forget and when I look at some of the others I think maybe she's right, cos some of them just sit and stare for hours or cry. With Mrs Reginald I've had the same conversation every day now for over a week, I'm sure of it. So maybe that's where the hours and the weeks and the months go, they trickle away like water as we think the same thoughts and say the same words over and over again. Until what? Until they mean something? Or until they mean nothing?

≈

8th June 1944

We've been talking about what I will do and where I will go when I leave this place. This place that's never been me home, but maybe, just maybe it has been a sanctuary.

Doris says she's been here all of her life and she too has years and years of memories missing. That's sad and she's so sweet to me. Would I want to stay here forever though? Is that what I want? I don't think it can be. Mum would say a body has to work and live a life, day by day, but this ain't living, I know that. Anyway, what would living mean for me now? How would me day by day go now and where would it be? I've got no home or family, not really, not anymore, just memories and they're often too painful to allow meself to visit or try and find some comfort in them. There ain't no answers, I know that, so I've stopped looking for them.

≈

9th June 1944

Alice came today. She says I can come and live with her. There's factories nearby that are always looking for people. Auntie Eth wrote and she says I can come and live with her and Walter. They seem happy and she says she understands. I wish I did, but maybe she will explain it all to me.

Mr R says me place is with them and Roberta. Elsie and Rita say they too have room for me and Viv would love to have me, but it's too dangerous to cross the ocean. It seems I have a lot of homes, but I wonder which is the right one?

≈

15th June 1944

Alice asked who I'll miss when I leave here. There's really only Doris and she's going herself tomorrow. Doris is a schoolteacher and she's been teaching me, but she says I'm her last pupil. She tells me that there won't be any more, because when she leaves here she'll retire. She has a house near the sea, where her son lives and she'll go and live with him. I hope she'll write.

She says the world outside will have changed and that she may not know it anymore, because she's been here since she was nineteen and she says that was in 1897. Imagine! I don't really believe her, but the nurses never tell her she's being silly, like what they do with Mrs Woolton, who tells everyone that her sister is a lady in waiting to the Queen of Spain and that her father was the Duke of Argyll.

≈

16th June 1944

I hear on the news that we're back in France. It seems so long ago that we were forced to leave in such a hurry. The lads came home then, when the battle for France was lost and over, those that survived did anyway and now they go back and hope to be in Berlin for Christmas. Will they all make it? Do the Jerries know they're going to lose and do they stop shooting at the lads that run at them? I don't s'pose they do though, I don't s'pose Hitler lets them. I don't really know how that makes me feel.

≈

Claire looks up as Louise comes in, red eyed, but composed. Her eyes dart about the room and she quickly glances outside into the empty garden.

"They've gone into town. Megan said she'd phone later to let us know if she'll be back for dinner, but I suspect not." Claire tells her as she sits down.

"I suspect not too." Louise agrees, pulling the package towards her and opening it.

"Will you be ok if I go and do a bit in the garage? I'd like to clear my thoughts, but Joe is still upstairs, sitting with Mum."

"Of course I will be. I've got Lillian to keep me company. I'll even bring you some tea and cake later, if you'd like that?" Claire smiles at her sister-in-law and Louise knows she means it, so she picks the box up, tells her that would be lovely and heads out.

Watching Louise walk to the garage, Claire is acutely aware that she is quite content with her life and that she has been for some considerable while. Her childhood was wonderfully boring and her family life was good and solid. Her parents lived and died without any major secrets ever being revealed and she doubts that there were ever any skeletons rattling about in the family closet.

There was a time when she almost envied Louise her slim figure, her sophistication and her energy, but she has long since realised that they are not an endowment of nature, but more a product of anxiety. She is genuinely sorry that her marriage seems to be unravelling, but she and Joe have often quietly discussed the fact that in their view, Louise deserves someone better, someone who will love her for who she is. She hopes that there is still time for this someone to come along and that Louise will recognise him when he does.

With this thought, her eyes move back to the diary. She is not aware of Lillian marrying later in life, but that doesn't mean it didn't happen. After all, she only met her a few times before she died; once at her own wedding, once at Arnold's funeral, the christening of someone or other's child and maybe a birthday or two. It was, she now realises, always a gathering of some sort. She and Joe never came just to visit and she wonders why not. Resolving to ask him later, she picks up the book and hopes that things turned out all right for Lillian. She feels that most people deserve a happy ending, while acknowledging that even if life always had enough to dole out, not everyone would want one.

22nd June 1944

I make meself listen to the news every evening. There's a big map on the wall in the day room and just like Alice, I help move little flags across the land and sea and we're able to see what's happening in the huge arena that is at war. The difference of course, is she knows the men that her flags represent, I don't, not anymore. Although of course Tommy and Rita's Tom are still out there somewhere. I s'pose I should write and ask.

It's interesting for me to look at North Africa and I do look, often. There's Cairo and Tobruk and the Nile. I try to remember where that hotel was and what it was called, the one he stayed at where he could see the jewel blue sea as he described it, lapping at the white sand. He said it was so white it blinded him. We were going to see it together afterwards, only now there ain't no afterwards, not for us and not for you love.

There ain't no German flag there now, there's only ours. We won that battle, we hold that land, so they can't take it back, not now. His life wasn't wasted then, was it? All his tomorrows weren't thrown away for nothing, were they?

≈

2nd July 1944

I walked all the way round the gardens today. The flowers are out along the wall and in tubs, but everywhere else is vegetables of course. I remembered that I like to grow things though, I like the feeling of the soil slipping through me fingers and the mud stuck to me boots. The gardener came to talk to me and we chatted for ages about his peas and his onions and the soil that he has here. It was only as I came back inside that I remembered everything else. It was peaceful talking to him, I'm going to go again tomorrow, he said I could.

≈

9th July 1944

That Hitler has a new terror for us now. He sends bombs on their own, bombs that don't need to be dropped by planes with pilots and crews that can be shot down. Who would sit down and dream that up? They come during the day and at night. Elsie and Auntie Eth say they're terrifying, you spend all your time straining to listen, trying to hear if one's on its way with your name on it.

Now that their dad's gone, Elsie's sister has persuaded their mum to move in with her in Southend, cos she's on her own now. Sad that, I missed the funeral. Elsie's sent the girls to Southend too, she says she can't bear the thought of anything happening to them. Fred manages to get his hands on enough petrol, so they get out most weekends to see them. Elsie don't understand how I don't want to see me own daughter, me own baby. How can I tell her that I do? I want to see her so much that I ache deep inside. I so want to hold her close to me, but I'm still so very afraid that me loving her might be the cause of her death, so maybe it's better that she don't know me.

Dr Smith never asks me about her, maybe because he's a man, but I know Bob and Vic would've. I think maybe it's because she's been adopted. I think he thinks, and part of me agrees, that she ain't mine no more and that it's healthy that I don't want her back. Really, I don't know what I think about it and there ain't no one left to ask anymore. At least Mrs R can tell her all about her dad, which'll be some comfort, won't it?

≈

19th July 1944

I spent today, like most days, out in the garden helping Old Tom. It was drizzling, but I didn't care, there's something nice about summer rain. Then he said, just like Mum would've, 'Make sure you don't come down with a chesty cough Miss Lillian, we can't have that!' For a minute I was taken back to so many other conversations and moments. Me heart almost stopped and I stood there like an idiot. I know that, because I saw him watching me, his face all unsure. But then the ticking started again, the blood started moving and I was unfrozen. 'Good milk and onion broth. That does the job!' I said to him and he laughed and said, 'Aye, so it does!'

≈

20th July 1944

The Poles have taken the Italian port of Ancona and from what I can see, if we hold it, we have a way in, a supply line. Bob always said you have to be able to get supplies to the troops, if they go too fast and get too far ahead, they'll come to a halt, cos they'll run out of everything. I told Dr Smith that as we were looking at the map. He said Bob had been right.

I also told him what Bob had said about the men from Poland and other places occupied by the Jerries, about them not getting any word from home and how hard that must be. No wonder they want to start taking places back, they must hope that soon, it'll be Poland itself. Dr Smith, like me, said he hadn't realised that. He smiled at me when he went off for his own dinner and said we would talk more tomorrow.

≈

29th July 1944

Dr Smith says I'm ready to return to me own life. I've given up trying to tell him it don't exist no more, so I just agree with him.

≈

31st July 1944

We've decided that I should go and live with Alice for a while. Mr and Mrs R agree and say that it's a good stepping stone and they want me to come and visit next time Alice goes home. I promised that I would think about it.

Elsie and Auntie Eth want me to go and visit them too. I should be able to, cos the underground runs into town from near where Alice is renting a flat with Angela.

I hope I'm ready.

Doris says I am, but she still hasn't gone yet. She says her son ain't well, but maybe next week she'll leave too. She's been saying that for such a long time though, that I'm starting to think that she'll never get away from here. I've promised her that I'll write and come to see her when I get the chance. She said she'd like that.

Might it all be over soon? I looked at the map in the day room and the allied flags are starting to take over bits of France, although we're not yet as far in as we were when we started retreating all those years ago, from the M line I think Bob called it.

Tommy's out there somewhere, I try not to think of him, but when I do, I see him as he was years ago, just a lad, not a man at all. He'll have seen things that no one should see, I hope he's ok.

But anyway, we're pushing and the Jerries seem to be running back towards Germany. Let em go. That's what we say, make em run!

≈

1st August 1944

Packed the few things I have here into one bag. It seems to me that as I get older I have less and less to carry about with me. Funny that, I never thought I had that much to start with, but I miss things that were mine and are now gone. I s'pose me wedding suit is still at the farm.

We should have been celebrating two years of marriage and happy times together as a family. I wonder if anyone ever ate the cake.

≈

4th August 1944

I am here. Alice has the weekend off, so we can spend it together. It's a nice little flat and the sun comes in through the kitchen window in the morning. The walls are yellow and the tiles are white, so even in the afternoon it's nice. Mum would've liked to sit in here and talk to me after a long day while our tea was cooking. I would've liked that too.

I'll be sharing the big bedroom with Alice. Angela has the smaller one on her own. But as Alice says, sometimes they don't get to come home much, it depends what's going on. Alice is driving now, so she goes everywhere the Air Vice Marshall she's attached to needs to go. She loves the job and loves being in London. She's looking better than I remember, less haggard, but her eyes still tell a different story. I bet mine do too, except there's no one left now who'd really notice the difference.

We went for a little walk about and had some dinner in a restaurant. Nothing fancy, but nice enough. I have to go and get me new ration book next week, but she says they hardly ever cook at the flat, cos for a few shillings you can get a good meal out, with no washing up. Something to think about I s'pose, cos after all, I never have cooked. Mum did it all at home with Auntie Eth and Mollie did it all up at the farm, so I think she might be right there.

I have to tell the War Ministry that I'm here too. I was released from the Land Army before... well before, but now I *need to get assigned to some war work here. I'll go on Tuesday.*

Poor London. So much is destroyed, yet I can smell something in the air that I recognise, something that tells me I'm home.

≈

Claire puts the diary down and looks up at her husband as he comes in. "Cup of tea love?" she asks. He grunts in the affirmative and pulls out a chair opposite her.

"I think we should stay awhile." he tells her. "Will the boys be ok, do you think?"

She reaches across the table and places her hand on his. "Of course they will. The freezer is full and Colin will cope. I can always go back midweek, to stock up if necessary and keep my eye on things, but I think you're right. It wouldn't be fair to Louise to go just yet and you need to be here too, don't you?" she asks softly.

"Yes on both counts. But I need you too love, if the boys can spare you. It's all such a mess. I don't know how I thought this would go..." He pushes his free hand through his hair. "You remember when Lou told me that Mum wanted to come home to die? Honestly I don't know what we were thinking, but I don't think any of us were really prepared, not really. I mean in the films it's all misty eyed and peaceful, but that room stinks and I know Lou does her best."

She squeezes his hand. "One day at a time, or even just one hour at a time, that's all we can do. Now let's have some tea."

Claire stands up purposefully. "I promised Louise some and maybe when your mum wakes up, you can bring her down for a while to have hers. I'll have a bit of a sort out up there, get the windows open for a bit, get some air going through and have a bit more of a scrub than she'll let us do while she's in bed."

He too stands up. "Good idea. I'll just go and stretch my legs a bit, up and down the garden for a minute." he tells her.

She smiles. "You do that love. You're never at your best if you're stuck indoors for too long and it's such a nice afternoon.

Go on... try and relax a bit. I'll get the tea made and I've made some of your favourite fruit cake to go with it. Give Louise a shout on your way back, will you?"

Jake and Megan are in a rather nice coffee shop, sitting very comfortably in big squishy chairs. He is teaching her how to play backgammon and they are surrounded by late Saturday afternoon shoppers, but the chatter and laughter doesn't penetrate their bubble. Between moves, they discuss the future and at their age, the future is a strange concept. On the one hand it goes no further than the first week of September, when Megan must return to London and school. On the other, it stretches into infinity after the middle of October, when Jake will go to college.

"Do you know the address of the halls you'll be allocated to yet?" she asks as she makes her move, looking up to check if it's allowed.

He nods in response and she places her piece back on the board. "I can't remember exactly, but it's near the college. Only a ten minute walk, I think the bumph said."

"Well that can't be far from us then..." she says, then smiles at him and he melts at the sight of it, knowing it is only for him. He wonders if he could say goodbye to her now, without knowing how it might still play out and he finds he really doesn't want to. His mind turns to Bob and Lillian, who were forced to do just that, over and over again. He feels the weight of it, for he cannot imagine being dead when there is still so much to live for.

"Did you know that Bob was going to die? I mean then, you know... and not later. What I mean is, did you already know that he never came back from the war?" he asks as he takes one of her pieces from the board with a flourish.

"Hey!" She grabs at the piece and puts it down carefully. While she rolls the dice, she answers his question.

"Sort of, but like Mum said, I forgot. I was still hoping, like her, just like Lillian was too and I guess like he was, that somehow it would all turn out all right. I mean none of them were bad people, none of them deserved that, did they?"

She looks up at him, uncertain and wistful. He smiles sadly, understanding what it is she is saying and tries to find the words to explain something that cannot really be explained, at least not by him.

"Like you said, seventy million people died. Some them of might have been evil, some might have been misguided and I'm sure lots of people did things they wouldn't have normally done, just because they were afraid. So no, I don't believe they were all bad; they were probably just ordinary people, not much different from us. Of course the times were different, but not the people... I don't think there's a simple answer."

She nods and looks up slyly as she takes one of his pieces.

"Ha! So, no longer the pupil!" he tells her. "This means war!"

Roberta is lost in the mist, no longer sure which version of herself she is. A variety of sensations and images from different times float and meld, then separate, leaving her confused. The only thing she is certain of is the pain and it is that that pulls her into her least favourite version of herself. It is, she realises, the last one and is saddened by the knowledge. Somehow she thought it would be different.

"I blame Hollywood..." she mutters crossly and is surprised by a laugh that appears to be quite close by, but is not immediately recognisable.

"Well you would now, wouldn't you?"

She struggles to open her eyes and finds her son-in-law sitting there. He looks tanned and as always, is relaxed and casual in exactly the right way.

"I thought you were somewhere else." she tells him, her voice straining to find some force.

"And so I was, but now I am here. How are you Roberta?"

He has never called her mum, or any other variation of mother. From their first meeting, he has always used her full name and up until now, she has always considered it a mark of respect. However, now she suspects it has never been anything of the sort. She recognises something of herself in this man and has always been aware that he does it better than she ever could.

She regards him silently for a moment, wondering, and not for the first time, if in another life she would have coveted him; if she would have suited him better than her daughter, or if he would have made her happy. After all, he is so different from her late husband, so polished and self-confident.

But, she remembers, Arnold had been just as self-assured in his own way and she fleetingly remembers the love she felt for him. It surges up and then disappears, but a soft glow is left behind and she is sure that Peter is less honest than Arnold ever was, despite their apparent similarities.

So would he have made me happy? She asks herself again. As always, she cannot quite find the answer, but the way she is looking at him makes him uncomfortable. He feels she is peeling away layers and as their eyes meet, they are both aware that he does not know what Louise may have told her. She sees his discomfort and smiles.

"I am suddenly feeling much better than I was..." she tells him truthfully.

Chapter twenty five

Louise is at the window of the back parlour looking out, while Claire is sitting on the sofa watching her, amazed that anyone can move so much while standing still. Her hands fly up to her hair, her cheeks and then drop down again. Then she wraps her arms around her as if holding herself in. But her fingers do not lie still on her shoulders and in a moment both arms have dropped back down again as she shifts her weight from one foot to the other.

Claire shakes her head. "If you don't want him to stay, we can ask him to take a room in town. Joe won't mind telling him if you don't want to." she suggests, struggling to keep her tone neutral, aware that it isn't her decision and not wishing to voice an opinion or possibly cause an awkward moment.

Louise turns round to face her, and her eyes look so young and immature, that Claire thinks she could be looking at Megan. All her sister-in-law's poise and sophistication are gone and she appears unsure and vulnerable. It breaks Claire's heart to see a grown woman reduced to this and she stands up and smiles.

"What would you prefer? Be honest now."

"It's late and Megan isn't back yet. It will only confuse things further if she doesn't get the chance to see him. He can stay tonight, but I'll ask him to leave in the morning. I need to do this Claire, but thank you for offering." She tries to smile. "I'll get Granddad's old room ready for him, I could do with something to do."

"You do that and I'll get some food on the go. Shall I phone Megan, and tell her to come home for dinner?" Claire asks, heading for the door.

"Yes please. Invite Jake too, so Peter can meet him. He'll have one less thing to worry about then."

Louise sighs and turns back to the garden, bathed in late afternoon sunlight. As the door clicks shut, she allows her shoulders to sag and indulges herself in a moment of deep self pity, before pulling herself together and heading out towards the stairs.

Bob's room was never intended to be a shrine. The fact that it had been used only rarely, was more to do with the scarcity of people in the post-war Robinson family, rather than a wish to leave it untouched by time. Louise stands in the doorway and looks in. It's not for the first time, but this room is one of the less familiar ones. It is larger than the one she is using, which had been Alice's and there is still the same old single bed and big old winged chair, probably the same one that Lillian sat in while waiting for him to recover from his wounds.

In one of the alcoves is an old writing bureau, and on it, as it has done for as long as she can remember, stands a model of a First World War biplane. It must have been made by him or for him when he was a boy, eighty, if not more years ago.

She looks at the wardrobe and chest of drawers. They are oak and appear to be from the twenties. They are not a style that has ever been chic, nor are they sought after antiques. They were probably always just plain useful, she thinks to herself, back in the days when things were meant to last a lifetime.

"Well you outlived them all..." she says sadly as she crosses the room and opens the windows, hoping to blow away the stale musty smell that comes from the ancient rug and eiderdown.

The wardrobe door creaks through lack of use and as she expected, there are clean sheets and pillowcases on the shelf. She pulls them out, wondering if they actually still count as 'clean' as they probably haven't been washed for years, but there again, she reminds herself, nor have they been slept in. As she shakes them out, stems and crumbs of lavender fall out and for a moment the scent is strong.

Lillian loved the smell of lavender and violets, and the memories conjured up by the scent make Louise smile as she is transported back to summers long gone. In that brief floral assault, so much of her life is brought back that she feels a new, but at the same time, familiar strength fill her.

"I am a whole person." she says to her reflection in the mirror. "I have lived a whole life. I am me, good and bad, but ALL ME!" she shouts and then looks around, feeling a bit silly.

While making the bed up, she wonders how old the mattress might actually be and at what point it becomes an obscenity or a health risk. Without coming to a conclusion, she returns to the wardrobe, to see if she can find something with which to have a quick dust. There is a tatty old pair of pyjamas and using the top, she quickly brings a bit of a shine to the bedside table and the headboard, then goes to the bureau and runs the cloth across the top, gently picking up the plane as she does.

Once it is carefully put back in its place, she moves away, but something of her clothing is caught on the drawer handle. As the desk wobbles, she turns and is able to catch the model before it falls. In trying to untangle herself, she pulls the drawer open and is surprised to find that it is not empty. There are bundles of papers in it and as she pulls one out, she realises that they are school reports.

Leafing through them, she sees one that is dated June 1924 and she opens it out. It is from Bob's first year at prep school and she does a quick calculation, working out that he must have been seven years old and had clearly been a boarder, as the school was in Warwickshire. She knows that she would not have been able to part with Megan at such a tender age, but perhaps times were different, she reminds herself. If she had lived then, it might have seemed normal to her.

She pushes the thought away and looks down at the fragile piece of paper, smiling as she reads that his attention easily wanders in geography and history and that he has no love for music, despite the best efforts of the teacher, who was clearly at a loss for what to do with one so ungifted in her class. Drawing and chemistry are a different story however. The young Bob appeared to be a delight to teach, always interested and had put forward work ahead of his years and while Latin and trigonometry had seemed to fascinate him, French and German left him cold. In sport however, he was a different lad; excelling at tennis and rugby as well as cross country running.

She carefully folds the thin paper and looks at a later one. It is from 1931, when he was fourteen and at a different school. This one was near Manchester, again as a boarder, as was the way back then. After a quick glance at it, she decides that the year seems to have been a difficult one for him. His form teacher appeared to have dished out a lot of detention, and more than one caning during the year, as well as frequent losses of privileges, including weekend out of school excursions, but still, young Bob seemed unrepentant. His saving grace was his importance on the school rugby and cricket teams and his ability to keep the headmaster's car running.

She puts the bundle back and closes the drawer, then opens the top. Inside is a glimpse of the adult Bob, the person he was on his last visit home. There are receipts for boot repairs and tools that he must have bought, either for the farm or to take back with him to the desert of North Africa. There is a note to himself to buy pipe cleaners, Golden Shred marmalade and brown shoe polish. There is a tobacco tin, but it has bolts and nuts in it instead of smoking paraphernalia and next to it is another tin, but this one had mints in it once. It is empty now, but she suspects it wasn't when he left, as there is still a faint smell of spearmint inside.

Pushed into one of the pigeonholes are letters from school friends, from before and during the war and a photograph of a boy sitting astride a rocking horse. She holds it up to the light and looks at it carefully, deciding that it must have been grey originally, probably dappled, although it's impossible to be sure. On the back, in adult handwriting, is 'Me aged two on Ro-Ro, June 1919.' Now her horse has a name and a past, and she hugs this gem to herself. This new knowledge makes her project more substantial and now it is important that she complete it and keep him in the family.

There is a ball of string and under it is a photograph of him and Lillian, leaning against a five bar gate. He is holding a walking stick in one hand and his other arm is draped around her shoulders. She has one arm around his waist and is holding his hand as it lies on her shoulder. She is wearing a dress instead of her uniform and there is a quiet air of intimacy about them, as though the photographer had intruded on something private. Next to it there is some change in old money, a shrivelled elastic band and some penny stamps. Such normal things, she thinks as she looks at them, yet little treasures nonetheless.

She knows that over the years her granny would have come and stood there every now and then, and would have looked, just as she is doing. For Louise they are almost museum pieces, but she wonders what they were for Lillian. A little time machine perhaps, one that transported her back to an ordinary moment in an extraordinary time, when a variety of possibilities still existed.

"Would you have made it through, for better and for worse? Would you have lasted the course?" she asks the photograph.

Of course they cannot tell her the answer, not because it is hidden in the mists of forgotten years, but because there never was one; there hadn't been enough time for them to find out.

"There never is," she whispers, "but we hope. That's all we can do, we hope."

She closes the lid of the bureau and takes her makeshift duster with her as she leaves the room. She finds Peter on the landing, just leaving her mother's room.

"She's sleeping for the moment." he tells her. She nods and shows him where he will be sleeping. He looks at the single bed and raises an eyebrow.

Louise shakes her head. "I didn't ask you to come. We can talk... we should talk in fact, but I'm not ready to do more than that yet. Come down when you've sorted your things out. Megan should be home soon and we've invited Jake to dinner. Be nice to him." she tells him and turns to leave.

He catches her round the waist and pulls her towards him, holding her fast and smiling down at her. "Lou I've missed you. Haven't you missed me, just a little bit...?"

She looks into his eyes and tries to fathom what he is really thinking. "Actually, I've missed you a lot, but I'm not sure if the person I've been missing is the one I'm married to now." she says and he releases her as though she has burnt him.

"Dad!"

From the top of the stairs there is whoop and Megan hurls herself towards them, enabling Louise to extricate herself from the situation with some grace and without having to say anything else.

Downstairs, Megan takes her father outside to meet Jake, who is sitting with Joe at the end of the garden. She has her fingers crossed and although she would never admit it, his approval is important to her, so it is with some trepidation that she does the introductions. Joe appreciates the moment and is happy to have had only sons; the worry is different and somehow easier for a man to bear. He nods at Peter sympathetically and leaves them to it, ambling back to the house, happy with his lot in life.

Claire and Louise decide to lay the big table in the dining room and hope that Joe can persuade Roberta to join them, for it would give them a chance to get some fresh air through her room.

"You know, it's only now that I fully appreciate just how little Mum has changed in the house over the years. I mean it's a huge old place and she's been here alone. Granny was alone too, after Mum left to marry Dad, and up there in Granddad's old room, it's pretty much as he must have left it seventy-odd years ago; same wallpaper, same rug, everything."

Louise turns to look at her sister-in-law. "Mum sold the orchard and the meadow, not Granny. We were all grown up by then, but what did she do with money? How did she enjoy herself? Do you know I've never asked, isn't that terrible?"

"If you had, I'd have told you to mind your own business." snaps her mother's voice from behind them.

"Well that would explain why I never bothered asking then." Louise says, trying to smile, but she can't help thinking that Claire looked uncomfortable for the briefest of moments. She shrugs, deciding that she probably imagined it.

Roberta is in Joe's arms and Claire can see from the way he is walking and the almost reverent way he is holding her that she weighs next to nothing. She remembers him holding each of their sons in the same way at the beginning, as if he was frightened of breaking them. Of course as they grew stronger the fear disappeared, but Roberta is getting frailer and now, instead of laughing at him, she shares his fear.

Joe sits at the head of the table and keeps order in a nice gentle way. He sticks up for Jake when necessary and asks Peter questions about his holiday and his business when the silence goes on too for long, or when he is giving someone a hard time in order to win the sympathy vote. Roberta eats next to nothing, but enjoys sitting there and takes her turn to ask Peter or Jake difficult questions whenever the opportunity arises.

Megan enjoys the meal tremendously, for she has both her parents there, her favourite uncle and Jake. She is pleased with the way he handles her family and she tells him this later, as the first stars are appearing in the evening sky and they are saying goodnight at the gate.

"I guess you'll be spending the day with your parents tomorrow?" he asks, trying to hide his disappointment.

She shrugs. "Probably not, I'm guessing they have things to talk about."

"Ok then, call me once you know." he tells her, drawing her into his arms and gently kissing her upturned face.

While Louise and Peter tackle the washing up, Joe sits with Roberta in the dining room and Claire takes the hoover upstairs with some disinfectant and a bucket of hot water.

"So this chat of ours... when exactly have you scheduled it for?" Peter asks his wife, with more than a hint of sarcasm in his voice.

She turns from the sink to look at him and to look more carefully at the face she has loved so well for so long. She smiles and puts her head to one side, watching his mouth twitch slightly under her scrutiny. She has always loved his mouth and the way it crinkles into a smile or a scowl was always something special for her.

Sighing, she realises she is confused. Her feelings seem to point only to the past, to memories of what has already been. She cannot find the anticipation for tomorrow that she is certain she used to feel, or see a future that at one time had contained the two of them.

She sees her confusion mirrored in his eyes and is aware that he does not understand her, but as she does not understand herself, she cannot hold this against him or even hold him responsible.

Holding a glass in a wet and soapy gloved hand, she looks at him and tries to explain.

"When I came here, I came for several reasons: One, because Mum needed me. Two, because I needed some space and three, because I hoped you would miss me and would realise that it was me you loved and so choose me, not her. I naïvely thought it was all going to be quite simple. But it isn't, is it? The reasons why you went to her in the first place, the reasons why I can't just feel happy that in the end you seem to be choosing me, or how we even got into this mess. None of it is simple, is it?"

He looks at her for a long moment and sees her fears, but at the same time, there is a new certainty. She looks different and he feels the need to answer honestly.

"No, it clearly isn't. I'm not sure if it ever was, not really." he tells her, moving away and sitting down at the table. She lets him go and watches him as he watches her.

"I don't know where we go from here. Do you?" he asks softly and from his tone, she thinks that he is being sincere and is genuinely puzzled, both by her and by their situation.

"No," she replies, "not really."

"New territory then. No map and no foregone conclusions. A clean canvas. What do you say?"

She nods in agreement and turns back to the washing up, just as their daughter comes in and begins questioning him on Greece; a calculated move on her part, attempting to put off the moment when he will pronounce judgement on Jake. But this he saves until later, almost catching her unawares, just before she goes up to bed.

"He seems nice enough, but for god's sake use precautions if you're going to have sex." he tells her and she physically squirms as she leaves them.

"God... Dad!" she mutters and goes pink, but still manages one of her better flounces as she goes up the stairs.

"I think that was uncalled for." Louise tells him as she pours herself a nightcap.

"Hopefully it will put her off, rather than spur her on. Either way, it's good advice." he says, pouring himself a large whiskey and heading out to the front parlour to watch TV.

Listening to the silence that settles on the house once everyone is asleep, Louise wonders what this new canvas of theirs might have painted on it. On their way upstairs to sleep in separate rooms, they had agreed that a period of getting to know each other all over again was needed. Her mind draws a blank as to how this might be achieved, so she gives up and turns the bedside light back on. Then punching the pillows into submission and struggling into a sitting position, she opens the diary.

5th September 1944

Well I've been lucky. I went to the work office and managed to get meself sorted out as a clippie on the buses. I think that's better for me, cos I'm really not sure how working in all that noise in a factory would have been for me. I started yesterday and seem to be doing all right. Of course I've only had the training day so far and today I went out to watch someone else, but still, I'm hopeful. Mum would have laughed. Mind you, I also know she would have told me to get back to the farm and me daughter and she would have been right miffed that she'd had to say it. But that was a different life and Mum ain't here.

Paris has been liberated and the Japs are being pushed out of India, so everyone's talking about the end. Only a matter of weeks or months now they say. It reminds me of before, when everyone thought war was coming, but no one knew when or where it would really start. Now it's the reverse and no one really knows when or where it'll finish. I don't dare believe them now, any more than I wanted to believe them then.

≈

7th September 1944

Met up with Auntie Eth and me new Uncle Walter last night. We chose a pub almost halfway between us, cos that made it easier for all of us to get home after. At first it was a bit strange sitting there, not having seen her for so long and so much has changed since then, but after a while we found our old selves again and that was a relief all round! He's a nice bloke and I can see they're happy together and that's the main thing. That's what Mum would've said. He's a greengrocer and they have a place over the shop and I make her right, Uncle Norm would still have liked him too!

We kept the conversation away from me, which suited me fine, but there was plenty of news about the cousins to keep us going for hours. Evan is still up in the North East, down the mines, but she said he's happy there and cos its important work he's not been called up. He's facing different dangers of course, but as luck or fate would have it, he's not been involved in any of them cave-ins or gas explosions.

Joyce and Charlie are doing well in Duxford with little Gordon, who Auntie Eth can't get enough of. That made me smile. Mum would've been happy to see her all alight like that. Fancy, her little sister a granny! Tish has taken up with a Canadian, so everyone's hoping all goes well there, when this is all over. Tommy writes now and then and the last time she saw him he was all right, chirpy as usual and full of life. For a non believer, I do pray that it stays that way.

It was nice hearing all about everyone, but as I left them, I knew that I'm not a part of that family anymore, not in the way I was when we were just the tribe as we called ourselves back then. It seems so long ago now. We was all different people then, how can that be?

Times have changed and I can't go back, cos back don't exist no more. Anyway, everyone's moved on and it seems I'm the only one who don't know how to.

≈

8th September 1944

Went over and had tea with Elsie yesterday. Their new place is really sweet, a little house with a yard out the back. Like she said, she always thought they would leave the flats one day, but of course the bombs changed everything and she was so glad none of her family were caught indoors when they went like that. Then she remembered Mum of course and went *pink. But like I said to her, it happened, no use pretending it didn't. Pretending don't change nothing and ain't going to bring her back after all. She had to agree with me, but still, a bit of an awkward moment.*

She said I talk all posh now! I said that was Doris at the hospital, she taught me to mind me p's and q's!

Her mum was there and the girls were too. How they've grown! I hardly recognised Rosie and she was a bit shy with me at first, but we soon got over that and had a lovely little game, which ended with me tickling her and blowing raspberries on her belly. Just as I was leaving, Elsie said, 'You're a natural, go and get your daughter.' But legally she ain't mine and well, I've not been there for her in any way at all. I don't have any rights, not anymore.

Made me think though, as Elsie was telling me what I was missing out on. I mean I never had many dreams, just one or two and they weren't nothing outlandish. Yet they were broken into pieces, just as they might have had a chance to become real. Why? Did I do something so wrong that I lost my right to have a proper life with someone who loved me and who I loved back? What did Mum do wrong, or Vic, or Viv, or Ginny and Ben? Why are we all being punished like this?

I can't see the specialness of anything no more, cos it's all just ordinary. Less than ordinary really. I mean there ain't nothing really ordinary anymore, not like it used to be. So now I've got all this new but not ordinary stuff filling me hours, me days, the weeks, the months and the years. What do I do with it all? I wish I knew.

≈

10th September 1944

Went to put flowers on Mum's grave this afternoon and sat there for a while, chatting to the stone. I wanted to believe that somehow she could hear me, that maybe she was there. Daft really, and after a while I gave up. That stone don't make her real, don't say what kind of life she'd lived and how she'd been loved. I know those things though, but there's only me and Auntie Eth to really keep them alive for each other now, so I mustn't forget. Sometimes I think to forget everything might be nice, to be numb again, but I know that ain't right neither.

Out of respect, I s'pose I'll go again and help Auntie Eth keep it looking nice, but I didn't get no comfort from being there. Silly h'apence to think I would really, that's what she'd have said!

≈

12th September 1944

Belgium is ours, and we've also taken our first German city, Aachen. Everyone's so sure that it can't be long now until they're defeated, that the blackouts have become dimouts. Mind you, those bastards have got yet another new terror and not only does this bomb fly by itself, it flies so high that it can't be shot down. The V2 it's called and when it comes down there ain't no warning, one minute you're there, the next you ain't.

Made me think. I mean while I don't actually feel that I've much to live for, I don't want to die neither.

≈

18th September 1944

Me and Alice was talking last night in bed and she said that Bob wouldn't want to see me so sad. I agreed, cos I know he wouldn't, no more than Mum or Vic would want me to be in this nowhere place. But the point is, they ain't here, so they don't have no right to ask nothing of me, not anymore, they left me.

Then I remember that letter of Vic's, and in Viv's last letter she reminded me that the first Christmas after this war is over, I have to go there. I have to meet my niece and nephew, we have to know each other, it's what he wanted and it's what she still wants.

I'm so angry with them all for leaving me that sometimes it takes over from the love I know I feel for them really, or what I used to feel. I want to feel it again, but I can't find it.

I told her about those last two letters he sent me. I get them out sometimes and look at the envelopes, but I can't open them. She said she understood, she wouldn't be able to neither.

≈

3rd October 1944

Maybe the end ain't coming after all. We lost the battle for some place called Arnhem in Holland and they reckon that over six thousand of our lads have been taken prisoner. Six thousand! Poor sods, I hope they get treated ok, I mean if things are as bad as they say with the Jerries, there won't be much food for anyone, let alone prisoners. Don't seem that there's any sense left at all, why don't they just surrender?

≈

9th October 1944

Had a long shift today. It was good really and we was busy, so I didn't have much time to meself. But I do enjoy being on the bus going round the city. Sometimes we have to change routes if there's been a bomb or a building has collapsed. There was a bit of a flood today, cos some of the big pipes what got fractured before, gave up the ghost last night! Oh the mess, don't suppose anyone will forget that in hurry.

There's so much damage. Even after it's been cleared to one side so life can go on, there's so many piles of rubble or holes where buildings used to be, where streets used to be even, where lives used to be lived and everyone had their day to day living to sort out. All gone, and in one way it's hard to look at, yet in another you get used to it, it sort of becomes normal in its own way. Odd that.

What will life be like I wonder, afterwards I mean, when the shooting stops and the bombs don't fall no more. I mean anywhere, not just here and not just me. Will we all just shake hands and get on with rebuilding our cities and our lives? Can they be rebuilt? Do we just forget? How can we forgive? I lay awake all last night, just thinking. There's no one to ask now, I have to find the answers, one at a time. I wonder if I can.

≈

11th October 1944

I went for a walk today after me shift was over and I weren't really paying attention to where I was going, lost in me own thoughts I s'pose. When I stopped to see where I was, I was over by the gasworks, or rather where the gasworks used to be. Mrs Perkins' shop was still there, well most of it was, so I recognised it. I didn't recognise nothing else though, mainly because there was nothing left to recognise. I felt a huge hole open in me and I had to stuff me hand in me mouth to try and close it again before the hole swallowed me up. I knew it was going to make me lie flat on the floor again, the real me, even if me body was still standing. But I just knew if that happened, I might never get up again, so I had to keep stuffing me hand into the hole. I had to look away and not let meself fall into it.

There ain't no words, or if there are, I don't know them. I feel like I've been crying for hours, yet me face is dry. It's like they're on the inside. Oh Mum, oh Bob, why ain't you here? Why did you leave me all alone? I can't bear it, honestly I can't.

≈

12th October 1944

Alice has got us both rail passes to go up to the farm for the weekend. I'm not sure though, really not sure. She says I've got to go one day and this way, she'll be there with me for the whole time. I'm really thankful that Alice is such a good friend. She tries so hard to understand, even when I can't say the words, but she still tries and in her eyes I can see that she knows something of what I feel and a lot of what I won't allow myself to feel, not now and maybe never.

≈

As Louise's eyelids begin to close, the diary begins to drop from her hand. She appreciates the need for a good friend in life and she hopes that if and when Cate might be in need, she will rise to the challenge. She knows that what Lillian is about to do must be harder than giving Roberta up in the first place, although at the time she must have been sure it was the right thing to do, no matter how crazy it must have seemed to everyone else. She remembers reading that intense grief can do that to a person and that it can change them beyond all recognition, at least for a time.

Louise also knows that Lillian's feelings for her daughter, and her own relationship with her later, were never simple and that so many doubts were never laid to rest, on either side. She sighs as sleep begins to overtake her, thankful that the relationship she enjoys with her own daughter is so different and as her head starts to droop, she almost hears her grandmother's voice from across the room.

"The future has to be different from the past, or else what's the point of it all?"

It is something she often said to her granddaughter, and once, she told her that it was a discussion she and Bob had had on his last visit home.

"Yes Granny," she mumbles, "yes, it has..." and drifts away on the darkness.

Chapter twenty six

A bird is singing in the branches outside Louise's window and although the song is sweet, it is also irritatingly repetitive and calls her awake, when really she would rather still be asleep. She tries to think about her husband along the landing, but her mind moves quickly from him to the bureau and its contents, then on to 'Ro-Ro', the rocking horse in the garage. She remembers all the junk that had been piled up in there and wonders about the attic. She has not been up there, *ever*, not on any of her visits, not even as a child. And then of course, there is Lillian's box and all the photo albums.

"I need to talk to Joe." she mumbles, trying to block out the song by burying her head under the covers.

The door creaks open and she moves her head slightly and opens one eye. Relieved to see it is only her daughter, she tries to push herself into a sitting position.

Megan slowly walks across the room, balancing a tray that is clearly laden with things.

"Breakfast in bed!" she announces a little too cheerfully and Louise is instantly suspicious.

"Erm, why...? Not that I don't appreciate it, but..." she says, as the tray is placed carefully across her lap.

"Oh Mum!" Megan says, sitting on the edge of the bed and helping herself to a piece of toast. "Dad and I just thought you deserved it."

"Aha. And where is your father...?" she asks, sipping the tea.

"Gone. But he left this for you and to be honest, it was him that got breakfast ready. I just sort of appeared at the right moment." she admits cheerfully, handing over an envelope. "But I would've, if I'd thought of it."

"Yes darling, of course you would have... in about fifteen year's time!"

"Well, if you're going to be like that, I shall go and phone Jake and see if he's awake!" Megan stands up and tries to appear insulted, but she can't help but grin at her mother.

"You do that darling and leave me to enjoy the breakfast that you would have made *if* you'd thought of it." Louise theatrically blows her daughter a kiss and eyes the envelope speculatively, wondering what her husband has written.

She leaves it on the bed while she nibbles the toast and drinks her orange juice, listening to the day unfolding outside the open window. The bird song is now mixed with other sounds of people moving about, both within the house and outside in the distance. Dogs bark, car doors slam, children's voices carry on the breeze and insects buzz. It is, she decides, all rather nice and very Sunday-ish.

Eventually she moves the tray to one side and picks up the envelope. She tries to recall other letters, but cannot and realises that their relationship has always been conducted in person or over the phone. There have been hurried notes of course, but this doesn't feel like a note and now that she is properly awake, her curiosity is fired up and she opens it.

Well Lou,

By the time you read this, Megan will have told you that I have gone. I am heading back to London to think about what we said, as well as the many things that we didn't say during my very brief visit to say goodbye to Roberta and to meet our daughter's boyfriend.

It was more than a little strange for us to be sleeping in the same house, but in such very different rooms and beds, and it brought home just how separate we have become. It is in fact, a deeper separation than I had realised, but perhaps this is not news for you. Perhaps you have known this for a while now and maybe this is why you are hurting and angry. I don't know, because we haven't spoken, properly spoken I mean, for some time now.

I found stacks of old letters in a box under the bed, all addressed to someone called Bob. They were written before and during the second world war by someone called Alice, and there are some from his mother and some from Lillian too, who if I recall correctly, was your grandmother.

I read some of them, well I couldn't sleep - that mattress really does need replacing, that is if you plan to keep the house after R has passed on.

Of course back then, in the 'good old days', so many relationships were conducted by letter. I seem to remember that Churchill and his wife wrote to each other almost every day, even when they were under the same roof. We of course have not been like that. Our relationship has always been physical and we have rarely been separated by distance. This last year or so has been an exception and we have not dealt with it well.

I use the word 'we' on purpose, because in my view, neither of us have Lou, not just me. I will not have all the blame laid at my door, that would not be fair and I do not think, or rather I hope, that is not what you intend to do. After all, it takes two to tango. I know the context is very different to when we used to say it to each other, but the meaning remains the same, even if there is little to laugh at in our present situation. At least it does for me and I do hope that you too can raise a smile as you remember other, happier times.

Reading those old letters and thinking about what we said about having to get to know each other again gave me the idea of writing to you. Perhaps we can write what we find so difficult to say and then once it has been written, read and carefully considered, perhaps it can be spoken of too.

Let me be blunt. I am not enjoying this phase of our marriage, it is not what I expected from us and it would be true to say, as I believe I did try to explain when we met in London a few weeks ago, that it is you who has changed. I honestly do not believe that I have. I became who I am a long time ago, and life and I muddle along quite happily most of the time. My needs and wants are much the same as they were when we met. Our circumstances may have changed, but in essence I am the same man you met and fell in love with all those years ago.

I don't know what you want of me, so I cannot be sure that I can give you what you need, but I am sure that right now, I am not getting what I need and want from my partner in life. Lou, I don't want to throw away the years we have had, but I cannot continue for much longer without some hope that we have both a present and a future. A future that has meaning for both of us and one in which we are not confused, hurt or angry with the other.

You told me last night, that of late, you have missed someone a great deal, but that you were not sure if the person you are missing is the one you are married to. That person is me. I am your husband, the same husband you have had for many years now, but as far as I am concerned, my wife is missing. Will you help me look for her?

I find I have no idea how to end this letter. Do I write 'with much love' or 'all my love' or even 'your loving hubby'? Probably not the last one - it's not really me, is it? So I guess I'll keep it simple...

Peter xx

Louise reads it several times and with each reading her emotions change. The first time she is indignant. The second time she concedes he has a point. The third time she smiles as she pictures him writing it, and then the fourth time she shakes her head sadly.

A gentle knock on the door breaks her thoughts. "Yes, come in." she calls out softly, and Claire pops her head round the door.

"You ok?" she asks, clearly concerned. "Would you like more tea...?"

She comes into the room carrying a tray with a fresh pot on it.

"Yes, I'm fine, honestly. How's Mum this morning?"

"Sleeping again. Apparently she and Peter were both up from about six this morning, chatting. He's gone now, but you know that, yes?" Her voice is uncertain and Louise puts her sister-in-law's mind at ease.

"Yes, I do. I thought about the attic when I woke up. I've never been up there... I mean never. Do you know if Joe has?" she asks, pushing the covers off, making to swing her legs down.

"I don't know, but it's a good idea. He's fretting and in need of something to do. I'll suggest it to him. You stay there and rest a while. The carer has been and gone and I'm getting lunch prepared. Megan has gone over to Jake's, so take it easy."

Louise smiles. "But I feel guilty."

Claire shrugs. "No need to feel guilty, no need at all. Everything is under control, for now at least."

Alone again, Louise pours herself some more tea, then leans back on the pillows and thinks about those last words that her husband wrote.

'My wife is missing. Will you help me look for her?'

Do I know where she is? Louise asks herself, turning her head towards the window. Then she spies the diary and remembers another lost woman.

"Is this what love does to us?" she asks the empty room, picking it up and opening it. Before she reads though, she is acutely aware that her granny did find herself again somehow, and that in learning how to be a different person, living a different life to the one she had hoped for, she had brought a great deal of happiness to many others. The thought makes her smile and she realises that really, she had never known just how difficult the journey had been for Lillian, but her strength and her hope had always been there for Louise and she finds that it has not deserted her now.

31st October 1944

I've been twice now, the first time with Alice and the second time on me own. Mrs R fusses about, but that's really how it should be I s'pose, given everything that I did. I mean I'm just visiting, I don't live there with them and she and the child are there every day together after all. That must make her the mother, not me and she is enjoying it and good at it too, so I don't know, I don't know nothing no more. Funny that, I used to know so much, but that was then, not now.

Me uniform was still there and I helped out in the fields on both occasions, which pleased Mr R, who said the others don't work as hard as I used to. We smiled when he told me that and we both knew that we were thinking about different futures from the ones we're getting, but there ain't no point dwelling on that.

I just gave meself over to the wind and the soil and it felt good. I felt freer and I know Mr R understands that sensation, cos he said that when he was demobbed and came back in 1918, that's how he'd worked things out for his self, by going straight onto the land. At least a body can sleep after all that work and the mind has to too, if only for a little while.

The first time, I didn't hold Roberta, I just sat with her while she slept and stroked her cheek. It were so soft. Her golden red hair is wavy and her eyes are naughty, just like her father's were. The second time, when she was having a bit of a toddle in the yard, she almost fell and I reached out and grabbed her before I'd even had the thought, it was that automatic, but anyone would've done the same. Mrs R came running, because she was crying and I handed her over. She stopped as soon as she was in her nana's arms. Natural really, she don't know me, don't know I'm her mum and I'm not, not really, more of an aunt maybe.

They asked me to join them at Christmas and I think I will. The buses won't be running after all, so I can't hide meself in work and forget all about it. Maybe it's time to try and remember happier Christmases, ones that are gone but not forgotten. I wish me and him had had the chance to spend one together. Just one would've been nice.

≈

5th *November 1944*

Angela told me about one of her friends who had gone to a clairvoyant to try and contact her boyfriend. Apparently they'd had a terrible row before he'd gone on his bombing mission and well, he didn't make it back, so she was beside herself of course. Anyway, Angela said this friend of hers had been pleased to hear that he was all right over there and that he wasn't angry with her. She'd actually been given a message from the other side, imagine!

Then she asked me if I'd ever thought of it and if I wanted the address of this woman. To be honest, I'd not thought of it and I'm not even sure I believe in it, but it did make me think. I mean, Bob and me, we never had a row. In all the time we knew each other, our time together was always precious, it always had a limit on it, right from our very first meeting.

I don't know even know what we would have rowed about, had times been different. I mean all couples argue, I know Vic and Viv did and Mum said she and Dad did, their biggest one being about the flat. Dad didn't want to move in there because it was so dirty. Mum always said he couldn't see that it just needed a bit of a scrub and some fresh paint. When he came back on leave the first time, he'd been amazed at how homely it was. Always made her smile when she told me that. All gone now of course. If there's anything left, it's just burnt rubble and dust.

Really, I ain't had the heart, not to mention the courage, to go back and see for meself. What'd be the point? And after fetching up by the gasworks that time, well I don't want to go any closer, that was hard enough.

But me and him, well we never had that luxury, or the inclination to have a real good screaming and shouting match about something that in the end didn't matter, that we could've enjoyed making up about afterwards. Our dreams weren't so big. Maybe there were lots of little things, but only the little things that a real life, a proper life is made up of. I never really wanted more than that.

So did I want to contact him on the other side? Or Mum or Vic, come to it? I decided not to, maybe because of the risk of disappointment. I mean if they couldn't be found, it would be too much to bear and frankly, I'm not sure I actually believe in the other side, but also because I'm starting to think that I know where to find them anyway. It makes me cry to know that, but it makes me smile too.

Don't make no sense really when I read those words back, but in another way it does, really it does. I went and sat under the pear tree one night while I was there and looked at the stars. All those stars, all the way up there. I cried me heart out, but it was different. I wasn't alone there and I don't always feel totally alone anymore neither, not now, even though I'm in a place that I never shared with any of them.

≈

Louise stops reading and thinks about what her granny had written. She suspects that it was also the moment she began to think about coming back to the farm to live, as a real possibility. She has started to forgive them for leaving her and Louise wonders if she can forgive herself for leaving Peter.

I pushed him away, she thinks to herself. He left me to go and find Lucy, but only because he didn't, and obviously still doesn't, know how to find me. I wonder why I did that, she says to herself as she puts the diary down. I mean, I never thought I could love anybody the way I loved him, so why?

She decides that it is time to get up and goes to the bathroom. She takes a long, hot shower and then gets dressed, then still mulling over the question in her mind, she goes in to see her mother.

Roberta's curiosity has been fighting a losing battle with her impatience, so she is pleased to see her.

"Well, he's gone then. Bit of a flying visit, I must say. Where does it leave you?" she asks, motioning for Louise to sit on the bed.

"It leaves me wondering where we go from here. Rightly or wrongly, he's parked it firmly at my door." she explains, then sighs heavily as she looks at her mother.

"Silly girl. He doesn't like responsibility, so of course he's parked it at your door. No surprises there! What does surprise me is that you see it for what it is. I'm happy about that. Whatever you choose from now on, well at least you choose with your eyes wide open, instead of your legs."

"Mum!" Louise is shocked, then realises she sounds just like her own daughter and sighs again.

"You'll be fine." Roberta says quietly.

"Yes, I know I will, but I'd like to be happy too. Is that really too much to ask?"

She remembers that Lillian had written about wanting only little things to make her happy. What, she wonders, are the little things that would fill her life now? What could fill the space that Peter used to occupy?

"Ah... well you've been happy before, and no doubt you will be again. But happiness is a bit elusive; not so easy to plan for, and anyway, it tends to sneak up on you unawares. Sometimes, doing what we're fairly sure won't make us unhappy is a better bet."

Her mother's watery blue eyes have a faint twinkle in them as she speaks and Louise smiles at her.

"Yes, perhaps that is a better thing to aspire to, but it's not just me, it's Megan too. That makes it all the more difficult."

Roberta shakes her head. "No, that's just you using your child as an excuse. Stand by your own decisions; that's what I've always tried to do."

For a moment, Louise is aware of the shadow of her grandmother hovering nearby. It is her own fancy, she knows that, but she also realises that she too, stood by and was judged by the same maxim.

"Granny did what she thought was best for you, because she loved you and because she had her own fears. And given the times and the circumstances... well they were real."

The words are spoken softly and are out before she has thought them through, but she doesn't regret them and as Roberta says nothing, she continues, with the aim of explaining what happened at the beginning of her mother's life. She tells her about the decisions that were made, because love is sometimes a prickly and painful thing.

As she comes to the end, she realises that this is not news for her mother and that she has known some, if not all of it for a long time and what she didn't know, doesn't actually matter to her.

Roberta stops staring into the distance and turns to look at her daughter. Her expression is harsh, one that Louise knows well.

"My nana never held that back from me, she was always my nana and never my mother. Knowing isn't the same as understanding and even understanding doesn't change things. You don't wipe out a feeling, a pain or a hurt by understanding why someone did it to you in the first place and knowing why doesn't make the hurt go away. In fact it changes nothing, nothing at all."

Louise looks carefully at her. She wants to speak, but cannot say the words, because of the pain she knows they will cause. She thinks them though and wonders why, if her mother knows that, if she really knows and believes what she has just said, why did she say what she said to Mark? And why has she always shut her only daughter out? Why did she want to hurt them both so much?

In a moment of sublime clarity, she sees why and understands that both she and her eldest brother had rejected their mother when they were too young to understand what they were doing, for as children, they had reacted to circumstances they had no control over. Their mother could never forgive them because she had never got over the pain of being rejected herself and subsequent occurrences just reopened the same wound, again and again.

She sees now that Roberta could never forgive Lillian for giving in to fear and terror, or understand how even in her darkest moment, she could abandon her child. For her, it was the greatest sin and so she punished her own children too. We are still being punished, she thinks, and in doing that, she's punishing herself. Her mother is right; understanding doesn't seem to change anything.

Shaking her head and forcing back a tear, like she has had to do so many times before, Louise stands up. "More tea Mum...?" she asks.

Chapter twenty seven

"Look, more treasures!" Joe announces as Louise pushes the kitchen door open.

He is looking flushed and pleased to see his sister. The table is covered in dusty old boxes from the attic and she smiles at him, asking what he has found.

"Well... lots more letters. Crikey Lou, this family really wrote to each to other, something that's gone now I suppose. I don't think I've ever written to the boys. There's the ones written between Nana and Grampy Robinson while they were courting and then some from after they were married, you know, during the first war. There's quite a few from his parents to him from the same period and even a couple from the days when his parents were courting! We need to think what we're going to do with all of them. It would be such a shame to just ditch them. After all, they're a bit of real family history.

"Then in here, we have a record collection of 78s. There might be a few that are worth something and there's even the old wind up gramophone to play them on, complete with a blooming great big horn. In this one we've got old lead soldiers and mechanical toys that we should get looked at and there's a box full of Christmas decorations that were obviously collected over a long period of time. There's a trunk of old clothes that's far too heavy for me to move by myself and record keeping books for the farm going back to 1809, along with some other old books, children's books mainly. There's a pile of old newspapers and magazines that were probably kept back as packaging, but which are very interesting in themselves. Quite a haul in fact!"

"Wow!" Louise exclaims. "Well, I suppose we could phone round in the morning and get a few people up to have a look and see. What do you think?" she asks, wandering around the table and peering into the boxes.

"Good idea. I'll look for some numbers this afternoon. And the family stuff?" he asks, looking at her carefully, thinking that it is more her line than his.

"Well, there's even more in Granddad's old room. I found his school reports in the bureau and Peter found a box of letters under the bed. I agree though, it would be a shame to discard them all. I mean Megan's had the chance to see them and the boys might be interested too, if not now, then later on. And who knows about the people to come in the future? Or Mark even? We might be able to get it all digitalised and preserved that way." she says, absentmindedly taking the biscuit tin from the top of the dresser and finding to her delight, that Claire has filled it. "The whole idea of family is so spread about now and I'm guessing that will only increase as the years roll by.

"We moved three times as children, same area but different houses, and none of them were ours. Mum had a jolly good clear out each time as I remember, not that we had that much. So far, Megan has lived in four places and who knows what we're going to do next, because we certainly don't. So this is probably the last time all these ghosts can speak to us in their own words. What will our generation leave? We've done everything by phone, email or possibly a blog, but it's all very fleeting. My great grandchildren will see nothing written by me, yet here we have letters to Lillian from her mother, others from Grampy Robinson's parents to him and to each other. I mean, when were they born?"

She does a quick calculation, reckoning that Virginia, Stanley and Muriel must have been born in the late 1880's or early 1890's.

"His parents must have come into the world during the 1850's or 60's." she announces.

"Wow..." They say together.

"I wonder what was happening then," Louise says, taking another biscuit.

"When?" asks Megan, coming in through the back door with Jake.

"In 1850. We were wondering what was going on then." Claire tells her niece, with a big smile on her face. While Joe was up in the attic, she had spent the morning preparing food. Now she is relaxed, happy that he and Louise have something to explore together.

"Quite a lot really." Jake says, with authority. "In Ireland the potato famine was still taking a terrible toll on the people, while the English continued to export the wheat and other crops grown there and did very little to help."

"I remember that," says Megan, "we did it in history. About a million people died, because over here we got 'famine fatigue' and felt that in some way the poor catholic Irish were not quite human."

"That's right." says Jake, continuing. "It's a terrible thing, classifying humans according to race or religion. Do that and you'll have those at the top regarding those at the bottom as a sub species." he trails off, shrugging his shoulders. Then on a brighter, but related note, adds, "The only other thing I can be sure of is that the Crystal Palace was being built for the Great Exhibition of 1851. Supposedly it was to demonstrate to the world what a modern country Britain was, but a lot of it was just trophies from the empire."

He takes a seat at the table and starts looking in the box with the mechanical toys in it. "Hey, these are amazing!" he says, taking one out and examining it.

He and Joe start discussing the mechanisms of some of them, while Claire checks on the roast; opening the oven door and filling the kitchen with the wonderful smell of meat and butter mixed with rosemary.

Megan and Louise smile at each other as they take in the scene. Megan is sorry that her father is not there and Louise is saddened that her mother cannot be part of it, if only for one last time.

"It'll be another half hour..." Claire announces. "I'll just take Roberta some soup and a fresh pot of tea. If I put the veg on, will you keep an eye on them?" she asks Louise, who smiles and assures her that she will and that Megan will lay the table.

"Is your mum at home?" Claire asks Jake, who nods as she passes him. "Give her a call and invite her up for lunch. There's plenty, after all." she tells him and he fishes out his mobile and does as he is asked.

Lunch is as lovely as everyone expected it to be. Megan is happy to learn that Louise has told Roberta the truth about Lillian, but saddened by the fact that it makes little difference to her grandmother and that she seems unable to see her mother in a kinder light.

"She's a bit mean really, isn't she?"

As soon as the words are out she feels bad, but Louise smiles at her honesty and says simply, "Yes, sometimes she is, but then sometimes we all are."

After Lunch, Joe and Jake offer to do the washing up while the 'girls' take themselves off to the front parlour with the remains of the wine that Jake's mother brought. Megan goes to check on her gran and finds her sleeping, so she returns to the kitchen, where her uncle tells her she is not needed.

She stays anyway, but is quickly bored by their conversation and spotting the diary on the dresser where her mother had left it, she smiles and pulls it towards it her, opening it at the page with the bookmark.

Christmas Eve 1944

I am twenty six and this is my first birthday that makes me older than he got to be. This winter will be followed by spring and so the seasons will keep changing, like they've always done and always will. The years will march on for me, one after another and if I'm lucky I'll go grey, me skin will wrinkle and I will have experiences that right now, today, I can't even think about or imagine. But I must do this without him, for he will stay the same, frozen forever in photographs, letters and memories. Him and so many more lads, so many. They won't get fat and bald, or become muddled and forgetful. Maybe I'll get that chance, but Bob won't and nor will me big brother. Hitler stole that from us, he stole our future and now we've only got the past.

I can't bear that thought. Maybe that's the real reason why I can't open the last two letters, because then there will nothing more to come. I don't want it to be over yet, I still feel a part of me and him and I don't want to lose it, not ever.

I know Viv feels the same and I can see the space where her pen stops when she signs Viv, Ben and Ginny. Her hovering over the space that should be Vic, means in a funny way he's still there.

There is no birthday wish, other than that this war end before too many more people who are loved and will be missed are killed.

≈

Christmas day 1944

Today has been easier than I dared hope. We arrived at eight o' clock this morning and Mr and Mrs R were really sweet, happy to see us both. Me room was all ready for me and they'd put a new bedspread in there. They want me to come back and live here, but not just yet, I told them. Soon maybe and they were pleased with that.

Little Roberta loved the tree and the presents, everyone's presents, not just hers! I bought her a toy rabbit and she hardly let it go once she'd opened it. She came and sat near me and watched me as I unwrapped a book from Alice. By teatime she was exhausted, but she's strong and growing well.

She got a bit of a second wind after a kip on the big chair in the front parlour and then later at bedtime, I went up with her and listened as Mrs R told her a story. It's hard to know what I feel when I'm there with her, but at the same time not with her. She don't know me anymore than she knows Alice. I tell meself it's for the best, because she's safe here, safer than she would be in London and safer than she would be with me.

Alice and I will drive back early tomorrow morning. It's been great that she was able to use the car. We have to pick up the air chief's wife on our way back, but even so.

≈

28th December 1944

I was told today that eight hundred American servicemen died on me birthday, because the troop ship they was on was *hit by a U-boat in the channel. Eight hundred lives snuffed out on Christmas Eve.*

Some V1 doodlebug bombs landed on Manchester and snuffed out more, with no warning or mercy and still it goes on and on.

They stood the Home Guard down earlier this month, because the threat of invasion is no more. So why does it go on? Why does Hitler carry on giving orders to fight and not surrender? Why have people got to keep dying?

≈

New Year 1945

I saw 1945 in with Elsie, Fred, Rita and Tish. Lord, that was strange.

It's been a long time, long in years as well as other things. Rita looks good and despite everything, she's happy down there being a navy wife. Tom is out somewhere in the pacific fighting the Japs and she's become a bit more religious than she used to be. Starts and ends each day with prayer, she says. To give her credit, so far so good, his ship ain't been sunk! Connor's a lovely strong lad with such a laugh on him, not a serious boy at all. At midnight we all drank a toast to the ones that weren't there and the hope of this being the last New Year at war. Amen to that!

≈

12th January 1945

≈

Nothing is written under the date, but the fact that it is blank means that it meant something important to Lillian and it takes Megan a moment or two for it to register.

"Of course, it would have been his birthday..." she murmurs to herself, sighing sadly. She looks up and asks Jake when exactly his is, remembering vaguely that when they'd first met and were exchanging little details about themselves, he'd said January.

"7th Jan. Why?" he asks.

"No reason," she tells him slyly and looks back down at the diary, having committed the date to memory. Joe whispers to Jake that hers is 7th September, a fact that he too stores away. She notices that the next page is discoloured and that some of the ink has run slightly, where her great grandmother's tears had fallen.

24th January 1945

We got held up today by a bombed out building finally giving up the ghost and keeling over. Lots of passengers got off to walk to the other side, but we had to wait for a few hours while things got tidied up. Kiddies came to watch, then got bored and started to play in the rubble. Made me think that did. All that mess, yet there they were playing, lost in a world of their own that looked more fun than the world I usually get lost in.

It made me realise that even in all this, this, whatever this is, that the world is still a wonderful place, but I can't find the wonder without you. I need you beside me so that I can see it for what it is again, because without you it is nothing. Help me Bob, please help me.

≈

18th February 1945

We bombed a city called Dresden a couple of nights ago. It's a long way into Germany and as far as I know from what's been reported and what Angela and Alice have both said, it weren't military targets that were bombed, just a lot of ordinary people, German people mind. The city centre has been flattened by fire and bombs now though, and by all accounts there's not much of it left standing.

I'm not altogether sure why we did it. Was it simply because we could? Because the Luftwaffe can't stop us no more and we want all of Germany to know that, or is it because they did it to us first? Because they started this bloody war and we mean to finish it?

Maurice, one of the old men at the depot, said the Jerries bombed our cities to soften us up for invasion and now we're just doing the same as what they did, except we'll march all the way to Berlin.

Maybe he's right, but I can't help remembering what Bob said. We must have respect, we can't forget our humanness. I think maybe we just did and despite everything they and this war have done to us all and to me, this really worries me. I don't want to be like them, because then they will have won and if that happens, what will have been the point of it all?

What is happening to us?

≈

18th March 1945

There's a picture of Tommy in the Daily Mirror. He's with some Canadian troops and they're taking food convoys to the people of Holland, those that the Nazis have been starving because the railway workers went on strike against them. He's standing by a jeep with a few lads, smiling away he is. The photo's a bit grainy of course, but it's so lovely to see him there and in one piece!

≈

The picture has been carefully cut out of the newspaper and stuck below the entry, exactly as Lillian describes it, with an arrow pointing to one cheerful looking solider. Megan stares at his face for a long time and wonders about him. No one has ever spoken of 'Uncle Tommy' or 'Cousin Tommy' and she wonders why as she slowly turns the page.

22nd March 1945

Viv wrote, to say that over there everyone's convinced war in Europe has only weeks left in it. The headlines the other day was that the Jerries are retreating across the Rhine and that the US air force firebombed Tokyo. How they've changed their tune in a couple of years, but I daresay in those same few years, too many of their lads have perished, so maybe it ain't no wonder. They say that maybe a hundred thousand Japanese people (not soldiers, but people) died in the attack. That shocks me to the core.

We've flown over Berlin with a huge number of aircraft. While that's probably full of ordinary people who might have had enough, it's also where all their troops are heading, as they say that's were Hitler is.

I miss Vic a lot. Every day I miss him, but I especially miss him at times like this. He'd help me know what to think of it all.

Getting some nice shiny dress material or a decent cut of meat and real eggs instead of powdered stuff is what's on most folk's minds though. Round here it is anyway, because all they can think about is food! In the canteen the other day me and Mavis were trying to remember oranges and jammy buns covered in that fine crunchy sugar, so much of the stuff that you had to lick your lips! Will it all come back, like it used to be before rationing?

≈

29th March 1945

Alice came home tonight with a strange tale. She said that up at their base everyone was talking about this prison camp in Poland that's been liberated by the Russians. Full it was, of people from all over Europe, all starving, like living skeletons, but not POWs, because there were men, women and children. There was talk she said, that they were slave labour, but worse than that, when they couldn't work they were killed. Not just left to die, but actually killed in their thousands. Not much has been reported about it on the news or in the papers here, so we don't really know what to make of it at all.

We went out to Ma Wilson's for a bite to eat, as neither of us felt like cooking and she does a big plateful for half a crown and no washing up! We had a walk around afterwards and stood outside a place where there was band and dancing going on inside. We laughed and thought of all those years ago, when we was getting to know each other and went dancing with Bob and a mate of his. Neither of us could remember his name though. Funny that, I wonder if he's still *alive. We didn't go in, but in a way it was nice, nice to be remembering together. We both said it was all right.*

≈

8th April 1945

We had what the Yanks call a pyjama party last night. Three of the girls from the ministry came and Mavis from the depot. Everyone brought something and we did our nails and our hair, got rid of the leg hair and dyed our legs, cos stockings is really hard to get hold of just now. We laughed and ate and drank. Angela made martinis, although she said not to ask where the vermouth came from. I must say though, never again. Two of them and I almost went blind!

Me head wouldn't get up from the pillow this morning, but that was no great problem, as I was on the twelve o' clock shift and by that time I could just about hold me own again.

≈

10th April 1945.

It's nearly all over, even I can see that. Tonight, while we was having a bite to eat at the terminal cafe, I asked Alice what she would do afterwards, go back to the farm or what? She said that there were plans for afterwards already being made and that some of the pen pushers and others would need to go to Germany and Japan and maybe other places, until their governments and whatnot could do their jobs properly. She said there were real fears of anarchy and civil unrest and they're worried about the Russians too. She told me that she's signed up to stay on, maybe get the chance to travel a bit. She laughed when I mentioned the farm and told me that was the past and there's no going back. I'm not sure I agree, but even so, what will I do? I'd have to find a new place to live, maybe even a new job if mine's one of the ones that the lads will be coming back to, so it don't seem like the upheaval is set to stop for some time. But still, it ain't over yet, so there's no real point in thinking about it.

≈

20th April 1945

I heard that Mr Dimbleby on the radio the other night. He was in one of the units that liberated a camp like the one in Poland and he told us what he'd seen there. I don't think anyone listening could believe what he was saying and I'm sure he couldn't believe it his self. Why? How? It beggars belief that anyone could treat another human being like that, or that a person just like me could get so used to being treated worse than a farm animal. The survivors are so hungry that they sit there, eating with all those dead people and rotting bodies around them.

Since then, there's been more reported and it makes me sick to the stomach. I wanted to leave the cinema while the Pathé news was on, but I wouldn't let meself. They had to live it, they never had the luxury to get up and leave when they'd had enough, so I sat there and watched it all, so that I could maybe understand what it'd been like for them.

Those poor, poor people. Starved, shot or gassed, or just worked to death.

Why? Because they were the wrong religion or nationality? Were they just in the wrong place at the wrong time? Was it as simple as that? Was that going to be our fate too, if we hadn't fought back, or if we'd lost?

It don't make no sense that someone sat down and thought all that up. Human beings, just like them, then others put it into practice. I just can't get me head round it. Why? Why would anyone do that?

This bloody war seems to have killed as many civilians as soldiers, but this? I can't close me eyes without seeing them. Is there no end to the horror of it all?

I keep thinking what Bob told me and what Vic said about why he made his decision to go back to sea. They couldn't allow Hitler to win.

I know we ain't perfect, I mean we've done some terrible things too, but nothing like this, nothing like what I heard on the radio and saw on the Pathé. We'll all be judged later and no doubt we'll judge ourselves, but what Hitler has been doing, that ain't the world we want, that ain't a future we planned for.

That's why Bob and Vic died, to keep what was good in this world and to not let that loss of humanness become normal. I have to remember that, I have to remember them the right way.

≈

6th May 1945

I'm at the farm for a week or two. Mr R had a tumble and broke his leg, put him in a right grumpy mood it has. Anyway, he phoned down and asked if I would come up. Says there's no one left here he can trust and of course now it's a real busy time. It's important work, so the bus depot let me go without having to argue and I got a rail pass without any trouble neither. Seems like this is where I need to be for the time being.

Not seen much of Roberta, as I'm in the fields all day and she's asleep when I leave and when I get back again, but Mrs R brought up her to the top field yesterday to play. She knows her own mind that one, despite her size.

I wonder what Mum would have made of her? Or Bob?

Right now I can't let me mind spend too long on those thoughts, but I think they'd have smiled and been proud of her.

≈

8th May 1945

It's over in Europe. They say Hitler is dead and the rest of them surrendered. The King said that faith and unity held us together and carried us to victory through times when the dangers seemed overwhelming.

I don't know about him of course, but for me lots of things still are overwhelming. Still, there's a deep sense of relief, a feeling that maybe tomorrow won't be all bad after all and *that our grandchildren will have a better life because we saw it through to the bitter end.*

I'm probably getting ahead of meself. Like Mr Churchill said, it's not over yet, not until Japan surrenders too, but surely we're on our way to peace. Surely the King is right.

≈

Megan thinks about the hope that her great grandmother must have felt. While she wishes fervently never to experience the awful darkness that descended on her, she can understand something of fear. She is sure that her fears are smaller than a lot of other people's in the world, whose lives are still precarious.

"But isn't hope always the same though, and isn't it always powerful?" she asks herself.

She is so deep in thought, that at first she doesn't notice that she is alone in the kitchen with just the ticking of the clock for company. She looks around the room and tries to see it the way Lillian and the Robinsons must have on that very important day all those decades ago and tries to imagine the joy they must have felt and their belief that what they had achieved, needed to be done, despite the enormous cost.

"For me..." she whispers to herself. "They did it for me."

Chapter twenty eight

"There you are! All by yourself?"

Megan nods to her aunt as she bustles in, clearly a woman on a mission.

"We're gasping in there; I'd forgotten just how much three women can talk!" Claire tells her. Then with a big smile, she fills the kettle and gets cups, saucers and plates from the cupboard. "Be a love and pop upstairs and tell Joe and Jake that tea will be ready in ten minutes and see how your gran is."

Megan puts the diary down and scoots off up the stairs to the top floor. She finds her uncle at the bottom of the attic ladder, carefully manoeuvring a large trunk that Jake has the other end of. She watches them working together and is pleased that they get on so well. Joe sees her and she delivers her message.

"Righty ho, we'll be down in a minute. Whoa! Hold it steady lad..."

He is caught off guard by the trunk coming down a little faster than he had been expecting and as he turns back to his task, Megan goes down to her grandmother's room, where she finds her deeply engrossed in a film.

"A cup of tea would be nice, yes. Shhh, I'm watching." she says, curtly dismissing her.

Back in the kitchen, Claire is still arranging trays and cutting cake.

"They'll be down in a minute and Gran would like tea." Megan tells her aunt, sitting back down at the table, eyeing the cakes and wishing her mother baked more.

"Was your grandfather in the war?" she asks, helping herself to a warm, buttery crumpet.

"Yes, they both were and my maternal grandmother too."

"What did they do?" Megan asks, wiping a greasy dribble from her chin and grinning happily.

"Well, my father's father was in the regular army and was sent to Burma. Sadly he was taken prisoner by the Japanese and he died in one of their POW camps, like a lot of other people did. Some died from starvation, lack of medicines, or were just worked till they dropped. Some were just shot or beaten of course." She shivers slightly as she speaks, although the kitchen is warm.

"The conditions were really bad. They didn't understand apparently, the Japanese I mean, they thought that you should never let yourself be taken prisoner. They didn't sign up to the Geneva Convention, or at least I don't think they did and they believed that you should fight to the bitter end and keep your honour intact, you know the sort of thing. So they felt little or no respect for their prisoners, only contempt, or so I was told by my father, who was ten when it was all over."

She shrugs sadly at the memory. "He was always angry about it and right to the end of his own life he wouldn't buy anything Japanese, not even a TV. So you can imagine what he had to say when...

"Anyway... my maternal grandparents were both in the navy, although my grandmother was on land for most of her service. They met during the war and married soon afterwards. So you see, there are some happy endings. They always said they would never have bumped into each other without the war and they were really happy together. I used to love visiting them, even after fifty years of marriage they could still giggle together! Pass me the milk dear, a fresh bottle from the scullery fridge please."

Megan is thoughtful as she does her aunt's bidding, but before she can ask anything else, her uncle comes in with Jake close behind him and they head for the sink to wash their hands, both of them happily eyeing the food on the trays.

Claire takes a tray up to Roberta, while the others stagger into the front parlour with theirs and settle down with Louise and Lynn, who are still deep in conversation about someone that Joe remembers from when they were all younger. Jake and Megan curl up together in a chair to share a plate laden with goodies and he tells her about some of the things he and her uncle found in the attic.

Upstairs, Roberta is glad to see her daughter-in-law and even happier to hear that they will not be leaving soon after all.

"What about his work?" she asks Claire. "Can he do that right now?"

"As he says, it's the beauty of being his own boss. We've got you to thank for that, don't think we ever forget it." she tells her, but Roberta waves the comment away, it is unnecessary in her eyes. Claire knows this and continues. "He's got good people at the office. They'll cope and he's only a call away if they need him. Everything's fine, don't worry. He wants to be here; here is where he belongs." She smiles sadly at Roberta, wishing there was something she could do to change things.

"You've always been a kind person Claire. I've admired and appreciated that, right from when he first brought you home, but there's nothing you can do to change this. The tea and the company make it easier though." She smiles mischievously and then winces in pain.

Claire reaches for the assortment of tablets on the bedside table, hands Roberta the pack she points at and then pours her some water to wash them down.

"They're all obsessed with that bloody diary of my mother's. Have you been reading it too?" she asks, more to take her mind off the pain.

"Off and on." Claire admits. "You forget just what a big thing the war was, how many lives it shaped as well as destroyed. Without it, I daresay my father would have been a different man and my life may have taken a turn down another road too. Who knows? If we had lost, well so much would have been different, probably horribly so... It just doesn't bear thinking about. So yes, it's interesting reading what someone who was there wrote about it at the time and I met her more than once remember, so she's not a complete stranger to me."

Roberta nods. She cannot be angry with Claire, her reasons are sensible and she knows there is no intention of inflicting any pain, unlike her daughter, who she mistakenly assumes does.

"Am I right in thinking that Megan has some sort of school project?" she asks instead.

"Yes," Claire tells her while refilling her teacup, "from what she has told me about it she should get a good mark. She's a clever girl, you should be proud of her."

"I am. I'm proud of all my grandchildren."

Roberta turns her head to look out of the window and watches clouds drift across a timeless summer sky, wishing she could go back to a different summer, one where she was the grandchild, not the grandmother.

Claire misunderstands the sigh and tries to help her feel part of something that she has all too often only been on the edges of. "I know that, and I believe they all know too." she says.

"You're a good girl Claire, a good girl."

Roberta pats her hand and closes her eyes. She is suddenly exhausted by everything and wishes to sleep, possibly forever.

Joe comes up a little while later and relieves his wife, happy to sit with his mother while day fades into evening. The birds sing loudly, proclaiming their roosting places and then as the sun dips below the horizon, they fall silent and a range of insects, bats and owls take their place.

Lynn insists that Jake comes home with her, as his room remains a tip, despite promises that it would be sorted out over the weekend. Claire smiles at their gentle bickering and as they are leaving, she sits on the stairs and phones home, issuing instructions to her boys about what should be done when and by whom and what should on no account be allowed to happen, without much hope of any of her words being taken seriously.

"I'll call for you in the morning and we can go into town together." Jake tells Megan outside on the drive. She squeezes his hand and promises to phone him later and he grins at her while his mother issues edicts about other chores he has been ignoring lately.

Louise and Megan head for the kitchen, with the idea of washing up the tea things and as they are working, Megan tells her mother that she needs to go to the library the following day, but that after that she hopes to have her project finished and then intends to relax a bit more.

"Jake said that he can take a week's holiday and still get paid and we thought we might take the bus to the coast one day. He wants to save a few days for when his friends get back the week after next." Her voice sounds a little troubled and her mother turns to look at her.

"Why are you worried about them?" she asks, slightly puzzled.

"Well they might not like me. I mean I can't go down the pub with them or do things like that, can I? Their girlfriends are older, well I don't actually know that, but they probably are and well..." she trails off unhappily.

"Silly girl!" her mother tells her, pulling her closer to her. "He clearly adores you and although I don't think any of us can ever know how complicated things like relationships will go, I don't see any signs of him turning his back on you just yet, quite the opposite in fact."

She smoothes her daughter's hair down, thinking back to his recent question about what Megan might like for her birthday. She doesn't want to spoil the surprise, so says nothing, but is able to feel quite confident about their immediate future, if not about anything else. However, it makes her think.

"By the way, have you thought about what you want from us for your birthday?" she asks her.

"Super duper phone, shiny pink one please, with..." she pauses and they both say together, "... all the bells and whistles!"

They laugh. It is her father's language, not theirs and they are united against him for a moment, but in a tender and familiar way.

"... and decent headphones, just like you said!" she pleads.

"I'll speak to your dad then! It's more his line anyway."

"Thanks Mum."

She smiles shyly and turns back to the drying up. They both know her gratitude is for far more than the promise of a new piece of technology, even if it is a shiny pink one.

Claire joins them and they turn the conversation to other more mundane things, while upstairs, Roberta has woken. She is cold and scared and Joe is trying to soothe her, so he sits on the edge of the bed with his arm about her shoulders and together they remember events from long ago. It enables her to regain her sense of reality and importance and it helps him to get some perspective on his own life and they smile as they recount things from their own points of view. They laugh and cry, bound even closer for a little while, before she gently drifts off to sleep again.

Louise lets the carer in as Megan heads up the stairs, planning to take a hot bath, then phone Jake from her room. Joe comes down and he and Claire make themselves comfortable in front of the TV for an hour or so, leaving Louise the space and time to phone Peter. Her mobile is upstairs however, and deciding it is too far away, she settles on the stairs and uses the house phone instead. The number is preset and she feels a bit like a teenager again, with the distant background noise of the TV and the ringing tone pulsating in her ear.

"Hello?"

A female voice answers breathlessly, clearly in mid conversation with someone else there, catching Louise completely off guard. For a moment she is stunned and then she says calmly, "Lucy, is that you?"

"Yes, who is this? Sorry, I don't recognise your voice."

"It's Louise, Peter's wife. Is he there?"

Silence.

Louise finds herself smiling, but a large tear also runs down her cheek. She senses the other woman's indecision as she listens to the light crackle on the line, but it is too late to take the words back and too late to hang up. Is she mouthing things to Peter? She can visualise him muttering 'Christ!'

Wiping her face, she takes charge of the situation. "Ask him to phone me, but tomorrow, not this evening." she says quietly and hangs up.

"I think I understand..." she says to herself as she stands up. "We are after all, in no man's land as far as our marriage is concerned."

Smiling sadly, she goes back to the kitchen and puts the kettle on, but before it has boiled, the carer appears in the doorway looking flustered.

"I've just phoned for an ambulance." she says. "Your mother has had a fall in the bathroom."

Louise rushes past her up the stairs, calling loudly for Joe as she goes. He is behind her in seconds and with Claire coming up at the rear, the three of them are with Roberta very quickly.

While Joe and Louise kneel beside their mother, Claire calls the GP, then goes out onto the landing to ask the carer what happened, before accompanying her to the front door. She has other clients to see, others who are waiting for her and her services are no longer required upstairs.

Roberta is dazed and confused, struggling to sit up, and she clutches at her son's hand as it comes into reach.

"My heart, son. My heart." she wheezes.

They gently help her into a more comfortable position, using a pillow and a blanket from the bed. They don't want to move her, not without precise instructions from a professional, so they sit with her and wait. Megan appears in the doorway, wrapped in a big bath towel and Louise takes her hand and leads her away.

"I think Gran has had a mild heart attack. We've called the doctor. There's not a lot you can do, but go and get dressed, just in case we have to go to the hospital. Can you do that?" she asks softly.

Megan nods, but she looks frightened. Louise hugs her tightly before releasing her and sending her off down the landing towards her room.

The ambulance and the GP arrive at the same time and Claire takes Megan to the kitchen to wait, sensing that decisions need to be made and they are for Louise and Joe to make. They make cocoa and sit at the table, listening to the ticking of the clock, trying not to imagine what might be going on upstairs.

A thought strikes Megan as she runs through what has happened that day, and remembers that when they had sat in that same place just a few short hours ago, she had been happy. She turns to Claire with a question.

"What did you mean earlier?" she asks, looking at her aunt expectantly. "You were telling me about your father not liking the Japanese, but you said something odd."

Claire smiles and stirs her drink thoughtfully. "Your great aunt Alice married a Japanese man. He'd been in an internment camp in America during the war. He and his family suffered and were not allowed to be 'American' for the duration, even though they were I believe, second or even third generation. He was never a soldier, but for my father and your gran's nana, the fact that he was Japanese was enough to blame him for all the acts of his people. For them he represented the enemy and the enemy had taken away the people and a way of life that they loved."

Megan needs a moment to take this in. "And Lillian?" she asks, "Did she hate Alice and her husband too?"

She tries to imagine Hannah marrying someone who was somehow associated with people who had hurt her family. Would she forget everything they had shared, if for instance she had lost her parents in the attack on the World Trade Centre in New York and if Hannah had later married a Muslim? But the question is too big and the emotions are unknown. Instead she turns back to her aunt.

"No, far from it. As I understand it, Lillian remained very close to her and her family. Alice died before her, of lung cancer I believe, and Lillian continued to visit her husband and the children. Of course they were grown up by then, but she stayed in touch, right up until her own death a few years later. She knew that he was not to blame for Bob's or her brother's deaths, or her mother's come to that. Someone killed them all, but it wasn't Alice's husband. I can't remember his name now. He was a really nice man, very polite and he had such a lovely sense of humour. I only met him once or twice of course, but...."

They hear the front door close and a few moments later Louise appears in the kitchen doorway.

"We're staying. It was a heart attack and there is the risk of another one in the next forty-eight hours. It may be less severe or more so, or she may just sleep peacefully, there's no way of knowing."

She sits down with a sigh and puts her arm around her daughter, but looks at Claire as she speaks. "We all agreed that staying here was the best option. It's what Mum wants. They've dosed her up with I don't know what and the doctor will come back in the morning, although we can phone at any time if we need him before that. She's sleeping now and Joe's up there with her. We don't think she should be left alone."

Claire nods. "We'll take turns."

Louise feels Megan go tense and smiles. "Not you sweetie, not you." She kisses the top of her daughter's head and strokes her cheek.

"Some strong coffee for Joe I think, and I'll go and take a nap for an hour or so then relieve him."

She releases Megan, who carefully picks up her mug of cocoa and heads upstairs to phone Jake. She is worried about what the night might have in store for them all and wonders if she should pop in and see her grandmother. After all, it might be the last time. She involuntarily shudders at the thought and spills chocolaty milk on the stair carpet and has to go back down for a cloth to wipe it up.

As she approaches the open door, she sees her mother and aunt holding each other. Both are crying and she feels she is intruding on something that she does not wish to be a part of. She cannot share their sadness, for her grandmother is an old woman and old people die. Hers is a more distant relationship and she has never been as close to her gran as she is to her aunt. Nor is it like the real affection she feels for her paternal grandmother, who is an altogether easier and therefore more lovable person.

She quietly closes the door and goes once more to the stairs, hoping she won't get into trouble for the stain, while at the same time, reasonably confident that no one will actually notice it.

Chapter twenty nine

Roberta is running through the orchard, shouting and singing at the top of her voice. The wind playfully catches her long hair, making it stream out behind her and life courses through her limbs, pushing her on and on until eventually she falls, laughing at nothing. She lies there for a few moments, trying to get her breath back, then rolls over and looks up through the apple blossom. Huge clouds race each other high above, and now and then, blue sky peeps through. Smiling, she sits up and brushes twigs and bits of grass from her dress, while higher up the hill, her nana is standing with her hands on her hips, calling for her to come back. She is trying to sound cross, but Roberta knows she isn't, not really. Nothing Roberta does ever makes Nana cross and she is always forgiven every word and action.

Grampy and her mother are different though; they sometimes shout at her and often scold her. If Nana is there, she shoos them away and tells her to pay them no heed, then they go off together, just the two of them and do something nice. 'We don't need anyone else,' she would say, which was just as well, as her mother rarely wanted to do anything with her.

She and Nana will have a picnic lunch in the orchard today, just the two of them, which is how they prefer things. Then later maybe, they will drive into town and do a little shopping. She has been promised new clothes for the coming season and the thought excites her, even though come September, she will be going to boarding school and will have to wear her uniform most of the time.

She smiles and looks to where Nana had been standing, only the vision has faded and she realises that she is looking at her daughter, who is looking back at her, but she looks perplexed and Roberta can't be bothered with it all. She closes her eyes again and tries to grab the fleeting memories, but they have slipped away and everything has become dark.

In the darkness, Roberta hears her beloved nana's voice. She is confused and calling for her, but when she goes to her, she no longer recognises her. She wants the child, not the young woman that Roberta has become and she starts to cry, still calling out for her granddaughter.

Her mother appears and tries to calm her. While Lillian is allowed to be close to Nana, who reaches out to her and calls for her when she can't see her, she pushes Roberta away harshly, as though she were a stranger. This rejection pierces her soul and makes her weep inside, though no tears ever run down her face.

"Nana, where are you? Where have you gone?" she whispers. "Why did you leave me...?"

"Mum...?" Louise asks uncertainly, "Mum...?"

Roberta's eyes had briefly flickered open, she is sure of that. But did she speak? Louise leans forward, relieved to hear her breathing and although it is quite faint, at least it is not laboured. She shakes her head and sits back in the chair, wondering how long this will go on for. While she does not wish her mother dead, she also knows this pain filled half-life is not what Roberta would choose for herself.

Sighing deeply, she looks down at the pad and rereads what she has written.

Peter

When I sat down to write this, I thought I was going to write a different kind of letter altogether. The words that originally came to me and sat in my mind are different to the ones that are here. You see, I thought I would be angry or sad and would rant and rave that I no longer understood you or trusted you, that your feelings for me were clearly all lies and other such rubbish and that this letter would be about making that clear to you. I imagine this is what you would be expecting and under the circumstances it would be natural.

It's funny really. I find, having realised that you are spending tonight with Lucy, that you are indeed the same man that you have always been. You were right when you wrote that it's not you that's changed, but me, and I think we both know that I rather naïvely wanted you to be different somehow. But that is not your wish. You are happy being the person that you have always been and I do not want to forget how happy I used to be just being with you and how much I loved you.

My mother is dying and a part of my life will come to an end sooner rather than later. Memories will no longer be shared or argued over and I will be left with mine to do as I please with. I will mourn her of course, and mourn the things that now will never be, for without her they cannot be, but it is too late to make them different. She would say, 'things are what they are, live with it.' And for the first time in my life, I think I just might agree with her.

It would be too easy to dismiss our years together as having been shallow and meaningless, but that would be to forget the one thing we do have to show for them. That is Megan and she is important in all of this. She is yours as much as mine and right now, she is moving towards being herself. We should be happy, for we made her together and together we have tried as best we could, to be the best that we could be, which is an achievement and something we should be proud of, or at least I think it is, don't you?

But us? I think it's time for me to be honest. Honest with myself and honest with you. I don't see how there can be 'us', not anymore. There is me and there is you. I don't think this is about Lucy as such, she is incidental, to me anyway and possibly to you too and that in itself is one of the reasons why I know that we are over.

You do not love her. We both know that and it's likely that she does too.

When we began, I believed that you loved both me and Deirdre and that the choice was therefore a difficult one for you to make. Knowing as I do now, that you were involved with another woman at the same time, makes me question that assumption, but I find that I want to hang on to it. I still need to believe it was true then, whatever may be true now.

You might choose Lucy after all this is over, but more because of circumstance, not because of real and enduring emotion. She is not the reason I am writing this, but she, the fact of her at least, has helped me see some of the things that I have been trying for too long to be blind to, things about myself as much as about you. Yes, it does take two to tango and sometimes, it would appear, it takes three.

I never for a single moment thought that I would be the one to say our marriage was over. The fact of being married always meant more to me than to you. Funny that, don't you think, now at the end of it? I believe that it still does mean something great and important to me, which is why I have to end ours. I do not want to lose that belief and I can no longer trust in you or believe that your feelings for me are what I actually need from you.

We will need to sort out all manner of stuff: legal, material, emotional and banal and we will no doubt get short tempered with each other as we go through this process of separating our lives. Despite this, I want you to know that I don't think I would have changed a thing. I am both where I need to be and who I need to be and that is in part due to the journey we have shared together.

Louise.

She is surprised by her words, but she instinctively knows they are the right ones. Before the morning she may rewrite it, but in essence it won't change much and for that reason she thinks it will be posted pretty much as it stands. She folds it and tells her mother that she has made her decision. She does not know if Roberta can hear her, but again, it feels like the right thing to do.

Claire comes a little while later to take over and Louise quietly goes to her room and lies fully clothed on top of the bed. The windows are open and a breeze lazily wafts through the curtains. She watches them sway and allows her mind to drift back through her life, giving it no real direction and is pleasantly surprised at some of the things that pop up.

"Everything is going to be different soon," she tells herself, "Everything. But am I strong enough? Can I actually do this?"

Shadows flit across the ceiling, a ceiling she has stared at so many times in the past, during other difficult moments in her life. She decides that it is right to be in that room, on that bed, asking herself the same question she has asked so many times before.

"Am I strong enough?"

She remembers her granny holding her while she sobbed, after yet another explosive and damaging argument with her mother. Her self esteem, her hopes and dreams lay in tatters and she had fled over the hill to the one place she always felt safe.

"Am I strong enough to ignore what she said?" she had pleaded, looking up into concerned blue eyes. "Am I strong enough to go on anyway...? Am I?"

She remembers feeling uncertain and fragile and Lillian had told her the truth, only back then, she hadn't appreciated just how her grandmother had come to this insight, or how much it had cost her.

"We never know the answer to that love, never. But we usually find that when we look back, we were stronger than we thought we were. We do find a way to go on, maybe just one tiny step at a time, but still... we keep going, and eventually we find that we can smile again, even though we once thought that there was nothing left in this world to smile about."

She feels a stirring of something warm, deep inside, a feeling of love and remembers how Lillian had helped her fight back and how she had given her the chance at freedom. They had filled out application forms together, gone to open days and interviews. She had held her hand throughout it all and after all that, she had given her the money she needed to not be dependent on anybody. Then she met Peter and willingly chained herself to him.

"Now it's time to break those chains." she whispers to herself.

She smiles as she realises the enormity of those words and closes her eyes, allowing sleep to take her for a while, knowing that tomorrow will be different, possibly difficult, but that it will be ok too.

Claire gently shakes her awake a few hours later.

"Come... it's time." she tells her and holds her hand out, helping her up and leading her down the dark landing towards her mother. Joe is already there holding her hand and she sees the tears pouring down his face.

She stands next to him and is aware that Claire has slipped out, probably to phone for someone. Her mother's chest heaves and shakes and her eyes flutter open, then close. Louise knows that she is being oversensitive, but at the same time she feels almost outside herself as she watches her mother breathe her last breath.

"Goodbye..." she whispers through parched lips as a strange rattling noise seems to fill the room. She shivers, even though the room is warm and stuffy.

Feeling numb, as if everything has been washed out of her, her eyes take in every detail and pattern, even the things she knows she cannot possibly see clearly in the gloom. She cannot look at her mother yet. She knows her face well in life, but she is not ready to see it dead, not yet, and her eyes continue to rove around the room until they find her brother.

Joe is kneeling beside the bed. His shoulders are shaking and she moves closer towards him, meaning to comfort him. She stands behind him and he takes her hand as she rests it on his shoulder. In life, he had always been the link between her and her mother, and death has not changed that.

Claire comes in and stands beside her, resting a hand on Joe's other shoulder. "I've called the Doctor, he's on his way." she tells them. Louise nods and continues to stand there, not knowing what else to do.

Her father had died in the ambulance on the way to hospital. She was in London at the time and only came home the day before the funeral. Roberta had taken care of everything and had been distant with her, letting her know that she was still not forgiven for leaving. She is sure that her mother never really forgave her for wanting a more exciting life, one that had different possibilities from what there would have been in the local market town.

She had played no part in the preparations to send her father off and had left the morning after the funeral, with excuses that were acceptable to everyone. Any mourning she had done for him, she had done alone; miles away from the place he had been born, lived and died in.

Thinking about her father brings her thoughts to Susan and she wonders who told her he'd died. She is surprised that she could even contemplate such a question at such a time, but also wonders why she knows so little of his wartime experiences.

Maybe Susan will know, she thinks to herself. After all, I can't ask him. Or Mum now..."

The reality of what has just happened begins to creep in from the edges of her mind and she shivers again. Claire wraps an arm around her and they stand for a while longer, each lost in their own thoughts, and just as Roberta had feared it would, life starts to move on without her.

Chapter thirty

Megan's hand hovers uncertainly over the back door handle. Everything looks the same, but she knows it isn't. The house has an almost spooky stillness to it and although the ambulance took the lifeless body of her grandmother away during the night, she is reluctant to go inside. A noise from the garage catches her attention and she turns and goes there instead, thankful for an excuse to put off the moment of entering.

Her mother is weaving silky black 'hair' together and sticking the last of it into the neck of the rocking horse, before standing back to admire it.

"It's really lovely Mum." Megan says, walking closer. "And you were right; it looks gorgeous as an appaloosa."

"Ro-Ro..." Louise says, turning round and smiling at her daughter. "His name is Ro-Ro and he's coming home with us, although I'm not altogether sure where home might end up being."

Megan walks to her mother's side and hugs her as they regard Ro-Ro in all his splendid glory.

"We made all the arrangements while you were at the library." Louise tells her. "The funeral will be on Monday next week, at ten in the morning. Claire will go and get the boys on Saturday and then on Monday the funeral directors will bring Gran back here and we'll all go together to the crematorium. Then later, probably in the afternoon, we'll go to the church and bury her ashes with Granddad's."

Megan nods. Her unspoken question has been answered; the house is 'safe'. "And afterwards?" she asks, "Are we staying here until the end of the holidays or going home?"

"Your father and I need to talk about that. He will come up for the funeral of course, but you know... we could take off to the sun for a week afterwards... Greece maybe, or Turkey or even the south of France. What do you think? You said Jake had a week's holiday, why waste it here? Invite him to come with us, would you like that?"

Megan is thoughtful for a moment before making a decision that her mother, in the same position, would never have made. "No, let's go. I mean just you and me."

Louise looks at her quizzically and Megan smiles. "We're fine, or as Lillian would have said, 'Me and him, we're strong!' But he'll be coming to London soon anyway and he's got his friends coming back from their holidays and all sorts of things he wants to sort out before leaving. He hasn't got much money, so I don't want to make him feel bad by asking something that he'll have to refuse. And if we can't be apart for a week or so and enjoy missing each other, well..." She shrugs and smiles self-consciously.

"What a difference a summer can make..." Louise murmurs, marvelling at this newly discovered maturity in her daughter. She is happy with the outcome and makes no effort to change Megan's mind. They will have this holiday together and it will be a little idyll before real life has to resume.

Turning off the light, they go back to the house together, talking about Megan's project, which is now finished and ready to be handed in. Claire is not in the kitchen, but there is the comforting smell of fresh baking.

Louise sighs sadly. "I will never be the cook that your aunt Claire is... it always makes me feel I've failed in some way, but I don't know why that should be."

"Mum, don't be so dramatic." Megan tells her, dumping her bag and books at the far end of the table. "Anyway, we'd be enormous if you were and then we'd have to go and live in a gym or something!"

"Yes, I suppose..."

She sits down and looks around the room. "I shall miss this place, but it isn't my home. A lot of my life has been lived here, but it's not where I need to be. Times are different and life is different too."

Now that Mum's gone, Louise thinks, but doesn't say.

Gone...

The word echoes in her mind.

Maisie rubs herself against her leg and purrs softly, bringing a welcome distraction. "You'll miss it though, won't you?" Louise says to the cat as she rubs her ears, causing her to purr louder.

Megan has the biscuit tin in her hands and having taken one, she puts it down on the table. Louise absentmindedly takes one too and munches thoughtfully.

"I'd like to keep the clock though, what do you think?"

"Mmm, why not. You can put it where that awful picture of me is in the alcove." Megan suggests hopefully, then reaches for the diary, which is lying open where Claire has left it, but slightly too far away for her to get without stretching.

"I happen to like that picture; I think you look very sweet in it. And as you were only four when it was taken, well what's not to like?" Louise says unsympathetically, but can't help smiling.

The diary had been left open at the last page and Megan has it in her hand.

"Yeah, whatever... Listen."

5th July 1955

We're back. Mr R and I arrived home yesterday, though I don't think Mrs R and Roberta missed us even for a minute. They're like two peas in a pod those two and there's no getting between them neither, mores the pity, but maybe it's too late now. Maybe the die was cast when I gave her up and that's that. Mum always said there are some things in life you just have to accept, so no point banging your head against a wall and maybe this is one of them things. I did what I did when I thought it was for the best and there ain't no going back now to change me mind. I'm not sure I could anyway. I mean I was lost, not able to find the way back through the fog, not then anyroads. I couldn't have taken care of meself, let alone a baby. No, what was done was done for what seemed like the best at the time.

It's funny, they ain't asked no questions at all about our trip, or shown any interest. I can understand Roberta, because she's so young, but not Mrs R. Maybe it's just too painful for her. I shouldn't judge her though, after all, I ain't lost a child. Well not in the same way, anyway.

We didn't talk much about it, Mr R and me, but it's left a lasting impression on both of us. When we walked between the headstones in the blinding sun, I was overwhelmed. There were palm trees of course and there's grass. I wasn't expecting that, not in a desert country, but it was like standing in a sea of white stones, stretching out in all directions. There are so many, so many just there in that one cemetery and there are other places like it, it's not the only one. Each stone is like a little piece of home and has a name, a date and some little fact about the life or death of the person, something that tells you that once they was as real as me or Mr R.

We stopped often and tried to picture them, wondering if they had known Bob. If they'd been friendly with each other, passed the time of day, shared a joke or a smoke maybe. We tried to imagine them full of life, fun and cheer, or the noise of the mess, with them eating, drinking and even singing perhaps, but instead found ourselves listening for the noise of battle.

Mr R could do that, cos he could remember his own experiences in the Great War, when he'd been in the Rifles, while I had only the memories of other people to call on. Either way, what you really notice there is that it's so silent. All those voices, that now have nothing more to say, but I suppose it's cos they've said it all in their deeds. They're all gone now, but what they did ain't and it ain't forgotten neither.

Have we learnt anything though? I hope the future will be different and I hope we will we stop trying to find other and more terrible ways of killing each other and murdering the children. I hope so, but really I ain't that sure, not anymore.

Bob always said we was going to see the desert together one day. Of course that weren't never going to be possible, but I think he'd like the fact that I've seen it for meself anyway. He was right, it really does seem to stretch out forever, and just like he wrote to me, it's two different places by day and by night. I stood out there in both of them, just staring out into the bright blue of the day and then into the inky black of the night.

When I was out there, I remembered what that Indian chap told him one night while they were under all them stars. He said, 'Whatever has been, can never not be,' or something like that.

We didn't understand it back then, but I think I do now and I'm glad of this truth. Bob was real and so was Vic, even though there ain't no grave that I can visit. All the lads there under those stones were real people, each and every one of them and not just them what fought, but all those others that got caught up in it, that couldn't avoid the bombs, the beatings, the gas, the fire or whatever. Those far out at sea, or up in the air, in those camps and even at home, they were all real people. I knew lots of them or people like them and I loved a few of them too. In fact I still love three of them very much indeed.

I wonder if he survived, that Indian chap, and if he's back home with his family, picking up his life and growing old. Or was he there too somewhere? I never knew his name, so I couldn't look for him.

Maybe I'll be able to open those letters now. Maybe I don't need to hang onto them no more. Maybe we can still have new conversations down in the orchard and as long as I remember them right, I'll never really be alone. But still I miss him, I miss them all and I miss the life that should've been ours. I hope it was worth it, really I do.

I'm glad we went, me and Mr R. We both said the same, 'There's some peace to be found in knowing, in seeing it for yourself.' It gives us a reason to keep going, to make sure it weren't all for nothing. We have to remember what they did, what they gave up and why, cos it was so we could go on, one step at a time, one day at a time, one life at a time. It made me realise that I have to be pleased to be living and that I have to live for all of us, not just me and even though that's a big, big responsibility, I know I can do it. For them, for him and for me.

It seems right that there ain't another page left in me diary, the one me big brother got for me when I was fifteen, with all those empty pages, waiting to be filled and now they are. All those days I'd never have dreamt possible, all those happy moments that are still mine in a funny way, and all those nightmares I'd have wanted to avoid, except it weren't a possibility, not for me and not for a lot of us. But would I have given up all the laughter, the wonder and the love I got and gave in return, in order not to feel the pain? Probably not!

A piece of me life.

Me, Lillian Loveday.

≈

Megan looks up at her mother and they smile at each other.

"It must have been really hard for her to keep going." Megan says sadly.

"Yes, for her and for a lot of people. And for some it still is, but on we must go. Always." Louise tells her, reaching for another biscuit.

I hope you've enjoyed reading this book. If you have, please leave a review on Amazon or Goodreads.

You can follow me on Facebook or Goodreads

http://www.facebook.com/pages/Jacqui-Henderson/149076491935857

http://www.goodreads.com/

Also by Jacqui Henderson and published on Amazon:

What about us?

Beyond the Horizon
and
Shifting Horizons

Printed in Great Britain
by Amazon.co.uk, Ltd.,
Marston Gate.